UNCLE TOM'S CABIN

UNCLE TOM'S
∾ CABIN ∾

BY

HARRIET BEECHER STOWE

ADAPTED BY

ANNE TERRY WHITE

· *A Venture Book* ·

GEORGE BRAZILLER · NEW YORK

Adaptation copyright © 1966 by Anne Terry White

All rights in this book are reserved.
For information, address the publisher:
George Braziller, Inc.
One Park Avenue, New York 16, New York

Library of Congress Catalog Card Number: 66-20534

SECOND PRINTING

Designed by Hilda Scott

Printed in the United States of America

Contents

An Introduction

"So you're the little woman who wrote the book that made this great war," President Lincoln said to the author of *Uncle Tom's Cabin* when she paid him a visit at the White House.

It is not recorded what answer Harriet Beecher Stowe made. But we do know that her book inflamed the North against slavery and was a mighty force in bringing about the Civil War. No novel before or since stirred this country so deeply—while throughout the civilized world it sold in millions of copies.

Mrs. Stowe claimed that she didn't compose *Uncle Tom's Cabin.* "It all came before me in visions," she said, "one after another, and I put them down in words." And again she said, "God wrote it. I merely did his dictation."

As edition after edition poured from the presses, Mrs. Stowe became "the most talked-of woman in the world." But that isn't important. The important thing is that her book "powerfully affected every mind that read it."

It still does. For *Uncle Tom's Cabin* is not just a story of "Life Among the Lowly." It does not merely tell us what a hard row the Negro had to hoe. It is a timeless plea for humanity and justice. It stirs our hearts today just as it did a century ago.

It was out of a desire to make the struggle for Freedom Now grippingly understandable to boys and girls that I was moved to put *Uncle Tom's Cabin* into a form acceptable to young readers. For the Negro's determination to "stand up" in our time is rooted in slavery, and nowhere else is that dark past depicted in such graphic, individual, and moving terms as in Harriet Beecher Stowe's novel.

True, to most Negroes "Uncle Tom" has come to be a derogatory term, an "odious symbol of one who accepts a status of racial inferiority." But Mrs. Stowe's hero has been condemned out of measure. As a note in "Harlem, U.S.A.," a recent symposium by fifty Negro writers, artists, and sculptors, tells us, "Uncle Tom" further symbolizes "one who in his efforts to keep on the good side of white folk often acts as an informer." This is outrageously wide of the truth, a complete distortion of the character. Mrs. Stowe's Uncle Tom lets himself be beaten to death rather than reveal the hiding place of Cassy and Emmeline, whom he himself has urged to escape from their master. What is more, a true perspective on Uncle Tom must take cognizance of the fact that he accepted his slave status not because he lacked natural dignity, but because wholly accepting, as he did, the teachings of Christianity, he believed that God had put him in his inferior place for a purpose.

Previous generations read *Uncle Tom's Cabin* as a matter of course, with deep involvement and wholesome tears. To previous generations Uncle Tom, little Eva, St. Clare, Miss Ophelia, Topsy, Legree, and especially the fugitive George Harris—whose ringing declarations of the Negro's right to manhood and equality match the most passionate outpourings of today—were living figures. Regrettably, boys and girls no longer read *Uncle Tom's Cabin.* This powerful human document, which so affected American history and which so illuminates the present, is unhappily a closed book to them.

My first thought was to present the novel as Harriet Beecher Stowe wrote it and to reinforce it with some background of slavery in general, African slavery in particular, slave ships, the triangle trade, the middle passage, slave revolts, abolitionists, John Brown, the underground railway, and so on. After such an introduction I began reading the book aloud to a group of ten- and eleven-year-old boys and girls. But I quickly found that to hold their absorbed attention I had to cut and, to a certain extent, adapt the original.

As I went on, I came to feel that the old-fashioned, discursive style, with its interruptions of the story by commentary and addresses to the reader, sets a bar between young readers and the message which the story itself fully carries. I realized that to make *Uncle Tom's Cabin* appealing to boys and girls, who today have an almost limitless choice among readable books written expressly for them, it must be made shorter, tighter, less tract-like, and less formidable.

I found, in working on the book, that very little so-called "adaptation" was actually necessary. Judicious cutting frequently excluded references to books, events, characters, and things outside a young reader's knowledge and understanding. It also often excluded vocabulary beyond the ten-to-fourteen level. Seldom did I need to substitute one word for another. I changed *inexorable* to "unyielding," *solicitude* to "concern," *vehemently* to "passionately," *embarrassments* to "debts," *incredulity* to "disbelief," *juncture* to "point," *elucidation of* to "notions of," and by so doing made possible an unhalted reading. Now and then, in the course of cutting, a transitional phrase or sentence was called for. But more than superficial adaptation was necessary only in a few places. Cassy's relation of her story to Tom is such a place, for example. Cassy is introduced into the book very late, when the reader wants to get on with the action, and her story is in any case emotionally beyond a child's level. Here not only cutting but a change of pace through partial substitution of indirect for direct discourse was indicated.

Another hurdle that had to be removed was the old-fashioned punctuation. Mrs. Stowe used an excess of commas and relied a great deal on the semicolon, while the dash she scattered quite arbitrarily. Today's young readers are accustomed

to short sentences and a minimum of punctuation. Commas
that set off every phrase and clause confuse them; they don't
understand the semicolon at all. I took care to break up the
endless sentences where possible, put commas in places of natural pause, and have used the dash and exclamation point
with restraint.

As for the cutting, I believe that in every instance it has
served not only to shorten the book and make the story flow
freely, but also to heighten the effect. A case in point is the
chapter, "An Evening in Uncle Tom's Cabin." Another is the
last part of the chapter, "In Which Property Gets into an
Improper State of Mind." For reasons of drama, this chapter
should logically end with George's ringing words, "If you
hear that I'm taken, you may know that I'm dead" and Mr.
Wilson's fumbling out of the room. But the author was not
content with this. She has George call Mr. Wilson back, and
there follows a sentimental, unconvincing, and anticlimactic
scene.

A definite drag on the story is the fact that Mrs. Stowe
frequently "explains" her characters. This is quite superfluous, for they reveal themselves in speech and action. She
also repeatedly develops character, incident, and description
beyond need and then rounds all up with commentary. It
adds nothing to the story that the slave-trader Haley intends
to repent before he dies—this only clutters. It adds nothing
that the reformed slave-catcher Tom Loker says of the Quakers that they "make jist the tallest kind o' broth and
knickknacks." This merely holds up the story. A detailed
description of Eva's room is not necessary—the reader already
knows that Eva has been given everything imaginable to make
her happy, and with so long a story before him, that is all
he wants or needs to know. The tongue-in-cheek description
of the Kentucky tavern is a needless excursion. So is Sam's
address to his fellow servants on returning from the pursuit of
Eliza—the interest falls badly here. So is the reaction of Miss
Ophelia's neighbors to her projected departure for New

Orleans. So is the despair of Legree's mother. So is the bickering of Marie and St. Clare. And on and on.

Being a daughter, sister, wife, and mother of ministers, it is not surprising that Mrs. Stowe should fill her book with religiosity. Much of it is essential in that religion, and especially a belief in a heaven filled with "spirits bright" was basic to Tom, Eva, Eliza, and many of the other characters. But much, again, merely weighs down the story and is incomprehensible to young readers. What, for example, can they make of the following?

"Ye who have wondered to hear, in the same evangel, that God is love, and that God is a consuming fire, see ye not how, to the soul resolved in evil, perfect love is the most fearful torture, the seal and sentence of the direst despair?"

Or, again:

"That submissive and silent man, whom taunts, nor threats, nor stripes, nor cruelties, could disturb, roused a voice within him, such as of old his Master roused in the demoniac soul, saying, 'What have we to do with thee, thou Jesus of Nazareth?—art thou come to torment us before the time?' "

I believe that leaving out unessential religious commentary and interpolation has in every instance made the book more readable and better suited to boys and girls of today, many of whom have little or no knowledge of the New Testament.

The total result of cutting, adapting, and modernizing both punctuation and spelling is that the story proceeds without halt or mechanical hindrance, yet is not anywhere hurried. The pace is such that the young reader can accommodate himself to it without effort and will remain throughout inside the covers of the book, for he will be continuously involved with the characters and the action. In all, I think I have cut the original by about twenty per cent. This still leaves the story long—but the book is no longer formidable, and this is of first importance.

Since Mrs. Stowe wrote *Uncle Tom's Cabin* in weekly installments, certain small inconsistencies crept in, and these I have corrected. For instance, as Eliza escapes across the ice, we are told that "Her shoes are gone—her stockings cut from her feet." But later, in the senator's house, she is presented "with one shoe gone, and the stocking torn away from the cut and bleeding foot." Or, again, when George Shelby meets Madame de Thoux on the Mississippi boat, she is "accompanied by a fine little daughter, a child of some twelve summers." Since this child is dropped from the story without explanation, her introduction was obviously a slip.

With inconsistencies of another kind, I did not feel free to tamper. For example, Mr. Wilson would never have asked George Harris where his wife was. Not knowing about her flight, the manufacturer would have taken it for granted that she was on the Shelby farm. That this is so is brought out by his astonishment when he is told that Eliza has fled. Clearly Mrs. Stowe in her haste resorted to an easy transition. It would have been simple for me to rectify it, but I did not.

I took particular pains to simplify the opening of the story, and this, obviously, was with the object of capturing the reader from the start. As the first three paragraphs read in my version, they will not discourage even a ten-year-old, yet all the necessary material is there—and without the language having been reduced to pap. Indeed, I will be bold to say that the opening reads all the better for the changes. Mrs. Stowe only misleads by the additional phrase "in the town of P——," since the setting is a farm. In describing Haley as no gentleman, such a sentence as, "One of the parties, however, when critically examined, did not seem, strictly speaking, to come under the species," is circuitous and wordy writing that puts a young reader on the defensive. As for "His conversation was in easy defiance of Murray's Grammar, and was garnished at convenient intervals with various profane expressions which not even the desire to be graphic in our account shall induce us to transcribe," very few young readers would get beyond that sentence. What is more, the statement is not needed, since Haley's language reveals itself in subsequent passages.

In adapting *Uncle Tom's Cabin*, I have been more faithful to the matter than to the manner, for Mrs. Stowe's manner often defeats her aim, which is to inform and to stir. You cannot inform or stir a reader unless you capture his absorbed attention, and you cannot get a young reader's attention unless you make a book readable. If I have succeeded in making *Uncle Tom's Cabin* acceptable to young readers and at the same time have left it essentially whole and true, I have done what I set out to do—which was to put this eminently moving story of slave days once more into children's hands.

ANNE TERRY WHITE

In Which the Reader Is Introduced to a Man of Humanity

LATE in the afternoon of a chilly day in February, two gentlemen were sitting alone over their wine. There were no servants in the dining parlor of the Kentucky house, and the gentlemen, with chairs close together, seemed to be discussing some subject with great earnestness.

We have said two *gentlemen*. One of the parties, however, was hardly that. He was a short, thick-set man with coarse, commonplace features, and that swaggering air which marks a low man who is trying to elbow his way up in the world. He was overdressed in a gaudy vest of many colors and a blue neckerchief bedropped gaily with yellow spots. His hands, large and coarse, were plentifully bedecked with rings. And he wore a heavy gold watch-chain with a bundle of large seals in a great variety of colors attached to it—which in the heat of conversation he was in the habit of jingling with evident satisfaction.

His companion, Mr. Shelby, had the appearance of a gentleman, and the arrangements of his house, and the general air of the housekeeping, indicated easy and even rich circumstances. As we said before, the two were in the midst of an earnest conversation.

"That is the way I should arrange the matter," said Mr. Shelby.

"I can't make trade that way—I positively can't, Mr. Shelby," said the other, holding up a glass of wine between his eye and the light.

"Why, the fact is, Haley, Tom is an uncommon fellow. He is certainly worth that sum anywhere—steady, honest, capable, manages my whole farm like a clock."

"You mean honest as niggers go," said Haley, helping himself to a glass of brandy.

"No, I mean really. Tom is a good, steady, sensible, pious fellow. He got religion at a camp-meeting four years ago, and I believe he really *did* get it. I've trusted him since then with everything I have—money, house, horses—and let him come and go round the country. And I always found him true and square in everything."

"Some folks don't believe there is pious niggers, Shelby," said Haley with a flourish of his hand, "but *I do*. I had a fellow, now, in this yer last lot I took to Orleans—'twas as good as a meetin', now, really, to hear that critter pray. And he was quite gentle and quiet like. He netted me a good sum, too, for I bought him cheap of a man that was 'bliged to sell out; so I realized six hundred on him. Yes, I consider religion a valeyable thing in a nigger, when it's the genuine article and no mistake."

"Well, Tom's got the real article, if ever a fellow had," rejoined the other. "Why, last fall I let him go to Cincinnati alone to do business for me and bring home five hundred dollars. 'Tom,' says I to him, 'I trust you because I think you're a Christian—I know you wouldn't cheat.' Tom comes back sure enough. I knew he would. Some low fellows, they say, said to him, 'Tom, why don't you make tracks for Canada?' 'Ah, master trusted me, and I couldn't'—they told me about it. I am sorry to part with Tom, I must say. You ought to let him cover the whole balance of the debt. And you would, Haley, if you had any conscience."

"Well, I've got just as much conscience as any man in business can afford to keep," said the trader jocularly, "and I'm ready to do anything in reason to 'blige friends. But this yer, you see, is a leetle too hard on a fellow—a leetle too hard." He sighed and poured out some more brandy.

"Well, then, Haley, how will you trade?" said Mr. Shelby after an uneasy silence.

"Well, haven't you a boy or gal that you could throw in with Tom?"

"Hum! None that I could well spare. To tell the truth, it's only hard necessity makes me willing to sell at all. I don't like parting with any of my hands, that's a fact."

Here the door opened, and a small quadroon boy, between four and five years of age, entered the room. There was something in his appearance remarkably beautiful and engaging. His black hair, fine as floss silk, hung in glossy curls about his round, dimpled face, while a pair of large dark eyes, full of fire and softness, looked out from beneath the long lashes as he peered curiously into the room. A comic air of assurance, blended with bashfulness, showed that he had not been unused to being petted and noticed by his master.

"Hulloa, Jim Crow!" said Mr. Shelby, whistling and snapping a bunch of raisins toward him. "Pick that up, now!"

The child scampered with all his little strength after the prize, while his master laughed.

"Come here, Jim Crow," said he. The child came up, and the master patted the curly head and chucked him under the chin.

"Now, Jim, show this gentleman how you can dance and sing."

The boy at once commenced a wild, grotesque song common among the Negroes, in a rich, clear voice, accompanying his singing with many comic movements of the hands, feet, and whole body, all in perfect time to the music.

"Bravo!" said Haley, throwing him a quarter of an orange.

"Now, Jim, walk like old Uncle Cudjoe when he has the rheumatism," said his master.

Instantly the childish limbs assumed the appearance of deformity as, with his back humped up and his master's stick in his hand, the child hobbled about the room, his face drawn into a doleful pucker, spitting from right to left in imitation of an old man.

Both gentlemen laughed uproariously.

"Now, Jim," said his master, "show us how old Elder Robbins leads the psalm."

The boy drew his chubby face down and commenced gravely toning a psalm tune through his nose.

"Hurrah! Bravo! What a young un!" said Haley. "That chap's a case, I'll promise. Tell you what," said he, suddenly clapping his hand on Mr. Shelby's shoulder, "fling in that chap and I'll settle the business—I will. Come now, if that ain't doing the thing up about the rightest!"

At this moment the door was pushed gently open, and a young quadroon woman, apparently about twenty-five, entered the room.

There needed only a glance from the child to her to identify her as its mother. There was the same rich, full, dark eye with its long lashes, the same ripples of silky black hair. The brown of her complexion gave way on the cheek to a flush, which deepened as she saw the gaze of the strange man fixed upon her in bold and undisguised admiration. Her dress was of the neatest possible fit and set off to advantage her finely molded shape. A delicately formed hand and a trim foot and ankle were items of appearance that did not escape the quick eye of the trader, well used to run up at a glance the points of a fine female article.

"Well, Eliza?" said her master as she stopped and looked hesitatingly at him.

"I was looking for Harry, please, sir." And the boy bounded toward her, showing his spoils, which he had gathered into the skirt of his robe.

"Well, take him away, then," said Mr. Shelby. And hastily she withdrew, carrying the child on her arm.

"By Jupiter," said the trader, "there's an article, now! You

might make your fortune on that ar gal in Orleans any day.
I've seen over a thousand, in my day, paid down for gals not a
bit handsomer."

"I don't want to make my fortune on her," said Mr. Shelby
dryly. And seeking to turn the conversation, he uncorked a
bottle of fresh wine and asked his companion's opinion of
it.

"Capital, sir—first chop!" said the trader. Then, turning
and slapping his hand familiarly on Shelby's shoulder, he
added:

"Come, how will you trade about the gal? What shall I say
for her—what'll you take?"

"Mr. Haley, she is not to be sold," said Shelby. "My wife
would not part with her for her weight in gold."

"Ay, ay! Women always say such things 'cause they ha'nt

no sort of calculation. Just show 'em how many watches, feathers, and trinkets one's weight in gold would buy, and that alters the case, *I* reckon."

"I tell you, Haley, this must not be spoken of. I say no, and I mean no," said Shelby decidedly.

"Well, you'll let me have the boy, though. You must own I've come down pretty handsome for him."

"What on earth can you want with the child?" said Shelby.

"Why, I've got a friend that's going into this yer branch of the business—wants to buy up handsome boys to raise for the market. Fancy articles entirely—sell for waiters and so on, to rich uns that can pay for handsome uns. It sets off one of yer great places—a real handsome boy to open door, wait, and tend. They fetch a good sum. And this little devil is such a comical, musical concern, he's just the article."

"I would rather not sell him," said Mr. Shelby thoughtfully. "The fact is, sir, I'm a humane man, and I hate to take the boy from his mother, sir."

"Oh, you do? La! Yes—I understand perfectly. It is mighty onpleasant getting on with women sometimes. I al'ays hates these yer screechin', screamin' times. They are *mighty* onpleasant. But as I manages business, I generally avoids 'em, sir. Now, what if you get the girl off for a day, or a week, or so. Then the thing's done quietly—all over before she comes home. Your wife might get her some earrings, or a new gown, or some such truck, to make up with her."

"I'm afraid not."

"Lor bless ye, yes! These critters an't like white folks, you know—they gets over things. Only manage right. Now, I've seen fellers as would pull a woman's child out of her arms and set him up to sell, and she screechin' like mad all the time. Very bad policy, damages the article—makes 'em quite unfit for service sometimes. I knew a real handsome gal, now, in Orleans, as was entirely ruined by this sort of handling. The fellow that was trading for her didn't want her baby. And she was one of your real high sort when her blood was up. I tell you, she squeezed up her child in her arms, and talked, and went on real awful. And when they carried off the child and locked her up, she jest went ravin' mad and died in a week. Clear waste, sir, of a thousand dollars, just for want of management—there's where 'tis. It's always best to do the humane thing, sir. That's been *my* experience." And the trader leaned back in his chair and folded his arms with an air of virtuous decision.

"It don't look well, now," he continued while Mr. Shelby thoughtfully peeled an orange, "for a feller to be praisin' himself, but I say it jest because it's the truth. I believe I'm reckoned to bring in about the finest droves of niggers that is brought in—fat and likely, and I lose as few as any man in the business. And I lays it all to my management, sir. And humanity, sir, I may say, is the great pillar of *my* management."

Mr. Shelby, not knowing what to say, said, "Indeed!"

"Now, I've been laughed at for my notions, sir, and I've been talked to. They an't pop'lar, and they an't common, but I've stuck to 'em, sir. I've stuck to 'em and realized well on 'em. Yes, sir, they have paid their passage, I may say." And the trader laughed at his joke.

There was something so original in these notions of humanity that Mr. Shelby could not help laughing with him.

"It's strange, now," the trader proceeded, encouraged by the laugh, "but I never could beat this into people's heads. Now there was Tom Loker, my old partner, down in Natchez. He was a clever fellow, Tom was, only the very devil with niggers—on principle 'twas, you see, for a better-hearted feller never broke bread. 'Twas his *system*, sir. I used to talk to Tom. 'Why, Tom,' I used to say, 'when your gals takes on and cry, what's the use o' crackin' on 'em over the head and knockin' on 'em round? It's ridiculous,' says I, 'and don't do no sort o' good. Why, I don't see no harm in their cryin',' says I. 'It's natur,' says I, 'and if natur can't blow off one way, it will another. Besides, Tom,' says I, 'it jest spiles your gals. They get sickly, and down in the mouth, and some-

times they gets ugly—particular yellow gals do—and it's the
devil and all gettin' on 'em broke in. Now,' says I, 'why can't
you kinder coax 'em up, and speak 'em fair? Depend on it,
Tom, a little humanity, thrown in along, goes a heap further
than all your jawin' and crackin'. And it pays better,' says I,
'depend on 't.' But Tom couldn't get the hang on 't. And he
spiled so many for me that I had to break off with him though
he was a good-hearted fellow, and as fair a business hand as is
goin'."

"And do you find your way of managing the business better than Tom's?" said Mr. Shelby.

"Why, yes, sir, I may say so. You see, when I anyways can,
I takes a leetle care about the onpleasant parts, like selling
young uns and that, get the gals out of the way—out of sight,
out of mind, you know. And when it's clean done, and can't
be helped, they naturally gets used to it. 'Tan't, you know, as
if it was white folks, that's brought up in the way of spectin'
to keep their children and wives, and all that. Niggers, you
know, that's fetched up properly ha'nt no kind of spectations
of no kind; so all these things come easier."

"I'm afraid mine are not properly brought up, then," said
Mr. Shelby.

"S'pose not. You Kentucky folks spile your niggers. You
mean well by 'em, but 'tan't no real kindness, after all. Now, a
nigger, you see, what's got to be hacked and tumbled round
the world and sold to Tom, and Dick, and the Lord knows
who, 'tan't no kindness to be givin' on him notions and spectations, and bringin' him up too well, for the rough and tumble
comes all the harder on him after. I think I treat niggers just
about as well as it's ever worth while to treat 'em."

"It's a happy thing to be satisfied," said Mr. Shelby with a
slight shrug.

"Well," said Haley after they had both silently picked their
nuts for a time, "what do you say?"

"I'll think the matter over and talk with my wife," said Mr.
Shelby. "Meanwhile, Haley, if you want the matter carried

on in the quiet way you speak of, you'd best not let your business in this neighborhood be known."

"Oh, certainly, by all means. Mum, of course. But I'll tell you, I'm in a devil of a hurry and shall want to know as soon as possible what I may depend on," said he, rising and putting on his overcoat.

"Well, call this evening between six and seven and you shall have my answer," said Mr. Shelby. And the trader bowed himself out of the room.

"I'd like to have been able to kick the fellow down the steps," Shelby said to himself as he saw the door fairly closed, "with his impudent assurance. But he knows how much he has me at advantage. If anybody had ever said to me that I should sell Tom down South to one of those rascally traders, I should have said, 'Is thy servant a dog?' And now it must come, for aught I see. And Eliza's child, too! I know that I shall have some fuss with wife about that. And, for that matter, about Tom, too. So much for being in debt—heigh-ho! The fellow sees his advantage and means to push it."

Mr. Shelby was a fair average kind of man, good-natured and kindly, and disposed to easy indulgence of those around him. There had never been a lack of anything which might contribute to the physical comfort of the Negroes on his estate. He had, however, speculated largely, had involved himself deeply, and his notes to a large amount had come into the hands of Haley. This was the key to the preceding conversation.

Now, it had so happened that in approaching the door, Eliza had caught enough of the talk to know that a trader was making offers to her master for somebody. She would gladly have stopped at the door to listen as she came out, but her mistress just then calling, she was obliged to hasten away. Still, she thought she heard the trader make an offer for her boy—could she be mistaken? Her heart swelled and throbbed, and she strained him so tightly that the little fellow looked up into her face in astonishment.

"Eliza, girl, what ails you today?" said her mistress when Eliza had upset the wash-pitcher, knocked down the work-stand, and finally was distractedly offering her mistress a long nightgown in place of the silk dress she had ordered her to bring from the wardrobe.

Eliza started. "Oh, Missis!" she said, raising her eyes. Then bursting into tears, she sat down in a chair and began sobbing.

"Why, Eliza child, what ails you?" said her mistress.

"Oh, Missis, Missis," said Eliza, "there's been a trader talking with master in the parlor. I heard him."

"Well, silly child, suppose there has."

"Oh, Missis, *do* you suppose Mas'r would sell my Harry?" And the poor creature threw herself into a chair and sobbed convulsively.

"Sell him! No, you foolish girl! You know your master never deals with those Southern traders and never means to sell any of his servants so long as they behave well. Why, you silly child, who do you think would want to buy your Harry? Do you think all the world are set on him as you are, you goosie? Come, cheer up, and hook my dress. There now, put my back hair up in that pretty braid you learnt the other day, and don't go listening at doors any more."

"Well, but Missis, *you* never would give your consent—to —to—"

"Nonsense, child! To be sure, I shouldn't. What do you talk so for? I would as soon have one of my own children sold. But really, Eliza, you are getting altogether too proud of that little fellow. A man can't put his nose in the door but you think he must be coming to buy him."

Reassured by her mistress' confident tone, Eliza proceeded nimbly with her toilet, laughing at her own fears as she proceeded.

Mrs. Shelby was a woman of a high class both intellectually and morally, who carried her principles out with great energy for the comfort, instruction, and improvement of her servants. Her husband, who made no professions to any particular character, nevertheless reverenced her opinion. The heaviest load on his mind, after his conversation with the trader, lay in the necessity of breaking to his wife the arrangement contemplated—meeting the opposition which he knew he should have reason to encounter.

Mrs. Shelby, being entirely ignorant of her husband's debts, and knowing only the general kindliness of his temper, had been quite sincere in the entire disbelief with which she had met Eliza's suspicions. In fact, she dismissed the matter from her mind without a second thought. And, being occupied in preparations for an evening visit, it passed out of her thoughts entirely.

The Mother

ELIZA had been brought up by her mistress, from girlhood, as a petted and indulged favorite. Safe under the protecting care of Mrs. Shelby, she had reached maturity without those temptations which make beauty so fatal an inheritance to a slave. She had been married to a bright and talented young mulatto man, who was a slave on a neighboring estate and bore the name of George Harris.

This young man had been hired out by his master to work in a bagging factory, where his adroitness and ingenuity caused him to be considered the first hand in the place. He had invented a machine for the cleaning of the hemp, which, considering the education and circumstances of the inventor, displayed quite as much mechanical genius as Whitney's cotton-gin.

He was possessed of a handsome person and pleasing manners and was a general favorite in the factory. Nevertheless, as this young man was in the eye of the law not a man, but a thing, all these superior qualifications were subject to the control of a vulgar, narrow-minded, and tyrannical master. This same gentleman, having heard of the fame of George's invention, took a ride over to the factory to see what this intelligent chattel had been about. He was received with great enthusiasm by the employer, who congratulated him on possessing so valuable a slave.

He was waited upon over the factory, and shown the machinery by George, who, in high spirits, talked so fluently, held himself so erect, looked so handsome and manly, that his master began to feel an uneasy consciousness of inferiority. What business had his slave to be marching round the country, inventing machines, and holding up his head among gentlemen? He'd soon put a stop to it. He'd take him back and put him to hoeing and digging, and "see if he'd step about so smart." Accordingly, the manufacturer and all hands concerned were astounded when he suddenly demanded George's wages, and announced his intention of taking him home.

"But, Mr. Harris," remonstrated the manufacturer, "isn't this rather sudden?"

"What if it is? Isn't the man *mine?*"

"We would be willing, sir, to increase the rate of compensation."

"No object at all, sir. I don't need to hire any of my hands out unless I've a mind to."

"But, sir, he seems peculiarly adapted to this business."

"Dare say he may be. Never was much adapted to anything that I set him about, I'll be bound."

"But only think of his inventing this machine," interposed one of the workmen, rather unluckily.

"Oh yes! A machine for saving work, is it? He'd invent that, I'll be bound. Let a nigger alone for that, any time. They are all labor-saving machines themselves, every one of 'em. No, he shall tramp!"

George had stood like one transfixed at hearing his doom thus suddenly pronounced by a power that he knew was irresistible. He folded his arms and tightly pressed in his lips, but a whole volcano of bitter feelings burned in his bosom and sent streams of fire through his veins. He breathed short. His large dark eyes flashed like live coals. He might have broken into some dangerous outburst, had not the kindly manufacturer touched him on the arm and said in a low tone:

"Give way, George. Go with him for the present. We'll try to help you yet."

The tyrant observed the whisper and guessed its meaning though he could not hear what was said. And he inwardly strengthened himself in his determination to keep the power he possessed over his victim.

George was taken home and put to the meanest drudgery of the farm. He had been able to repress every disrespectful word. But the flashing eye, the gloomy and troubled brow, were part of a natural language that could not be repressed— they were signs which showed too plainly that the man could not become a thing.

It was during the happy period of his employment in the factory that George had seen and married his wife. During that period, being much trusted and favored by his employer, he had liberty to come and go. The marriage was highly approved of by Mrs. Shelby, who felt pleased to unite her handsome favorite with one of her own class who seemed in every way suited to her. So they were married in her mistress' great parlor, and her mistress herself adorned the bride's beautiful hair with orange-blossoms, and threw over it the bridal veil, which certainly could scarce have rested on a fairer head. And there was no lack of white gloves, and cake and wine, and of admiring guests to praise the bride's beauty and her mistress' liberality.

For a year or two Eliza saw her husband frequently, and there was nothing to interrupt their happiness except the loss of two infant children, to whom she was passionately attached, and whom she mourned with intense grief. After the birth of little Harry, however, she had gradually become quieted and settled. Entwined with that little life, her spirit had become sound and healthful, and Eliza was a happy woman up to the time that her husband was rudely torn from his kind employer and brought under the iron sway of his legal owner.

The manufacturer, true to his word, visited Mr. Harris a week or two after George had been taken away, and tried every possible inducement to lead him to restore him to his former employment.

"You needn't trouble yourself to talk any longer," Mr. Harris said doggedly. "I know my own business, sir."

"I did not presume to interfere with it, sir. I only thought that you might think it for your interest to let your man to us on the terms proposed."

"Oh, I understand the matter well enough. I saw your winking and whispering the day I took him out of the factory. But you don't come it over me that way. It's a free country, sir. The man's *mine*, and I do what I please with him—that's it!"

And so fell George's last hope—nothing before him but a life of toil and drudgery, rendered more bitter by every little smarting vexation and indignity which tyranny could devise.

The Husband and Father

MRS. SHELBY had gone on her visit, and Eliza stood on the verandah, looking after the retreating carriage, when a hand was laid on her shoulder. She turned, and a bright smile lighted up her fine eyes.

"George, is it you? Well, I am so glad you's come! Missis is gone to spend the evening. So come into my little room, and we'll have the time all to ourselves."

Saying this, she drew him into a neat little apartment opening on the verandah, where she generally sat at her sewing, within call of her mistress.

"How glad I am!—Why don't you smile?—And look at Harry—how he grows." The boy stood shyly regarding his father through his curls, holding close to the skirts of his mother's dress. "Isn't he beautiful?" said Eliza, lifting his curls and kissing him.

"I wish he'd never been born!" said George bitterly. "I wish I'd never been born myself!"

Surprised and frightened, Eliza sat down, leaned her head on her husband's shoulder, and burst into tears.

"There now, Eliza, it's too bad for me to make you feel so, poor girl!" said he fondly. "It's too bad. Oh, how I wish you never had seen me—you might have been happy!"

"George! George! How can you talk so? What dreadful thing has happened, or is going to happen? I'm sure we've been very happy, till lately."

"So we have, dear," said George. Then drawing his child on his knee, he gazed intently on his glorious dark eyes and passed his hands through his long curls.

"Just like you, Eliza—and you are the handsomest woman I ever saw, and the best one I ever wish to see. But, oh, I wish I'd never seen you, nor you me!"

"Oh, George, how can you!"

"Yes, Eliza, it's all misery, misery, misery! My life is bitter as wormwood—the very life is burning out of me. I'm a poor, miserable, forlorn drudge. I shall only drag you down with me, that's all. What's the use of our trying to do anything, trying to know anything, trying to be anything? What's the use of living? I wish I was dead!"

"Oh, now, dear George, that is really wicked! I know how you feel about losing your place in the factory, and you have

a hard master. But pray be patient, and perhaps something—"

"Patient!" said he, interrupting her. "Haven't I been patient? Did I say a word when he came and took me away, for no earthly reason, from the place where everybody was kind to me? I'd paid him truly every cent of my earnings—and they all say I worked well."

"Well, it *is* dreadful," said Eliza. "But, after all, he is your master, you know."

"My master! And who made him my master? That's what I think of—what right has he to me? I'm a man as much as he is. I'm a better man than he is. I know more about business than he does. I am a better manager than he is. I can read better than he can. I can write a better hand. And I've learned it all myself, too, no thanks to him—I've learned it in spite of him. And now what right has he to make a dray-horse out of me—to take me from things I can do, and do better than he can, and put me to work that any horse can do? He says he'll bring me down and humble me, and he puts me to just the hardest, meanest, and dirtiest work on purpose!"

"Oh, George! George! You frighten me! Why I never heard you talk so. I'm afraid you'll do something dreadful. I don't wonder at your feelings at all. But oh, do be careful—do, do, for my sake, for Harry's!"

"I have been careful, and I have been patient, but it's growing worse and worse—flesh and blood can't bear it any longer. Every chance he can get to insult and torment me he takes. I thought I could do my work well, and keep on quiet, and have some time to read and learn out of work hours. But the more he sees I can do, the more he loads on. He says that though I don't say anything, he sees I've got the devil in me, and he means to bring it out. And one of these days it will come out in a way that he won't like, or I'm mistaken!"

"Oh dear! What shall we do?" said Eliza mournfully.

"It was only yesterday," said George, "as I was busy loading stones into a cart, that young Mas'r Tom stood there, slashing his whip so near the horse that the creature was frightened. I asked him to stop, as pleasant as I could—he just kept right on. I begged him again, and then he turned on me and began striking me. I held his hand, and then he screamed and kicked and ran to his father and told him that I was fighting him. He came in a rage and said he'd teach me who was my master. And he tied me to a tree, and cut switches for young master, and told him that he might whip me till he was tired—and he did do it! If I don't make him remember it sometime!" And the brow of the young man grew dark, and his eyes burned with an expression that made his young wife tremble. "Who made this man my master? That's what I want to know!" he said.

"Well," said Eliza mournfully, "I always thought that I must obey my master and mistress, or I couldn't be a Christian."

"There is some sense in it in your case—they have brought

you up like a child, fed you, clothed you, indulged you, and taught you so that you have a good education. That is some reason why they should claim you. But I have been kicked and cuffed and sworn at, and at the best only let alone. And what do I owe? I've paid for all my keeping a hundred times over. I *won't* bear it. No, I *won't!*" he said, clenching his hand with a fierce frown.

Eliza trembled and was silent. She had never seen her husband in this mood before.

"You know poor little Carlo, that you gave me," added George. "The creature has been about all the comfort that I've had. He has slept with me nights, and followed me around days, and kind o' looked at me as if he understood how I felt. Well, the other day I was just feeding him with a few scraps I picked up by the kitchen door, and Mas'r came along and said I was feeding him up at his expense, and that he couldn't afford to have every nigger keeping his dog, and ordered me to tie a stone to his neck and throw him in the pond."

"Oh, George, you didn't do it!"

"Do it? Not I! But he did. Mas'r and Tom pelted the poor drowning creature with stones. Poor thing! He looked at me so mournful, as if he wondered why I didn't save him. I had to take a flogging because I wouldn't do it myself. I don't care. Mas'r will find out that I'm one that whipping won't tame. My day will come yet if he don't look out."

"What are you going to do? Oh, George, don't do anything wicked. If you only trust in God, and try to do right, he'll deliver you."

"I an't a Christian like you, Eliza—my heart's full of bitterness. I can't trust in God. Why does he let things be so?"

"Oh, George, we must have faith. Mistress says that when all things go wrong to us, we must believe that God is doing the very best."

"That's easy to say for people that are sitting on their sofas and riding in their carriages. But let 'em be where I am, I guess it would come some harder. I wish I could be good, but my heart burns and can't be reconciled anyhow. You couldn't in my place—you can't now if I tell you all I've got to say. You don't know the whole yet."

"What can be coming now?"

"Well, lately Mas'r has been saying that he was a fool to let me marry off the place, that he hates Mr. Shelby and all his tribe because they are proud and hold their heads up above him, and that I've got proud notions from you. And he says he won't let me come here any more, and that I shall take a wife and settle down on his place. At first he only scolded and grumbled these things. But yesterday he told me that I should take Mina for a wife, and settle down in a cabin with her, or he would sell me down river."

"Why—but you were married to *me*, by the minister, as much as if you'd been a white man!" said Eliza simply.

"Don't you know a slave can't be married? There is no law in this country for that. I can't hold you for my wife if he chooses to part us. That's why I wish I'd never seen you— why I wish I'd never been born. It would have been better for us both—it would have been better for this poor child if he had never been born. All this may happen to him yet!"

"Oh, but Master is so kind!"

"Yes, but who knows? He may die, and then Harry may be sold to nobody knows who. What pleasure is it that he is handsome, and smart, and bright? I tell you, Eliza, that a sword will pierce through your soul for every good and pleasant thing your child is or has. It will make him worth too much for you to keep!"

The words smote heavily on Eliza's heart. The vision of the trader came before her eyes, and as if someone had struck her a deadly blow, she turned pale and gasped for breath. She looked nervously out on the verandah where the boy, tired of the grave conversation, had retired, and where he was riding triumphantly up and down on Mr. Shelby's walking-stick. She would have spoken to tell her husband her fears, but checked herself.

"No, no—he has enough to bear, poor fellow!" she thought.

"No, I won't tell him. Besides, it an't true. Missis never deceives us."

"So, Eliza, my girl," said the husband mournfully, "bear up, now. And good-bye, for I'm going."

"Going, George! Going where?"

"To Canada," said he, straightening himself up. "And when I'm there, I'll buy you. That's all the hope that's left us. You have a kind master, that won't refuse to sell you. I'll buy you and the boy—God helping me, I will!"

"Oh, dreadful! If you should be taken?"

"I won't be taken, Eliza—I'll *die* first! I'll be free, or I'll die!"

"You won't kill yourself!"

"No need of that. They will kill me, fast enough. They never will get me down the river alive!"

"Oh, George, for my sake, do be careful! Don't do anything wicked—don't lay hands on yourself, or anybody else! You are tempted too much, too much. But don't—go you must—but go carefully, prudently. Pray God to help you."

"Well, then, Eliza, hear my plan. Mas'r took it into his head to send me right by here, with a note to Mr. Symmes, that lives a mile past. I believe he expected I should come here to tell you what I have. It would please him if he thought it would aggravate 'Shelby's folks,' as he calls 'em. I'm going home quite resigned, you understand, as if all was over. I've got some preparations made—and there are those that will help me. And in the course of a week or so, I shall be among the missing. Pray for me, Eliza. Perhaps the good Lord will hear *you*."

"Oh, pray yourself, George, and go trusting in him. Then you won't do anything wicked."

"Well, now *good-bye*," said George, holding Eliza's hands and gazing into her eyes without moving. They stood silent. Then there were last words, and sobs, and bitter weeping— such parting as those may make whose hope to meet again is as the spider's web—and the husband and wife were parted.

An Evening in Uncle Tom's Cabin

THE cabin of Uncle Tom was a small log building close to "the house," as the Negro calls his master's dwelling. In front, it had a neat garden patch where, every summer, strawberries, raspberries, and a variety of fruits, vegetables, and flowers flourished under careful tending. The whole front of the cabin, moreover, was covered by a large scarlet bignonia and a native rose which, twisting and interlacing, left scarce a vestige of the rough logs to be seen.

Let us enter the dwelling. The evening meal at the house is over, and Aunt Chloe, who presided over its preparation as head cook, has come out into her own snug territories to "get her ole man's supper." Therefore doubt not that it is her you see by the fire, presiding with anxious interest over certain frizzling items in a stewpan, and anon lifting the cover of a bake-kettle. A round, black, shining face is hers. It beams with contentment from under her well-starched checked turban, yet bears on it a little of that tinge of self-consciousness which becomes the first cook of the neighborhood.

But let us finish our picture of the cottage. In one corner stood a bed, covered neatly with a snowy spread, and by the side of it was a piece of carpeting of some considerable size. That corner, made sacred from the inroads of little folks, was the *drawing room* of the establishment. In the other corner was a bed of much humbler pretensions and evidently designed for *use*.

On a rough bench in the corner, a couple of woolly-headed boys with glistening black eyes and fat, shining cheeks, were busy superintending the first walking operations of the baby, which, as is usually the case, consisted in getting up on its feet, balancing a moment, and then tumbling down—each successive failure being violently cheered as something decidedly clever.

A table was drawn out in front of the fire and covered with a cloth, displaying cups and saucers of a brilliant pattern, with other symptoms of an approaching meal. At this table was seated Uncle Tom, Mr. Shelby's best hand. He was a large, broad-chested, powerfully made man, of a full glossy black, and a face whose truly African features were characterized by an expression of grave and steady good sense, united with much kindness and good will. There was something about his whole air self-respecting and dignified, yet united with a confiding and humble simplicity.

He was very busily intent at this moment on a slate lying before him, on which he was carefully endeavoring to copy some letters, an operation overlooked by young Mas'r George, a smart boy of thirteen, who appeared fully to realize the dignity of his position as instructor.

"Not that way, Uncle Tom, not that way," said he briskly as Uncle Tom laboriously brought up the tail of his *g* the wrong side out. "That makes a *q*, you see."

"La sakes, now, does it?" said Uncle Tom, looking with a respectful, admiring air as his young teacher flourishingly scrawled *q*'s and *g*'s innumerable. Then, taking the pencil in his big, heavy fingers, he patiently recommenced.

"How easy white folks al'ays does things!" said Aunt Chloe, pausing while she was greasing a griddle with a scrap of bacon on her fork, and regarding young Master George with pride. "The way he can write, now! And read, too! And then to come out here evenings and read his lessons to us—it's mighty interestin'!"

"But, Aunt Chloe, I'm getting mighty hungry," said George. "Isn't that cake in the skillet almost done?"

"Mos' done, Mas'r George," said Aunt Chloe, lifting the lid and peeping in, "browning beautiful—a real lovely brown. Ah, let me alone for dat! Missis let Sally try to make some

cake t' other day, jes to *larn* her, she said. 'Oh, go way, Missis,' says I. It really hurts my feelin's, now, to see good vittles spiled dat ar way. Cake ris all to one side—no shape at all, no more dan my shoe. Go way!''

And with this final expression of contempt, Aunt Chloe whipped the cover off the bake-kettle and disclosed to view a neatly-baked pound cake, of which no city confectioner need to have been ashamed. This being evidently the central point of the entertainment, Aunt Chloe began now to bustle about earnestly in the supper department.

"Here you, Mose and Pete! Get out de way, you niggers! Get away, Polly, honey—Mammy'll give her baby somefin by and by. Now, Mas'r George, you jes take off dem books and set down now with my old man, and I'll take up de sausages and have de first griddleful of cakes on your plates in less dan no time.''

"They wanted me to come to supper in the house," said George, "but I knew what was what too well for that, Aunt Chloe."

"So you did, honey," said Aunt Chloe, heaping the smoking battercakes on his plate. "You know'd your old Aunty'd keep de best for you. Oh, let you alone for dat! Go way!" And with that, Aunty turned again to her griddle.

"Now for the cake," said Mas'r George when the activity of the griddle department had somewhat subsided. And the youngster flourished a large knife over the article in question.

"La bless you, Mas'r George!" said Aunt Chloe with earnestness, catching his arm. "You wouldn't be for cuttin' it wid dat ar great heavy knife! Smash all down—spile all de pretty rise of it. Here I've got a thin old knife I keeps sharp a purpose. Dar now, see! Comes apart light as a feather! Now eat away—you won't get anything to beat dat ar."

"Tom Lincon says," said George, speaking with his mouth full, "that their Jinny is a better cook than you."

"Dem Lincons an't much 'count, no way!" said Aunt Chloe contemptuously. "I mean longside *our* folks. Set Mas'r Lincon, now, longside Mas'r Shelby! Good Lord! And Missis Lincon—can she kinder sweep it into a room like my Missis, so kinder splendid, yer know! Oh, go way! Don't tell me nothin' o 'dem Lincons!" And Aunt Chloe tossed her head as one who hoped she did know something of the world.

"Well, though, I've heard you say," said George, "that Jinny was a pretty fair cook."

"So I did," said Aunt Chloe. "I may say dat. Good, plain, common cookin' Jinny'll do—make a good pone o' bread, bile her tater fa'r. Her corn cakes isn't extra, not extra now, Jinny's corn cakes isn't, but then they's fa'r. But, Lor, come to de higher branches, and what *can* she do? "Why, she makes pies—sartin she does. But what kinder crust? Can she make your real flecky paste as melts in your mouth and lies all up like a puff? Now, I went over thar when Miss Mary was gwine to be married, and Jinny she jes showed me de weddin' pies. Jinny and I is good friends, ye know. I never said nothin'. But go long, Mas'r George! Why, I shouldn't sleep for a week if I had a batch of pies like dem ar."

"I suppose Jinny thought they were ever so nice," said George.

"Thought so! Thar she was, showin' 'em as innocent—she can't be spected to know. Lor, de family an't nothin'! Ah, Mas'r George, you doesn't know half your privileges in yer family and bringin' up!"

"I'm sure, Aunt Chloe, I understand all my pie and pudding privileges," said George. "Ask Tom Lincon if I don't crow over him every time I meet him."

Aunt Chloe sat back in her chair and indulged in a hearty guffaw of laughter at this witticism, telling Mas'r George to go way, and that he was a case, that he was fit to kill her, and that he sartin would kill her one of these days.

"Now, Mas'r George," she added, "ye oughter jest ask him here to dinner, some o' dese times. It would look quite pretty of ye."

"Well, I mean to ask Tom here some day next week," said George, "and you do your prettiest, Aunt Chloe, and we'll make him stare."

"Yes, yes—sartin," said Aunt Chloe, delighted. "You'll see. Lor, to think of some of our dinners! Yer mind dat ar great chicken pie I made when we guv de dinner to Gineral Knox? I and Missis, we come pretty near quarrelin' about dat ar crust. What does get into ladies sometimes, I don't know. But sometimes when a body has de heaviest kind o' 'sponsibility on 'em, as ye may say, and is all kinder *seris* and taken up, dey takes dat ar time to be hangin' round and kinder interferin'! Now, Missis she wanted me to do dis way, and she wanted me to do dat way. And finally I got kinder sarcy and says I, 'Now Missis, do jes look at dem beautiful white hands o' yourn, with long fingers, and all a sparklin' with rings, like my white lilies when de dew's on 'em. And look at my great black stumpin' hands. Now, don't ye think dat de Lord must have meant *me* to make de pie crust, and you to stay in de parlor?' Dar! I was jes so sarcy, Mas'r George."

"And what did Mother say?" said George.

"Say? Why, she kinder larfed in her eyes—dem great handsome eyes o' hern—and says she, 'Well, Aunt Chloe, I think you are about in the right on 't,' says she, and she went off in de parlor. She oughter cracked me over de head for bein' so sarcy. But dar's whar 'tis—I can't do nothin' with ladies in de kitchen!"

"Well, you made out well with that dinner—I remember everybody said so," said George.

"Didn't I? And wan't I behind de dinin' room door dat bery day? And didn't I see de Gineral pass his plate three times for some more dat bery pie? And says he, 'You must have an uncommon cook, Mrs. Shelby!' Lor, I was fit to split myself."

By this time Master George had arrived at that pass when he really could not eat another morsel and, therefore, he was at leisure to notice the pile of woolly heads and glistening eyes which were regarding their operations hungrily from the opposite corner.

"Here, you Mose, Pete," he said, breaking off liberal bits and throwing them. "You want some, don't you? Come, Aunt Chloe, bake them some cakes."

And George and Tom moved to a comfortable seat in the chimney-corner while Aunt Chloe, after baking a goodly pile of cakes, took her baby on her lap and began alternately filling its mouth and her own, and distributing to Mose and Pete, who seemed rather to prefer eating theirs as they rolled about on the floor under the table, tickling each other and occasionally pulling the baby's toes.

"Oh, go long, will ye?" said the mother, giving now and then a kick, in a kind of general way, under the table. "Can't ye be decent when white folks comes to see ye?"

"La, now!" said Uncle Tom. "They are so full of tickle all the while, they can't behave theirselves."

Here the boys emerged from under the table and, with hands and faces plastered with molasses, began a vigorous kissing of the baby.

"Get along wid ye!" said the mother, pushing away their woolly heads. "Ye'll all stick together and never get clar if ye do dat fashion. Go long to de spring and wash yerselves. Did ye ever see such aggravatin' young uns?" she continued complacently as, producing an old towel, she poured a little water out of the cracked teapot on it and began rubbing off the molasses from the baby's face and hands. And having polished her till she shone, she set her down in Tom's lap while she busied herself in clearing away supper.

"An't she a peart young un?" said Tom, holding her from him to take a full-length view. Then, getting up, he set her on his broad shoulder and began capering and dancing with her, while Mas'r George snapped at her with his pocket handkerchief, and Mose and Pete, now returned, roared after her like bears, till Aunt Chloe declared that they "fairly took her head off" with their noise.

"Well, now, I hopes you're done," said Aunt Chloe, who had been busy pulling out a rude box of a trundle-bed. "And now, you Mose and you Pete, get into thar, for we's goin' to have the meetin'."

"Oh, Mother, we don't wanter. We wants to sit up to meetin'—meetin's is so curis. We likes 'em."

"La, Aunt Chloe, shove it under and let 'em sit up," said Mas'r George decisively, giving a push to the rude machine.

Aunt Chloe, having thus saved appearances, seemed highly delighted to push the thing under.

"What we's to do for cheers, now *I* declare I don't know," she said. But as the meeting had been held at Uncle Tom's weekly for an indefinite length of time without any more "cheers," there seemed some encouragement to hope that a way would be discovered at present.

"Well, ole man," said Aunt Chloe, "you'll have to tote in them ar bar'ls."

Two empty casks were rolled into the cabin, and being secured from rolling by stones on each side, boards were laid across them, which arrangement, together with the turning down of certain tubs and pails and the disposing of the rickety chairs, at last completed the preparation.

"Mas'r George is such a beautiful reader, now, I know he'll stay to read for us," said Aunt Chloe, to which George very readily assented.

The room was soon filled with a motley assemblage, from the old grayhead of eighty to the young girl and lad of fifteen. A little harmless gossip ensued on various themes, such as where old Aunt Sally got her new red handkerchief, and how "Missis was going to give Lizy that spotted muslin gown," and how Mas'r Shelby was thinking of buying a new sorrel colt that was going to prove an addition to the glories of the place. A few of the worshipers belonging to families hard by, who had got permission to attend, brought in various choice scraps of information about the sayings and doings at the house and on the place, which circulated as freely as the same sort of small change does in higher circles.

After a while the singing commenced, to the evident delight of all present. The words were sometimes the well-known and common hymns sung in the churches about, and sometimes of a wilder, more indefinite character, picked up at camp-meetings. The chorus of one of them, which ran as follows, was sung with great energy:

> Die on the field of battle,
> Die on the field of battle,
> Glory in my soul.

Another special favorite had the oft-repeated words:

> O, I'm going to glory—won't you come along with me?
> Don't you see the angels beck'ning, and a calling me away?
> Don't you see the golden city and the everlasting day?

Various relations of experience followed. One old gray-headed woman, long past work, but much revered, rose, and leaning on her staff, said:

"Well, chil'en! Well, I'm mighty glad to hear ye all and see ye all once more, 'cause I don't know when I'll be gone to glory. But I've done got ready, chil'en—'pears like I'd got my little bundle all tied up and my bonnet on, jest a-waitin' for the stage to come along and take me home. Sometimes in the night, I think I hear the wheels a rattlin', and I'm lookin' out all the time. Now, you jest be ready, too, for I tell ye all, chil'en," she said, striking her staff hard on the floor, "Dat ar *glory* is a mighty thing! It's a mighty thing, chil'en—you don' know nothin' about it—it's *wonderful*." And the old creature sat down, with streaming tears, as wholly overcome, while the whole circle struck up:

> O Canaan, bright Canaan,
> I'm bound for the land of Canaan.

Mas'r George, by request, read the last chapters of Revelation, often interrupted by such exclamations as "The *sakes* now!" "Only hear that!" "Jest think on 't!" "Is all that a comin' sure enough?"

George, who was well trained in religious things by his mother, finding himself an object of general admiration, threw in expositions of his own from time to time, for which he was admired by the young and blessed by the old. And it was agreed on all hands that "a minister couldn't lay it off better than he did, and that 'twas reely 'mazin'."

Uncle Tom was looked up to with great respect as a sort of minister among them, and he spoke in a simple, hearty, sincere style. But it was in prayer that he especially excelled. Nothing could exceed the touching simplicity, the child-like earnestness, of his prayer, enriched with the language of Scripture, which seemed so entirely to have wrought itself into his being as to have become a part of himself and to drop from his lips unconsciously. In the language of a pious old Negro, he "prayed right up." And so much did his prayer always work on the devotional feelings of his audiences that there seemed often a danger that it would be lost altogether in the abundance of the responses which broke out everywhere around him.

———

While this scene was passing in the cabin of the man, one quite different passed in the halls of the master. The trader and Mr. Shelby were seated together in the dining room aforenamed, at a table covered with papers and writing utensils. Mr. Shelby was busy in counting some bundles of bills, which, as they were counted, he pushed over to the trader, who counted them likewise.

"All fair," said the trader. "And now for signing these yer."

Mr. Shelby hastily drew the bills of sale toward him and signed them like a man that hurries over some disagreeable business, then pushed them over with the money. Haley produced a parchment which, after looking over it a moment, he handed to Mr. Shelby, who took it with a gesture of suppressed eagerness.

"Wal, now, the thing's *done!*" said the trader, getting up.

"It's *done!*" said Mr. Shelby in a musing tone, and fetching a long breath, he repeated, "It's done!"

"Yer don't seem to feel much pleased with it, 'pears to me," said the trader.

"Haley," said Mr. Shelby, "I hope you'll remember that you promised, on your honor, you wouldn't sell Tom without knowing what sort of hands he's going into."

"Why, you've just done it, sir," said the trader.

"Circumstances, you well know, *obliged* me," said Shelby haughtily.

"Wal, you know, they may 'blige *me*, too," said the trader. "Howsomever, I'll do the very best I can in gettin' Tom a good berth. As to my treatin' on him bad, you needn't be a grain afeard. If there's anything that I thank the Lord for, it is that I'm never noways cruel."

Mr. Shelby did not feel particularly reassured by these declarations. But as they were the best comfort the case admitted of, he allowed the trader to depart in silence and betook himself to a solitary cigar.

Showing the Feelings of Living Property on Changing Owners

MR. AND Mrs. Shelby had retired to their apartment for the night. He was lounging in the large easy-chair, looking over some letters that had come in the afternoon mail, and she was standing before her mirror, brushing out the complicated braids and curls in which Eliza had arranged her hair. For, noticing her maid's pale cheeks and haggard eyes, she had excused her attendance that night and ordered her to bed. The employment, naturally enough, suggested her conversation with the girl in the afternoon, and turning to her husband, she said carelessly:

"By the by, Arthur, who was that low-bred fellow that you lugged in to our dinner table today?"

"Haley is his name," said Shelby, turning himself rather uneasily in his chair and continuing with his eyes fixed on a letter.

"Haley! Who is he, and what may be his business here, pray?"

"Well, he's a man that I transacted some business with, last time I was at Natchez," said Mr. Shelby.

"And he presumed on it to make himself quite at home, and call and dine here, ay?"

"Why, I invited him. I had some accounts with him," said Shelby.

"Is he a Negro-trader?" said Mrs. Shelby, noticing a certain embarrassment in her husband's manner.

"Why, my dear, what put that into your head?" said Shelby, looking up.

"Nothing, only Eliza came in here after dinner in a great worry, crying and taking on, and said you were talking with a trader, and that she heard him make an offer for her boy—the ridiculous little goose!"

"She did, hey?" said Mr. Shelby, returning to his paper, which he seemed for a few minutes quite intent upon, not perceiving that he was holding it bottom upwards.

"It will have to come out," said he mentally. "As well now as ever."

"I told Eliza," said Mrs. Shelby, as she continued brushing her hair, "that she was a little fool for her pains, and that you never had anything to do with that sort of person. Of course, I knew you never meant to sell any of our people—least of all to such a fellow."

"Well, Emily," said her husband, "so I have always felt and said. But the fact is that my business lies so that I cannot get on without. I shall have to sell some of my hands."

"To that creature? Impossible! Mr. Shelby, you cannot be serious."

"I'm sorry to say that I am," said Mr. Shelby. "I've agreed to sell Tom."

"What! Our Tom? That good, faithful creature—been your faithful servant from a boy! Oh, Mr. Shelby! And you have promised him his freedom, too—you and I have spoken to him a hundred times of it. Well, I can believe anything now—I can believe *now* that you could sell little Harry, poor Eliza's only child!" said Mrs. Shelby, in a tone between grief and indignation.

"Well, since you must know all, it is so. I have agreed to sell Tom and Harry both. And I don't know why I am to be rated, as if I were a monster, for doing what everyone does every day."

"But why, of all others, choose these?" said Mrs. Shelby. "Why sell them, of all on the place, if you must sell at all?"

"Because they will bring the highest sum of any—that's why. I could choose another, if you say so. The fellow made me a high bid on Eliza, if that would suit you any better," said Mr. Shelby.

"The wretch!" said Mrs. Shelby forcefully.

"Well, I didn't listen to it a moment—out of regard to your feelings I wouldn't. So give me some credit."

"My dear," said Mrs. Shelby, recollecting herself, "forgive me. I was surprised, and entirely unprepared for this. But surely you will allow me to intercede for these poor creatures. Tom is a noble-hearted, faithful fellow, if he is black. I do believe, Mr. Shelby, that if he were put to it, he would lay down his life for you."

"I know it. But what's the use of all this? I can't help myself."

"Why not make a financial sacrifice? I'm willing to bear my part. Oh, Mr. Shelby, I have tried—tried most faithfully, as a Christian woman should—to do my duty to these poor, simple, dependent creatures. I have cared for them, instructed them, watched over them, and known all their little cares and joys, for years. And how can I ever hold up my head again among them if, for the sake of a little paltry gain, we sell such a faithful, excellent, confiding creature as poor Tom, and tear from him in a moment all we have taught him to love and value? I have taught them the duties of the family, of parent and child, and husband and wife. And how can I bear to have this open acknowledgment that we care for no tie, no duty, no relation, however sacred, compared with money? I have talked with Eliza about her boy—her duty to him as a Christian mother, to watch over him, pray for him, and bring him up in a Christian way. And now what can I say if you tear him away and sell him to an unprincipled man, just to save a little money? I have told her that one soul is worth more than all the money in the world. And how will she believe me when she sees us turn round and sell her child—sell him, perhaps, to certain ruin of body and soul?"

"I'm sorry you feel so about it, Emily—indeed, I am," said Mr. Shelby. "And I respect your feelings, too, though I don't pretend to share them to their full extent. But I tell you now solemnly, it's no use—I cannot help myself. I didn't mean to tell you this, Emily, but, in plain words, there is no choice between selling these two and selling everything. Either they must go, or *all* must. Haley has come into possession of a mortgage, which, if I don't clear off with him directly, will take everything before it. I've raked, and scraped, and borrowed, and all but begged—and the price of these two was needed to make up the balance, and I had to give them up. Haley fancied the child. He agreed to settle the matter that way and no other. I was in his power and *had* to do it. If you feel so to have them sold, would it be any better to have *all* sold?"

Mrs. Shelby stood like one stricken. Finally, turning to her toilet table, she rested her face in her hands and gave a sort of groan.

"This is God's curse on slavery—a bitter, bitter, most accursed thing—a curse to the master and a curse to the slave! I was a fool to think I could make anything good out of such a deadly evil. It is a sin to hold a slave under laws like ours. I always felt it was. I always thought so when I was a girl. I thought so still more after I joined the church. But I thought I could gild it over. I thought by kindness, and care, and instruction I could make the condition of mine better than freedom—fool that I was!"

"Why, wife, you are getting to be an abolitionist, quite."

"Abolitionist! If they knew all I know about slavery, they *might* talk! We don't need them to tell us. You know I never thought that slavery was right—never felt willing to own slaves."

"Well, therein you differ from many wise and pious men," said Mr. Shelby. "You remember Mr. B's sermon the other Sunday?"

"I don't want to hear such sermons. I never wish to hear Mr. B in our church again. Ministers can't help the evil, perhaps, can't cure it, any more than we can—but defend it! It always went against my common sense. And I think you didn't think much of that sermon either."

"Well," said Shelby, "I must say these ministers sometimes carry matters further than we poor sinners would exactly dare to do. But now, my dear, I trust you see the necessity of the thing, and you see that I have done the very best that circumstances would allow."

"Oh yes, yes!" said Mrs. Shelby, hurriedly and distractedly fingering her gold watch. "I haven't any jewelry of any amount," she added thoughtfully, "but would not this watch do something? It was an expensive one when it was bought. If

I could only at least save Eliza's child, I would sacrifice anything I have."

"I'm sorry, very sorry, Emily," said Mr. Shelby. "I'm sorry
this takes hold of you so. But it will do no good. The fact is,
Emily, the thing's done. The bills of sale are already signed
and in Haley's hands, and you must be thankful it is no worse.
That man has had it in his power to ruin us all—and now he is
fairly off. If you knew the man as I do, you'd think that we
had had a narrow escape."

"Is he so hard, then?"

"Why, not a cruel man exactly, but a man of leather—a
man alive to nothing but trade and profit—cool, and unhesitating, and unrelenting as death and the grave. He'd sell his
own mother at a good percentage—not wishing the old
woman any harm, either."

"And this wretch owns that good, faithful Tom and Eliza's
child!"

"Well, my dear, the fact is that this goes rather hard with
me—it's a thing I hate to think of. Haley wants to drive
matters and take possession tomorrow. I'm going to get out
my horse bright and early and be off. I can't see Tom, that's a
fact. And you had better arrange a drive somewhere and
carry Eliza off. Let the thing be done when she is out of
sight."

"No, no," said Mrs. Shelby. "I'll be in no sense accomplice
or help in this cruel business. I'll go and see poor old Tom,
God help him, in his distress! They shall see, at any rate, that
their mistress can feel for and with them. As to Eliza, I dare
not think about it. The Lord forgive us! What have we done
that this cruel necessity should come on us?"

There was one listener to this conversation whom Mr. and
Mrs. Shelby little suspected.

Communicating with their apartment was a large closet,
opening by a door into the outer passage. When Mrs. Shelby
had dismissed Eliza for the night, her feverish and excited
mind had suggested the idea of this closet. She had hidden

herself there, and with her ear pressed close against the crack of the door, had lost not a word of the conversation.

When the voices died into silence, she rose and crept stealthily away. Pale and shivering, with rigid features and compressed lips, she looked an entirely altered being from the soft and timid creature she had been hitherto. She moved cautiously along the entry, paused one moment at her mistress' door and raised her hands in mute appeal to heaven, then turned and glided into her own room. It was a quiet, neat apartment, on the same floor with her mistress. There was the pleasant, sunny window where she had often sat singing at her sewing, there a little case of books, and various little fancy articles ranged by them, the gifts of Christmas holidays. There was her simple wardrobe in the closet and in the drawers. Here was, in short, her home—and, on the whole, a happy one it had been to her. But there, on the bed, lay her slumbering boy, his long curls falling negligently around his unconscious face, his rosy mouth half open, his little fat hands thrown out over the bedclothes.

"Poor boy! Poor fellow!" said Eliza. "They have sold you! But your mother will save you yet!"

No tear dropped over that pillow. In such straits as these the heart has no tears to give—it drops only blood, bleeding itself away in silence. She took a piece of paper and a pencil and wrote hastily:

"Oh, Missis! Dear Missis! Don't think me ungrateful—don't think hard of me, anyway. I heard all you and Master said tonight. I am going to try to save my boy—you will not blame me! God bless and reward you for all your kindness!"

Hastily folding and directing this, she went to a drawer and made up a little package of clothing for her boy, which she tied with a handkerchief firmly round her waist. And, so fond is a mother's remembrance, that even in the terrors of that hour she did not forget to put in the little package one or two of his favorite toys, reserving a gaily painted parrot to amuse him when she should be called on to awaken him. It was some trouble to arouse the little sleeper. But after some effort, he sat up, and was playing with his bird while his mother was putting on her bonnet and shawl.

"Where are you going, Mother?" said he, as she drew near the bed with his little coat and cap.

His mother drew near and looked so earnestly into his eyes that he at once divined that something unusual was the matter.

"Hush, Harry," she said, "mustn't speak loud, or they will hear us. A wicked man was coming to take little Harry away from his mother and carry him way off in the dark. But Mother won't let him—she's going to put on her little boy's cap and coat and run off with him, so the ugly man can't catch him."

Saying these words, she had tied and buttoned on the child's simple outfit, and taking him in her arms, she whispered to him to be very still. And opening the door in her room which led into the outer verandah, she glided noiselessly out.

It was a sparkling, frosty, starlit night, and the mother wrapped the shawl close round her child as he clung round her neck.

Old Bruno, a great Newfoundland, who slept at the end of the porch, rose with a low growl as she came near. She gently spoke his name, and the animal, an old pet and playmate of hers, instantly wagging his tail, prepared to follow her, though apparently revolving much, in his simple dog's head, what such an indiscreet midnight promenade might mean. He often stopped as Eliza glided forward, and looked wistfully first at her and then at the house, and then, as if reassured by reflection, he pattered along after her again. A few minutes brought them to the window of Uncle Tom's cottage, and Eliza, stopping, tapped lightly on the window pane.

The prayer-meeting had been protracted to a very late hour. As Uncle Tom had indulged himself in a few lengthy solos afterwards, he and his worthy helpmeet were not yet asleep, though it was now between twelve and one o'clock.

"Good Lord! What's that?" said Aunt Chloe, starting up and hastily drawing the curtain. "My sakes alive, if it ain't Lizy! Get on your clothes, old man, quick. There's old Bruno, too, a-pawin' round. What on airth!"

The door flew open, and the light of the tallow candle, which Tom had hastily lighted, fell on the haggard face and dark, wild eyes of the fugitive.

"Lord bless you! I'm skeered to look at ye, Lizy! Are ye tuck sick, or what's come over ye?"

"I'm running away, Uncle Tom and Aunt Chloe, carrying off my child—Master sold him!"

"Sold him?" echoed both, lifting up their hands in dismay.

"Yes, sold him!" said Eliza firmly. "I crept into the closet by Mistress' door tonight, and I heard Master tell Missis that he had sold my Harry and you, Uncle Tom, both, to a trader, and that he was going off this morning on his horse, and that the man was to take possession today."

Tom had stood, during this speech, with his hands raised and his eyes dilated, like a man in a dream. Slowly and gradually, as its meaning came over him, he collapsed, rather than seated himself, on his old chair, and sunk his head down upon his knees.

"The good Lord have pity on us!" said Aunt Chloe. "Oh, it don't seem as if it was true! What has he done that Mas'r should sell *him?*"

"He hasn't done anything—it isn't for that. Master don't want to sell, and Missis—she's always good. I heard her plead and beg for us. But he told her 'twas no use, that he was in this man's debt, and that this man had got the power over him, and that if he didn't pay him off clear, it would end in his having to sell the place and all the people, and move off. Yes, I heard him say there was no choice between selling these two and selling all, the man was driving him so hard. Master said he was sorry. But oh, Missis—you ought to have heard her talk! If she an't a Christian and an angel, there never was one. I'm a wicked girl to leave her so, but then I can't help it. She said, herself, one soul was worth more than the world. And this boy has a soul, and if I let him be carried off, who knows what'll become of it? It must be right. But if it an't right, the Lord forgive me, for I can't help doing it!"

"Well, old man!" said Aunt Chloe. "Why don't you go, too? Will you wait to be toted down river, where they kill niggers with hard work and starving? I'd a heap rather die than go there, any day! There's time for ye. Be off with Lizy—you've got a pass to come and go any time. Come, bustle up, and I'll get your things together."

Tom slowly raised his head, looked sorrowfully but quietly around, and said:

"No, no—I an't going. Let Eliza go—it's her right! I wouldn't be the one to say no—'tan't in *natur* for her to stay. But you heard what she said. If I must be sold, or all the people on the place, and everything go to rack, why, let me be sold. I s'pose I can b'ar it as well as any on 'em," he added, while something like a sob and a sigh shook his broad, rough chest convulsively. "Mas'r always found me on the spot—he always will. I never have broke trust, nor used my pass no ways contrary to my word, and I never will. It's better for me alone to go than to break up the place and sell all. Mas'r an't to blame, Chloe, and he'll take care of you and the poor—"

Here he turned to the rough trundle-bed, full of little woolly heads, and broke fairly down. He leaned over the back of the chair and covered his face with his large hands. Sobs, heavy, hoarse, and loud, shook the chair, and great tears fell through his fingers on the floor: just such tears, sir, as you dropped into the coffin where lay your first-born son—such tears, woman, as you shed when you heard the cries of your dying babe. For, sir, he was a man—and you are but another man. And, woman, though dressed in silk and jewels, you are but a woman, and in life's great straits and mighty griefs, ye feel but one sorrow!

"And now," said Eliza, as she stood in the door, "I saw my husband only this afternoon, and I little knew then what was to come. They have pushed him to the very last standing-place, and he told me today that he was going to run away. Do try, if you can, to get word to him. Tell him how I went, and why I went. And tell him I'm going to try and find Canada. You must give my love to him, and tell him, if I never see him again"—she turned away and stood with her back to them for a moment, and then added in a husky voice—"tell him to be as good as he can, and try and meet me in the kingdom of heaven.

"Call Bruno in there," she added. "Shut the door on him, poor beast. He mustn't go with me."

A few last words and tears, a few simple adieus and blessings, and clasping her wondering and affrighted child in her arms, she glided noiselessly away.

Discovery

MR. AND Mrs. Shelby, after their protracted discussion of the night before, did not readily sink to repose, and in consequence slept somewhat later than usual the next morning.

"I wonder what keeps Eliza," said Mrs. Shelby, after giving her bell repeated pulls to no purpose.

Mr. Shelby was standing before his dressing-glass, sharpening his razor. Just then the door opened, and a colored boy entered with his shaving water.

"Andy," said his mistress, "step to Eliza's door and tell her I have rung for her three times. Poor thing!" she added to herself with a sigh.

Andy soon returned, with eyes very wide in astonishment.

"Lor, Missis! Lizy's drawers is all open, and her things all lyin' every which way. And I believe she's just done clared out!"

The truth flashed upon Mr. Shelby and his wife at the same moment. He exclaimed:

"Then she suspected it, and she's off!"

"The Lord be thanked!" said Mrs. Shelby. "I trust she is."

"Wife, you talk like a fool. Really, it will be something pretty awkward for me if she is. Haley saw that I hesitated about selling this child, and he'll think I connived at it, to get him out of the way. It touches my honor!" And Mr. Shelby left the room hastily.

There was great running and exclaiming, and opening and shutting of doors, and appearances of faces in all shades of color in different places for about a quarter of an hour. One person only, who might have shed some light on the matter, was entirely silent, and that was the head cook, Aunt Chloe. Silently, and with a heavy cloud settled down over her once joyous face, she proceeded making out her breakfast biscuits, as if she heard and saw nothing of the excitement around her.

Very soon about a dozen young imps were roosting, like so many crows, on the verandah railings, each one determined to be the first one to inform the strange Mas'r of his ill luck.

"He'll be rael mad, I'll be bound," said Andy.

"Won he swar!" said little black Jake.

When at last Haley appeared, booted and spurred, he was saluted with the bad tidings on every hand. The young imps on the verandah were not disappointed in their hope of hearing him "swar," which he did with an ardor that delighted them all amazingly, as they ducked and dodged hither and thither, to be out of the reach of his riding-whip.

"If I had the little devils!" muttered Haley between his teeth.

"But you han't got 'em though!" said Andy, making a string of indescribable mouths at the unfortunate trader's back when he was fairly beyond hearing.

"I say now, Shelby, this yer's a most extr'or'nary business!" said Haley as he abruptly entered the parlor. "It seems that gal's off with her young un."

"Mr. Haley, Mrs. Shelby is present," said Mr. Shelby.

"I beg pardon, ma'am, " said Haley, bowing slightly, with a still lowering brow. "But still I say, as I said before, this yer's a sing'lar report. Is it true, sir?"

"Sir," said Mr. Shelby, "if you wish to communicate with me, you must observe something of the decorum of a gentleman. Andy, take Mr. Haley's hat and riding-whip. Take a seat, sir. Yes, sir, I regret to say that the young woman, excited by overhearing, or having reported to her, something of this business, has taken her child in the night and made off."

"I did expect fair dealing in this matter, I confess," said Haley.

"Well, sir," said Mr. Shelby, turning sharply round upon him, "what am I to understand by that remark? If any man calls my honor in question, I have but one answer for him."

The trader cowered at this, and in a somewhat lower tone said that "it was plaguey hard on a fellow, that had made a fair bargain, to be gulled that way."

"Mr. Haley," said Mr. Shelby, "if I did not think you had some cause for disappointment, I should not have borne from you the rude and unceremonious style of your entrance into my parlor this morning. I say this much, however. I shall allow of no insinuations cast upon me, as if I were at all partner to any unfairness in this matter. Moreover, I shall feel bound to give you every assistance in the use of horses, servants, et cetera, in the recovery of your property. So, in short, Haley," said he, suddenly dropping from the tone of dignified coolness to his ordinary one of easy frankness, "the best way for you is to keep good-natured and eat some breakfast, and we will then see what is to be done."

Mrs. Shelby now rose and said her engagements would prevent her being at the breakfast-table that morning. And ordering a very respectable mulatto woman to attend to the gentlemen's coffee at the sideboard, she left the room.

Never did fall of any prime minister at court cause greater sensation than the report of Tom's fate. It was the topic in every mouth, everywhere. And nothing was done in the house or in the field but to discuss its probable results. Eliza's flight also greatly stimulated the general excitement.

Black Sam, as he was commonly called from his being about three shades blacker than any other on the place, was revolving the matter profoundly—with a strict lookout to his own personal well-being.

"It's an ill wind dat blows nowhar—dat ar a fact," said Sam, giving an additional hoist to his pantaloons, and adroitly substituting a long nail in place of a missing suspender-button. "Now dar, Tom's down—wal, course der's room for some nigger to be up, and why not dis nigger? Dat's de idee. Tom, a ridin' round de country—boots blacked, pass in his pocket, all grand as Cuffee. Now, why shouldn't Sam? Dat's what I want to know."

"Halloo, Sam—Oh Sam! Mas'r wants you to cotch Bill and Jerry," said Andy, cutting short Sam's soliloquy.

"High! What's afoot now young un?"

"Why, you don't know, I s'pose, that Lizy's cut stick and clared out with her young un?"

"You teach your granny!" said Sam with infinite contempt. "Knowed it a heap sight sooner than you did. This nigger an't so green, now!"

"Well, anyhow, Mas'r wants Bill and Jerry geared right up. And you and I's to go with Mas'r Haley to look arter her."

"Good, now! Dat's de time o' day!" said Sam. "It's Sam dat's called for in dese yer times. He's de nigger. See if I don't cotch her, now. Mas'r'll see what Sam can do!"

"Ah, but Sam!" said Andy. "You'd better think twice. For Missis don't want her cotched, and she'll be in yer wool."

"High!" said Sam, opening his eyes. "How you know dat?"

"Heard her say so my own self, dis blessed mornin', when I bring in Mas'r's shaving-water. She sent me to see why Lizy didn't come to dress her. And when I telled her she was off, she jest ris up, and ses she, 'The Lord be praised.' And Mas'r, he seemed rael mad, and ses he, 'Wife, you talk like a fool.' But Lor! She'll bring him to! I knows well enough how that'll be—it's allers best to stand Missis' side the fence, now I tell yer."

Black Sam, upon this, scratched his woolly pate and again gave a hitch to his pantaloons.

"Der an't no sayin'—never—'bout no kind o' thing in *dis* yer world," he said at last. "Now, sartin I'd a said that Missis would a scoured the varsal world after Lizy."

"So she would," said Andy. "But can't ye see through a ladder, ye black nigger? Missis don't want dis yer Mas'r Haley to get Lizy's boy—dat's de go!"

"High!" said Sam.

"And I'll tell yer more'n all," said Andy. "I specs you'd better be makin' tracks for dem hosses—mighty sudden, too —for I hearn Missis 'quirin' after yer. So you've stood foolin' long enough."

Sam, upon this, began to bestir himself in real earnest, and after a while appeared, bearing down gloriously toward the house, with Bill and Jerry in full canter. Throwing himself off before they had any idea of stopping, he brought them up alongside the horse-post like a tornado. Haley's horse, which was a skittish young colt, winced and bounced and pulled hard at his halter.

"Ho, ho!" said Sam. "Skeery, ar ye?" And his black visage lighted up with a curious, mischievous gleam. "I'll fix ye now!" said he.

There was a large beech tree overshadowing the place, and

the small, sharp, triangular beechnuts lay scattered thickly on the ground. With one of these in his fingers, Sam approached the colt, stroked and patted, and seemed apparently busy in soothing his agitation. On pretense of adjusting the saddle, he adroitly slipped under it the sharp little nut in such a manner that the least weight brought upon the saddle would annoy the animal, without leaving any visible graze or wound.

"Dar!" he said, rolling his eyes with an approving grin. "Me fix 'em."

At this moment Mrs. Shelby appeared on the balcony, beckoning to him.

"Why have you been loitering so, Sam? I sent Andy to tell you to hurry."

"Lord bless you, Missis!" said Sam. "Horses won't be cotched all in a minit. They'd done clared out way down to the south pasture, and the Lord knows whar!"

"Sam, how often must I tell you not to say 'Lord bless you,' and 'the Lord knows,' and such things? It's wicked."

"Oh Lord bless my soul, I done forgot, Missis! I won't say nothing of de sort no more."

"Why, Sam, you just *have* said it again."

"Did I? Oh, Lord! I mean—I didn't go fur to say it."

"You must be *careful*, Sam."

"Jest let me get my breath, Missis, and I'll start fair. I'll be bery careful."

"Well, Sam, you are to go with Mr. Haley, to show him the road and help him. Be careful of the horses, Sam—you know Jerry was a little lame last week. *Don't ride them too fast.*"

Mrs. Shelby spoke the last words with a low voice and strong emphasis.

"Let dis child alone for dat!" said Sam, rolling up his eyes with a volume of meaning. "Lord knows! High! Didn't say dat!" said he, suddenly catching his breath with an absurd gesture, which made his mistress laugh in spite of herself. "Yes, Missis, I'll look out for de hosses!"

"Now, Andy," said Sam, returning to his stand under the beech trees, "you see I wouldn't be 'tall surprised if dat ar gen'lman's crittur should gib a fling by and by, when he comes to be a-gettin' up. You know, Andy, critturs *will* do such things." And therewith Sam poked Andy in the side in a highly suggestive manner.

"High!" said Andy with an air of instant comprehension.

"Yes, yer see, Andy, Missis wants to make time—dat ar's clar to der most or'nary 'bserver. I jist make a little for her. Now, yer see, get all dese yer hosses loose, caperin' permiscus round dis yer lot and down to de wood dar, and I spec Mas'r won't be off in a hurry."

Andy grinned.

"Yer see," said Sam, "yer see, Andy, if any such thing should happen as that Mas'r Haley's horse *should* begin to act contrary, and cut up, you and I jist lets go of ourn to help him, and *we'll help him*—oh, yes!" And Sam and Andy laid their heads back on their shoulders and broke into a low, immoderate laugh, snapping their fingers and flourishing their heels with exquisite delight.

At this instant Haley appeared on the verandah. Somewhat soothed by certain cups of very good coffee, he came out smiling and talking, in tolerably restored humor. Sam and Andy flew to the horse-posts, to be ready to "help Mas'r."

"Well, boys," said Haley, "look alive now. We must lose no time."

"Not a bit of him, Mas'r!" said Sam, putting Haley's reins in his hand and holding his stirrup, while Andy was untying the other two horses.

The instant Haley touched the saddle, the mettlesome creature bounded from the earth with a sudden spring that threw his master sprawling, some feet off, on the soft, dry turf. Sam, with frantic exclamations, made a dive at the reins, but only succeeded in brushing his tattered palm-leaf hat into the horse's eyes, which by no means tended to soothe its nerves. So, with great violence, he overturned Sam, and giving two or

three contemptuous snorts, flourished his heels in the air and
was soon prancing away toward the lower end of the lawn,
followed by Bill and Jerry, whom Andy had not failed to let
loose according to plan, speeding them off with various
dreadful exclamations. And now followed a scene of confusion. Sam and Andy ran and shouted, dogs barked here and
there, and Mike, Mose, Mandy, Fanny, and all the smaller
specimens on the place raced, clapped hands, whooped, and
shouted with untiring zeal.

Haley's horse, which was very fleet and spirited, appeared
to enter into the spirit of the scene with great gusto. And
having for his coursing ground a lawn of nearly half a mile in
extent, gently sloping down on every side into indefinite
woodland, he appeared to take infinite delight in seeing how
near he could allow his pursuers to approach him, and then,
when within a hand's breadth, whisk off with a start and a
snort and career far down into some alley of the wood-lot.

Nothing was further from Sam's mind than to have any one of the troop taken until such season as should seem to him befitting—and the exertions that he made were certainly most heroic. Like the sword of Coeur de Lion, which always blazed in the front and thickest of the battle, Sam's palm-leaf was to be seen everywhere when there was the least danger that a horse could be caught. There he would bear down full tilt, shouting, "Now for it! Cotch him! Cotch him!" in a way that would set everything to rout in a moment.

Haley ran up and down and cursed and swore and stamped. Mr. Shelby in vain tried to shout directions from the balcony, and Mrs. Shelby from her chamber window alternately laughed and wondered—not without some inkling of what lay at the bottom of all this confusion.

At last, about twelve o'clock, Sam appeared triumphant, mounted on Jerry, with Haley's horse by his side, reeking with sweat, but with flashing eyes and dilated nostrils, showing that the spirit of freedom had not yet entirely subsided.

"He's cotched!" he exclaimed triumphantly. "If it hadn't been for me, they might a bust theirselves, all on 'em. But I cotched him!"

"You!" growled Haley, in no amiable mood. "If it hadn't been for you, this never would have happened."

"Lord bless us, Mas'r," said Sam in a tone of the deepest concern. "And me that has been racin' and chasin' till the sweat jest pours off me!"

"Well, well!" said Haley. "You've lost me near three hours with your cursed nonsense. Now let's be off and have no more fooling."

"Why, Mas'r," said Sam in a protesting tone, "I believe you mean to kill us all clar, horses and all. Here we are all just ready to drop down, and the critters all in a reek of sweat. Why, Mas'r won't think of startin' on now till arter dinner. Mas'r's hoss wants rubben down—see how he splashed hisself. And Jerry limps, too. Don't think Missis would be willin' to have us start dis yer way nohow. Lord bless you, Mas'r, we can ketch up, if we do stop. Lizy never was no great of a walker."

Mrs. Shelby, who greatly to her amusement had overheard this conversation from the verandah, now resolved to do her part. She came forward, and courteously expressing her concern for Haley's accident, pressed him to stay to dinner, saying that the cook should bring it on the table immediately.

Thus, all things considered, Haley, with rather questionable grace, proceeded to the parlor, while Sam, rolling his eyes after him with unutterable meaning, proceeded gravely with the horses to the stable-yard, where he and Andy laughed to their hearts' content.

"Did yer see him, Andy? *Did* yer see him when I brought the hoss up? Lord, he'd a killed me if he durs' to—and there I was a standin' as innercent and as humble."

"Lor, I seed you," said Andy. "An't you an old hoss, Sam?"

"Rather specks I am," said Sam. "Did you see Missis upstairs at the winder? I seed her laughin'."

"I'm sure I was racin' so, I didn't see nothin'," said Andy.

"Well, yer see," said Sam, proceeding gravely to wash down Haley's pony, "I'se 'quired what yer may call a habit o' bobservation, Andy. It's a very 'portant habit, Andy, and I 'commend yer to be cultivatin' it, now yer young. Yer see, Andy, it's bobservation makes all de difference in niggers. Didn't I see which way the wind blew dis yer mornin'? Didn't I see what Missis wanted, though she never let on? Dat ar's bobservation, Andy."

"I guess if I hadn't helped your bobservation dis mornin', yer wouldn't have seen your way so smart," said Andy.

"Andy," said Sam, "you's a promisin' child, der an't no manner o' doubt. I thinks lots of yer, Andy, and I don't feel no way ashamed to take idees from you. We oughtenter overlook nobody, Andy, cause the smartest on us gets tripped up sometimes. And so, Andy, let's go up to the house now. I'll be boun' Missis'll give us an uncommon good bite dis yer time."

The Mother's Struggle

IT is impossible to conceive of a human creature more wholly desolate and forlorn than Eliza when she turned her footsteps from Uncle Tom's cabin.

Her husband's suffering and dangers, and the danger of her child, all blended in her mind with a confused and stunning sense of the risk she was running in leaving the only home she had ever known and cutting loose from the protection of a friend whom she loved and revered. Then there was the parting from every familiar object—the place where she had grown up, the trees under which she had played, the groves where she had walked many an evening in happier days by the side of her young husband. Everything, as it lay in the clear, frosty starlight, seemed to speak reproachfully to her and ask her whither could she go from a home like that?

But stronger than all was maternal love, wrought into frenzy by the near approach of a fearful danger. Her boy was old enough to have walked by her side. Now the bare thought of putting him out of her arms made her shudder, and she strained him to her bosom with a convulsive grasp, as she went rapidly forward.

The frosty ground creaked beneath her feet, and she trembled at the sound. Every quaking leaf and fluttering shadow quickened her footsteps. She wondered within herself at the strength that seemed to have come upon her, for she felt the weight of her boy as if it had been a feather. Every flutter of fear seemed to increase the supernatural power that bore her on, while from her pale lips burst forth the prayer to a Friend above—"Lord, help! Lord, save me!"

If it were *your* Harry, mother, or your Willie, that was

going to be torn from you by a brutal trader tomorrow morning—if you had seen the man, and heard that the papers were signed and delivered, and you had only from twelve o'clock till morning to make good your escape—how fast could *you* walk? How many miles could you make in those few brief hours, with the darling at your bosom, the little sleepy head on your shoulder, the small, soft arms trustingly holding on to your neck?

For the child slept. At first, the novelty and alarm kept him waking. But his mother so hurriedly repressed every breath or sound, and so assured him that if he were only still she would certainly save him, that he clung quietly round her neck, only asking as he found himself sinking to sleep:

"Mother, I don't need to keep awake, do I?"

"No, my darling. Sleep if you want to."

"But, Mother, if I do get asleep, you won't let him get me?"

"No, so may God help me!" said his mother, with a paler cheek and a brighter light in her large dark eyes.

The boundaries of the farm, the grove, the wood-lot passed by her dizzily as she walked on. And still she went, leaving one familiar object after another, slacking not, pausing not, till reddening daylight found her many a long mile from all traces of any familiar objects upon the open highway.

She had often been with her mistress to visit some connections in the little village of T——, not far from the Ohio River, and knew the road well. To go thither, to escape across the Ohio River, were the first hurried outlines of her plan of escape—beyond that she could only hope in God.

When horses and vehicles began to move along the highway, she became aware that her headlong pace and distracted air might bring remark and suspicion. She therefore put the boy on the ground, and adjusting her dress and bonnet, walked on at as rapid a pace as she dared. In her little bundle she had provided a store of cakes and apples, which she used to quicken the speed of the child, rolling the apple some yards before them, when the boy would run with all his might after it. And this ruse, often repeated, carried them over many a half-mile.

After a while they came to a thick patch of woodland, through which murmured a clear brook. As the child complained of hunger and thirst, she climbed over the fence with him, and sitting down behind a large rock which concealed them from the road, she gave him a breakfast out of her little package. The boy wondered and grieved that she could not eat.

"No, no, Harry darling! Mother can't eat till you are safe! We must go on—on—till we come to the river!" And she hurried again into the road, and again forced herself to walk regularly and composedly forward.

She was many miles past any neighborhood where she was personally known. If she should chance to meet any who knew her, she reflected that the well-known kindness of the family would be of itself a blind to suspicion, as making it an unlikely supposition that she could be a fugitive. As she was also so white as not to be known as of colored lineage, without a critical survey, and her child was white also, it was much easier for her to pass on unsuspected.

On this presumption, she stopped at noon at a neat farmhouse to rest herself and buy some dinner for her child and self. For as the danger decreased with the distance, she found herself both weary and hungry.

The good woman, kindly and gossiping, seemed rather pleased than otherwise with having somebody in to talk with, and accepted without examination Eliza's statement that she "was going on a little piece to spend a week with her friends."

An hour before sunset, she entered the village of T——, by the Ohio River, weary and footsore, but still strong in heart. Her first glance was at the river, which lay, like Jordan, between her and the Canaan of liberty on the other side.

It was now early spring, and the river was swollen and turbulent. Great cakes of floating ice were swinging heavily to and fro in the turbid waters. Owing to the peculiar form of the shore on the Kentucky side, the land bending far out into the water, the ice had been lodged and detained in great quantities, and the narrow channel which swept round the bend was full of ice, piled one cake over another, thus forming a temporary barrier to the descending ice, which lodged and formed a great, undulating raft, filling up the whole river and extending almost to the Ohio shore.

Eliza stood for a moment contemplating this unfavorable aspect of things, which she saw at once must prevent the usual ferryboat from running, and then turned into a small public house on the bank to make a few inquiries.

The hostess, who was busy in various fizzing and stewing operations over the fire, stopped with a fork in her hand as Eliza's sweet voice arrested her.

"What is it?" she said.

"Isn't there any ferry or boat that takes people over to B——now?" she said.

"No, indeed!" said the woman. "The boats has stopped running."

Eliza's look of dismay struck the woman, and she said inquiringly:

"Maybe you're wanting to get over? Anybody sick? Ye seem mighty anxious."

"I've got a child that's very dangerous," said Eliza. "I never heard of it till last night, and I've walked quite a piece today in hopes to get to the ferry."

"Well, now, that's onlucky," said the woman, whose motherly sympathies were much aroused. "I'm re'lly consarned for ye. Solomon!" she called from the window toward a small back building.

A man in leather apron appeared at the door.

"I say, Sol," said the woman, "is that ar man going to tote them bar'ls over tonight?"

"He said he should try, if 'twas any way prudent," said the man.

"There's a man a piece down here that's going over with some truck this evening, if he durs' to. He'll be in here to supper tonight, so you'd better set down and wait. That's a sweet little fellow," added the woman, offering him a cake.

But the child, wholly exhausted, cried with weariness.

"Poor fellow! He isn't used to walking, and I've hurried him on so," said Eliza.

"Well, take him into this room," said the woman, opening the door into a small bedroom, where stood a comfortable bed. Eliza laid the weary boy upon it and held his hands in hers till he was fast asleep. For her there was no rest. As a fire in her bones, the thought of the pursuer urged her on. And she gazed with longing eyes on the sullen, surging waters that lay between her and liberty. . . .

Here we must take leave of her for the present, to follow the course of her pursuers.

Though Mrs. Shelby had promised that the dinner should be hurried on table, yet it was soon seen that it required more than one to make a bargain. So, although the order was fairly given out in Haley's hearing and carried to Aunt Chloe by at least half a dozen juvenile messengers, she only gave certain very gruff snorts, and tosses of her head, and went on with every operation in an unusually leisurely manner.

For some singular reason, an impression seemed to reign among the servants generally that Missis would not be particularly disobliged by delay, and it was wonderful what a number of accidents occurred constantly to retard the course of things. One luckless wight contrived to upset the gravy. And then gravy had to be got up anew, Aunt Chloe watching and stirring with dogged precision, answering shortly, to all suggestions of haste, that she "warn't going to have raw gravy on the table, to help nobody's catchings." One tumbled down with the water and had to go to the spring for more. Another dropped the butter. And there was from time to time giggling news brought into the kitchen that "Mas'r Haley was mighty oneasy, and that he couldn't sit in his cheer no ways, but was a walkin' and stalkin' to the winders, and through the porch."

"Sarves him right!" said Aunt Chloe indignantly. "He'll get wuss nor oneasy, one of these days, if he don't mend his ways. *His* master'll be sending for him, and then see how he'll look!"

"He'll go to torment, and no mistake," said little Jake.

"He desarves it," said Aunt Chloe grimly. "He's broke a many, many, many hearts—I tell ye all!" she said, stopping with a fork uplifted in her hands. "It's like what Mas'r George reads in Ravelations—souls callin' on the Lord for vengeance on sich! And by and by the Lord'll hear 'em—so he will!"

Aunt Chloe, who was much revered in the kitchen, was listened to with open mouth, and the dinner being now fairly sent in, the whole kitchen was at leisure to gossip with her and to listen to her remarks.

"Sich'll be burnt up forever, and no mistake, won't ther?" said Andy.

"I'd be glad to see it, I'll be boun'," said little Jake.

"Chil'en!" said a voice that made them all start. It was Uncle Tom, who had come in and stood listening to the conversation at the door.

"Chil'en!" he said. "I'm afeard you don't know what ye're sayin'. Forever is a *dre'ful* word, chil'en. It's awful to think on 't. You oughtenter wish that ar to any human crittur."

"We wouldn't to anybody but the soul-drivers," said Andy. "Nobody can help wishin' it to them, they's so awful wicked."

"Don't natur herself kinder cry out on 'em?" said Aunt Chloe. "Don't dey tear der suckin' baby right off his mother's breast and sell him, and der little children as is cryin' and holdin' on by her clothes—don't dey pull 'em off and sells 'em? Don't dey tear wife and husband apart," said Aunt Chloe, beginning to cry, "when it's jest takin' de bery life on 'em? And all de while does dey feel one bit—don't dey drink and smoke, and take it oncommon easy? Lor, if de debil don't get them, what's he good for?" And Aunt Chloe covered her face with her checked apron and began to sob in good earnest.

"Pray for them that spitefully use you, the good book says," said Tom.

"Pray for 'em!" said Aunt Chloe. "Lor, it's too tough! I can't pray for 'em."

"It's natur, Chloe, and natur's strong," said Tom, "but the Lord's grace is stronger. Besides, you oughter think what an awful state a poor crittur's soul's in that'll do them ar things— you oughter thank God that you an't *like* him, Chloe. I'm sure I'd rather be sold ten thousand times over than to have all that ar poor crittur's got to answer for."

"So'd I, a heap," said Jake. "Lor, *shouldn't* we cotch it, Andy?"

"I'm glad Mas'r didn't go off this morning, as he looked to," said Tom. "That ar hurt me more than sellin', it did. Mebbe it might have been natural for him, but 'twould have come desp't hard on me, as has known him from a baby. But I've seen Mas'r, and I begin ter feel sort o' reconciled to the Lord's will now. Mas'r couldn't help hisself. He did right, but I'm feared things will be kinder goin' to rack when I'm gone. Mas'r can't be spected to be a pryin' round everywhar, as I've done, a keepin' up all the ends. The boys all means well, but they's powerful car'less. That ar troubles me."

The bell here rang, and Tom was summoned to the parlor.

"Tom," said his master kindly, "I want you to notice that I give this gentleman bonds to forfeit a thousand dollars if you are not on the spot when he wants you. He's going today to look after his other business, and you can have the day to yourself. Go anywhere you like, boy."

"Thank you, Mas'r," said Tom.

"And mind yerself," said the trader, "and don't come it over your master with any o' yer nigger tricks. For I'll take every cent out of him if you an't thar. If he'd hear to me, he wouldn't trust any on ye—slippery as eels!"

"Mas'r," said Tom—and he stood very straight—"I was jist eight years old when ole Missis put you into my arms, and you wasn't a year old. 'Thar,' says she, 'Tom, that's to be *your* young Mas'r. Take good care on him,' says she. And now I jist ask you, Mas'r, have I ever broke word to you, or gone contrary to you, 'specially since I was a Christian?"

Mr. Shelby was fairly overcome, and the tears rose to his eyes.

"My good boy," said he, "the Lord knows you say but the truth. And if I was able to help it, all the world shouldn't buy you."

"And sure as I am a Christian woman," said Mrs. Shelby, "you shall be redeemed as soon as I can any way bring together means. Sir," she said to Haley, "take good account of who you sell him to, and let me know."

"Lor, yes. For that matter," said the trader, "I may bring him up in a year, not much the wuss for wear, and trade him back."

"I'll trade with you then, and do it to your advantage," said Mrs. Shelby.

"Of course," said the trader. "All's equal with me. I'd as soon trade 'em up as down, so I does a good business. All I want is a livin', you know, ma'am. That's all any on us wants, I s'pose."

Mr. and Mrs. Shelby both felt annoyed and degraded by the familiar impudence of the trader, and yet both saw the absolute necessity of putting a constraint on their feelings. The more hopelessly insensible he appeared, the greater became Mrs. Shelby's dread of his succeeding in recapturing Eliza and her child, and, of course, the greater her motive for detaining him by every female artifice. She therefore graciously smiled, assented, chatted familiarly, and did all she could to make the time pass imperceptibly.

At two o'clock Sam and Andy brought the horses up to the posts, apparently greatly refreshed by the scamper of the morning.

"Your master, I s'pose, don't keep no dogs," said Haley thoughtfully as he prepared to mount.

"Heaps on 'em," said Sam triumphantly. "Thar's Bruno—he's a roarer! And, besides that, 'bout every nigger of us keeps a pup of some natur or other."

"Poh!" said Haley—and he said something else, too, with regard to the said dogs, at which Sam muttered:

"Don't see no use cussin' on 'em no way."

"But your master don't keep no dogs (I pretty much know he don't) for trackin' out niggers."

Sam knew exactly what he meant, but he kept on a look of earnest simplicity.

"Our dogs all smells round considable sharp. I spect they's the kind, though they han't never had no practice. They's fa'r dogs, though, at most anythin', if you'd get 'em started. Here, Bruno," he called, whistling to the lumbering Newfoundland, who came pitching toward them.

"You go hang!" said Haley, getting up. "Come, tumble up now."

Sam tumbled up accordingly, cleverly contriving to tickle Andy as he did so, which occasioned Andy to split out into a laugh, greatly to Haley's indignation, who made a cut at him with his riding-whip.

"I's astonished at yer, Andy," said Sam with awful gravity. "This yer's a seris bisness, Andy. Yer mustn't be a-makin' game. This yer an't no way to help Mas'r."

"I shall take the straight road to the river," said Haley decidedly, after they had come to the boundaries of the estate. "I know the way of all of 'em—they makes tracks for the underground."

"Sartin," said Sam, "dat's de idee. Mas'r Haley hits de thing right in de middle. Now, der's two roads to de river—de dirt road and der pike. Which Mas'r mean to take? Course, I'd rather be 'clined to 'magine that Lizy'd take de dirt road, bein' it's the least traveled."

Haley, notwithstanding that he was a very old bird, and naturally inclined to be suspicious of chaff, was rather brought up by this view of the case.

"If ye warn't both on yer such cussed liars!" he said as he pondered a moment.

"Course," said Sam, "Mas'r can do as he'd ruther. Go de straight road if Mas'r thinks best—it's all one to us. Now, when I study 'pon it, I think de straight road de best, *decidedly*."

"She would naturally go a lonesome way," said Haley, thinking aloud, and not minding Sam's remark.

"Dar an't no sayin'," said Sam. "Gals is pecular. Dey never does nothin' ye thinks dey will. Mose gen'lly de contrar. Gals is nat'lly made contrar. And so, if you thinks dey've gone one road, it is sartin you'd better go t'other, and then you'll be sure to find 'em. Now, my private 'pinion is, Lizy took der dirt road; so I think we'd better take de straight one."

This profound view of the female sex did not seem to dispose Haley particularly to the straight road, and he announced decidedly that he should go the other and asked Sam when they should come to it.

"A little piece ahead," said Sam, giving a wink to Andy with the eye which was on Andy's side of the head. And he added gravely, "But I've studded on de matter, and I'm quite clar we ought not to go dat ar way. I nebber been over it no way. It's desp't lonesome, and we might lose our way—what we'd come to, de Lord only knows."

"Nevertheless," said Haley, "I shall go that way."

"Now I think on't, I think I hearn 'em tell that dat ar road was all fenced up and down by der creek. An't it, Andy?"

Andy wasn't certain. He'd only "hearn tell" about that road, but never been over it.

Haley, accustomed to choosing between greater and lesser

lies, thought the probability lay in favor of the dirt road. When, therefore, Sam indicated the road, Haley plunged briskly into it, followed by Sam and Andy.

Now, the road, in fact, was an old one that had formerly been a thoroughfare to the river, but abandoned for many years after the building of the new pike. It was open for about an hour's ride, and after that it was cut across by various farms and fences. Sam knew this fact perfectly well. He therefore rode along with an air of dutiful submission, only groaning and voicing occasionally that 'twas "desp't rough, and bad for Jerry's foot."

"Now, I jest give yer warning," said Haley, "I know yer. Yer won't get me to turn off this yer road with all yer fussin' —so you shet up!"

"Mas'r will go his own way!" said Sam with submission, at the same time winking to Andy, whose delight was now very near to the explosive point.

Sam was in wonderful spirits. He professed to keep a very brisk look-out—at one time exclaiming that he saw "a gal's bonnet" on the top of some distant height, or calling to Andy "if that thar wasn't Lizy down in the hollow," always making these exclamations in some rough or craggy part of the road, where the sudden quickening of speed was a special inconvenience to all parties concerned, and thus keeping Haley in a state of constant commotion.

After riding about an hour in this way, the whole party made a sudden descent into a barnyard belonging to a large farm. Not a soul was in sight, all the hands being employed in the fields. But as the barn stood square across the road, it was evident that their journey in that direction had reached a decided end.

"Wan't dat ar what I telled Mas'r?" said Sam with an air of injured innocence. "How does strange gentleman spect to know more about a country dan de natives born and raised?"

"You rascal!" said Haley. "You knew all about this."

"Didn't I tell yer I *know'd*, and yer wouldn't believe me? I telled Mas'r 'twas all shet up, and fenced up, and I didn't spect we could get through—Andy heard me."

It was all too true to be disputed, and the unlucky man had to pocket his wrath. All three faced to the right about and took up their line of march for the highway.

In consequence of the various delays, it was about three-quarters of an hour after Eliza had laid her child to sleep in the village tavern that the party came riding into the same place. Eliza was standing by the window, looking out in another direction, when Sam's quick eye caught a glimpse of her. Haley and Andy were two yards behind. At this crisis, Sam contrived to have his hat blown off and uttered a loud exclamation, which startled her at once. She drew suddenly back. The whole train swept by the window, round to the front door.

A thousand lives seemed to be concentrated in that one moment to Eliza. Her room opened by a side door to the river. She caught her child and sprang down the steps toward it. The trader caught a full glimpse of her just as she was disappearing down the bank, and throwing himself from his horse, and calling loudly on Sam and Andy, he was after her like a hound after a deer. In that dizzy moment her feet scarce seemed to her to touch the ground, and a moment brought her to the water's edge. Right on behind they came, and nerved with strength such as God gives only to the desperate, with one wild cry and flying leap, she vaulted sheer over the current by the shore on to the raft of ice beyond. It was a desperate leap—impossible to anything but madness and despair. And Haley, Sam, and Andy instinctively cried out and lifted up their hands as she did it.

The huge green fragment of ice on which she alighted pitched and creaked as her weight came on it, but she stayed there not a moment. With wild cries and desperate energy she leaped to another and still another cake—stumbling—leaping —slipping—springing upward again! Her shoes were gone, her stockings cut from her feet, while blood marked every

step. But she saw nothing, felt nothing, till dimly, as in a dream, she saw the Ohio side, and a man helping her up the bank.

"Yer a brave gal, now, whoever ye are!" said the man, with an oath.

Eliza recognized the voice and face of a man who owned a farm not far from her old home.

"Oh, Mr. Symmes! Save me—do save me—do hide me!" said Eliza.

"Why, what's this?" said the man. "Why, if 'tan't Shelby's gal!"

"My child—this boy—he's sold him! There is his Mas'r," said she, pointing to the Kentucky shore. "Oh, Mr. Symmes, you've got a little boy!"

"So I have," said the man, as he roughly, but kindly, drew

her up the steep bank. "Besides, you're a right brave gal. I like grit, wherever I see it."

When they had gained the top of the bank, the man paused.

"I'd be glad to do something for ye," said he, "but then there's nowhar I could take ye. The best I can do is to tell ye to go *thar*," said he, pointing to a large white house which stood by itself, off the main street of the village. "Go thar. They're kind folks. Thar's no kind o' danger but they'll help you—they're up to all that sort o' thing."

"The Lord bless you!" said Eliza earnestly.

"No 'casion, no 'casion in the world," said the man. "What I've done's of no 'count."

"And oh, surely sir, you won't tell anyone!"

"Go to thunder, gal! What do you take a feller for? Of course not," said the man. "Come now, go along like a likely, sensible gal, as you are. You've arnt your liberty, and you shall have it, for all me."

The woman folded her child to her bosom and walked firmly and swiftly away. The man stood and looked after her.

"Shelby, now, mebbe won't think this yer the most neighborly thing in the world. But what's a feller to do? If he catches one of my gals in the same fix, he's welcome to pay back. Somehow I never could see no kind o' crittur a strivin' and pantin', and trying to clar theirselves, with the dogs arter 'em, and go agin 'em. Besides, I don't see no kind of 'casion for me to be hunter and catcher for other folks neither."

Haley had stood a perfectly amazed spectator of the scene till Eliza disappeared up the bank, when he turned a blank, inquiring look on Sam and Andy.

"That ar was a tolable fair stroke of business," said Sam.

"The gal's got seven devils in her, I believe!" said Haley. "How like a wildcat she jumped!"

"Wal, now," said Sam, scratching his head, "I hope Mas'r'll 'scuse us trying dat ar road. Don't think I feel spry enough for dat ar, no way!" and Sam gave a hoarse chuckle.

"*You* laugh!" said the trader with a growl.

"Lord bless you, Mas'r, I couldn't help it, now," said Sam, giving way to the long pent-up delight of his soul. "She looked so curis, a-leapin' and springin'—ice a-crackin'—and only to hear her—plump! ker chunk! ker splash! Spring—Lord, how she goes it!" And Sam and Andy laughed till the tears rolled down their cheeks.

"I'll make ye laugh t'other side yer mouths!" said the trader, laying about their heads with his riding-whip.

Both ducked, and ran shouting up the bank, and were on their horses before he was up.

"Good evening, Mas'r!" said Sam with much gravity. "I bery much spect Missis be anxious 'bout Jerry. Mas'r Haley won't want us no longer. Missis wouldn't hear of our ridin' the critturs over Lizy's bridge tonight." And with a poke into Andy's ribs, he started off, followed by the latter at full speed, their shouts of laughter coming faintly on the wind.

Eliza's Escape

ELIZA made her desperate retreat across the river just in the dusk at twilight. The gray mist of evening, rising slowly from the river, enveloped her as she disappeared up the bank, and the swollen current and floundering masses of ice presented a hopeless barrier between her and her pursuer. Haley therefore slowly and discontentedly returned to the little tavern to ponder further what was to be done. The woman opened to him the door of a little parlor, and here Haley sat him down to meditate.

"What did I want with the little cuss, now," he said to himself, "that I should have got myself treed like a coon, as I am, this yer way?"

He was startled by the loud and harsh voice of a man who

was apparently dismounting at the door. He hurried to the window.

"By the land! If this yer an't the nearest, now, to what I've heard folks call Providence," said Haley. "I do b'lieve that ar's Tom Loker."

Haley hastened out. Standing by the bar in the corner of the room, was a brawny, muscular man, full six feet in height and broad in proportion. He was dressed in a coat of buffalo-skin made with the hair outward, which gave him a shaggy and fierce appearance. Every feature and line of his head and face expressed brutal and unhesitating violence. Indeed, could our readers fancy a bulldog come unto man's estate and walking about in a hat and coat, they would have no unapt idea of the general style and effect of his physique. He was accompanied by a traveling companion, in many respects an exact contrast to himself. He was short and slender, lithe and cat-like in his motions, and had a peering, mousing expression about his keen black eyes.

The great big man poured out a big tumbler half full of raw spirits and gulped it down without a word. The little man stood tiptoe, and putting his head first to one side and then to the other, and snuffing the various bottles, ordered at last a mint julep, and proceeded to dispose of it in short sips.

"Wal, now, who'd a thought this yer luck 'ad come to me? Why, Loker, how are ye?" said Haley, coming forward and extending his hand to the big man.

"The devil!" was the civil reply. "What brought you here, Haley?"

The mousing man, who bore the name of Marks, instantly stopped his sipping and looked shrewdly on the new acquaintance, as a cat sometimes looks at a moving dry leaf, or some other possible object of pursuit.

"I say, Tom, this yer's the luckiest thing in the world. I'm in a devil of a hobble, and you must help me out."

"Ugh? Aw, like enough!" grunted Loker. "A body may be pretty sure of that when *you're* glad to see 'em. What's the blow now?"

"You've got a friend here?" said Haley, looking doubtfully at Marks. "Partner, perhaps?"

"Yes, I have. Here, Marks! Here's that ar feller that I was in with in Natchez."

"Shall be pleased with his acquaintance," said Marks, thrusting out a long, thin hand, like a raven's claw. "Mr. Haley, I believe?"

"The same, sir," said Haley. "And now, gentlemen, seein' as we've met so happily, I think I'll stand up to a small matter of a treat in this here parlor. So, now, old coon," said he to the man at the bar, "get us hot water, and sugar, and cigars, and plenty of the *real stuff*, and we'll have a blow-out."

Behold, then, the candles lighted, the fire stimulated to the burning point in the grate, and our three worthies seated round a table.

Haley began a pathetic recital of his peculiar troubles. Loker listened to him with gruff and surly attention. Marks, who was compounding a tumbler of punch to his own peculiar taste, occasionally looked up from his employment, and poking his sharp nose and chin almost into Haley's face, gave the most earnest heed to the whole narrative. The conclusion of it appeared to amuse him extremely, for he shook his shoulders and sides in silence and perked up his thin lips with an air of great internal enjoyment.

"So, then, ye're fairly sewed up, an't ye?" he said. "He! he! he! It's neatly done, too."

"This yer young-un business makes lots of trouble in the trade," said Haley dolefully.

"If we could get a breed of gals that didn't care, now, for their young uns," said Marks, "I think 'twould be 'bout the greatest mod'rn improvement I knows on."

"Jest so," said Haley. "I never could see into it. Young uns is heaps of trouble to 'em. One would think, now, they'd be glad to get clar on 'em, but they an't. And the more trouble a young un is, and the more good for nothing, as a gen'l thing the tighter they sticks to 'em."

"Wal, Mr. Haley," said Marks, "you say jest what I feel

and al'us have. Now, I bought a gal once when I was in the trade—a tight, likely wench she was, too, and quite considerable smart—and she had a young un that was mis'able sickly. It had a crooked back or something. And I jest give't away to a man that thought he'd take his chance raising on 't, being it didn't cost nothin'. Never thought, yer know, of the gal's takin' on about it. But, Lord, yer oughter seen how she went on. Why, re'lly, she did seem to me to valley the child more 'cause 'twas sickly and cross and plagued her. And she warn't making b'lieve, neither—cried about it, she did, and lopped round as if she'd lost every friend she had. It re'lly was droll to think on 't. Lord, there an't no end to women's notions."

"Wal, jest so with me," said Haley. "Last summer, down on Red River, I got a gal traded off on me with a likely lookin' child enough, and his eyes looked as bright as yourn. But come to look, I found him stone blind. Fact—he was stone blind. Wal, ye see, I thought there warn't no harm in my jest passing him along and not sayin' nothin'. And I got him nicely swapped off for a keg o' whiskey. But come to get him away from the gal, she was jest like a tiger. So 'twas before we started, and I hadn't got my gang chained up. So what should she do but ups on a cotton-bale, like a cat, ketches a knife from one of the deck hands, and I tell ye she made all fly for a minit, till she saw 'twan't no use. And she jest turns round and pitches head first, young un and all, into the river—went down plump and never ris."

"Bah!" said Tom Loker, who had listened to these stories with ill-repressed disgust. "Shiftless, both on ye! *My* gals don't cut up no such shines, I tell ye!"

"Indeed! How do you help it?" said Marks briskly.

"Help it? Why, I buys a gal, and if she's got a young un to be sold, I jest walks up and puts my fist to her face and says 'Look here, now, if you give me one word out of your head, I'll smash yer face in. I won't hear one word—not the beginning of a word.' I says to 'em, 'This yer young un's mine, and not yourn, and you've no kind o' business with it. I'm going to sell it, first chance. Mind, you don't cut up none o' yer shines about it, or I'll make ye wish ye'd never been born.' I tell ye, they sees it an't no play when I gets hold. And if one on 'em begins and gives a yelp, why—" And Mr. Loker brought down his fist with a thump.

"That ar's what ye may call *emphasis*," said Marks, poking Haley in the side and going into another small giggle. "If you an't the devil, Tom, you's his twin brother, I'll say that for ye."

Tom received the compliment with becoming modesty, while Haley said:

"Wal, now, Tom, ye re'lly is too bad, as I al'ays have told ye. Ye know, Tom, you and I used to talk over these yer matters down in Natchez, and I used to prove to ye that we made full as much, and was as well off for this yer world, by treatin' on 'em well, besides keepin' a better chance for comin' in the kingdom at last."

"Bah!" said Tom. "*Don't* I know? Don't make me too sick with any yer stuff—my stomach is a little riled now." And Tom drank half a glass of raw brandy.

"I say," said Haley, leaning back in his chair and gesturing impressively, "I'll say this now, I al'ays meant to drive my trade so as to make money on't, *fust and foremost*, as much as any man. But I b'lieve in religion, and one of these days, when I've got matters tight and snug, I calculates to tend to my soul and them ar matters. And so what's the use of doin' any more wickedness than's re'lly necessary? It don't seem to me it's 'tall prudent."

"Tend to yer soul!" repeated Tom contemptuously. "Take a bright look-out to find a soul in you—save yerself any care on that score. If the devil sifts you through a hair sieve, he won't find one."

"Why, Tom, ye're cross," said Haley. "Why can't ye take it pleasant now, when a feller's talking for your good?"

"Stop that ar jaw o' yourn, there," said Tom gruffly. "I can stand most any talk o' yourn but your pious talk—that kills me right up. After all, what's the odds between me and you? 'Tan't that you care one bit more, or have a bit more feelin'— it's clean, sheer, dog meanness, wanting to cheat the devil and save your own skin. Don't I see through it? And your gettin' religion, as you call it, after all, is too p'ison mean for any crittur—run up a bill with the devil all your life, and then sneak out when pay time comes! Bah!"

"Come, come, gentlemen, I say. This isn't business," said Marks. "There's different ways, you know, of looking at all subjects. Mr. Haley is a very nice man, no doubt, and has his own conscience. And, Tom, you have your ways, and very good ones, too, Tom. But quarreling, you know, won't an-swer no kind of purpose. Let's go to business. Now, Mr. Haley, what is it? You want us to undertake to catch this yer gal?"

"The gal's no matter of mine—she's Shelby's. It's only the boy. I was a fool for buying the monkey!"

"You're generally a fool!" said Tom gruffly.

"Come, now, Loker, none of your huffs," said Marks, lick-ing his lips. "You see, Mr. Haley's a-puttin' us in a way of a good job, I reckon. This yer gal, Mr. Haley, what is she?"

"Wal, white and handsome—well brought up. I'd a gi'n Shelby eight hundred or a thousand, and then made well on her."

"White and handsome—well brought up!" said Marks, his sharp eyes, nose, and mouth all alive with enterprise. "Look here, now, Loker, a beautiful opening. We'll do a business here on our own account. We does the catchin'. The boy, of course, goes to Mr. Haley—we takes the gal to Orleans to speculate on. An't it beautiful?"

Tom, whose great heavy mouth had stood ajar during this communication, now suddenly snapped it together, as a big dog closes on a piece of meat, and seemed to be digesting the idea at his leisure.

"Ye see," said Marks to Haley, stirring his punch as he did

so, "ye see, we has justices, convenient at all p'ints along shore, that does up any little jobs in our line quite reasonable. Tom, he does the knockin' down, and I come in, all dressed up, when the swearin's to be done. You oughter see, now," said Marks, in a glow of professional pride, "how I can tone it off. One day I'm Mr. Twickem from New Orleans, 'nother day I'm just come from my plantation on Pearl River, where I works seven hundred niggers. Then, again, I come out a distant relation of Henry Clay, or some old cock in Kentuck. Talents is different, you know. Now, Tom's a roarer when there's any thumping or fighting to be done. But at lying he an't good, Tom an't—ye see, it don't come natural to him. But, Lord, if thar's a feller in the country that can swear to anything and everything, and put in all the circumstances and flourishes with a longer face, and carry 't through better'n I can, why, I'd like to see him, that's all!"

Tom Loker, who was a man of slow thoughts and movements, here interrupted Marks by bringing his heavy fist down on the table so as to make all ring again. *"It'll do!"* he said.

"Lord bless ye, Tom, ye needn't break all the glasses!" said Marks. "Save your fist for time o' need."

"But, gentlemen, an't I to come in for a share of the profits?" said Haley.

"An't it enough we catch the boy for ye?" said Loker. "What do ye want?"

"Wal," said Haley, "if I gives you the job, it's worth something—say ten per cent on the profits, expenses paid."

"Now," said Loker with a tremendous oath and striking the table with his heavy fist, "don't I know *you*, Dan Haley? Don't you think to come it over me! Suppose Marks and I have taken up the catchin' trade jest to 'commodate gentlemen like you, and get nothin' for ourselves? Not by a long chalk! We'll have the gal out and you keep quiet, or, ye see, we'll have both—what's to hinder? Han't you show'd us the game? It's as free to us as you, I hope. If you or Shelby wants to chase us, look where the partridges was last year. If you find them or us, you're quite welcome."

"Oh, wal, certainly, jest let it go at that," said Haley, alarmed. "You catch the boy for the job—you allers did trade *fa'r* with me, Tom, and was up to yer word."

"Ye know that," said Tom. "I don't pretend none of your sniveling ways, but I won't lie in my 'counts with the devil himself. What I ses I'll do, I will do—you know *that*, Dan Haley."

"Jest so, jest so—I said so, Tom," said Haley. "And if you'd only promise to have the boy for me in a week, at any point you'll name, that's all I want."

"But it an't all I want, by a long jump," said Tom. "Ye don't think I did business with you down in Natchez for nothing, Haley. I've learned to hold an eel when I catch him. You've got to fork over fifty dollars, flat down, or this child don't start a peg. I know yer."

"Why, when you have a job in hand that may bring a clean profit of somewhere about a thousand or sixteen hundred, why, Tom, you're onreasonable," said Haley.

"Yes, and hasn't we business booked for five weeks to come —all we can do? And suppose we leaves all and goes to bush-whacking round arter yer young un, and finally doesn't catch the gal—and gals allers is the devil *to* catch—what's then? Would you pay us a cent—would you? I think I see you a doin' it—ugh! No, no. Flap down your fifty. If we get the job, and it pays, I'll hand it back. If we don't, it's for our trouble—that's *fa'r*, an't it, Marks?"

"Certainly, certainly," said Marks. "Tom'll have the boy for yer anywhere ye'll name. Won't ye, Tom?"

"If I find the young un, I'll bring him on to Cincinnati and leave him at Granny Belcher's on the landing," said Loker.

"So now let's come to the particulars," said Marks. "You saw this yer gal when she landed, Mr. Haley?"

"To be sure—plain as I see you."

"And a man helpin' on her up the bank?" said Loker.

"To be sure, I did."

"Most likely," said Marks, "she's took in somewhere. But where's a question. Tom, what do you say?"

"We must cross the river tonight, no mistake," said Tom.

"But there's no boat about," said Marks. "The ice is running awfully, Tom. An't it dangerous?"

"Don' know nothing 'bout that—only it's got to be done," said Tom decidedly.

"Dear me," said Marks, fidgeting, "it'll be—I say," he said, walking to the window, "it's dark as a wolf's mouth, and, Tom—"

"The long and short is you're scared, Marks. But I can't help that—you've got to go. Suppose you want to lie by a day or two till the gal's been carried on the underground line up to Sandusky or so, before you start."

"Oh, no, I an't a grain afraid," said Marks, "only—"

"Only what?" said Tom.

"Well, about the boat. Yer see, there an't any boat."

"I heard the woman say there was one coming along this evening, and that a man was going to cross over in it. Neck or nothing, we must go with him," said Tom.

"I s'pose you've got good dogs," said Haley.

"First rate," said Marks. "But what's the use? You han't got nothin' o' hers to smell on."

"Yes, I have," said Haley triumphantly. "Here's her shawl she left on the bed in her hurry. She left her bonnet, too."

"That ar's lucky," said Loker. "Fork over."

"Though the dogs might damage the gal if they come on her unawars," said Haley.

"That ar's a consideration," said Marks. "Our dogs tore a feller half to pieces once, down in Mobile, 'fore we could get 'em off."

"Wal, ye see, for this sort, that's to be sold for their looks, that ar won't answer, ye see," said Haley.

"I do see," said Marks. "Besides, if she's got took in, 'tan't no go, neither. Dogs is no 'count in these yer up states where these critturs gets carried—ye can't get on their track. They only does down in plantations, where niggers, when they runs, has to do their own running and don't get no help."

"Well," said Loker, who had just stepped out to the bar to make some inquiries, "they say the man's come with the boat. So, Marks—"

Marks cast a rueful look at the comfortable quarters he was leaving, but slowly rose to obey. After exchanging a few words of further arrangement, Haley handed over the fifty dollars to Tom, and the worthy trio separated.

While this scene was going on at the tavern, Sam and Andy, in a state of high delight, pursued their way home, and between ten and eleven their heels resounded on the gravel at the end of the balcony. Mrs. Shelby flew to the railings.

"Is that you, Sam? Where are they?"

"Mas'r Haley's a-restin' at the tavern. He's dreffful fatigued, Missis."

"And Eliza, Sam?"

"Wal, she's clar 'cross Jordan. As a body may say, in the land o' Canaan."

"Why, Sam, what *do* you mean?" said Mrs. Shelby, breathless and almost faint as the possible meaning of these words came over her.

"Wal, Missis, de Lord he persarves his own. Lizy's done gone over the river into 'Hio, as 'markably as if de Lord took her over in a charrit of fire and two hosses," said Sam.

"Come up here, Sam," said Mr. Shelby, who had followed on to the verandah, "and tell your mistress what she wants. Come, come, Emily," said he, passing his arm round her, "you are cold and all in a shiver. You allow yourself to feel too much."

"Feel too much! Am not I a woman—a mother? Are we not both responsible to God for this poor girl? My God, lay not this sin to our charge!"

"What sin, Emily? You see yourself that we have only done what we were obliged to."

"There's an awful feeling of guilt about it, though," said Mrs. Shelby. "I can't reason it away."

"Now, Sam," said Mr. Shelby as Sam appeared, palm-leaf in hand, at the parlor door, "tell us distinctly how the matter was. Where is Eliza, if you know?"

"Wal, Mas'r, I saw her, with my own eyes, a-crossin' on the floatin' ice. She crossed most 'markably. It wasn't no less nor a miracle. And I saw a man help her up the 'Hio side, and then she was lost in de dusk."

"Sam, crossing on floating ice isn't easily done," said Mr. Shelby.

"Easy! Couldn't nobody a done it widout de Lord. Why, now," said Sam, " 'twas jist dis yer way. Mas'r Haley and me and Andy, we comes up to de little tavern by de river, and I rides a leetle ahead—I's so zealous to be a cotchin' Lizy that I couldn't hold in, no way—and when I comes by de tavern winder, sure nuff thar she was, right in plain sight, and dey diggin' on behind. Wal, I loses off my hat and sings out nuff to raise de dead. Course Lizy she hars, and she dodges back, when Mas'r Haley he goes past de door. And then, I tell ye, she clared out de side door. She went down de river bank. Mas'r Haley he seed her and yelled out, and him and me and Andy, we took arter. Down she come to de river, and thar was de current running ten feet wide by de shore, and over t'other side ice a-sawin' and a-jiggling up and down, kinder as 'twere a great island. We come right behind her, and I thought my soul he'd got her sure nuff—when she gi'n sich a screech as I never hearn, and thar she was, clar over t'other side de current, on de ice, and then on she went, a-screechin' and a-jumpin'. De ice went crack! c'wallop! cracking! chunk!

and she a-boundin' like a buck! Lord, de spring dat ar gal's got in her an't common, I'm o' 'pinion."

Mrs. Shelby sat perfectly silent, pale with excitement, while Sam told his story.

"God be praised, she isn't dead!" she said. "But where is the poor child now?"

"De Lord will pervide," said Sam, rolling up his eyes piously. "As I've been a-sayin', dis yer's a providence and no mistake, as Missis has allers been instructin' on us. Thar's allers instruments ris up to do de Lord's will. Now, if 't hadn't been for me today, she'd a been took a dozen times. Warn't it I started off de hosses, dis yer mornin', and kept 'em chasin' till nigh dinner time? And didn't I car Mas'r Haley nigh five miles out of de road, dis evening, or else he'd come up with Lizy as easy as a dog arter a coon? These yer's all providences."

"They are a kind of providences that you'll have to be pretty sparing of, Master Sam. I allow no such practices with gentlemen on my place," said Mr. Shelby, with as much sternness as he could command under the circumstances.

Sam was in no wise disheartened by this rebuke, though he assumed an air of doleful gravity as he said, "Mas'r's quite right—quite. It was ugly on me—thar's no disputin' dat ar. And of course Mas'r and Missis wouldn't encourage no such works. I'm sensible of dat ar. But a poor nigger like me's 'mazin' tempted to act ugly sometimes, when fellers will cut up such shines as dat ar Mas'r Haley. He an't no gen'lman no way—anybody's been raised as I've been can't help a seein' dat ar."

"Well, Sam," said Mrs. Shelby, "as you appear to have a proper sense of your errors, you may go now and tell Aunt Chloe she may get you some of that cold ham that was left of dinner today. You and Andy must be hungry."

"Missis is a heap too good for us," said Sam, making his bow with alacrity, and departing.

In Which It Appears That
a Senator Is but a Man

THE light of the cheerful fire shone on the rug and carpet of a cosy parlor and glittered on the teacups and well-brightened teapot as Senator Bird was drawing off his boots, preparatory to inserting his feet in a pair of new, handsome slippers, which his wife had been working for him while he was away on his senatorial tour. Mrs. Bird, looking the very picture of delight, was superintending the arrangements of the table, and ever and anon addressing remarks to a number of frolicsome children.

"Tom, let the doorknob alone—there's a man! Mary! Mary! Don't pull the cat's tail—poor pussy! Jim, you mustn't climb on that table—no, no! You don't know, my dear, what a surprise it is to us all to see you here tonight!" said she at last, when she found a space to say something to her husband.

"Yes, yes, I thought I'd just make a run down, spend the night, and have a little comfort at home. I'm tired to death, and my head aches."

Mrs. Bird cast a glance at a camphor bottle, which stood in the half-open closet, and appeared to meditate an approach to it, but her husband interposed.

"No, no, Mary, no doctoring! A cup of your good hot tea and some of our good home living is what I want. It's a tiresome business, this legislating!"

"Well," said his wife, after the business of the tea-table was getting rather slack, "and what have they been doing in the Senate?"

Now, it was a very unusual thing for gentle little Mrs. Bird ever to trouble her head with what was going on in the house of the State. Mr. Bird, therefore, opened his eyes in surprise and said:

"Not very much of importance."

"Well, but is it true that they have been passing a law forbidding people to give meat and drink to those poor colored folks that come along? I heard they were talking of some such law, but I didn't think any Christian legislature would pass it!"

"Why, Mary, you are getting to be a politician all at once."

"No, nonsense! I wouldn't give a flip for all your politics, generally, but I think this is something downright cruel and un-Christian. I hope, my dear, no such law has been passed."

"There has been a law passed forbidding people to help off the slaves that come over from Kentucky, my dear. So much of that thing has been done by these reckless Abolitionists that our brethren in Kentucky are very strongly excited, and it seems necessary, and no more than Christian and kind, that something should be done by our State to quiet the excitement."

"And what is the law? It don't forbid us to shelter these poor creatures a night, does it, and to give 'em something comfortable to eat, and a few old clothes, and send them quietly about their business?"

"Why, yes, my dear. That would be aiding and abetting, you know."

Mrs. Bird was a timid, blushing little woman of about four feet in height, and with mild blue eyes, and a peach-blow complexion, and the gentlest, sweetest voice in the world. As for courage, a moderate-sized cock-turkey had been known to put her to rout at the very first gobble, and a stout house-dog would bring her into subjection merely by a show of his teeth. Her husband and children were her entire world, and in these she ruled more by entreaty and persuasion than by command or argument. There was only one thing that was capable of arousing her—anything in the shape of cruelty would throw her into a passion.

On the present occasion, Mrs. Bird rose quickly with very red cheeks, walked up to her husband with quite a resolute air, and said in a determined tone:

"Now, John, I want to know if you think such a law as that is right and Christian?"

"You won't shoot me, now, Mary, if I say I do?"

"I never could have thought it of you, John. You didn't vote for it?"

"Even so, my fair politician."

"You ought to be ashamed, John! Poor, homeless, houseless creatures! It's a shameful, wicked, abominable law, and I'll break it, for one, the first time I get a chance. And I hope I *shall* have a chance, I do! Things have got to a pretty pass if a woman can't give a warm supper and a bed to poor, starving creatures, just because they are slaves and have been abused and oppressed all their lives, poor things!"

"But, Mary, just listen to me. Your feelings are all quite right, dear, and I love you for them. But then, dear, we mustn't suffer our feelings to run away with our judgment. You must consider it's not a matter of private feeling—there are great public interests involved. There is such a state of public agitation rising that we must put aside our private feelings."

"Now, John, I don't know anything about politics, but I can read my Bible. And there I see that I must feed the hungry, clothe the naked, and comfort the desolate. And that Bible I mean to follow."

"But in cases where your doing so would involve a great public evil—"

"Obeying God never brings on public evils. I know it can't. It's always safest, all round, to *do as He* bids us."

"Now, listen to me, Mary, and I can state to you a very clear argument to show—"

"Oh, nonsense, John! You can talk all night, but you wouldn't do it. I put it to you, John—would *you* now turn away a poor, shivering, hungry creature from your door because he was a runaway? *Would* you, now?"

Now, if the truth must be told, our senator had the misfortune to be a man who had a particularly humane nature, and turning away anybody that was in trouble never had been his strong point. And what was worse for him in this particular pinch of the argument was that his wife knew it, and, of course, was making an assault on rather an indefensible point. So he had recourse to the usual means of gaining time for such cases. He said "ahem," and coughed several times, and took out his pocket handkerchief and began to wipe his glasses. Mrs. Bird had no more conscience than to push her advantage.

"I should like to see you doing that, John—I really should! Turning a woman out of doors in a snowstorm, for instance. Or maybe you'd take her up and put her in jail, wouldn't you? You would make a great hand at that!"

"Of course, it would be a very painful duty," began Mr. Bird in a moderate tone.

"Duty, John! Don't use that word! You know it isn't a duty—it can't be a duty! If folks want to keep their slaves from running away, let 'em treat 'em well—that's my doctrine. If I had slaves (as I hope I never shall have), I'd risk their wanting to run away from me, or you either, John. I tell you folks don't run away when they are happy. And when they do run, poor creatures, they suffer enough with cold and hunger and fear, without everybody's turning against them. And, law or no law, I never will, so help me God!"

"Mary! Mary! My dear, let me reason with you."

"I hate reasoning, John—especially reasoning on such subjects. There's a way you political folks have of coming round and round a plain right thing, and you don't believe in it yourselves when it comes to practice. I know *you* well enough, John. You don't believe it's right any more than I do, and you wouldn't do it any sooner than I."

At this critical point, old Cudjoe, the black man-of-all-work, put his head in at the door and wished "Missis would come into the kitchen." And our senator, tolerably relieved, seated himself in the armchair and began to read the papers.

After a moment, his wife's voice was heard at the door in a quick, earnest tone: "John! John! I do wish you'd come here a moment."

He laid down his paper, and went into the kitchen, and started, quite amazed at the sight that presented itself: A young and slender woman, with garments torn and frozen, her shoes gone and the stockings torn away from the cut and bleeding feet, was laid back in a deadly swoon upon two chairs. There was the impress of the despised race on her face, yet none could help feeling its mournful and pathetic beauty, while its cold, fixed, deathly aspect struck a solemn chill over him. He drew his breath short and stood in silence. His wife and their only colored domestic, old Aunt Dinah, were busily engaged in restorative measures, while old Cudjoe had got the boy on his knee and was busy pulling off his shoes and stockings and chafing his little cold feet.

"Sure, now, if she an't a sight to behold!" said old Dinah compassionately. " 'Pears like 'twas the heat that made her faint. She was tol'able peart when she cum in, and asked if she couldn't warm herself here a spell. And I was just a-askin' her where she cum from, and she fainted right down. Never done much hard work, guess, by the looks of her hands."

"Poor creature!" said Mrs. Bird compassionately as the woman slowly opened her large, dark eyes and looked vacantly at her. Suddenly an expression of agony crossed her face, and she sprang up, saying, "Oh, my Harry! Have they got him?"

The boy, at this, jumped from Cudjoe's knee, and running to her side, put up his arms. "Oh, he's here! He's here!"

"Oh, ma'am!" said she wildly to Mrs. Bird, "do protect us!

Don't let them get him!"

"Nobody shall hurt you here, poor woman," said Mrs. Bird encouragingly. "You are safe; don't be afraid."

"God bless you!" said the woman, covering her face and sobbing, while the little boy, seeing her crying, tried to get into her lap.

With many gentle and womanly offices, which none knew better how to render than Mrs. Bird, the poor woman was in time rendered more calm. A temporary bed was provided for her on the settle, near the fire. And after a short time she fell into a heavy slumber, with the child, who seemed no less weary, soundly sleeping on her arm—for the mother resisted the kindest attempts to take him from her, and even in sleep her arm encircled him with an unrelaxing clasp.

Mr. and Mrs. Bird had gone back to the parlor where, strange as it may appear, no reference was made, on either side, to the preceding conversation. Mrs. Bird busied herself with her knitting-work, and Mr. Bird pretended to be reading the paper.

"I wonder who and what she is," said Mr. Bird at last as he laid it down.

"When she wakes up and feels a little rested, we will see," said Mrs. Bird.

"I say, wife!" said Mr. Bird, after musing in silence over his newspaper.

"Well, dear."

"She couldn't wear one of your gowns, could she, by any letting down, or such matter? She seems to be rather larger than you are."

A quite perceptible smile glimmered on Mrs. Bird's face as she answered, "We'll see."

Another pause, and Mr. Bird again broke out:

"I say, wife!"

"Well! What now?"

"Why, there's that old bombazine cloak that you keep on purpose to put over me when I take my afternoon's nap. You might as well give her that—she needs clothes."

At this instant Dinah looked in to say that the woman was awake and wanted to see Missis.

Mr. and Mrs. Bird went into the kitchen, followed by the two eldest boys, the smaller fry having by this time been safely disposed of in bed.

The woman was now sitting up on the settle by the fire. She was looking steadily into the blaze with a calm, heartbroken expression, very different from her former agitated wildness.

"Did you want me?" said Mrs. Bird in gentle tones. "I hope you feel better now, poor woman!"

A long-drawn, shivering sigh was the only answer. But she lifted her dark eyes and fixed them on her with such a forlorn and imploring expression that the tears came into the little woman's eyes.

"You needn't be afraid of anything—we are friends here,

poor woman. Tell me where you came from and what you want," said she.

"I came from Kentucky," said the woman.

"When?" said Mr. Bird, taking up the questioning.

"Tonight."

"How did you come?"

"I crossed on the ice."

"Crossed on the ice!" said everyone present.

"Yes," said the woman slowly, "I did. God helping me, I crossed on the ice. For they were behind me—right behind—and there was no other way!"

"Law, Missis," said Cudjoe, "the ice is all in broken-up blocks, a-swinging and a-teetering up and down in the water!"

"I know it was—I know it!" said she wildly. "But I did it! I wouldn't have thought I could—I didn't think I should get over, but I didn't care! I could but die, if I didn't. The Lord helped me—nobody knows how much the Lord can help 'em till they try," said the woman, with a flashing eye.

"Were you a slave?" said Mr. Bird.

"Yes, sir. I belonged to a man in Kentucky."

"Was he unkind to you?"

"No, sir. He was a good master."

"And was your mistress unkind to you?"

"No, sir—no! My mistress was always good to me."

"What could induce you to leave a good home, then, and run away, and go through such dangers?"

The woman looked up at Mrs. Bird with a keen, scrutinizing glance, and it did not escape her that she was dressed in deep mourning.

"Ma'am," she said suddenly, "have you ever lost a child?"

The question was unexpected, and it was a thrust on a new wound, for it was only a month since a darling child of the family had been laid in the grave.

Mr. Bird turned around and walked to the window, and

Mrs. Bird burst into tears. But recovering her voice, she said:

"Why do you ask that? I have lost a little one."

"Then you will feel for me. I have lost two, one after another—I left 'em buried there when I came away—and I had only this one left. I never slept a night without him. He was all I had. He was my comfort and pride, day and night. And, ma'am, they were going to take him away from me—to *sell* him, sell him down South, ma'am, to go all alone, a baby that had never been away from his mother in his life! I couldn't stand it, ma'am. I knew I never should be good for anything if they did. And when I knew the papers were signed, and he was sold, I took him and came off in the night. And they chased me—the man that bought him and some of Mas'r's folks—and they were coming down right behind me, and I heard 'em. I jumped right on to the ice, and how I got across I don't know—but first I knew, a man was helping me up the bank."

The woman did not sob nor weep. She had gone to a place where tears are dry. But every one around her was showing signs of hearty sympathy.

The two little boys, after a desperate rummaging in their pockets in search of those pocket handkerchiefs which mothers know are never to be found there, had thrown themselves into the skirts of their mother's gown, where they were sobbing and wiping their eyes and noses to their hearts' content. Mrs. Bird had her face fairly hidden in her pocket handkerchief. And old Dinah, with tears streaming down her black, honest face, was exclaiming, "Lord have mercy on us!" with all the fervor of a camp-meeting, while old Cudjoe, rubbing his eyes very hard with his cuffs, occasionally responded in the same key, with great fervor. Our senator was a statesman, and of course could not be expected to cry, like other mortals. So he turned his back to the company and looked out of the window, and seemed particularly busy in clearing his throat, wiping his spectacles, and occasionally blowing his nose.

"How came you to tell me you had a kind master?" he suddenly exclaimed, gulping down very resolutely some kind of rising in his throat.

"Because he *was* a kind master—I'll say that of him, anyway—and my mistress was kind. But they couldn't help themselves. They were owing money, and there was some way, I can't tell how, that a man had a hold on them, and they were obliged to give him his will. I listened and heard him telling Mistress that, and she begging and pleading for me—and he told her he couldn't help himself, and that the papers were all drawn. And then it was I took him and left my home and came away. I knew 'twas no use of my trying to live if they did it, for 't 'pears like this child is all I have."

"Have you no husband?"

"Yes, but he belongs to another man. His master is real hard to him, and won't let him come to see me hardly ever. And he's grown harder and harder upon us, and he threatens to sell him down South—it's like I'll never see *him* again!"

"And where do you mean to go, my poor woman?" said Mrs. Bird.

"To Canada, if I only knew where that was. Is it very far off, is Canada?" said she, looking up, with a simple, confiding air, to Mrs. Bird's face.

"Poor thing!" said Mrs. Bird.

"Is't a very great way off, think?" said the woman earnestly.

"Much further than you think, poor child!" said Mrs. Bird. "But we will try to think what can be done for you. Here, Dinah, make her up a bed in your own room, close by the kitchen, and I'll think what to do for her in the morning. Meanwhile, never fear, poor woman. Put your trust in God—he will protect you."

Mrs. Bird and her husband reentered the parlor. She sat down in her little rocking-chair before the fire, swaying thoughtfully to and fro. Mr. Bird strode up and down the room, grumbling to himself: "Pish! pshaw! Confounded awkward business!" At length, striding up to his wife, he said:

"I say, wife, she'll have to get away from here this very night. That fellow will be down on the scent bright and early tomorrow morning. If 'twas only the woman, she could lie quiet till it was over, but that little chap can't be kept still by a troop of horse and foot, I'll warrant me. He'll bring it all out, popping his head out of some window or door. A pretty kettle of fish it would be for me, too, to be caught with them both here just now! No, they'll have to be got off tonight."

"Tonight! How is it possible? Where to?"

"Well, I know pretty well where to," said the senator, beginning to put on his boots, with a reflective air. "You see," he said, there's my old client, Van Trompe, has come over from Kentucky and set all his slaves free. And he has bought a place seven miles up the creek here, back in the woods, where nobody goes unless they go on purpose. It's a place that isn't found in a hurry. There she'd be safe enough. But the plague of the thing is, nobody could drive a carriage there tonight but *me*."

"Why not? Cudjoe is an excellent driver."

"Ay, ay, but here it is. The creek has to be crossed twice, and the second crossing is quite dangerous unless one knows it as I do. I have crossed it a hundred times on horseback and know exactly the turns to take. And so, you see, there's no help for it. Cudjoe must put in the horses, as quietly as may be, about twelve o-clock, and I'll take her over. And then, to give color to the matter, he must carry me on to the next tavern to take the stage for Columbus, that comes by about three or four. And so it will look as if I had had the carriage only for that. I shall get into business bright and early in the morning. But I'm thinking I shall feel rather cheap there, after all that's been said and done. But, hang it, I can't help it!"

"Your heart is better than your head in this case, John," said the wife, laying her little white hand on his. "Could I ever have loved you, had I not known you better than you know yourself?" And the little woman looked so handsome, with the tears sparkling in her eyes, that the senator thought he must be a decidedly clever fellow to get such a pretty creature into such a passionate admiration of him. And so, what could he do but walk off soberly to see about the carriage? At the door, however, he stopped a moment, and then coming back, he said, with some hesitation:

"Mary, I don't know how you'd feel about it, but there's that drawer full of things—of—of—poor little Henry's." So saying he turned quickly on his heel and shut the door after him.

His wife opened the little bedroom door adjoining her room, and taking the candle, set it down on the top of a bureau there. Then from a small recess she took a key and put it thoughtfully in the lock of a drawer, and made a sudden pause, while the two boys, who had followed close on her heels, stood looking with silent, significant glances at their mother. And oh, mother that reads this, has there never been in your house a drawer, or a closet, the opening of which has been to you like the opening again of a little grave? Ah, happy mother that you are, if it has not been so.

Mrs. Bird slowly opened the drawer. There were little coats of many a form and pattern, piles of aprons, rows of small stockings, and even a pair of little shoes, worn and rubbed at the toes. There was a toy horse and wagon, a top, a ball—memorials gathered with many a tear and many a heart-break. She sat down by the drawer, and leaning her head on her hands over it, wept till the tears fell through her fingers into the drawer. Then suddenly raising her head, she began, with nervous haste, selecting the plainest and most substantial articles and gathering them into a bundle.

"Mamma," said one of the boys, gently touching her arm, "are you going to give away *those* things?"

"My dear boys," she said softly and earnestly, "if our dear, loving little Henry looks down from heaven, he would be glad to have us do this. I could not find it in my heart to give them away to any common person—to anybody that was happy. But I give them to a mother more heartbroken and sorrowful than I am, and I hope God will send his blessings with them!"

After a while Mrs. Bird opened a wardrobe, and taking from thence a plain, serviceable dress or two, she sat down busily to her worktable and quietly commenced the "letting down" process which her husband had recommended, and continued busily at it till the old clock in the corner struck twelve and she heard the low rattling of wheels at the door.

"Mary," said her husband, coming in with his overcoat in his hand, "you must wake her up now—we must be off."

Mrs. Bird hastily deposited the various articles she had collected in a small plain trunk, and locking it, desired her husband to see it in the carriage, and then proceeded to call the woman. Soon, arrayed in a cloak, bonnet, and shawl that had belonged to her benefactress, she appeared at the door with her child in her arms. Mr. Bird hurried her into the carriage, and Mrs. Bird pressed on after her to the carriage steps. Eliza leaned out of the carriage and put out her hand—a hand as soft and beautiful as was given in return. She fixed her large, dark eyes, full of earnest meaning, on Mrs. Bird's face, and seemed about to speak. Her lips moved—she tried once or twice, but there was no sound—and pointing upward, with a look never to be forgotten, she fell back in the seat and covered her face. The door was shut, and the carriage drove on.

What a situation, now, for a patriotic senator that had been all the week before spurring up the legislature of his native state to pass stricter resolutions against escaping fugitives, their harborers and abettors! How he had scorned all sentimental weakness of those who would put the welfare of a few miserable fugitives before great state interests!

He was as bold as a lion about it and "mightily convinced" not only himself, but everybody that heard him. But then, his idea of a fugitive was only an idea of the letters that spell the word—or, at the most, the image of a little newspaper picture of a man with a stick and bundle, with "Ran away from the subscriber" under it. The magic of the real presence of distress—the imploring human eye, the frail, trembling human hand, the despairing appeal of helpless agony—these he had never tried. He had never thought that a fugitive might be a hapless mother, a defenseless child—like that one who was now wearing his lost boy's well-known little cap. And so, as our poor senator was not stone or steel, as he was a man and a downright noble-hearted one, too, he was, as everybody must see, in a sad case for his patriotism.

And you need not exult over him, good brother of the Southern States, for we have some inklings that many of you, under similar circumstances, would not do much better. We have reason to know, in Kentucky, as in Mississippi, are noble and generous hearts, to whom never was tale of suffering told in vain. Ah, good brother! Is it fair for you to expect of us services which your own brave, honorable heart would not allow you to render, were you in our place?

Be that as it may, if our good senator was a political sinner, he was in a fair way to expiate it that night. There had been a long, continuous period of rainy weather, and the soft, rich earth of Ohio, as everyone knows, is admirably suited to the manufacture of mud—and the road was an Ohio "railroad" of the good old times.

"And pray, what sort of a road may that be?" says some Eastern traveler, accustomed to connect no ideas with a railroad but those of smoothness and speed.

Know, then, that in regions of the West, where the mud is of unfathomable depth, roads are made of round rough logs, laid side by side and coated over with earth, turf, and whatsoever may come to hand. In time, the rains wash off all the turf and grass, move the logs hither and thither—up, down, and crosswise—with chasms and ruts of black mud intervening.

Over such a road as this our senator went stumbling along, the carriage proceeding much as follows: Bump! bump!

bump! slush! down in the mud! The senator, woman, and child, suddenly reversing their positions, come against the windows of the down-hill side. Carriage sticks fast while Cudjoe on the outside is heard making a great muster among the horses. Just as the senator is losing all patience, the carriage suddenly rights itself with a bounce—two front wheels go down into another abyss, and senator, woman, and child all tumble on to the front seat. Senator's hat is jammed over his eyes and nose, and he considers himself fairly extinguished. Child cries, and Cudjoe on the outside delivers addresses to the horses, who are kicking, and floundering, and straining under repeated cracks of the whip. Carriage springs up with another bounce—down go the hind wheels. Senator, woman, and child fly over onto the back seat, his elbows encountering her bonnet, and both her feet being jammed into his hat. After a few moments the "slough" is passed, and the horses stop, panting. The senator finds his hat, the woman straightens her bonnet and hushes her child, and they brace themselves firmly for what is yet to come.

For a while only the continuous bump! bump! They begin to flatter themselves that they are not so badly off, after all. Then with a square plunge, which puts all on to their feet and then down into their seats, the carriage stops, and after much outside commotion, Cudjoe appears at the door.

"Please, sir, it's a powerful bad spot, this yer. I don't know how we's to get clar out. I'm a thinkin' we'll have to be a gettin' rails."

The senator despairingly steps out. Down goes one foot an immeasurable depth. He tries to pull it up, loses his balance, and tumbles over into the mud, and is fished out, in a very despairing condition, by Cudjoe. . . .

It was full late in the night when the carriage emerged, dripping and bespattered, out of the creek, and stood at the door of a large farmhouse.

It took no small effort to arouse the inmates. But at last the proprietor appeared and undid the door. He was a great, tall, bristling fellow, full six feet and some inches in his stockings, and arrayed in a red flannel hunting-shirt. A very heavy mat of sandy hair and a beard of some days' growth gave the worthy man an appearance not particularly prepossessing. He stood for a few minutes holding the candle aloft and blinking on our travelers with a mystified expression that was truly humorous. It cost some effort of our senator to make him comprehend the case fully. And while he is doing his best at that, we shall give him a little introduction to our readers.

Honest old John Van Trompe was once quite a landholder and slave-owner in Kentucky. Having "nothing of the bear about him but the skin," and being gifted by nature with a great, honest, just heart, he had been for some years witnessing with uneasiness the workings of a system equally bad for oppressor and oppressed. At last, one day, John's great heart had swelled altogether too big to wear his bonds any longer. So he just took his pocketbook out of his desk, went over into Ohio and bought a quarter of a township of good, rich land, made out free papers for all his people—men, women, and children—packed them up in wagons, and sent them off to settle down. And then honest John turned his face up the creek and sat quietly down on a snug, retired farm.

"Are you the man that will shelter a poor woman and child from slave-catchers?" said the senator.

"I rather think I am," said honest John, with some considerable emphasis.

"I thought so," said the senator.

"If there's anybody comes," said the good man, stretching his tall, muscular form upward, "why here I'm ready for him —and I've got seven sons, each six foot high, and they'll be ready for 'em. Give our respects to 'em," said John. "Tell 'em it's no matter how soon they call—make no kinder difference to us," said John, running his fingers through his hair and bursting out into a great laugh.

Weary, jaded, and spiritless, Eliza dragged herself up to the door with her child lying in a heavy sleep on her arm. The rough man held the candle to her face. Uttering a kind of compassionate grunt, he opened the door of a small bedroom adjoining to the large kitchen where they were standing, and motioned her to go in. He took down a candle, and lighting it, set it upon the table. Then he addressed himself to Eliza.

"Now, I say, gal, you needn't be a bit afeard, let who will come here. I'm up to all that sort o' thing," said he, pointing to two or three goodly rifles over the mantelpiece. "And most people that know me know that 'twouldn't be healthy to try to get anybody out o' my house when I'm agin it. So you jist go to sleep now, as quiet as if yer mother was a rockin' ye," said he as he shut the door.

"Why, this is an uncommon handsome un," he said to the senator. "Ah, well, handsome uns has the greatest cause to run, sometimes, if they has any kind o' feelin' such as decent women should. I know all about that."

The senator in a few words explained Eliza's history.

"Oh! ou! aw! Now, I want to know!" said the good man pitifully. "Sho, now, sho! That's natur now, poor crittur, hunted down like a deer—hunted down just for havin' natural feelin's, and doin' what no kind o' mother could help a-doin'! I tell ye what, these yer things make me come the nighest to swearin', now, o' most anything," said honest John, as he wiped his eyes with the back of a great, freckled, yellow hand. "I tell yer what, stranger, it was years and years before I'd jine the church, 'cause the minister round in our parts used to preach that the Bible went in for these 'ere cuttings up. I couldn't be up to 'em with their Greek and Hebrew, and so I took up agin 'em, Bible and all. I never j'ined the church till I found a minister that said right the contrary. And then I took right hold—I did now, fact," said John, who had been all this time uncorking some very frisky bottled cider, which at this point he presented.

"Ye'd better just put up here, now, till daylight," said he heartily, "and I'll call up the old woman and have a bed got ready for you in no time."

"Thank you, my good friend," said the senator, "I must be along, to take the night stage for Columbus."

"Ah, well, then, if you must, I'll go a piece with you and

show you a crossroad that will take you there better than the road you came on. That road's mighty bad."

John equipped himself, and with a lantern in hand was soon seen guiding the senator's carriage towards a road that ran down in a hollow back of his dwelling. When they parted, the senator put into his hand a ten-dollar bill.

"It's for her," he said briefly.

"Ay, ay," said John.

They shook hands and parted.

The Property Is Carried Off

THE February morning looked gray and drizzling through the window of Uncle Tom's cabin. It looked on downcast faces, reflecting mournful hearts. The little table, covered with an ironing-cloth, stood out before the fire. A coarse but clean shirt or two, fresh from the iron, hung on the back of a chair by the fire, and Aunt Chloe had another spread out before her on the table. Carefully she rubbed and ironed every fold and every hem, now and then raising her hand to her face to wipe off the tears that were coursing down her cheeks.

Tom sat by, with his Testament open on his knee and his head leaning upon his hands. But neither spoke. It was yet early, and the children lay all asleep together in their little rude trundle-bed.

Tom got up and walked silently to look at his children.

"It's the last time," he said.

Aunt Chloe did not answer, only rubbed away over and over on the coarse shirt, already as smooth as hands could make it. Finally, setting her iron suddenly down with a despairing plunge, she sat down to the table, and "lifted up her voice and wept."

"S'pose we must be resigned. But oh Lord, how ken I? If I know'd anythin' whar you's goin', or how they'd sarve ye! Missis says she'll try and 'deem ye, in a year or two. But Lord! Nobody never comes up that goes down thar! They kills 'em! I've hearn 'em tell how dey works 'em up on dem ar plantations."

"There'll be the same God there, Chloe, that there is here."

"Well," said Aunt Chloe, "s'pose dere will. But de Lord lets drefful things happen sometimes. I don't seem to get no comfort dat way."

"I'm in the Lord's hands," said Tom. "Nothin' can go no furder than he lets it. And thar's *one* thing I can thank him for—it's *me* that's sold and going down, and not you nur the chil'en. Here you're safe—what comes will come only on me. And the Lord, he'll help me—I know he will."

Tom spoke with thick utterance, and with a bitter choking in his throat, but he spoke brave and strong.

"Let's think on our marcies!" he added, as if he were quite sure he needed to think on them very hard indeed.

"Marcies!" said Aunt Chloe. "Don't see no marcy in't! Tan't right! Tan't right it should be so! Mas'r never ought ter left it so that ye *could* be took for his debts. Ye've arnt him all he gets for ye, twice over. He owed ye yer freedom, and ought ter gi'n 't to yer years ago. Mebbe he can't help himself now, but I feel it's wrong. Nothin' can't beat that ar out o' me. Sich a faithful crittur as ye've been—and allers sot his business 'fore yer own every way, and reckoned on him more than yer own wife and chil'en! Them as sells heart's love and heart's blood to get out thar scrapes, de Lord'll be up to 'em."

"Chloe! Now, if ye love me, ye won't talk so, when perhaps it's jest the last time we'll ever have together! And I'll tell ye, Chloe, it goes agin me to hear one word agin Mas'r. Warn't he put in my arms a baby? It's natur I should think a heap of him. And he couldn't be spected to think so much of poor Tom. Mas'rs is used to havin' all these yer things done for 'em, and nat'lly they don't think so much on 't. They can't be spected to, no way. Set him 'longside of other Mas'rs —who's had the treatment and the livin' I've had? And he never would have let this yer come on me if he could have seed it aforehand. I know he wouldn't."

"Wal, anyway, thar's wrong about it somewhar," said Aunt Chloe. "I can't jest make out whar 't is, but thar's wrong somewhar, I'm *clar* o' that."

"Yer ought to look up to the Lord above—he's above all—thar don't a sparrow fall without him."

"It don't seem to comfort me, but I spect it orter," said Aunt Chloe. "But thar's no use talkin'—I'll jest wet up de corn cake and get ye one good breakfast, 'cause nobody knows when you'll get another."

Mrs. Shelby had excused Aunt Chloe's attendance at the great house that morning, and the poor soul had expended all her little energies on the farewell feast—had killed and dressed her choicest chicken, prepared her corn cake just to her husband's taste, and brought out certain mysterious jars on the mantelpiece, some preserves that were never produced except on extreme occasions.

"Lor, Pete," said Mose triumphantly, "han't we got a buster of a breakfast!" at the same time catching at a fragment of the chicken.

Aunt Chloe gave him a sudden box on the ear. "Thar now! Crowin' over the last breakfast yer poor daddy's gwine to have to home!"

"Oh, Chloe!" said Tom gently.

"Wal, I can't help it," said Aunt Chloe, hiding her face in her apron. "I's so tossed about, it makes me act ugly."

The boys stood quite still, looking first at their father and then at their mother, while the baby, climbing up her clothes, began an urgent, commanding cry.

"Thar!" said Aunt Chloe, wiping her eyes and taking up the baby. "Now I's done, I hope—now do eat something. This yer's my nicest chicken. Thar, boys, ye shall have some, poor critturs! Yer mammy's been cross to yer."

The boys needed no second invitation and went in with great zeal for the eatables. And it was well they did so, as otherwise there would have been very little performed to any purpose by the party.

"Now," said Aunt Chloe, bustling about after breakfast, "I must put up yer clothes. Jest like as not, he'll take 'em all away. I know thar ways—mean as dirt, dey is. Wal, now, yer flannels for rheumatis is in this corner—so be car'ful, 'cause thar won't nobody make ye no more. Then here's yer old shirts, and these yer is new ones. I toed off these yer stockin's last night and put de ball in 'em to mend with. But Lor! Who'll ever mend for ye?" And Aunt Chloe, again overcome, laid her head on the box side and sobbed. "To think on't! No crittur to do for ye, sick or well!"

The boys, having eaten everything there was on the breakfast table, began now to take some thought of the case, and seeing their mother crying and their father looking very sad, began to whimper and put their hands to their eyes. Uncle Tom had the baby on his knee and was letting her enjoy herself to the utmost extent, scratching his face and pulling his hair, and occasionally breaking out into explosions of delight.

"Ay, crow away, poor crittur!" said Aunt Chloe. "Ye'll have to come to it, too! Ye'll live to see yer husband sold, or mebbe be sold yerself. And dese yer boys, dey's to be sold, I s'pose, too, jest like as not, when dey gets good for somethin'. An't no use in niggers havin' nothin'!"

Here one of the boys called, "Thar's Missis a-comin' in!"

"She can't do no good; what's she comin' for?" said Aunt Chloe.

Mrs. Shelby entered. Aunt Chloe set a chair for her in a manner decidedly gruff and crusty. She did not seem to notice either the action or the manner. She looked pale and anxious.

"Tom," she said, "I come to—" and stopping suddenly and regarding the silent group, she sat down in the chair, and covering her face with her handkerchief, began to sob.

"Lor, now, Missis, don't—don't!" said Aunt Chloe, bursting out in her turn. For a few moments they all wept in company. And in those tears they all shed together, the high and the lowly, melted away all the heartburnings and anger of the oppressed.

"My good fellow," said Mrs. Shelby, "I can't give you anything to do you any good. If I give you money, it will only be taken from you. But I tell you solemnly, and before God, that I will keep trace of you and bring you back as soon as I can command the money—and, till then, trust in God!"

Here the boys called out that Mas'r Haley was coming, and then an unceremonious kick pushed open the door. Haley stood there in very ill humor, having ridden hard the night before, and being not at all pacified by his ill success in recapturing his prey.

"Come," said he, "ye nigger, ye're ready? Servant, Ma'am!" said he, taking off his hat as he saw Mrs. Shelby.

Aunt Chloe shut and corded the box, and getting up, looked gruffly on the trader, her tears seeming suddenly turned to sparks of fire.

Tom rose up meekly to follow his new master and raised up his heavy box on his shoulder. His wife took the baby in her arms to go with him to the wagon, and the children, still crying, trailed on behind.

Mrs. Shelby, walking up to the trader, detained him for a few moments, talking with him in an earnest manner. And while she was thus talking, the whole family party proceeded to a wagon that stood ready harnessed at the door. A crowd of all the old and young hands on the place stood gathered around it, to bid farewell to their old associate. Tom had been looked up to, both as a head servant and a Christian teacher, by all the place, and there was much honest sympathy and grief about him, particularly among the women.

"Why, Chloe, you b'ar it better'n we do!" said one of the women, who had been weeping freely, noticing the gloomy calmness with which Aunt Chloe stood by the wagon.

"I's done *my* tears!" she said, looking grimly at the trader, who was coming up. "I does not feel to cry 'fore dat ar old limb, nohow!"

"Get in!" said Haley to Tom, as he strode through the crowd of servants, who looked at him with lowering brows.

Tom got in, and Haley, drawing out from under the wagon seat a heavy pair of shackles, made them fast around each ankle.

A smothered groan of indignation ran through the whole circle, and Mrs. Shelby spoke from her verandah:

"Mr. Haley, I assure you that precaution is entirely unnecessary."

"Don't know, ma'am. I've lost one five hundred dollars from this yer place, and I can't afford to run no more risks."

"What else could she spect on him?" said Aunt Chloe indignantly, while the two boys, who now seemed to comprehend at once their father's destiny, clung to her gown, sobbing.

"I'm sorry," said Tom, "that Mas'r George happened to be away."

George had gone to spend two or three days with a companion on a neighboring estate, and having departed early in the morning, before Tom's misfortune had been made public, had left without hearing of it.

"Give my love to Mas'r George," he said earnestly.

Haley whipped up the horse, and with a steady, mournful look fixed to the last on the old place, Tom was whirled away.

Mr. Shelby at this time was not at home. He had sold Tom under the spur of a driving necessity, to get out of the power of a man whom he dreaded—and his first feeling after the completion of the bargain had been that of relief. But it was in vain that he said to himself that he had a *right* to do it—that everybody did it, and that some did it without even the excuse of necessity. He could not satisfy his own feelings. And he had gone on a short business tour up the country, hoping that all would be over before he returned.

Tom and Haley rattled on along the dusty road, whirling past every old familiar spot until the bounds of the estate were fairly passed and they found themselves out on the open pike. After they had ridden about a mile, Haley suddenly drew up at the door of a blacksmith's shop, when taking out with him a pair of handcuffs, he stepped into the shop to have a little alteration in them.

"These yer's a little too small for his build," said Haley, showing the fetters and pointing out to Tom.

"Lor, now, if thar an't Shelby's Tom! He han't sold him, now?" said the smith.

"Yes, he has," said Haley.

"Now, ye don't! Well, reely," said the smith, "who'd a thought it! Why, ye needn't go to fetterin' him up this yer way. He's the faithfullest, best crittur—"

"Yes, yes," said Haley, "but your good fellows are just the critturs to want ter run off. Them stupid ones, as doesn't care whar they go, and shiftless, drunken ones, as don't care for nothin', they'll stick by, and like as not be rather pleased to be toted around. But these yer prime fellers, they hates it like sin. No way but to fetter 'em—got legs, they'll use 'em, no mistake."

"Well," said the smith, feeling among his tools, "them plantations down thar, stranger, an't just the place a Kentuck nigger wants to go—they dies thar tol'able fast, don't they?"

"Wal, yes, tol'able fast, ther dying is. What with the 'climating and one thing and another, they dies so as to keep the market up pretty brisk," said Haley.

"Wal, now, a feller can't help thinkin' it's a mighty pity to have a nice, quiet, likely feller, as good as Tom is, go down to be fairly ground up on one of them ar sugar plantations."

"Wal, he's got a fa'r chance. I promised to do well by him. I'll get him in house-servant in some good old family, and then, if he stands the fever and 'climating, he'll have a berth good as any nigger ought ter ask for."

"He leaves his wife and chil'en up here, s'pose?"

"Yes, but he'll get another thar. Lord, thar's women enough everywhar," said Haley.

Tom was sitting very mournfully while this conversation was going on. Suddenly he heard the quick, short click of a horse's hoofs behind him, and before he could fairly awake from his surprise, young Master George sprang into the wagon, threw his arms round his neck, and was sobbing and scolding with energy.

"I declare, it's real mean! I don't care what they say, any of 'em! It's a nasty, mean shame! If I was a man, they shouldn't do it—they should *not*, so!" said George, with a kind of subdued howl.

"Oh, Mas'r George! This does me good!" said Tom. "I couldn't bar to go off without seein' ye! It does me real good. ye can't tell!" Here Tom made some movement of his feet, and George's eyes fell on the fetters.

"What a shame!" he exclaimed, lifting his hands. "I'll knock that old fellow down—I will."

"No you won't Mas'r George. And you must not talk so loud. It won't help me any to anger him."

"Well, I won't then, for your sake. But only to think of it—isn't it a shame? They never sent for me, nor sent me any word, and if it hadn't been for Tom Lincon, I shouldn't have heard it. I tell you, I blew 'em up well, all of 'em, at home!"

"That ar wasn't right, I'm 'feard, Mas'r George."

"Can't help it! I say it's a shame! Look here, Uncle Tom," said he, turning his back to the shop and speaking in a mysterious tone, "I've brought you my dollar!"

"Oh! I couldn't think o' takin' on 't, Mas'r George, no ways in the world!" said Tom, quite moved.

"But you *shall* take it!" said George. "Look here—I told Aunt Chloe I'd do it, and she advised me just to make a hole in it and put a string through, so you could hang it round your neck and keep it out of sight. Else this mean scamp would take it away. I tell ye, Tom, I want to blow him up! It would do me good!"

"No, don't, Mas'r George, for it won't do *me* any good."

"Well, I won't for your sake," said George, busily tying his dollar round Tom's neck. "But there, now, button your coat tight over it, and keep it, and remember every time you see it that I'll come down after you and bring you back. Aunt Chloe and I have been talking about it. I told her not to fear. I'll see to it, and I'll tease Father's life out if he don't do it."

"Oh, Mas'r George, ye mustn't talk so 'bout yer father!"

"Lor, Uncle Tom, I don't mean anything bad."

"And now, Mas'r George," said Tom, "ye must be a good boy. 'Member how many hearts is sot on ye. Al'ays keep close to yer mother. Don't be gettin' into any of them foolish ways boys has of gettin' too big to mind their mothers. Tell ye what, Mas'r George, the Lord gives good many things twice over, but he don't give ye a mother but once. Ye'll never see sich another woman, Mas'r George, if ye live to be a hundred years old. So, now, you hold on to her, and grow up and be a comfort to her, thar's my own good boy—you will now, won't ye?"

"Yes, I will, Uncle Tom," said George seriously.

"And be careful of yer speaking, Mas'r George. Young boys, when they comes to your age, is willful sometimes—it's natur they should be. But real gentlemen, such as I hopes you'll be, never lets fall no words that isn't 'spectful to thar parents. Ye an't 'fended, Mas'r George?"

"No, indeed, Uncle Tom. You always did give me good advice."

"I's older, ye know," said Tom, stroking the boy's fine, curly head with his large, strong hand, but speaking in a voice as tender as a woman's, "and I sees all that's bound up in you. Oh, Mas'r George, you has everything—larnin', privileges, readin', writin'—and you'll grow up to be a great, larned, good man, and all the people on the place and your mother and father'll be so proud on ye! Be a good mas'r, like yer father, and be a Christian, like yer mother. 'Member yer Creator in the days o' yer youth, Mas'r George."

"I'll be *real* good, Uncle Tom, I tell you," said George. "I'm going to be a *first-rater*. And don't you be discouraged. I'll have you back to the place yet. As I told Aunt Chloe this morning, I'll build your house all over, and you shall have a room for a parlor, with a carpet on it when I'm a man. Oh, you'll have good times yet!"

Haley now came to the door with the handcuffs in his hands.

"Look here, now, Mister," said George with an air of great

superiority, as he got out, "I shall let father and mother know how you treat Uncle Tom."

"You're welcome," said the trader.

"I should think you'd be ashamed to spend all your life buying men and women, and chaining them like cattle! I should think you'd feel mean!" said George.

"So long as your grand folks wants to buy men and women, I'm as good as they is," said Haley. " 'Tant' any meaner sellin' on 'em than 'tis buyin'!"

"I'll never do either, when I'm a man," said George. "I'm ashamed this day that I'm a Kentuckian. I always was proud of it before." And George sat very straight on his horse and looked round with an air as if he expected the State would be impressed with his opinion.

"Well, good-by, Uncle Tom. Keep a stiff upper lip," said George.

"Good-by, Mas'r George," said Tom, looking fondly and admiringly at him. "God Almighty bless you! Ah, Kentucky han't get many like you!" he said in the fullness of his heart as the frank, boyish face was lost to his view. Away he went, and Tom looked till the clatter of his horse's hoofs died away, the last sound or sight of his home. But over his heart there seemed to be a warm spot, where those young hands had placed that precious dollar. Tom put up his hand and held it close to his heart.

"Now I tell ye what, Tom," said Haley as he came up to the wagon and threw in the handcuffs, "I mean to start fa'r with ye, as I gen'ally do with my niggers. And I'll tell ye now, to begin with, you treat me fa'r, and I'll treat you fa'r. I an't never hard on my niggers. Calculates to do the best for 'em I can. Now, ye see, you'd better just settle down comfortable and not be tryin' no tricks, because nigger's tricks of all sorts I'm up to, and it's no use. If niggers is quiet, and don't try to get off, they has good times with me, and if they don't, why it's their fault and not mine."

Tom assured Haley that he had no intentions of running

off. In fact, the address seemed rather a superfluous one to a man with a great pair of iron fetters on his feet. But Mr. Haley had got in the habit of commencing his relations with his stock with little addresses of this nature, calculated, as he deemed, to inspire cheerfulness and confidence and prevent the necessity of any unpleasant scenes.

And here, for the present, we take our leave of Tom, to pursue the fortunes of other characters in our story.

In Which Property Gets into an Improper State of Mind

It was on a drizzly afternoon that a traveler alighted at the door of a small country hotel in the village of N——, in Kentucky. In the barroom he found assembled quite a company of great, tall, rawboned, loose-jointed Kentuckians, attired in hunting shirts. Rifles stacked away in the corner, shot-pouches, game-bags, hunting-dogs, and little Negroes, all rolled together in the corners were the characteristic features in the picture. At each end of the fireplace sat a long-legged gentleman, with his chair tipped back, his hat on his head, and the heels of his muddy boots reposing on the mantelpiece.

Mine host, who stood behind the bar, was great of stature, good-natured, and loose-jointed, and like all his guests wore a hat on top of his head. Several Negroes in very free-and-easy pantaloons were scuttling about hither and thither, without bringing to pass any very particular results, except expressing a willingness to turn over everything in creation generally for the benefit of Mas'r and his guests. Add to this picture a crackling, rollicking fire, going rejoicing up a great, wide chimney, and you have an idea of the jollities of a Kentucky tavern.

Into such an assembly of the free and easy our traveler entered. He was a short, thick-set man, carefully dressed, with a round, good-natured countenance and something rather fussy and particular in his appearance. He was very careful of his valise and umbrella, bringing them in with his own hands and resisting all offers from the various servants to relieve him of them. He looked round the barroom with rather an anxious air. Then, retreating with his valuables to the warmest corner, he disposed them under his chair, sat down, and looked rather apprehensively up at the worthy whose heels illustrated the end of the mantelpiece, who was spitting from right to left with a courage and energy rather alarming to gentlemen of weak nerves and particular habits.

"I say, stranger, how are ye?" said the aforesaid gentleman, firing an honorary salute of tobacco juice in the direction of the new arrival.

"Well, I reckon," was the reply of the newcomer as he dodged, with some alarm, the threatening honor.

"Any news?" said the other, taking out a strip of tobacco and a large hunting-knife from his pocket.

"Not that I know of," said the man.

"Chaw?" said the first speaker, handing the old gentleman a bit of tobacco with a decidedly brotherly air.

"No, thank ye—it don't agree with me," said the little man, edging off.

"Don't, eh?" the long-legged man said, stowing away a morsel in his own mouth, in order to keep up the supply of tobacco juice.

The old gentleman uniformly gave a little start whenever the man fired in his direction. And this being observed by his companion, he very good-naturedly turned his artillery to another quarter, and proceeded to storm one of the fire-irons.

"What's that?" asked the old gentleman, observing some of the company formed in a group around a large handbill.

"Nigger advertised," said one of the company briefly.

Mr. Wilson, for that was the old gentleman's name, rose up and after carefully adjusting his valise and umbrella, proceeded to take out his spectacles and fix them on his nose. This being performed, he read as follows:

> Ran away from the subscriber, my mulatto boy, George. Said George six feet in height, a very light mulatto, brown curly hair; is very intelligent, speaks handsomely, can read and write; will probably try to pass for a white man; is deeply scarred on his back and shoulders; has been branded in his right hand with the letter H.
>
> I will give four hundred dollars for him alive, and the same sum for satisfactory proof that he has been killed.

The old gentleman read this advertisement from end to end, in a low voice, as if he were studying it.

The long-legged veteran who had been besieging the fire-iron, as before related, now took down his legs, and rearing aloft his tall form, walked up to the advertisement and very deliberately spit a full discharge of tobacco juice on it.

"There's my mind upon that!" said he briefly and sat down again.

"Why, now, stranger, what's that for?" said mine host.

"I'd do it all the same to the writer of that ar paper, if he was here," said the long man, coolly resuming his old employment of cutting tobacco. "Any man that owns a boy like that and can't find any better way o' treating on him, *deserves* to lose him. Such papers as these is a shame to Kentucky—that's my mind right out, if anybody wants to know!"

"Well, now, that's a fact," said mine host, as he made an entry in his book.

"I've got a gang of boys, sir," said the long man, resuming his attack on the fire-irons, "and I jest tells 'em—'Boys,' says I, '*run* now, dig, put, jest when ye want to! I never shall come to look after you!' That's the way I keep mine. Let 'em know they are free to run any time, and it jest breaks up their wanting to. More'n all, I've got free papers for 'em all recorded, in case I gets keeled up any o' these times, and they knows it. And I tell ye, stranger, there an't a fellow in our parts gets more out of his niggers than I do. Why, my boys have been to Cincinnati, with five hundred dollars' worth of colts, and brought me back the money, all straight, time and agin. It stands to reason they should. Treat 'em like dogs, and you'll have dogs' works and dogs' actions. Treat 'em like men, and you'll have men's works."

"I think you're altogether right, friend," said Mr. Wilson. "And this boy described here *is* a fine fellow—no mistake about that. He worked for me some half-dozen years in my bagging factory, and he was my best hand, sir. He is an ingenious fellow, too. He invented a machine for the cleaning of hemp—a really valuable affair. It's gone into use in several factories. His master holds the patent of it."

"I'll warrant ye," said the long-legged drover, "holds it and makes money out of it, and then turns round and brands the boy in his right hand. If I had a fair chance, I'd mark him, I reckon, so that he'd carry it *one* while."

"These yer knowin' boys is allers aggravating and sarcy," said a coarse-looking fellow from the other side of the room. "That's why they gets cut up and marked so. If they behaved themselves, they wouldn't."

"That is to say, the Lord made 'em men, and it's a hard squeeze getting 'em down into beasts," said the drover dryly.

"Bright niggers isn't no kind of 'vantage to their masters," continued the other. "What's the use o' talents and them things if you can't get the use on 'em yourself? Why, all the use they make on 't is to get round you. I've had one or two of these fellers, and I jest sold 'em down river. I knew I'd got to lose 'em, first or last, if I didn't."

"Better send orders up to the Lord to make you a set and leave out their souls entirely," said the drover.

Here the conversation was interrupted by the approach of a small one-horse buggy to the inn. It had a genteel appearance, and a well-dressed, gentlemanly man sat on the seat, with a colored servant driving.

The whole party examined the newcomer with the interest with which a set of loafers on a rainy day usually examine every newcomer. He was very tall, with a dark, Spanish complexion, fine, expressive black eyes, and close-curling hair, also of a glossy blackness. His well-formed aquiline nose, straight, thin lips, and the admirable outline of his finely-formed limbs, impressed the whole company instantly with the idea of something uncommon. He walked easily in among the company, and with a nod indicated to his waiter where to place his trunk, bowed to the company, and, with his hat in his hand, walked up leisurely to the bar and gave in his name as Henry Butler, Oaklands, Shelby County. Turning with an

indifferent air, he sauntered up to the advertisement and read it over.

"Jim," he said to his man, "seems to me we met a boy something like this up at Bernan's, didn't we?"

"Yes, Mas'r," said Jim, "only I an't sure about the hand."

"Well, I didn't look, of course," said the stranger, with a careless yawn. Then, walking up to the landlord, he desired him to furnish him with a private apartment, as he had some writing to do immediately.

The landlord was all dutiful, and a relay of about seven Negroes, old and young, male and female, little and big, were soon whizzing about like a covey of partridges, bustling, hurrying, treading on each other's toes, and tumbling over each other in their zeal to get Mas'r's room ready, while he seated himself easily on a chair in the middle of the room and entered into conversation with the man who sat next to him.

The manufacturer, Mr. Wilson, from the time of the entrance of the stranger, had regarded him with an air of disturbed and uneasy curiosity. He seemed to himself to have met and been acquainted with him somewhere, but he could not recollect. Every few moments, when the man spoke, or moved, or smiled, he would start and fix his eyes on him, and then suddenly withdraw them as the bright, dark eyes met his with such unconcerned coolness. At last a sudden recollection seemed to flash upon him, for he stared with such an air of blank amazement and alarm that the stranger walked up to him.

"Mr. Wilson, I think," said he, in a tone of recognition, and extending his hand. "I beg your pardon, I didn't recollect you before. I see you remember me—Mr. Butler, of Oaklands, Shelby County."

"Ye—yes—yes, sir," said Mr. Wilson, like one speaking in a dream.

Just then a Negro boy entered and announced that Mas'r's room was ready.

"Jim, see to the trunks," said the gentleman carelessly.

Then, addressing himself to Mr. Wilson, he added, "I should like to have a few moments' conversation with you on business in my room, if you please."

Mr. Wilson followed him as one who walks in his sleep, and they proceeded to a large upper chamber, where a new-made fire was crackling, and various servants flying about, putting finishing touches to the arrangements.

When all was done, and the servants departed, the young man deliberately locked the door, and putting the key in his pocket, faced about, and folding his arms on his bosom, looked Mr. Wilson full in the face.

"George!" said Mr. Wilson.

"Yes, George," said the young man.

"I couldn't have thought it!"

"I am pretty well disguised, I fancy," said the young man, with a smile. "A little walnut bark has made my yellow skin a genteel brown, and I've dyed my hair black; so you see I don't answer to the advertisement at all."

"Oh, George! But this is a dangerous game you are playing. I could not have advised you to do it."

"I can do it on my own responsibility," said George, with the same proud smile.

Mr. Wilson ambled up and down the room, appearing divided between his wish to help George, and a certain confused notion of maintaining law and order.

"Well, George," he said as he shambled about, "I s'pose you're running away—leaving your lawful master, George— I don't wonder at it—at the same time, I'm sorry, George— yes, decidedly—I think I must say that, George—it's my duty to tell you so."

"Why are you sorry, sir?" said George calmly.

"Why, to see you, as it were, setting yourself in opposition to the laws of your country."

"*My* country!" said George, with a strong and bitter emphasis. "What country have I but the grave—and I wish to God that I was laid there!"

"Why, George, no—no—it won't do. This way of talking

is wicked. George, you've got a hard master—in fact, he is—well, he conducts himself very badly—I can't pretend to defend him. But you know how the angel commanded Hagar to return to her mistress and submit herself under her hand. And the apostle sent back Onesimus to his master."

"Don't quote Bible at me that way, Mr. Wilson," said George, with a flashing eye. "Don't. For my wife is a Christian, and I mean to be, if ever I get to where I can. But to quote Bible to a fellow in my circumstances is enough to make him give it up altogether. I appeal to God Almighty—I am willing to go with the case to Him and ask Him if I do wrong to seek my freedom."

"These feelings are quite natural, George," said the good-natured man, blowing his nose. "Yes, they're natural, but it is my duty not to encourage 'em in you. Yes, my boy, I'm sorry for you, now. It's a bad case—very bad. But the apostle says, 'Let every one abide in the condition in which he is called.' We must all submit to the indications of Providence, George, don't you see?"

George stood with his head drawn back, his arms folded tightly over his broad breast, and a bitter smile curling his lips.

"I wonder, Mr. Wilson, if the Indians should come and take you a prisoner away from your wife and children, and want to keep you all your life hoeing corn for them, if you'd think it your duty to abide in the condition in which you were called. I rather think that you'd think the first stray horse you could find an indication of Providence—shouldn't you?"

The little old gentleman stared with wide eyes at this illustration of the case, but, though not much of a reasoner, he had the sense of saying nothing where nothing could be said. So, as he stood carefully stroking his umbrella and folding and patting down all the creases in it, he proceeded with his advice in a general way.

"You see, George, you know, now, I always have stood your friend, and whatever I've said, I've said for your good. Now here, it seems to me, you're running an awful risk. You can't hope to carry it out. If you're taken, it will be worse with you than ever. They'll only abuse you, and half kill you, and sell you down river."

"Mr. Wilson, I know all this," said George. "I *do* run a risk, but—" he threw open his overcoat and showed two pistols and a bowie knife—"there!" he said. "I'm ready for 'em. Down South I never *will* go. No! If it comes to that, I can earn myself at least six feet of free soil—the first and last I shall ever own in Kentucky!"

"Why, George, this state of mind is awful—it's getting really desperate, George. I'm concerned. Going to break the laws of your country!"

"My country again! Mr. Wilson, *you* have a country. But what country have *I*, or any one like me, born of slave mothers? What laws are there for us? We don't make them—we don't consent to them—we have nothing to do with them. All they do for us is to crush us, and keep us down. Haven't I heard your Fourth-of-July speeches? Don't you tell us all, once a year, that governments derive their just power from the consent of the governed? Can't a fellow *think*, that hears such things? Can't he put this and that together and see what it comes to?"

Mr. Wilson's mind was like a bale of cotton—downy, soft, fuzzy, and confused. He really pitied George with all his heart, and had a sort of dim idea of the feeling that agitated him. But he deemed it his duty to go on talking *good* to him.

"George, this is bad. I must tell you, you know, as a friend, you'd better not be meddling with such notions. They are bad, George, very bad, for boys in your condition—very." And Mr. Wilson sat down to a table and began nervously chewing the handle of his umbrella.

"See here, now, Mr. Wilson," said George, coming up and sitting himself down in front of him. "Look at me, now. Don't I sit before you, every way, just as much a man as you are? Look at my face—look at my hands—look at my body," and the young man drew himself up proudly. "Why am I *not* a man, as much as anybody? Well, Mr. Wilson, hear what I can tell you. I had a father—one of your Kentucky gentlemen—who didn't think enough of me to keep me from being sold with his dogs and horses when he died. I saw my mother put up at sheriff's sale, with her seven children. They were sold before her eyes, one by one, all to different masters, and I was the youngest. She came and kneeled down before old Mas'r and begged him to buy her with me, that she might have at least one child with her. And he kicked her away with his heavy boot. I saw him do it. And the last that I heard was her moans and screams when I was tied to his horse's neck to be carried off to his place."

"Well, then?"

"Well, sir, I grew up—long years and years—no father, no mother, no sister, not a living soul that cared for me more than a dog. Nothing but whipping, scolding, starving. Why, sir, I've been so hungry that I have been glad to take the bones they threw to their dogs. And yet, when I was a little fellow, and lay awake whole nights and cried, it wasn't the hunger, it wasn't the whipping I cried for. No, sir. It was for my mother and my sisters—it was because I hadn't a friend to love me on earth. I never knew what peace or comfort was. I never had a kind word spoken to me till I came to work in your factory. Mr. Wilson, you treated me well, you encouraged me to do well, and to learn to read and write, and to try to make something of myself—and God knows how grateful I am for it.

"Then, sir, I found my wife. You've seen her—you know how beautiful she is. When I found she loved me, when I married her, I scarcely could believe I was alive, I was so happy. And, sir, she is as good as she is beautiful. But now what? Why, now comes my master, takes me right away from my work, and my friends, and all I like, and grinds me down into the very dirt! And why? Because, he says, I forgot who I was. He says, to teach me that I am only a nigger.

After all, and last of all, he comes between me and my wife, and says I shall give her up and live with another woman.

"And all this your laws give him power to do, in spite of God or man. Mr. Wison, look at it! There isn't *one* of all these things that have broken the hearts of my mother, and my sisters, and my wife, and myself, but your laws allow, and give every man power to do in Kentucky, and none can say to him nay! Do you call these the laws of *my* country? Sir, I haven't any country, any more than I have any father. But I'm going to have one. I don't want anything of *your* country except to be let alone—to go peaceably out of it. And when I get to Canada, where the laws will own me and protect me, *that* shall be my country, and its laws I will obey. But if any man tries to stop me, let him take care, for I am desperate. I'll fight for my liberty to the last breath I breathe. You say your fathers did it. If it was right for them, it is right for me!"

This speech, delivered partly while sitting at the table and partly walking up and down the room—delivered with tears, and flashing eyes, and despairing gestures—was altogether too much for the good-natured old body to whom it was addressed. He had pulled out a great yellow silk pocket-handkerchief and was mopping up his face with great energy.

"Blast 'em all!" he suddenly broke out. "Haven't I always said so—the infernal old cusses! I hope I an't swearing, now. Well! Go ahead, George, go ahead. But be careful, my boy. Don't shoot anybody, George, unless—well—you *better* not shoot, I reckon. At least, I wouldn't *hit* anybody, you know. Where is your wife, George?" he added, as he nervously rose and began walking the room.

"Gone, sir, gone with her child in her arms, the Lord only knows where—gone after the North Star. And when we ever meet, or whether we meet at all in this world, no creature can tell."

"Is it possible! Astonishing! From such a kind family?"

"Kind families get in debt, and the laws of *our* country

allow them to sell the child out of its mother's bosom to pay its master's debts," said George bitterly.

"Well, well," said the honest old man, fumbling in his pocket. "I s'pose, perhaps, I an't following my judgment—hang it, I *won't* follow my judgment!" he added suddenly. "So here, George." And taking out a roll of bills from his pocketbook, he offered them to George.

"No, my kind, good sir!" said George. "You've done a great deal for me, and this might get you into trouble. I have money enough, I hope, to take me as far as I need it."

"No, but you must, George. Money is a great help everywhere—can't have too much, if you get it honestly. Take it—*do* take it, *now*—do, my boy!"

"On condition, sir, that I may repay it at some future time, I will," said George, taking up the money.

"And now, George, how long are you going to travel in this way? Not long or far, I hope. It's well carried on, but too bold. And this black fellow—who is he?"

"A true fellow, who went to Canada more than a year ago. He heard, after he got there, that his master was so angry at him for going off that he had whipped his poor old mother. And he has come all the way back to get her away."

"Has he got her?"

"Not yet. He has been hanging about the place and found no chance yet. Meanwhile he is going with me as far as Ohio, to put me among his friends that helped him, and then he will come back after her."

"Dangerous, very dangerous!" said the old man.

George drew himself up and smiled disdainfully.

The old gentleman eyed him from head to foot with a sort of innocent wonder.

"George, something has brought you out wonderfully. You hold up your head and speak and move like another man," said Mr. Wilson.

"Because I'm a free man!" said George proudly. "Yes, sir. I've said Mas'r for the last time to any man. I'm free!"

"Take care! You are not sure—you may be taken."

"All men are free and equal *in the grave,* if it comes to that, Mr. Wilson," said George.

"I'm perfectly dumfounded with your boldness!" said Mr. Wilson. "To come right here to the nearest tavern!"

"Mr. Wilson, it is *so* bold, and this tavern is so near, that they will never think of it. They will look for me on ahead, and you yourself wouldn't know me. Jim's master don't live in this county. He isn't known in these parts. Besides, he is given up—nobody is looking after him. And nobody will take me up from the advertisement, I think."

"But the mark on your hand?"

George drew off his glove and showed a newly-healed scar in his hand.

"That is a parting proof of Mr. Harris' regard," he said scornfully. "A fortnight ago he took it into his head to give it to me because he said he believed I should try to get away one of these days. Looks interesting, doesn't it?" he said, drawing his glove on again.

"I declare, my very blood runs cold when I think of it—your condition and your risks!" said Mr. Wilson.

"Mine has run cold a good many years, Mr. Wilson. At present it's about up to the boiling point," said George.

"Well, my good sir," continued George after a few moments' silence, "I saw you knew me. I thought I'd just have this talk with you, lest your surprised looks should bring me out. I leave here early tomorrow morning, before daylight. By tomorrow night I hope to sleep safe in Ohio. I shall travel by daylight, stop at the best hotels, go to the dinner-tables with the lords of the land. So, good-by, sir. If you hear that I'm taken, you may know that I'm dead!"

George stood up like a rock, and put out his hand with the air of a prince. The friendly little old man shook it heartily, and after a little shower of caution, he took his umbrella and fumbled his way out of the room.

Select Incident of Lawful Trade

Mr. Haley and Tom jogged onward in their wagons, each for a time absorbed in his own reflections. Now, the reflections of two men sitting side by side are a curious thing. Seated on the same seat, having the same eyes, ears, hands, and organs of all sorts, and having pass before their eyes the same objects— it is wonderful what a variety we shall find in these same reflections.

As, for example, Mr. Haley. He thought first of Tom's length, and breadth, and height, and what he would sell for, if he was kept fat and in good case till he got him into market. He thought of how he should make out his gang. He thought of the market value of the men and women and children who were supposedly to compose it, and other kindred topics of business. Then he thought of himself, and how humane he was, that whereas other men chained their "niggers" hand and foot both, he only put fetters on the feet, and left Tom the use of his hands, as long as he behaved well. He had been taken in so by "niggers" whom he had favored. But still he was astonished to consider how good-natured he yet remained.

As to Tom, he was thinking over some words of an unfashionable old book, which kept running through his head again and again, as follows: "We have here no continuing city, but we seek one to come; wherefore God himself is not ashamed to be called our God; for he hath prepared for us a city."

Mr. Haley pulled out of his pocket sundry newspapers and began looking over their advertisements with absorbed interest. He was not a fluent reader and was in the habit of reading half-aloud. In this manner he slowly recited the following paragraph:

EXECUTOR'S SALE—NEGROES!—Agreeable to order of court, will be sold, on Tuesday, February 20, before the Court-house door, in the town of Washington, Kentucky, the following Negroes: Hagar, aged 60; John, aged 30; Ben, aged 21, Saul, aged 25; Albert, aged 14. Sold for the benefit of the creditors and heirs of the estate of Jesse Blutchford, Esq.

SAMUEL MORRIS
THOMAS FLINT
Executors.

"This yer I must look at," said he to Tom, for want of somebody else to talk to. "Ye see, I'm going to get up a prime gang to take down with ye, Tom. It'll make it sociable and pleasantlike—good company will, ye know. We must drive right to Washington first and foremost, and then I'll clap you into jail while I does the business."

Tom received this agreeable intelligence quite meekly, simply wondering, in his own heart, how many of these doomed men had wives and children, and whether they would feel as he did about leaving them. It is to be confessed, too, that the offhand information that he was to be thrown into jail by no means produced an agreeable impression on a poor fellow who had always prided himself on a strictly honest and upright course of life. However, the day wore on, and in the evening saw Haley and Tom comfortably accommodated in Washington—the one in a tavern, and the other in jail.

About eleven o'clock the next day, a mixed throng was gathered around the courthouse steps—smoking, chewing, spitting, swearing, and conversing, according to their respective tastes—waiting for the auction to commence. The men and women to be sold sat in a group apart, talking in a low tone to each other. The woman who had been advertised by the name of Hagar was a regular African in feature and figure. She might have been sixty, but was older than that by hard work and disease, was partially blind, and somewhat crippled with rheumatism. By her side stood her only remaining son, Albert, a bright-looking little fellow of fourteen years. The boy was the only survivor of a large family, who had been successively sold away from her to a Southern market. The mother held on to him with both her shaking hands, and eyed with intense alarm every one who walked up to examine him.

"Don't be feared, Aunt Hagar," said the oldest of the men. "I spoke to Mas'r Thomas 'bout it, and he thought he might manage to sell you in a lot both together."

"Dey needn't call me worn out yet," said she, lifting her shaking hands. "I can cook yet, and scrub, and scour—I'm wuth a-buying, if I do come cheap. Tell 'em dat ar—you *tell* 'em," she added earnestly.

Haley forced his way into the group, walked up to the man, pulled his mouth open and looked in, felt of his teeth, made him stand and straighten himself, bend his back, and perform various motions to show his muscles. Then he passed on to the next, and put him through the same trial. Walking up last to the boy, he felt of his arms, straightened his hands, and looked at his fingers, and made him jump to show his agility.

"He an't gwine to be sold widout me!" said the old woman with passionate eagerness. "He and I goes in a lot together. I's rael strong yet, Mas'r, and can do heaps o' work—heaps on it, Mas'r."

"On plantation?" said Haley, with a contemptuous glance. "Likely story!" And, as if satisfied with his examination, he walked out and stood with his hands in his pockets, his cigar in his mouth, and his hat cocked on one side, ready for action.

"What think of 'em?" said a man who had been following Haley's examination, as if to make up his own mind from it.

"Wal," said Haley, spitting, "I shall put in, I think, for the youngerly ones and the boy."

"They want to sell the boy and the old woman together," said the man.

"Find it a tight pull—why, she's an old rack o' bones, not worth her salt."

"You wouldn't, then?" said the man.

"Anybody'd be a fool 'twould. She's half blind, crooked with rheumatis, and foolish to boot."

"Some buys up these yer old critturs and ses there's a sight more wear in 'em than a body'd think," said the man reflectively.

"No go 'tall," said Haley. "Wouldn't take her for a present —fact."

"Wal, 'tis kinder pity, now, not to buy her with her son— her heart seems so sot on him—s'pose they fling her in cheap."

"Them that's got money to spend that ar way, it's all well enough. I shall bid off on that ar boy for a plantation hand. Wouldn't be bothered with her no way—not if they'd give her to me," said Haley.

"She'll take on desp't," said the man.

"Nat'lly she will," said the trader coolly.

The conversation was here interrupted by a busy hum in the audience, and the auctioneer, a short, bustling, important fellow, elbowed his way into the crowd. The old woman drew in her breath and caught instinctively at her son.

"Keep close to yer mammy, Albert—close. Dey'll put us up togedder," she said.

"Oh, mammy, I'm feard they won't," said the boy.

"Dey must, child. I can't live no ways, if they don't," said the old creature passionately.

The loud tones of the auctioneer, calling out to clear the way, now announced that the sale was about to commence. A place was cleared, and the bidding began. The different men on the list were soon knocked off at prices which showed a pretty brisk demand in the market. Two of them fell to Haley.

"Come, now, young un," said the auctioneer, giving the boy a touch with his hammer, "be up and show your springs, now."

"Put us two up togedder, togedder—do, please, Mas'r," said the old woman, holding fast to her boy.

"Be off," said the man gruffly, pushing her hands away. "You come last. Now, darkey, spring." And with a word, he pushed the boy toward the block while a deep, heavy groan rose behind him. The boy paused and looked back. But there was no time to stay, and dashing the tears from his large, bright eyes, he was up in a moment.

His fine figure, alert limbs, and bright face, raised an instant competition, and half a dozen bids met the ear of the auctioneer. Anxious, half frightened, the boy looked from side to side as he heard the clatter of contending bids—now here, now there—till the hammer fell. Haley had got him. He was pushed from the block toward his new master, but stopped one moment and looked back, when his poor old mother, trembling in every limb, held out her shaking hands toward him.

"Buy me, too, Mas'r, for de dear Lord's sake! Buy me—I shall die if you don't!"

"You'll die if I do, that's the kink of it," said Haley. "No!" And he turned on his heel.

The bidding for the poor old creature was brief. The man who had addressed Haley, and who seemed not without compassion, bought her for a trifle, and the spectators began to disperse.

The poor victims of the sale, who had been brought up in one place together for years, gathered round the despairing old mother, whose agony was pitiful to see.

"Couldn't dey leave me one? Mas'r allers said I should have one—he did," she repeated over and over in heartbroken tones.

"Trust in the Lord, Aunt Hagar," said the oldest of the men sorrowfully.

"What good will it do?" said she, sobbing.

"Mother, Mother—don't, don't!" said the boy. "They say you's got a good master."

"I don't care—I don't care. Oh, Albert! Oh, my boy! You's my last baby. Lord, how ken I?"

"Come, take her off—can't some of ye?" said Haley dryly. "Don't do no good for her to go on that ar way."

The older men of the company, partly by persuasion and partly by force, loosed the poor creature's last despairing hold, and as they led her off to her new master's wagon, strove to comfort her.

"Now!" said Haley, pushing his three purchases together and producing a bundle of handcuffs, which he proceeded to put on their wrists. And fastening each handcuff to a long chain, he drove them before him to the jail.

A few days saw Haley, with his possessions, safely deposited on one of the Ohio boats. It was the commencement of his gang, to be increased, as the boat moved on, by various other merchandise of the same kind, which he, or his agent, had stored for him in various points along shore.

The *La Belle Riviere* was floating gaily down the stream under a brilliant sky, the stripes and stars of free America waving and fluttering overhead, the upper deck crowded with well-dressed ladies and gentlemen walking and enjoying the delightful day. All was full of life, buoyant, and rejoicing—all but Haley's gang, who were stored, with other freight, on the lower deck, and who, somehow, did not seem to appreciate their various privileges as they sat in a knot, talking to each other in low tones.

"Boys," said Haley, coming up briskly, "I hope you keep up good heart and are cheerful. Now, no sulks, ye see. Keep stiff upper lip, boys. Do well by me, and I'll do well by you."

The boys addressed responded the invariable "Yes, Mas'r." But they did not look particularly cheerful.

"I've got a wife," spoke out the article listed as "John, aged thirty," and he laid his chained hand on Tom's knee. "She don't know a word about this, poor girl!"

"Where does she live?" said Tom.

"In a tavern a piece down here," said John. "I wish, now, I *could* see her once more in this world," he added.

Poor John! It *was* rather natural. And the tears that fell, as he spoke, came as naturally as if he had been a white man. Tom drew a long breath from a sore heart, and tried in his poor way to comfort him.

And overhead, in the cabin, sat fathers and mothers, husbands and wives. And merry, dancing children moved round among them, like so many little butterflies, and everything was going on quite easy and comfortable.

"Oh, Mamma," said a boy who had just come up from below, "there's a Negro trader on board, and he's brought four or five slaves down there."

"Poor creatures!" said the mother, in a tone between grief and indignation.

"What's that?" said another lady.

"Some poor slaves below," said the mother.

"And they've got chains on," said the boy.

"What a shame to our country that such sights are to be seen!" said another lady.

"Oh, there's a great deal to be said on both sides of the subject," said a genteel woman who sat at her stateroom door sewing while her little girl and boy were playing round her. "I've been South, and I must say I think the Negroes are better off than they would be to be free."

"In some respects some of them are well off, I grant," said the lady to whose remark she had answered. "The most dreadful part of slavery, to my mind, is its outrages on the feelings and affections—the separating of families, for example."

"That *is* a bad thing, certainly," said the other lady, holding up a baby's dress she had just completed and looking intently on its trimmings. "But then, I fancy, it don't occur often."

"Oh, it does," said the first lady eagerly. "I've lived many years in Kentucky and Virginia both, and I've seen enough to make anyone's heart sick. Suppose, ma'am, your two children there should be taken from you and sold?"

"We can't reason from our feeling to those of this class of persons," said the other lady, sorting out some worsteds on her lap.

"Indeed, ma'am, you can know nothing of them if you say so," answered the first lady warmly. "I was born and brought up among them. I know they *do* feel, just as keenly—even more so, perhaps, than we do."

The lady said "Indeed!" She yawned, looked out the cabin window, and finally repeated the remark with which she had begun: "After all, I think they are better off than they would be to be free."

"It's undoubtedly the intention of Providence that the African race should be servants—kept in a low condition," said a clergyman seated by the cabin door. " 'Cursed be Canaan; a servant of servants shall he be,' the Scripture says."

"I say, stranger, is that ar what that text means?" said a tall man standing by.

"Undoubtedly. It pleased Providence to doom the race to bondage ages ago."

"Well, then, we'll all go ahead and buy up niggers," said the man, "if that's the way of Providence. Won't we, Squire?" said he, turning to Haley, who had been standing with his hands in his pockets by the stove and intently listening to the conversation.

"Yes," continued the tall man, "we must all be resigned to the decrees of Providence. Niggers must be sold, and trucked round, and kept under. It's what they's made for. 'Pears like this yer view's quite refreshing, an't it, stranger?" said he to Haley.

"I never thought on 't," said Haley. "I couldn't have said as much myself—I han't no larning. I took up the trade just to make a living. If 'tan't right, I calculated to 'pent on 't in time, ye know."

"And now you'll save yerself the trouble, won't ye?" And the stranger, who was none other than the honest drover whom we introduced to our readers in the Kentucky tavern, sat down and began smoking, with a curious smile on his long, dry face.

The boat swept proudly on her way, and all went on merrily. Men talked, and loafed, and read, and smoked. Women sewed and children played.

One day when she lay to for a while at a small town in Kentucky, Haley went up into the place on a little matter of business.

Tom, whose fetters did not prevent his slowly walking around, had drawn near the side of the boat and stood listlessly gazing over the railings. After a time he saw the trader returning in company with a colored woman, bearing in her arms a young child. She was dressed quite respectably, and a colored man followed her, bringing along a small trunk. The woman came cheerfully onward, talking as she came with the man who bore her trunk, and so passed up the plank into the boat. The bell rang, the steamer whizzed, the engine groaned and coughed, and away swept the boat down the river.

The woman walked forward among the boxes and bales of the lower deck, and sitting down, busied herself with chirruping to her baby.

Haley made a turn or two about the boat, and then coming up, seated himself near her and began saying something to her in an undertone.

Tom soon noticed a heavy cloud passing over the woman's brow, and that she answered rapidly and with great heat.

"I don't believe it—I won't believe it!" he heard her say. "You're jist a-foolin' with me."

"If you won't believe it, look here!" said the man, drawing out a paper. "This yer's the bill of sale, and there's your master's name to it. And I paid down good solid cash for it, too, I can tell you—so, now!"

"I don't believe Mas'r would cheat me so. It can't be true!" said the woman, with increasing agitation.

"You can ask any of these men here that can read writing. Here!" he said to a man that was passing by. "Jist read this yer, won't you? This yer gal won't believe me when I tell her what 'tis."

"Why, it's a bill of sale, signed by John Fosdick," said the man, "making over to you the girl Lucy and her child. It's all straight enough, for aught I see."

The woman's passionate exclamations collected a crowd around her, and the trader briefly explained to them the cause of the agitation.

"He told me that I was going down to Louisville, to hire out as cook to the same tavern where my husband works—that's what Mas'r told me his own self. And I can't believe he'd lie to me," said the woman.

"But he has sold you, my poor woman. There's no doubt about it," said a good-natured looking man who had been examining the papers. "He has done it, and no mistake."

"Then it's no account talking," said the woman, suddenly growing quite calm. And clasping her child tighter in her arms, she sat down on her box, turned her back round, and gazed listlessly into the river.

"Going to take it easy after all!" said the trader. "Gal's got grit, I see."

The woman looked calm as the boat went on. She saw sunshine sparkling on the water and heard gay voices, full of ease and pleasure, talking around her everywhere. But her heart lay as if a great stone had fallen on it. Her baby raised himself up against her and stroked her cheeks with his little hands, and springing up and down, crowing and chatting, seemed determined to arouse her. She strained him suddenly and tightly in her arms, and slowly one tear after another fell on his wondering, unconscious face. Gradually she seemed to grow calmer, and busied herself with tending and nursing him.

The child, a boy of ten months, was uncommonly large and strong for his age and very vigorous in his limbs. Never for a moment still, he kept his mother constantly busy in holding him and guarding his springing activity.

"That's a fine chap!" said a man, suddenly stopping opposite to him. "How old is he?"

"Ten months and a half," said the mother.

The man whistled to the boy and offered him part of a stick of candy, which he eagerly grabbed and very soon had in his mouth.

"Rum fellow!" said the man. "Knows what's what!" And he whistled and walked on. When he had got to the other side of the boat, he came across Haley, who was smoking on top of a pile of boxes.

The stranger produced a match and lighted a cigar, saying as he did so:

"Decentish kind o' wench you've got round there, stranger."

"Why, I reckon she *is* tol'able fair," said Haley, blowing the smoke out of his mouth.

"Taking her down South?" said the man.

Haley nodded and smoked on.

"Plantation hand?" said the man.

"Wal," said Haley, "I'm fillin' out an order for a planta-tion, and I think I shall put her in. They told me she was a good cook. They can use her for that, or set her at the cotton-picking. She's got the right fingers for that—I looked at 'em. Sell well either way." And Haley resumed his cigar.

"They won't want the young un on a plantation," said the man.

"I shall sell him, first chance I find," said Haley, lighting another cigar.

" 'Spose you'd be selling him tol'able cheap," said the stran-ger, mounting the pile of boxes and sitting down comforta-bly.

"Don't know 'bout that," said Haley. "He's a pretty smart young un—straight, fat, strong—flesh as hard as a brick!"

"Very true, but then there's all the bother and expense of raisin'."

"Nonsense!" said Haley. "They is raised as easy as any kind of crittur going. They an't a bit more trouble than pups. This yer chap will be running all round in a month."

"I've got a good place for raisin', and I thought of takin' in a little more stock," said the man. "One cook lost a young un last week—got drownded in a washtub while she was hangin' out clothes—and I reckon it would be well enough to set her to raisin' this yer."

Haley and the stranger smoked a while in silence, neither seeming willing to broach the test question of the interview. At last the man resumed:

"You wouldn't think of wantin' more than ten dollars for that ar chap, seeing you *must* get him off yer hands anyhow?"

Haley shook his head and spit impressively.

"That won't do no ways," he said and began his smoking again.

"Well, stranger, what will you take?"

"Well, now," said Haley, "I *could* raise that ar chap myself, or get him raised. He's oncommon likely and healthy, and he'd fetch a hundred dollars six months hence. And in a year or two he'd bring two hundred, if I had him in the right spot. So I shan't take a cent less nor fifty for him now."

"Oh, stranger! That's ridiculous altogether," said the man.

"Fact!" said Haley with a decisive nod of his head.

"I'll give thirty for him," said the stranger, "but not a cent more."

"Now, I'll tell ye what I will do," said Haley, spitting again, with renewed decision. "I'll split the difference and say forty-five. And that's the most I will do."

"Well, agreed!" said the man after an interval.

"Done!" said Haley. "Where do you land?"

"At Louisville," said the man.

"Louisville," said Haley. "Very fair. We get there about dusk. Chap will be asleep—all fair—get him off quietly, and no screaming. Happens beautiful—I like to do everything quietly. I hates all kind of agitation and fluster." And so, after a transfer of certain bills from the man's pocketbook to the trader's, he resumed his cigar.

It was a bright, tranquil evening when the boat stopped at the wharf at Louisville. The woman had been sitting with her baby in her arms, now wrapped in a heavy sleep. When she heard the name of the place called out, she hastily laid the child down in a little cradle formed by the hollow among the boxes, first carefully spreading under it her cloak. Then she sprang to the side of the boat in hopes that among the various hotel waiters who thronged the wharf she might see her husband. In this hope she pressed forward to the front rails, and stretching far over them, strained her eyes intently on the moving heads on the shore. The crowd pressed in between her and the child.

"Now's your time," said Haley, taking the sleeping child up and handing him to the stranger. "Don't wake him up and set him to crying, now—it would make a devil of a fuss with the gal." The man took the bundle carefully and was soon lost in the crowd that went up the wharf.

When the boat, creaking and groaning and puffing, had loosed from the wharf and was beginning slowly to strain herself along, the woman returned to her old seat. The trader was sitting there—and the child was gone.

"Why, why—where . . . ?" she began in bewildered surprise.

"Lucy," said the trader, "your child's gone—you may as well know it first as last. You see, I know'd you couldn't take him down South. And I got a chance to sell him to a first-rate family that'll raise him better than you can."

The wild look of anguish and utter despair that the woman cast on him might have disturbed one less practiced. But Haley was used to it. He had seen that same look hundreds of times. So the trader only regarded the mortal anguish which he saw working in those dark features, those clenched hands, and suffocating breathings, as necessary incidents of the trade. He merely calculated whether she was going to scream and get up a commotion on the boat.

But the woman did not scream. The shot had passed too straight and direct through the heart for cry or tear.

Dizzily she sat down. Her slack hands fell lifeless by her side. Her eyes looked straight forward, but she saw nothing. All the noise and hum of the boat, the groaning of the machinery, mingled dreamily in her bewildered ear, and the poor, dumb-stricken heart had neither cry nor tear to show for its utter misery. She was quite calm.

The trader seemed to feel called on to administer such consolation as the case admitted of.

"I know this yer comes kinder hard at first, Lucy," said he. "But such a smart, sensible gal as you are won't give way to it. You see, it's *necessary* and can't be helped."

"Oh, don't, Mas'r, don't!" said the woman with a voice like one that is smothering.

"You're a smart wench, Lucy," he persisted. "I mean to do well by ye and get ye a nice place down river. And you'll soon get another husband—such a likely gal as you—"

"Oh, Mas'r, if you *only* won't talk to me now," said the

woman in a voice of such living anguish that the trader felt that there was something at present in the case beyond his style of operation. He got up, and the woman turned away and buried her head in her cloak.

The trader walked up and down for a time and occasionally stopped and looked at her.

"Takes it hard, rather," he thought, "but quiet, tho'. Let her sweat a while—she'll come right by and by."

Tom had watched the whole transaction from first to last and had a perfect understanding of its results. To him it looked like something unutterably horrible and cruel because —poor, ignorant black soul—he had not learned to generalize and to take enlarged views. If he had only been instructed by certain ministers of Christianity, he might have thought better of it and seen in it an everyday incident of a lawful trade. But Tom, as we see, being a poor, ignorant fellow, whose reading had been confined entirely to the New Testament, could not comfort himself with views like these. His very soul bled within him for what seemed to him the *wrongs* of the poor, suffering thing that lay like a crushed reed on the boxes—the feeling, living, bleeding, yet immortal *thing* which American state law coolly classes with the bundles, and bales, and boxes among which she is lying.

Tom drew near and tried to say something. But she only groaned. Honestly, and with tears running down his own cheeks, he spoke of a heart of love in the skies, of a pitying Jesus, and an eternal home. But the ear was deaf with anguish, and the palsied heart could not feel.

Night came on—night calm, unmoved, and glorious, shining down with her innumerable and solemn angel eyes, twinkling, beautiful, but silent. There was no speech nor language, no pitying voice or helping hand from that distant sky. One after another the voices of business or pleasure died away. All on the boat were sleeping, and the ripples at the prow were plainly heard. Tom stretched himself out on a box, and there, as he lay, he heard ever and anon a smothered sob or cry from the prostrate creature: "Oh, what shall I do? Oh, Lord! Oh, good Lord, do help me!" And so ever and anon until the murmur died away in silence.

At midnight Tom waked with a sudden start. Something black passed quickly by him to the side of the boat, and he heard a splash in the water. No one else saw or heard anything. He raised his head—the woman's place was vacant. He got up and sought about him in vain. The poor, bleeding heart was still at last, and the river rippled and dimpled just as brightly as if it had not closed above it.

The trader waked up bright and early and came out to see his livestock. It was now his turn to look about in perplexity.

"Where alive is that gal?" he said to Tom.

Tom, who had learned the wisdom of keeping counsel, did not feel called on to state his observations and suspicions, but said he did not know.

"She surely couldn't have got off in the night at any of the landings, for I was awake and on the look-out whenever the boat stopped. I never trust these yer things to other folks."

This speech was addressed to Tom quite confidentially, as if it was something that would be specially interesting to him. Tom made no answer.

The trader searched the boat from stem to stern, among boxes, bales, and barrels, around the machinery, by the chimneys, in vain.

"Now, I say, Tom, be fair about this yer," he said when after a fruitless search he came where Tom was standing. "You know something about it, now. Don't tell me—I know you do. I saw the gal stretched out here about ten o'clock, and ag'in at twelve, and ag'in between one and two, and then at four she was gone, and you was a-sleeping right there all the time. Now, you know something—you can't help it."

"Well, Mas'r," said Tom, "toward morning something brushed by me, and I kinder half woke. And then I heard a great splash, and then I clar woke up, and the gal was gone. That's all I know on 't."

The trader was not shocked nor amazed, because, as we said before, he was used to a great many things that you are not used to. Even the awful presence of Death struck no solemn chill upon him. He had seen Death many times—met him in the way of trade and got acquainted with him. And so he only swore that the gal was a baggage, and that he was devilish unlucky, and that if things went on in this way, he should not make a cent on the trip. In short, he seemed to consider himself an ill-used man decidedly. But there was no help for it, as the woman had escaped into a state which *never will* give up a fugitive—not even at the demand of the whole glorious Union. The trader, therefore, sat discontentedly down with his little account book, and put down the missing body and soul under the head of *losses*.

In concluding these little incidents of lawful trade, we must beg the world not to think that American legislators are entirely lacking in humanity, as might, perhaps, be unfairly supposed from the great efforts made in our national body to protect and perpetuate this species of traffic. Who does not know how our great men are outdoing themselves in crying out against the *foreign* slave-trade. Trading Negroes from Africa, dear reader, is so horrid! It is not to be thought of! But trading them from Kentucky—that's quite another thing!

The Quaker Settlement

A QUIET scene in Indiana now rises before us. A large, roomy, neatly-painted kitchen, its yellow floor glossy and smooth and without a particle of dust. A neat, well-blacked cooking stove. Rows of shining tin. Glossy green wood chairs, old and firm. A small flag-bottomed rocking chair with a patchwork cushion in it, and a larger-sized one, motherly and old. And in the chair, gently swaying back and forward, her eyes bent on some fine sewing, sat our old friend Eliza.

Yes, there she is, paler and thinner than in her Kentucky home, with a world of quiet sorrow lying under the shadow of her long eyelashes. It was plain to see how old and firm the girlish heart was grown under the discipline of heavy sorrow. And when, anon, her large dark eyes were raised to follow the gambols of her little Harry, who was sporting like some tropical butterfly, hither and thither over the floor, she showed a depth of firmness and steady resolve that was never there in her earlier and happier days.

By her side sat a woman with a bright tin pan in her lap, into which she was carefully sorting some dried peaches. Rachel Halliday might be fifty-five or sixty. But hers was one of those faces that time seems to touch only to brighten and adorn. The snowy cap, made after the Quaker pattern, the plain white muslin handkerchief lying in placid folds across her bosom, the drab shawl and dress, showed at once the community to which she belonged. Her face was round and rosy, with a healthful downy softness suggestive of a ripe peach. Her hair, partially silvered by age, was parted smoothly back from a high, placid forehead, on which time had written no inscription except peace on earth, good will to men. And beneath shone a large pair of clear, loving, brown eyes.

"And so thee still thinks of going to Canada, Eliza?" she said as she quietly looked over her peaches.

"Yes, ma'am," said Eliza firmly. "I must go onward. I dare not stop."

"And what'll thee do when thee gets there? Thee must think about that, my daughter."

Eliza's hands trembled, and some tears fell on her fine work, but she answered firmly:

"I shall do—anything I can find. I hope I can find something."

"Thee knows thee can stay here, as long as thee pleases," said Rachel.

"Oh, thank you," said Eliza, "but"—she pointed to Harry —"I can't sleep nights. I can't rest. Last night I dreamed I saw the man coming into the yard."

"Poor child!" said Rachel. "But thee mustn't feel so. The Lord hath ordered it so that never hath a fugitive been stolen from our village. I trust thine will not be the first."

The door here opened, and a little short, round, pincushiony woman stood at the door, with a cheery, blooming face, like a ripe apple. She, too, was dressed in sober gray, with the muslin folded neatly across her round, plump little chest.

"Ruth Stedman," said Rachel, coming joyfully forward. "How is thee, Ruth?"

"Nicely," said Ruth, taking off her little drab bonnet and displaying, as she did so, a round little head on which the Quaker cap sat with a sort of jaunty air. Then the newcomer, who might have been five-and-twenty, turned from the small looking-glass where she had been tucking in stray locks of decidedly curly hair.

"Ruth, this friend is Eliza Harris, and this is the little boy I told thee of."

"I am glad to see thee, Eliza—very," said Ruth, shaking hands as if Eliza were an old friend she had long been expecting. "And this is thy dear boy—I brought a cake for him," she said, holding out a little heart to the boy, who came up, gazing through his curls, and accepted it shyly.

"Where's thy baby, Ruth?" said Rachel.

"Oh, he's coming. But thy Mary caught him as I came in and ran off with him to the barn to show him to the children."

At this moment the door opened, and Mary, an honest, rosy-looking girl with large brown eyes like her mother's came in with the baby.

"Aha!" said Rachel, coming up and taking the great white,

fat fellow in her arms. "How good he looks, and how he does grow!"

"To be sure he does," said little bustling Ruth as she took the child and began taking off a little blue silk hood and various layers and wrappers of outer garments. And having given a twitch here, and a pull there, and variously adjusted and arranged him, and kissed him heartily, she set him on the floor to collect his thoughts. Baby appeared quite used to this mode of proceeding, for he put his thumb in his mouth and seemed soon absorbed in his own reflections, while she seated herself, and taking out a long stocking of mixed blue and white yarn, began to knit with briskness.

"Mary, thee'd better fill the kettle, hadn't thee?" gently suggested the mother.

Mary took the kettle to the well and, reappearing, placed it over the stove, where it was soon purring and steaming. The peaches, moreover, in obedience to a few gentle whispers from Rachel, were deposited by the same hand in a stewpan over the fire.

Rachel now took down a snowy molding-board, and tying on an apron, proceeded quietly to making up some biscuits, first saying to Mary: "Mary, hadn't thee better tell John to get a chicken ready?" And Mary disappeared accordingly.

Simeon Halliday, a tall, straight, muscular man in a drab coat and pantaloons and broad-brimmed hat, now entered.

"How is thee, Ruth?" he said warmly as he spread his broad hand for her little fat palm.

"Any news, Father?" said Rachel.

"Peter Stebbins told me that they should be along tonight with *friends*," said Simeon significantly, as he was washing his hands at a neat sink in a little back porch.

"Indeed!" said Rachel, looking thoughtful and glancing at Eliza.

"Did thee say thy name is Harris?" said Simeon to Eliza as he reentered.

Rachel glanced quickly at her husband as Eliza tremulously answered, "Yes."

"Mother!" called Simeon, standing in the porch.

"What does thee want, Father?" said Rachel, rubbing her floury hands as she went to him.

"This child's husband is in the settlement and will be here tonight."

"Now, thee doesn't say that, Father?" said Rachel, all her face radiant with joy.

"It's really true. Peter was down yesterday with the wagon to the other stand, and there he found an old woman and two men. One said his name was George Harris. And from what he told of his history, I am certain who he is. He is a bright, likely fellow, too. Shall we tell her now?"

"Let's tell Ruth," said Rachel. "Here, Ruth—come here."

Ruth laid down her knitting-work and was in the back porch in a moment.

"Ruth, what does thee think?" said Rachel. "Father says Eliza's husband is in the last company and will be here tonight."

A burst of joy from the little Quakeress interrupted the speech. She gave such a bound from the floor as she clapped her little hands that two stray curls fell from under her Quaker cap and lay brightly on her white neckerchief.

"Hush thee, dear!" said Rachel gently. "Tell us, shall we tell her now?"

"Now, to be sure—this very minute. Why, now, suppose 'twas my John—how should I feel? Do tell her right off." And she laid her hands persuasively on Rachel's arm. "Take her into thy bedroom, and let me fry the chicken while thee does it."

Rachel came out into the kitchen, and opening the door of a small bedroom, said gently, "Come in here with me, my daughter. I have news to tell thee."

The blood flushed in Eliza's pale face. She rose, trembling with nervous anxiety, and looked toward her boy.

"No, no," said little Ruth, darting up and seizing her hands. "Never thee fear—it's good news, Eliza. Go in, go in!" And she gently pushed her to the door, which closed after her. And then, turning round, Ruth caught little Harry in her arms and began kissing him.

"Thee'll see thy father, little one. Does thee know it? Thy father is coming," she said over and over again as the boy looked wonderingly at her.

Meanwhile, within the door, another scene was going on. Rachel Halliday drew Eliza toward her and said, "The Lord hath had mercy on thee, daughter. Thy husband hath escaped from the house of bondage."

The blood flushed to Eliza's cheek in a sudden glow and went back with as sudden a rush. She sat down, pale and faint.

"Have courage, child," said Rachel, laying her hand on her head. "He is among friends, who will bring him here to-night."

"Tonight!" Eliza repeated. "Tonight!" The words lost all meaning to her. Her mind was dreamy and confused, and all was mist for a moment.

———

When she awoke, she found herself snugly tucked up on the bed, with a blanket over her and little Ruth rubbing her hands with camphor. She opened her eyes in a state of dreamy, delicious languor, such as one who has long been bearing a heavy load and now feels it gone. As she lay with her large, dark eyes open, she followed, as in a quiet dream, the motions of those about her. She saw the door open into the other room, saw the supper table with its snowy cloth, heard the murmur of the singing teakettle; saw Ruth tripping backward and forward with plates of cake and saucers of preserves, and ever and anon stopping to put a cake into Harry's hand, or pat his head, or twine his long curls round her snowy fingers. She saw the ample, motherly form of

Rachel as she came to the bedside and smoothed and arranged something about the bedclothes. She saw Ruth's husband come in—saw her fly up to him and commence whispering very earnestly. She saw her, with the baby in her arms, sitting down to tea. She saw them all at table, and little Harry in a high chair, under the shadow of Rachel's wing. There were low murmurs of talk, gentle tinkling of teaspoons, musical clatter of cups and saucers, and all mingled in a delightful dream of rest. And Eliza slept as she had not slept since the fearful midnight hour when she had taken her child and fled through the frosty starlight.

She dreamed of a land of green shores, pleasant islands, and glittering water. And there, in a house which kind voices told her was a home, she saw her boy playing, a free and happy child. She heard her husband's footsteps—she felt him coming near. His arms were around her, his tears falling on her face. And she awoke. . . . The daylight had long faded.

Her child lay calmly sleeping by her side. A candle was burning dimly on the stand. And her husband was sobbing by her pillow.

———————

The next morning was a cheerful one at the Quaker house. "Mother" was up betimes and surrounded by busy girls and boys, who all moved obediently to Rachel's gentle "Thee had better," or more gentle "Hadn't thee better?" in the work of getting breakfast. While, therefore, John ran to the spring for fresh water, and Simeon the Second sifted meal for corn-cakes, and Mary ground coffee, Rachel moved gently and quietly about, making biscuits, cutting up chicken, and diffusing a sort of sunny radiance over the whole proceeding generally.

While all other preparations were going on, Simeon the Elder stood in his shirt-sleeves before a little looking-glass, engaged in shaving. Everything went on so sociably, so quietly, so harmoniously in the great kitchen—it seemed so pleasant to everyone to do just what they were doing, there was such an atmosphere of mutual confidence and good fellowship everywhere—even the knives and forks had a social clatter as they went on to the table, and the chicken and ham had a cheerful and joyous sizzle in the pan, as if they rather enjoyed being cooked than otherwise. And when George and Eliza and little Harry came out, they met such a hearty, rejoicing welcome, no wonder it seemed to them like a dream.

At last they were all seated at breakfast, while Mary stood at the stove baking griddlecakes, which, as they gained the true exact golden-brown tint of perfection, were transferred quite handily to the table.

It was the first time that ever George had sat down on equal terms at any white man's table, and he sat down at first with some constraint and awkwardness. But they all went off like fog in the genial morning rays of the simple, overflowing kindness.

This, indeed, was a home—*home*—a word that George had

never yet known a meaning for. And a belief in God and trust in His providence began to encircle his heart.

"Father, what if thee should get found out again?" said Simeon the Second as he buttered his cakes.

"I should pay my fine," said Simeon quietly.

"But what if they put thee in prison?"

"Couldn't thee and Mother manage the farm?" said Simeon, smiling.

"Mother can do almost everything," said the boy. "But isn't it a shame to have such laws?"

"Thee mustn't speak evil of thy rulers, Simeon," said his father gravely. "The Lord only gives us our worldly goods that we may do justice and mercy. If our rulers require a price of us for it, we must deliver it up."

"Well, I hate those old slaveholders!" said the boy.

"I am surprised at thee, son," said Simeon. "Thy mother never taught thee so. I would do even the same for the slaveholder as for the slave, if the Lord brought him to my door in affliction."

Simeon the Second blushed scarlet. But his mother only smiled and said, "Simeon is my good boy. He will grow older by and by, and then he will be like his father."

"I hope, my good sir, that you are not exposed to any difficulty on our account," said George anxiously.

"Fear nothing, George. If we would not meet trouble for a good cause, we were not worthy of our name."

"But for *me*," said George. "I could not bear it."

"Fear not, then, friend George. It is not for thee, but for God and man we do it," said Simeon. "And now thou must lie by quietly this day, and tonight, at ten o'clock, Phineas Fletcher will carry thee onward to the next stand—thee and the rest of thy company. The pursuers are hard after thee. We must not delay."

"If that is the case, why wait till evening?" said George.

"Thou art safe here by daylight, for everyone in the settlement is a Friend, and all are watching. It has been found safer to travel by night."

Evangeline

THE slanting light of the setting sun quivers on the sea-like expanse of the Mississippi. The shivery canes and the tall dark cypress, hung with wreaths of dark moss, glow in the golden ray as the heavily-laden steamboat marches onward.

Piled with cotton-bales from many a plantation till she seems in the distance a square, massive block of gray, she moves heavily onward to the nearing mart. We must look some time among its crowded decks before we shall find again our humble friend Tom. High on the upper deck, in a little nook among the cotton-bales, at last we may find him.

Partly from confidence inspired by Mr. Shelby's representations, and partly from the remarkably quiet character of the man, Tom had won his way far into the confidence even of such a man as Haley. At first the trader had watched him narrowly through the day and never allowed him to sleep at night unfettered. But the uncomplaining patience and apparent contentment of Tom's manner led him gradually to discontinue these restraints, and for some time Tom had enjoyed a sort of parole of honor, being permitted to come and go freely where he pleased on the boat.

Ever quiet and obliging, and more than ready to lend a hand in every emergency which occurred among the workmen below, he had won the good opinion of all the hands and spent many hours in helping them with as hearty a good will as ever he worked on a Kentucky farm.

When there seemed to be nothing for him to do, he would climb to a nook among the cotton-bales of the upper deck and busy himself in studying over his Bible—and it is there we see him now.

For a hundred or more miles above New Orleans, the river

is higher than the surrounding country and rolls between levees twenty feet in height. Tom, therefore, saw spread out full before him, in plantation after plantation, a map of the life to which he was approaching.

He saw the distant slaves at their toil. He saw afar their villages of huts gleaming out in long rows on many a plantation, distant from the stately mansions and pleasure-grounds of the master. And as the moving picture passed on, his poor, foolish heart would be turning backward to the Kentucky farm with its old, shadowy beeches, to the master's house with its wide, cool halls and, near by, the little cabin overgrown with the rose and bignonia. There he seemed to see familiar faces of comrades who had grown up with him from infancy. He saw his busy wife, bustling in her preparations for his evening meal. He heard the merry laugh of his boys at their play, and the chirrup of the baby at his knee. And then, with a start, all faded and he saw again the canebrakes and cypresses and gliding plantations, and heard again the creaking and groaning of the machinery, all telling him too plainly that all that phase of life had gone by forever.

In such a case, you write to your wife, and send messages to your children. But Tom could not write—the mail for him had no existence, and the gulf of separation was unbridged by even a friendly word or signal.

Is it strange, then, that some tears fall on the pages of his Bible, as he lays it on the cotton-bale, and with patient finger threading his slow way from word to word, traces out its promises? Having learned to read late in life, Tom was but a slow reader. Let us follow him a moment as, pointing to each word and pronouncing each half-aloud, he reads:

"Let—not—your—heart—be—troubled.   In—my—Father's—house—are—many—mansions. I—go—to—prepare—a—place—for—you."

It had been his custom to get the Bible read to him by his master's children, in particular by young Master George. And, as they read, he would designate, by bold, strong marks

and dashes with pen and ink the passages which more particularly gratified his ear or affected his heart. His Bible was thus
marked through from one end to the other. So he could in a
moment seize upon his favorite passages, and while it lay there
before him, every passage breathing of some old home scene,
his Bible seemed to him all of this life that remained, as well as
the promise of a future one.

Among the passengers on the boat was a young gentleman
of fortune and family, resident in New Orleans, who bore the
name of St. Clare. He had with him a daughter between five
and six years of age, together with a lady who seemed to
claim relationship to both, and to have the little one especially
under her charge.

Tom had often caught glimpses of this little girl, who, once
seen, could not be easily forgotten. Her form was the perfection of childish beauty, while her face had a dreamy earnestness of expression by which the dullest were impressed without knowing exactly why. The shape of her head and the
turn of her neck were peculiarly noble. And the long golden-
brown hair that floated like a cloud around her face, the deep
spiritual gravity of her violet-blue eyes, shaded by heavy
fringes of golden-brown, all marked her out from other children and made every one turn and look after her as she glided
hither and thither on the boat.

Nevertheless, the little one was not what you would have
called either a grave child or a sad one. On the contrary, an
innocent playfulness seemed to flicker over her childish face
and around her figure. She was always in motion, always,
with a half smile on her rosy mouth, flying hither and thither,
singing to herself as she moved as in a happy dream. Her
father and female guardian were incessantly busy in pursuit of
her—but when caught, she melted from them again like a
summer cloud. And as no word of chiding or reproof ever fell
on her ear for whatever she chose to do, she pursued her own
way all over the boat. Always dressed in white, she seemed to
move without contracting spot or stain. And there was not a

corner or nook, above or below, where those fairy footsteps had not glided.

Tom, who had the soft, impressible nature of his race, watched the little creature with daily increasing interest. To him she seemed something almost divine. And whenever her golden head and deep blue eyes peered out upon him from behind some dusky cotton-bale, or looked down upon him over some ridge of packages, he half believed that he saw one of the angels stepped out of his New Testament.

Often and often she walked mournfully round the place where Haley's gang of men and women sat in their chains. She would glide in among them and look at them with an air of perplexed and sorrowful earnestness, and sometimes she would lift their chains with her slender hands, and then sigh woefully as she glided away. Several times she appeared suddenly among them with her hands full of candy, nuts, and oranges, which she would distribute joyfully to them, and then be gone again.

Tom watched the little lady a great deal before he ventured on any overtures toward acquaintanceship. He knew an abundance of simple acts to invite the approaches of the little people, and he resolved to play his part right skillfully. He could cut cunning little baskets out of cherry-stones, could make grotesque faces on hickory nuts, or odd, jumping figures out of elder-pith, and he was a very Pan in the manufacture of whistles. His pockets were full of articles of attraction which he had hoarded in days of old for his master's children, and which he now produced one by one.

The little one was shy, and it was not easy to tame her. For a while she would perch like a canary-bird on some box or package near Tom, while busy in the little arts aforenamed, and take from him, with a kind of grave bashfulness, the little articles he offered. But at last they got on quite confidential terms.

"What's little missy's name?" said Tom at last when he thought matters were ripe to push such an inquiry.

"Evangeline St. Clare," said the little one, "though Papa and everybody else call me Eva. Now, what's your name?"

"My name's Tom—the little chil'en used to call me Uncle Tom, way back thar in Kentuck."

"Then I mean to call you Uncle Tom, because, you see, I like you," said Eva. "So, Uncle Tom, where are you going?"

"I don't know, Miss Eva."

"Don't know?" said Eva.

"No. I am going to be sold to somebody. I don't know who."

"My papa can buy you," said Eva quickly. "And if he buys you, you will have good times. I mean to ask him to, this very day."

"Thank you, my little lady," said Tom.

The boat here stopped at a small landing to take in wood, and Eva, hearing her father's voice, bounded nimbly away.

Tom rose up and went forward to offer his services in wood-ing, and soon was busy among the hands.

Eva and her father were standing together by the railings to see the boat start from the landing-place, the wheel had made two or three revolutions in the water, when by some sudden movement the little one suddenly lost her balance and fell sheer over the side of the boat into the water. Her father, scarce knowing what he did, was plunging in after her, but was held back by some behind him, who saw that more efficient aid had followed his child.

Tom was standing just under her on the lower deck as she fell. He saw her strike the water and sink, and was after her in a moment. A broad-chested, strong-armed fellow, it was nothing for him to keep afloat in the water till, in a moment or two, the child rose to the surface. Then he caught her in his arms, and swimming with her to the boat-side, handed her up to the grasp of hundreds of hands which, as if they had all belonged to one man, were stretched eagerly out to receive her. A few moments more and her father bore her, dripping and senseless, to the ladies' cabin.

———

It was a sultry, close day the next day as the steamer drew near to New Orleans. A general bustle of expectation and preparation was spread through the boat. In the cabin, one and another were gathering their things together and arrang-ing them, preparatory to going ashore. On the lower deck sat our friend Tom, with his arms folded, and anxiously from time to time turning his eyes toward a group on the other side of the boat.

There stood the fair Evangeline, a little paler than the day before but otherwise exhibiting no traces of the accident which had befallen her. A graceful, elegantly-formed young man stood by her, carelessly leaning one elbow on a bale of cotton, while a large pocketbook lay open before him. It was quite evident, at a glance, that the gentleman was Eva's father.

There was the same noble cast of the head, the same large blue eyes, the same golden-brown hair. Yet the expression was wholly different. In the large, clear blue eyes there was wanting that misty, dreamy depth of expression—all was clear, bold and bright, but with a light wholly of this world. The beautifully cut mouth had a proud and somewhat sarcastic expression, while an air of free-and-easy superiority sat not ungracefully in every turn and movement of his fine form. He was listening with a good-humored, careless air, half comic, half contemptuous, to Haley, who was glibly describing the quality of the article for which they were bargaining.

"All the moral and Christian virtues bound in black morocco, complete!" the gentleman said when Haley had finished. "Well, now, my good fellow, what's the damage, as they say in Kentucky? In short, what's to be paid out for this business? How much are you going to cheat me, now? Out with it!"

"Wal," said Haley, "if I should say thirteen hundred dollars for that ar fellow, I shouldn't but just save myself--I shouldn't, now re'ly."

"Poor fellow!" said the young man, fixing his keen, mocking blue eye on him. "But I suppose you'd let me have him for that, out of a particular regard for me."

"Wal, the young lady here seems to be sot on him, and nat'lly enough."

"Oh, certainly, there's a call on your benevolence, my friend. Now, as a matter of Christian charity, how cheap could you afford to let him go, to oblige a young lady that's particular sot on him?"

"Wal, now, just think on't," said the trader. "Just look at them limbs, broad-chested, strong as a horse. Look at his head. Them high forrards allays shows calculatin' niggers, that'll do any kind o' thing. I've marked that ar. Now, a nigger of that ar heft and build is worth considerable just, as you may say, for his body, supposin' he's stupid. But come to put in his calculatin' faculties, and them which I can show he has oncommon, why, of course, it makes him come higher. Why, that ar fellow managed his master's whole farm. He has a extr'or'nary talent for business."

"Bad, bad, very bad—knows altogether too much!" said the young man, with the same mocking smile playing about his mouth. "Never will do in the world. Your smart fellows are always running off, stealing horses, and raising the devil generally. I think you'll have to take off a couple of hundred for his smartness."

"Wal, there might be something in that ar, if it warn't for his character. But I can show recommends from his master and others to prove he is one of your real pious—the most humble, prayin', pious crittur ye ever did see. Why, he's been called a preacher in them parts he came from."

"And I might use him for a family chaplain, possibly," added the young man dryly. "That's quite an idea. Religion is a remarkably scarce article at our house."

"You're joking, now."

"How do you know I am? Didn't you just warrant him for a preacher? Come, hand over your papers."

The trader laid down a greasy pocketbook and began anxiously studying over certain papers in it. The young man stood by the while, looking down on him with an air of careless, easy drollery.

"Papa, do buy him! It's no matter what you pay," whispered Eva softly, getting up on a package and putting her arm around her father's neck. "You have money enough, I know. I want him."

"What for, Pussy? Are you going to use him for a rattlebox, or a rocking-horse, or what?"

"I want to make him happy."

"An original reason, certainly."

Here the trader handed up a certificate signed by Mr. Shelby, which the young man took with the tips of his long fingers and glanced over carelessly.

"A gentlemanly hand," he said, "and well spelt, too. Well,

now, but I'm not sure, after all, about this religion," said he, the old wicked expression returning to his eye. "I have not looked in the papers lately to see how it sells. How many hundred dollars, now, do you put on for this religion?"

"You like to be jokin', now," said the trader. "I know there's differences in religion. Some kinds is mis'rable, but ye see in this letter what Tom's old master says about him."

"Now," said the young man, stooping gravely over his book of bills, "if you can assure me that it will be set down to my account in the book up above, as something belonging to me, I wouldn't care if I did go a little extra for it. There, count your money, old boy," he added as he handed the roll to the trader.

"All right," said Haley, his face beaming with delight. And pulling out an old inkhorn, he proceeded to fill out a bill of sale, which, in a few moments, he handed to the young man.

"I wonder, now, if I was divided up," said the latter as he ran over the paper, "how much I might bring. . . . But come, Eva!"

Taking the hand of his daughter, he stepped across the boat, and carelessly putting the tip of his finger under Tom's chin, said good-humoredly, "Look up, Tom, and see how you like your new master."

Tom looked up. It was not in nature to look into that gay, young, handsome face without a feeling of pleasure, and Tom felt the tears start in his eyes as he said heartily, "God bless you, Mas'r!"

"Well, I hope he will. What's your name? Tom? Quite as likely to do it for your asking as mine, from all accounts. Can you drive horses, Tom?"

"I've been al'ays used to horses," said Tom. "Mas'r Shelby raised heaps on 'em."

"Well, I think I shall put you in coachy, on condition that you won't be drunk more than once a week, unless in cases of emergency, Tom."

Tom looked surprised and rather hurt, and said, "I never drink, Mas'r."

"I've heard that story before, Tom. But then we'll see. It will be a special accommodation to all concerned if you don't. Never mind, my boy," he added good-humoredly, seeing Tom still looked grave. "I don't doubt you mean to do well."

"I sartin do, Mas'r," said Tom.

"And you shall have good times," said Eva. "Papa is very good to everybody, only he always will laugh at them."

"Papa is much obliged to you for his recommendation," said St. Clare, laughing, as he turned on his heel and walked away.

Of Tom's New Master,
and Various Other Matters

SINCE the thread of our humble hero's life has now become interwoven with that of higher ones, it is necessary to give some brief introduction to them.

Augustine St. Clare was one of two sons born to a wealthy planter of Louisiana. Having inherited from his mother an exceeding delicacy of constitution, during many years the boy was sent to the care of an uncle in Vermont, in order that his body might be strengthened by the cold of a more bracing climate. In childhood he was remarkable for an extreme sensitiveness of character. Time, however, overgrew this softness with the rough bark of manhood, and but few knew how living and fresh it still lay at the core.

Soon after the completion of his college course, his whole nature was kindled into one intense romantic passion. He saw and won the love of a high-minded and beautiful woman in one of the Northern states, and they were affianced. He returned South to make arrangements for their marriage, when most unexpectedly his letters were returned to him by mail with a short note from her guardian, stating that ere this reached him, the lady would be the wife of another. Stung to madness, he vainly hoped, as many another has done, to fling the whole thing from his heart by one desperate effort. Too proud to plead or seek explanation, he threw himself at once into a whirl of fashionable society, and in a fortnight from the time of the fatal letter was the accepted lover of the reigning belle of the season. And as soon as arrangements could be made, he became the husband of a fine figure, a pair of bright dark eyes, and a hundred thousand dollars. Of course, everybody thought him a happy fellow.

The married couple were enjoying their honeymoon and entertaining a brilliant circle of friends in their splendid villa near Pontchartrain, when a letter was brought to him in *that* well-remembered writing. It was handed to him while he was in the full tide of gay conversation, in a whole roomful of company. He turned deadly pale when he saw the writing, but still preserved his composure, and a short time after was missed from the circle.

In his room alone, he opened and read the letter. It was from her, giving a long account of a persecution to which she had been exposed by her guardian's family to lead her to unite herself with their son. And she related how, for a long time, his letters had ceased to arrive; how she had written time and again till she became weary and doubtful; how her health had failed under her anxieties; and how, at last, she had discovered the whole fraud which had been practiced on them both. The letter ended with expressions of hope and thankfulness and professions of undying affection, which were more bitter than death to the unhappy young man. He wrote to her immediately:

"I have received yours—but too late. I believed all I heard.

I was desperate. *I am married*, and all is over. Only forget—it is all that remains for either of us."

And thus ended the whole romance of life for Augustine St. Clare. But the *real* remained—the *real*, like the flat, bare, oozy tide mud when the blue, sparkling wave has gone down, and there it lies, flat, slimy, bare.

Of course, in a novel people's hearts break and they die and that is the end of it. But in real life we do not die when all that makes life bright dies to us. There is a most busy and important round of eating, drinking, dressing, walking, visiting, buying, selling, talking, reading, and all that makes up what is commonly called *living* yet to be gone through. And this yet remained to Augustine. Had his wife been a whole woman, she might yet have done something—as a woman can—to mend the broken threads of life and weave it again into a tissue of brightness. But Marie St. Clare could not even see that they had been broken. As before stated, she consisted of a fine figure, a pair of splendid eyes, and a hundred thousand dollars.

When Augustine, pale as death, was found lying on the sofa and pleaded sudden sick headache as the cause of his distress, she recommended to him to smell of hartshorn. And when the paleness and headache came on week after week, she only said that she never thought Mr. St. Clare was sickly, and that it was a very unfortunate thing for her, because he didn't enjoy going into company with her, and it seemed odd to go so much alone when they were just married.

Marie never had possessed much capability of affection or much sensitiveness. From her infancy she had been surrounded with servants who lived only to study her whims. The idea that they had either feelings or rights had never dawned upon her. Her father, whose only child she had been, had never denied her anything, and when she entered life—beautiful, accomplished, and an heiress—she had, of course, all the other sex sighing at her feet, and she had no doubt that Augustine was a most fortunate man in having obtained her.

When, therefore, St. Clare began to drop off those gallantries and small attentions which flowed at first through the habit of courtship, he found his sultana no way ready to resign her slave. There were abundance of tears, pouting, and small tempests. There were discontents, pinings, upbraidings. St. Clare was good-natured and self-indulgent and sought to buy off with presents and flatteries. And when Marie became mother to a beautiful daughter, he really felt awakened, for a time, to something like tenderness.

St. Clare's mother had been a woman of uncommon purity of character, and he gave to this child his mother's name, fondly fancying that she would prove her image. The thing had been remarked with jealousy by his wife, and she regarded her husband's devotion to the child with suspicion and dislike. All that was given to Eva seemed so much taken from herself. From the time of birth of this child, her health gradually sank. A few years changed the blooming young belle into a yellow, faded, sickly woman, whose time was divided among a variety of fanciful diseases, and who considered herself the most ill-used and suffering person in existence.

There was no end of her various complaints. But the principal one appeared to be sick headache, which sometimes would confine her to her room three days out of six. As, of course, all family arrangements fell into the hands of servants, St. Clare found his household anything but comfortable. His only daughter was exceedingly delicate, and he feared that, with no one to look after her and attend to her, her health and life might yet fall a sacrifice to her mother's inefficiency. He had taken her with him on a tour to Vermont and had persuaded his cousin, Miss Ophelia Sinclare, to return with him to his Southern residence. And they are now returning on this boat, where we have introduced them to our readers.

And now, while the distant domes and spires of New Orleans rise to our view, there is yet time for an introduction to Miss Ophelia.

Whoever has traveled in the New England states will remember, in some cool village, the large farmhouse with its clean-swept grassy yard, shaded by the dense foliage of the sugar maple, and remember the air of order and stillness that seemed to breathe over the whole place. Nothing lost, or out of order—not a picket loose in the fence, not a particle of litter in the turfy yard with its clumps of lilacs bushes growing up under the windows. Within, he will remember wide, clean rooms, where nothing ever seems to be doing or going to be done, where everything is once and forever rigidly in place, and where all household arrangements move with the punctual exactness of the old clock in the corner. There are no servants in the house, but the lady in the snowy cap, with the spectacles, who sits sewing every afternoon among her daughters as if nothing ever had been done, or were to be done—she and her girls, in some long-forgotten forepart of the day "*did up the work*," and for the rest of the time, probably, at all hours when you would see them, it is "*done up.*" The old kitchen floor never seems stained or spotted, the table, the chairs, and the various cooking utensils never seem disordered—though three and sometimes four meals a day are got there, though the family washing and ironing is there performed, and though pounds of butter and cheese are in some silent and mysterious manner there brought into existence.

On such a farm, in such a house and family, Miss Ophelia had spent a quiet existence of some forty-five years when her cousin invited her to visit his Southern mansion. The eldest of a large family, she was still considered by her father and mother as one of "the children," and the proposal that she should go to Orleans was a most momentous one to the family circle. The good mother inquired anxiously "if Orleans wasn't an awful wicked place," saying "that it seemed to her most equal to going to the Sandwich Islands, or anywhere among the heathen."

It was known at the minister's, and at the doctor's, and at

Miss Peabody's millinery shop that Ophelia Sinclare was "talking about" going away down to Orleans with her cousin. And, of course, the whole village could do no less than help this very important process of *talking about* the matter. It was said that Squire Sinclare had counted out fifty dollars and given them to Miss Ophelia and told her to buy any clothes she thought best, and that two new silk dresses and a bonnet had been sent for from Boston. All parties agreed that there had been no such parasol seen in those parts as had been sent on from New York, and that she had one silk dress so stiff that it might fairly be trusted to stand alone. There were rumors also of a hemstitched pocket handkerchief, and report even went so far as to state that Miss Ophelia had one pocket handkerchief with lace all around it.

Miss Ophelia, as you now behold her, stands before you in a very shining brown linen traveling-dress, tall, square-formed, and angular. Her face was thin and rather sharp in its outlines, the lips compressed, like those of a person who is in the habit of making up her mind definitely on all subjects, while the keen, dark eyes traveled over everything as if they were looking for something to take care of.

All her movements were sharp, decided, and energetic. And though she was never much of a talker, her words were remarkably direct and to the purpose when she did speak. In her habits, she was all order, method, and exactness. The sin of sins, in her eyes, was expressed by one very common and important word in her vocabulary—"shiftlessness." People who did nothing, or who did not know exactly what they were going to do, or who did not take the most direct way to accomplish what they set their hands to, were objects of her contempt—a contempt shown less frequently by anything she said than by a kind of stony grimness, as if she scorned to say anything about the matter. Miss Ophelia was the absolute slave of the "*ought.*" Once make her certain that the "path of duty" lay in any given direction, and fire and water could not keep her from it. She would walk straight down into a well, or up to a loaded cannon's mouth, if she were only quite sure that there the path lay.

But how in the world can Miss Ophelia get along with Augustine St. Clare—gay, easy, unpunctual, unpractical, sceptical—in short, walking over every one of her most cherished habits and opinions?

To tell the truth, then, Miss Ophelia loved him. When he was a boy, it had been hers to teach him his catechism, mend his clothes, comb his hair, and bring him up generally in the way he should go. And her heart having a warm side to it, Augustine had, as he usually did with most people, taken a large share of it for himself, and therefore it was that he succeeded very easily in persuading her that the "path of duty" lay in the direction of New Orleans, and that she must go with him to take care of Eva and keep everything from going to wrack and ruin during the frequent illnesses of his wife. The idea of a house without anybody to take care of it went to her heart. Then she loved the lovely little girl. And though she regarded Augustine as very much of a heathen, yet she loved him, laughed at his jokes, and forbore with his failings to an extent which those who knew him thought perfectly unbelievable. But what more or other is to be known of Miss Ophelia our reader must discover by a personal acquaintance.

There she is, sitting now in her stateroom, surrounded by a mixed multitude of little and big carpetbags, boxes, baskets, which she is tying, binding up, packing, or fastening, with a face of great earnestness.

"Now, Eva, have you kept count of your things? Of course you haven't—children never do. There's the spotted carpetbag, and the little blue bandbox with your best bonnet—that's two. Then the India-rubber satchel is three. And my tape and needle box is four. And my hand-box, five. And my collarbox, six. And that little hair trunk, seven. What have you done with your sunshade? Give it to me, and let me put a paper round it and tie it to my umbrella with my shade—there, now."

"Why, Aunty, we are only going up home—what is the use?"

"To keep it nice, child. People must take care of their things if they ever mean to have anything. And now, Eva, is your thimble put up?"

"Really, Aunty, I don't know."

"Well, never mind. I'll look your box over—thimble, wax, two spools, scissors, knife, tape-needle. All right—put it in here. What did you ever do, child, when you were coming on with only your papa? I should have thought you'd a lost everything you had."

"Well, Aunty, I did lose a great many, and then, when we stopped anywhere, Papa would buy some more of whatever it was."

"Mercy on us, child—what a way!"

"It was a very easy way, Aunty," said Eva.

"It's a dreadful shiftless one," said Aunty.

"Why, Aunty, what'll you do now?" said Eva. "That trunk is too full to be shut down."

"It *must* shut down," said Aunty, with the air of a general, as she squeezed the things in and sprung upon the lid. Still a little gap remained about the mouth of the trunk.

"Get up here, Eva!" said Miss Ophelia courageously. "What has been done can be done again. This trunk has *got to be* shut and locked—there are no two ways about it."

And the trunk, intimidated, doubtless, by this resolute statement, gave in. Miss Ophelia turned the key and pocketed it in triumph.

"Now we're ready. Where's your papa? I think it time this baggage was set out. Do look out, Eva, and see if you see your papa."

"Oh, yes, he's down the other end of the gentlemen's cabin, eating an orange."

"He can't know how near we are coming," said Aunty.

"Hadn't you better run and speak to him?"

"Papa never is in a hurry about anything," said Eva, "and we haven't come to the landing. Do step on the deck, Aunty. Look! There's our house, up that street!"

The boat now began, with heavy groans, to prepare to push up among the steamers at the levee. Eva joyously pointed out the various spires, domes, and way-marks by which she recognized her native city.

"Yes, yes, dear, very fine," said Miss Ophelia. "But mercy on us, the boat has stopped! Where is your father?"

Now ensued the usual turmoil of landing, everybody crowding to the plank. Miss Ophelia seated herself resolutely on the lately vanquished trunk, and marshalling all her goods and chattels in fine military order, seemed resolved to defend them to the last.

"Shall I take your trunk, ma'am?" "Shall I take your baggage?" "Shan't I carry out these yer, Missis?" rained down upon her unheeded. She sat with grim determination, upright as a darning-needle stuck in a board, holding on to her bundle of umbrella and parasols, and wondering to Eva "what upon earth her papa could be thinking of. He couldn't have fallen over, now—but something must have happened." And just as she had began to work herself into a real distress, he came up with his usual careless motion, and giving Eva a quarter of the orange he was eating, said:

"Well, Cousin Vermont, I suppose you are all ready."

"I've been ready, waiting, nearly an hour," said Miss Ophelia. "I began to be really concerned about you."

"Well, the carriage is waiting," he said, "and the crowd are now off, so that one can walk out in a decent and Christian manner and not be pushed and shoved. Here," he added to a driver who stood behind him, "take these things."

"I'll go and see to his putting them in," said Miss Ophelia.

"Oh, pshaw, Cousin, what's the use?" said St. Clare.

"Well, at any rate, I'll carry this, and this, and this," said Miss Ophelia, singling out three boxes and a small carpetbag.

"My dear Miss Vermont, positively you mustn't walk out under all that load. They'll take you for a waiting-maid. Give them to this fellow—he'll put them down as if they were eggs, now."

Miss Ophelia looked despairingly as her cousin took all her treasures from her, and rejoiced to find herself once more in the carriage with them in a state of preservation.

"Where's Tom?" said Eva.

"Oh, he's on the outside, Pussy. I'm going to take Tom up to Mother for a peace-offering, to make up for that drunken fellow that upset the carriage."

"Oh, Tom will make a splendid driver, I know," said Eva. "He'll never get drunk."

The carriage stopped in front of an ancient mansion built in the Moorish fashion, a square building enclosing a courtyard, into which the carriage drove through an arched gateway. Wide galleries all around the four sides, Moorish arches, and slender pillars carried the mind back to the reign of oriental romance in Spain. In the middle of the court a fountain threw high its silvery water, falling in a never-ceasing spray into a marble basin, fringed with a deep border of violets. The water in the fountain, clear as crystal, was alive with myriads of gold and silver fishes, twinkling and darting through it like so many living jewels. Around the fountain ran a walk paved with a mosaic of pebbles. And this, again, was surrounded by turf, smooth as green velvet, while a carriage-drive enclosed the whole. Two large orange-trees, now fragrant with blossoms, threw a delicious shade. And round upon the turf were marble vases containing the choicest flowering plants of the tropics. Huge pomegranate trees with their glossy leaves and flame-colored flowers, dark-leaved Arabian jessamines with their silvery stars, geraniums, luxuriant roses bending beneath their heavy abundance of flowers, golden jessamines, lemon-scented verbena, all united their bloom and fragrance.

As the carriage drove in, Eva seemed like a bird ready to burst from a cage with the wild eagerness of her delight.

"Oh, isn't it beautiful, lovely! My own dear, darling home!" she said to Miss Ophelia. "Isn't it beautiful?"

" 'Tis a pretty place," said Miss Ophelia as she alighted, "though it looks rather old and heathenish to me."

St. Clare smiled as Miss Ophelia made her remark, and turning to Tom, who was standing looking round, his beaming black face perfectly radiant with admiration, he said:

"Tom, my boy, this seems to suit you."

"Yes, Mas'r, it looks about the right thing," said Tom.

All this passed in a moment while trunks were being hustled off, hackman paid, and while a crowd of all ages and sizes—men, women, and children—came running through the galleries, both above and below, to see Mas'r come in. Foremost among them was a highly-dressed young mulatto man, attired in the last extreme of fashion and gracefully waving a scented cambric handkerchief in his hand.

This personage had been exerting himself in driving all the flock of servants to the other end of the verandah.

"Back, all of you! I am ashamed of you," he said in a tone of authority. "Would you intrude on Master's domestic relations in the first hour of his return?"

All looked abashed at this elegant speech, delivered with quite an air, and stood huddled together at a respectful distance, except two stout porters, who came up and began conveying away the baggage.

Owing to Mr. Adolph's arrangements, when St. Clare turned round from paying the hackman, there was nobody in view but Mr. Adolph himself, conspicuous in satin vest, gold guard-chain, and white pants, and bowing with inexpressible grace.

"Oh, Adolph, is it you? How are you, boy?" said his master, offering his hand to him, while Adolph poured forth a speech which he had been preparing with great care for a fortnight before.

"Well, well," said St. Clare, passing on, with his usual air of careless drollery, "that's very well got up, Adolph. See that the baggage is well bestowed. I'll come to the people in a minute." And so saying, he led Miss Ophelia to a large parlor that opened onto the verandah.

While this had been passing, Eva had flown like a bird through the porch and parlor to a little boudoir opening likewise on the verandah.

A tall, dark-eyed, sallow woman half rose from a couch on which she was reclining.

"Mamma!" said Eva in a sort of rapture, throwing herself on her neck and embracing her over and over again.

"That'll do—take care, child—don't. You make my head ache," said the mother after she had languidly kissed her.

St. Clare came in, embraced his wife in true husbandly fashion, and then presented to her his cousin. Marie lifted her large eyes on her cousin with an air of some curiosity and received her with languid politeness. A crowd of **servants** now pressed to the entry door, and among them a middle-aged mulatto woman of very respectable appearance stood foremost, in a tremor of expectation and joy, at the door.

"Oh, there's Mammy!" said Eva as she flew across the room. And throwing herself into her arms, she kissed her repeatedly.

This woman did not tell her that she made her head ache, but on the contrary, she hugged her, and laughed, and cried, till her sanity was a thing to be doubted of. And when released from her, Eva flew from one to another, shaking hands and kissing in a way that Miss Ophelia afterwards declared fairly turned her stomach.

"Well!" said Miss Ophelia. "Your Southern children can do something that I couldn't."

"What, now, pray?" said St. Clare.

"Well, I want to be kind to everybody, and I wouldn't have anything hurt. But as to kissing—"

"Niggers," said St. Clare. "That you're not up to—hey?"

"Yes, that's it. How can she?"

St. Clare laughed as he went into the passage. "Halloa, here, what's to pay out here? Here, you all—Mammy, Jimmy, Polly, Sukey—glad to see Mas'r?" he said, as he went shaking hands from one to another. "Look out for the babies!" he added, as he stumbled over a sooty little urchin who was crawling upon all fours. "If I step upon anybody, let 'em mention it."

There was an abundance of laughing and blessing Mas'r, as St. Clare distributed small pieces of change among them.

"Come, now, take yourselves off, like good boys and girls," he said. And the whole assemblage, dark and light, disappeared through a door into a large verandah, followed by Eva, who carried a large satchel which she had been filling with apples, nuts, candy, ribbons, laces, and toys of every description during the whole homeward journey.

As St. Clare turned to go back, his eye fell upon Tom, who was standing uneasily shifting from one foot to the other, while Adolph stood carelessly leaning against the banisters, examining Tom through an opera glass with an air that would have done credit to any dandy living.

"Puh! You puppy!" said his master, striking down the opera glass. "Is that the way you treat your company? Seems to me, Dolph," he added, laying his finger on the elegant figured satin vest that Adolph was sporting, "seems to me that's *my* vest."

"Oh, Master, this vest all stained with wine—of course, a gentleman in Master's standing never wears a vest like this. I understood I was to take it. It does for a poor nigger-fellow like me." And Adolph tossed his head and passed his fingers through his scented hair with a grace.

"So that's it, is it?" said St. Clare carelessly. "Well, here, I'm going to show this Tom to his mistress, and then you take him to the kitchen. And mind you don't put on any of your airs to him. He's worth two such puppies as you."

"Master always will have his joke," said Adolph, laughing. "I'm delighted to see Master in such spirits.'

"Here, Tom," said St. Clare, beckoning.

Tom entered the room. He looked wistfully on the velvet carpets and the before unimagined splendors of mirrors, pictures, statues, and curtains, and like the Queen of Sheba before Solomon, there was no spirit in him. He looked afraid even to set his feet down.

"See here, Marie," said St. Clare to his wife, "I've bought you a coachman, at last to order. I tell you, he's a regular hearse for blackness and sobriety and will drive you like a funeral, if you want. Open your eyes, now, and look at him. Now, don't say I never think about you when I'm gone."

Marie opened her eyes and fixed them on Tom.

"I know he'll get drunk," she said.

"No, he's warranted a pious and sober article."

"Well, I hope he may turn out well," said the lady. "It's more than I expect, though."

"Dolph," said St. Clare, "show Tom downstairs. And mind yourself," he added. "Remember what I told you."

Adolph tripped gracefully forward, and Tom, with lumbering tread, went after.

"He's a perfect behemoth!" said Marie.

"Come, now, Marie," said St. Clare, seating himself on a stool beside her sofa, "be gracious and say something pretty to a fellow."

"You've been gone a fortnight beyond the time," said the lady, pouting.

"Well, you know I wrote you the reason."

"Such a short, cold letter!" said the lady.

"Dear me! The mail was just going, and it had to be that or nothing."

"That's the way always," said the lady. "Always something to make your journeys long and letters short."

"See here, now," he said, drawing an elegant velvet case out of his pocket and opening it. "Here's a present I got for you in New York."

It was a daguerreotype, clear and soft as an engraving, representing Eva and her father sitting hand in hand.

Marie looked at it with a dissatisfied air.

"What made you sit in such an awkward position?" she said.

"Well, the position may be a matter of opinion. But what do you think of the likeness?"

"If you don't think anything of my opinion in one case, I suppose you wouldn't in another," said the lady, shutting the daguerreotype.

"Hang the woman!" said St. Clare mentally. But aloud he added, "Come, now, Marie, what do you think of the likeness? Don't be nonsensical, now."

"It's very inconsiderate of you, St. Clare," said the lady, "to insist on my talking and looking at things. You know I've been lying all day with the sick headache. And there's been such a tumult made ever since you came, I'm half dead."

"You're subject to the sick headache, ma'am?" said Miss Ophelia, suddenly rising from the depths of the large armchair where she had sat quietly, taking an inventory of the furniture and calculating its expense.

"Yes, I'm a perfect martyr to it," said the lady.

"Juniper-berry tea is good for sick headache," said Miss Ophelia. "At least, Auguste, Deacon Abraham Perry's wife, used to say so, and she was a great nurse."

"I'll have the first juniper berries that get ripe in our garden by the lake brought in for that especial purpose," said St. Clare, gravely pulling the bell as he did so. "Meanwhile, Cousin, you must be wanting to retire to your apartment and refresh yourself after your journey. Dolph," he added, "tell Mammy to come here."

The decent mulatto woman whom Eva had caressed so rapturously soon entered. She was dressed neatly, with a high red and yellow turban on her head, the recent gift of Eva, and which the child had been arranging on her head.

"Mammy," said St. Clare, "I put this lady under your care. She is tired and wants rest. Take her to her chamber and be sure she is made comfortable." And Miss Ophelia disappeared in the rear of Mammy.

Tom's Mistress and Her Opinions

"AND now, Marie," said St. Clare, "your golden days are dawning. Here is our practical, business-like New England cousin, who will take the whole budget of cares off your shoulders and give you time to refresh yourself and grow young and handsome. The ceremony of delivering the keys had better come off forthwith."

This remark was made at the breakfast table, a few mornings after Miss Ophelia had arrived.

"I'm sure she's welcome," said Marie, leaning her head languidly on her hand. "I think she'll find one thing if she does, and that is—that it's we mistresses that are the slaves down here."

"Oh, certainly, she will discover that, and a world of wholesome truths besides, no doubt," said St. Clare.

"Talk about our keeping slaves, as if we did it for our *convenience*," said Marie. "I'm sure if we consulted *that*, we might let them all go at once."

Evangeline fixed her large, serious eyes on her mother's face with a perplexed expression and said simply, "What do you keep them for, Mamma?"

"I don't know, I'm sure, except for a plague. They are the plague of my life. I believe that more of my ill health is caused by them than by any one thing. And ours, I know, are the very worst that ever anybody was plagued with."

"Oh, come, Marie, you've got the blues this morning," said St. Clare. You know 'tisn't so. There's Mammy, the best creature living—what could you do without her?"

"Mammy is the best I ever knew," said Marie. "And yet Mammy, now, is selfish—dreadfully selfish. It's the fault of the whole race."

"Selfishness *is* a dreadful fault," said St. Clare gravely.

"Well, now, there's Mammy," said Marie. "I think it's selfish of her to sleep so sound nights. She knows I need little attentions almost every hour when my worst turns are on, and yet she's so hard to wake. I absolutely am worse this very morning for the efforts I had to make to wake her last night."

"Hasn't she sat up with you a good many nights lately, Mamma?" said Eva.

"How should you know that?" said Marie sharply. "She's been complaining, I suppose."

"She didn't complain. She only told me what bad nights you'd had—so many in succession."

"Why don't you let Jane or Rosa take her place a night or two," said St. Clare, "and let her rest?"

"How can you propose it?" said Marie. "St. Clare, you really are inconsiderate. So nervous as I am—the least breath disturbs me. And a strange hand about me would drive me absolutely frantic. If Mammy felt the interest in me she ought to, she'd wake easier—of course she would. I've heard of people who had such devoted servants, but it never was *my* luck." And Marie sighed.

Miss Ophelia had listened to this conversation with an air of shrewd, observant gravity, and she still kept her lips tightly compressed.

"Now, Mammy has a *sort* of goodness," said Marie. "She's smooth and respectful, but she's selfish at heart. Now, she never will be done fidgeting and worrying about that husband of hers. You see, when I was married and came to live here, of course I had to bring her with me, and her husband my father couldn't spare. He was a blacksmith and, of course, very necessary. And I thought and said at the time that Mammy and he had better give each other up, as it wasn't likely to be convenient for them ever to live together again. I wish now I'd insisted on it and married Mammy to somebody else. But I was foolish and indulgent and didn't want to insist. I told Mammy at the time that she mustn't ever expect to see him more than once or twice in her life again, for the air of Father's place doesn't agree with my health, and I can't go there. And I advised her to take up with somebody else. But no—she wouldn't. Mammy has a kind of obstinacy about her, in spots, that everybody don't see as I do."

"Has she children?" said Miss Ophelia.

"Yes, she has two."

"I suppose she feels the separation from them."

"Well, of course, I couldn't bring them. They were little dirty things—I couldn't have them about. And besides, they took up too much of her time. But I believe that Mammy has always kept up a sort of sulkiness about this. She won't marry anybody else. And I do believe, now, though she knows how necessary she is to me and how feeble my health is, she would go back to her husband tomorrow if she only could. I *do*, indeed," said Marie. "They are just so selfish, now, the best of them."

"It's distressing to reflect upon," said St. Clare dryly.

Miss Ophelia looked keenly at him and saw the flush of vexation and the sarcastic curl of the lip as he spoke.

"Now, Mammy has always been a pet with me," said Marie. "I wish some of your Northern servants could look at her closets of dresses—silks and muslins, and one real linen cambric she has hanging there. I've worked sometimes whole afternoons trimming her caps and getting her ready to go to a party. As to abuse, she don't know what it is. She never was whipped more than once or twice in her whole life. She has her strong coffee or her tea every day, with white sugar in it. It's abominable, to be sure, but St. Clare will have high life below-stairs, and they every one of them live just as they please. The fact is, our servants are over-indulged. I suppose it is partly our fault that they are selfish and act like spoiled children. But I've talked to St. Clare till I am tired."

"And I, too," said St. Clare, taking up the morning paper.

Eva, the beautiful Eva, had stood listening to her mother with that expression of deep earnestness which was peculiar to her. She walked softly round to her mother's chair and put her arms round her neck.

"Well, Eva, what now?" said Marie.

"Mamma, couldn't I take care of you one night—just one? I know I shouldn't make you nervous, and I shouldn't sleep. I often lie awake nights, thinking—"

"Oh, nonsense, child—nonsense!" said Marie. "You are such a strange child!"

"But may I, Mamma? I think," she said timidly, "that Mammy isn't well. She told me her head ached all the time lately."

"Oh, that's just one of Mammy's fidgets! Mammy is just like all the rest of them—makes such a fuss about every little headache or finger-ache. It'll never do to encourage it—never! I'm principled about this matter," said she, turning to Miss Ophelia. "You'll find the necessity of it. If you encourage servants in giving way to every little disagreeable feeling, you'll have your hands full. I never complain myself—nobody knows what I endure. I feel it a duty to bear it quietly, and I do."

Miss Ophelia's round eyes expressed an undisguised amazement at this, and St. Clare burst into a loud laugh.

"St. Clare always laughs when I make the least allusion to my ill health," said Marie, with the voice of a suffering martyr. "I only hope the day won't come when he'll remember it!" And Marie put her handkerchief to her eyes.

Of course, there was rather a foolish silence. Finally St. Clare got up, looked at his watch, and said he had an engagement down street. Eva tripped away after him, and Miss Ophelia and Marie remained at the table alone.

"Now, that's just like St. Clare!" said the latter. "He never realizes, never can, never will, what I suffer, and have, for years. If I was one of the complaining sort, or ever made any fuss about my ailments, there would be some reason for it. Men do get tired, naturally, of a complaining wife. But I've kept things to myself, and borne, and borne, till St. Clare has got in the way of thinking I can bear anything."

Miss Ophelia did not exactly know what she was expected to answer to this. While she was thinking what to say, Marie gradually wiped away her tears and began a housewifely chat with Miss Ophelia concerning cupboards, closets, linen-presses, store-rooms, and other matters, of which the latter was to assume the direction.

"And now," said Marie, "I believe I've told you everything, so that when my next sick turn comes on, you'll be able to go forward entirely without consulting me—only about Eva. She requires watching."

"She seems to be a good child, very," said Miss Ophelia. "I never saw a better child."

"Eva's peculiar," said her mother, "very. There are things about her so singular. She isn't like me, now, a particle," and Marie sighed.

Miss Ophelia in her own heart said, "I hope she isn't," but had prudence enough to keep it down.

"Eva always was disposed to be with servants, and I think that well enough with some children. Now, I always played with father's little Negroes—it never did me any harm. But Eva somehow always seems to put herself on an equality with every creature that comes near her. It's a strange thing about that child. I never have been able to break her of it. St. Clare, I believe, encourages her in it. The fact is, St. Clare indulges every creature under this roof but his own wife."

Again Miss Ophelia sat in blank silence.

"Now, there's no way with servants," said Marie, "but to *put them down* and keep them down. It was always natural to me, from a child. Eva is enough to spoil a whole houseful. What she will do when she comes to keep house herself, I'm sure I don't know. I hold to being *kind* to servants—I always am. But you must make 'em *know their place*. Eva never does. There's no getting into the child's head the first beginning of an idea what a servant's place is! You heard her offering to take care of me nights, to let Mammy sleep!"

"Why," said Miss Ophelia bluntly, "I suppose you think your servants are human creatures and ought to have some rest when they are tired."

"Certainly, of course. I'm very particular in letting them have everything that comes convenient—anything that doesn't put one at all out of the way, you know. Mammy can make up her sleep, some time or other—there's no difficulty about that. She's the sleepiest concern that ever I saw. Sewing, standing, or sitting, that creature will go to sleep, and sleep anywhere and everywhere. No danger but Mammy gets sleep enough. But this treating servants as if they were exotic flowers, or china vases, is really ridiculous," said Marie, as she plunged languidly into the depths of a pillowy lounge.

"You see," she continued, "you see, Cousin Ophelia, I don't often speak of myself. It isn't my *habit*. 'Tisn't agreeable to me. In fact, I haven't strength to do it. But there are points where St. Clare and I differ. St. Clare never understood me, never appreciated me. I think it lies at the root of all my ill health. St. Clare means well, I am bound to believe, but men are constitutionally selfish and inconsiderate to women. That, at least is my impression."

Miss Ophelia, who had a very particular horror of being drawn into family difficulties, now began to foresee something of this kind coming. So, composing her face into a grim neutrality, and drawing out of her pocket about a yard and a quarter of stocking, she proceeded to knit most energetically, shutting her lips together in a way that said, as plain as words could, "You needn't try to make me speak. I don't want anything to do with your affairs." In fact, she looked about as sympathizing as a stone lion. But Marie didn't care about that.

"You see," she went on, "I brought my own property and servants when I married St. Clare, and I am legally entitled to manage them my own way. St. Clare had his fortune and his servants, and I'm well enough content he should manage them in his way. But St. Clare will be interfering. He has wild notions about the treatment of servants. He really does act as if he set his servants before me, and before himself, too. For he lets them make him all sorts of trouble and never lifts a finger. Now, about some things, St. Clare is really frightful—he frightens me—good-natured as he looks in general. Now, he has set down his foot that, come what will, there shall not be a blow struck in this house except what he or I strike. And he does it in a way that I really dare not cross him. Well, you may see what that leads to. For St. Clare wouldn't raise his hand if every one of them walked over him, and I—you see how cruel it would be to require me to make the exertion.

Now, you know, these servants are nothing but grown-up children."

"I don't know anything about it, and I thank the Lord that I don't!" said Miss Ophelia shortly.

"Well, but you will have to know something, and know it to your cost, if you stay here. You don't know what a provoking, stupid, careless, unreasonable, childish, ungrateful set of wretches they are."

Marie now opened her eyes and seemed quite to forget her languor.

"You don't know, and you can't, the daily, hourly trials that beset a housekeeper from them. But it's no use to complain to St. Clare. He talks the strangest stuff. He says we have made them what they are, and ought to bear with them. He says their faults are all owing to us, and that it would be cruel to make the fault and punish it, too. He says we shouldn't be any better in their place—just as if one could reason from them to us, you know."

"Don't you believe that the Lord made them of one blood with us?" said Miss Ophelia shortly.

"No, indeed, not I! A pretty story, truly! They are a degraded race."

"Don't you think they've got immortal souls?" said Miss Ophelia with increasing indignation.

"Oh, well," said Marie, yawning, "that, of course—nobody doubts that. But as to putting them on any sort of equality with us, you know, as if we could be compared, why, it's impossible! Now, St. Clare really has talked to me as if keeping Mammy from her husband was like keeping me from mine. There's no comparing in this way. Mammy couldn't have the feelings that I should. It's a different thing altogether—of course, it is—and yet St. Clare pretends not to see it. And just as if Mammy could love her little dirty babies as I love Eva! Yet St. Clare once really and soberly tried to persuade me that it was my duty, with my weak health and all I suffer, to let Mammy go back, and take somebody else in her place. That was a little too much even for *me* to bear."

Miss Ophelia looked very much as if she was afraid she should say something. But she only rattled away with her needles in a way that had volumes of meaning in it.

"So you just see," Marie continued, "what you've got to manage. A household without any rule: where servants have it all in their own way, do what they please and have what they please, except so far as I, with my feeble health, have kept up government. I keep my cowhide about, and sometimes I do lay it on. But the exertion is always too much for me. If St. Clare would only have this thing done as others do—"

"And how's that?"

"Why, send them to the calaboose, or some of the other places, to be flogged. That's the only way. If I wasn't such a poor, feeble piece, I believe I should manage with twice the energy that St. Clare does."

"And how does St. Clare contrive to manage?" said Miss Ophelia. "You say he never strikes a blow."

"Well, men have a more commanding way, you know—it is easier for them. Besides, if you ever looked full in his eye, it's peculiar—that eye—and if he speaks decidedly, there's a kind of flash. I'm afraid of it myself. And the servants know they must mind. I couldn't do as much by a regular storm as St. Clare can by one turn of his eye, if once he is in earnest. But you'll find, when you come to manage, that there's no getting along without severity—they are so bad, so deceitful, so lazy."

"The old tune," said St. Clare, sauntering in. "What an awful account these wicked creatures will have to settle at last, especially for being lazy! You see, Cousin," said he as he stretched himself at full length on a lounge opposite to Marie, "it's wholly inexcusable in them, in the light of the example that Marie and I set them—this laziness."

"You do really try to be provoking," said Marie.

"Oh, come, Marie, the day is growing warm, and I have just had a long quarrel with Dolph, which has fatigued me excessively. So pray be agreeable, now, and let a fellow repose in the light of your smile."

"What's the matter about Dolph?" said Marie. "That fellow's impudence has been growing to a point that is perfectly intolerable to me. I only wish I had the undisputed management of him a while. I'd bring him down!"

"What you say, my dear, is marked with your usual acuteness and good sense," said St. Clare. "As to Dolph, the case is this: that he has so long been engaged in imitating my graces and perfections that he has, at last, really mistaken himself for his master. And I have been obliged to give him a little insight into his mistake."

"How?" said Marie.

"Why, I was obliged to let him understand explicitly that I preferred to keep *some* of my clothes for my own personal wearing. Also, I put his magnificence upon an allowance of cologne-water, and actually was so cruel as to restrict him to one dozen of my cambric handkerchiefs. Dolph was particularly huffy about it, and I had to talk to him like a father to bring him round."

"Oh, St. Clare! When will you learn how to treat your servants? It's abominable, the way you indulge them!" said Marie.

"Why, after all, what's the harm of the poor dog's wanting to be like his master? And if I haven't brought him up any better than to find his chief good in cologne and cambric handkerchiefs, why shouldn't I give them to him?"

"And why haven't you brought him up better?" said Miss Ophelia.

"Too much trouble—laziness, Cousin, laziness—which ruins more souls than you can shake a stick at. If it weren't for laziness, I should have been a perfect angel myself."

"I think you slaveholders have an awful responsibility upon

you," said Miss Ophelia. "I wouldn't have it for a thousand worlds. You ought to educate your slaves, and treat them like reasonable creatures—like immortal creatures that you've got to stand before the bar of God with. That's my mind," said the good lady, breaking suddenly out with a tide of zeal that had been gaining strength all the morning.

"Oh, come, come!" said St. Clare, getting up quickly. "What do you know about us?" And he sat down to the piano and rattled a lively piece of music. He played piece after piece, like a man who is trying to play himself into a good humor. After pushing the music aside, he rose up and said gaily, "Well, now, Cousin, you've given us a good talk and done your duty. On the whole, I think the better of you for it. I make no manner of doubt that you threw a very diamond of truth at me, though, you see, it hit me so directly in the face that it wasn't exactly appreciated, at first."

"For my part, I don't see any use in such sort of talk," said Marie. "I'm sure, if anybody does more for servants than we do, I'd like to know who. And it don't do 'em a bit of good—not a particle—they get worse and worse. As to talking to them, I'm sure I have talked till I was tired and hoarse, telling them their duty and all that. And I'm sure they can go to church when they like, though they don't understand a word of the sermon, more than so many pigs—so it isn't of any great use for them to go, as I see. But they do go, and so they have every chance. But, as I said before, they are a degraded race, and always will be, and there isn't any help for them—you can't make anything of them if you try. You see, Cousin Ophelia, I've tried and you haven't. I was born and bred among them, and I know."

A gay laugh from the court rang through the silken curtains of the verandah, and St. Clare, stepping out and lifting the curtain, laughed too.

"What is it?" said Miss Ophelia, coming to the railing.

There sat Tom on a little mossy seat in the court, every one of his button-holes stuck full of cape jessamines, and Eva, gaily laughing, was hanging a wreath of roses round his neck. And then she sat down on his knee, like a chip-sparrow, still laughing.

"Oh, Tom, you look so funny!"

Tom had a sober, benevolent smile, and seemed in his quiet way to be enjoying the fun quite as much as his little mistress. He lifted his eyes, when he saw his master, with a half-apologetic air.

"How can you let her?" said Miss Ophelia.

"Why not?" said St. Clare.

"Why, I don't know, it seems so dreadful!"

"You would think no harm in a child's caressing a large dog, even if he was black. But a creature that can think, and reason, and feel, and is immortal, you shudder at. Confess it, Cousin. I know the feeling among some of your Northerners well enough. You loathe them as you would a snake or a toad, yet you are indignant at their wrongs. You would not have them abused, but you don't want to have anything to do with them yourselves. You would send them to Africa, out of your sight and smell, and then send a missionary or two. Isn't that it?"

"Well, Cousin," said Miss Ophelia thoughtfully, "there may be some truth in this."

"What would the poor and lowly do without children?" said St. Clare, leaning on the railing and watching Eva as she tripped off, leading Tom with her. "Your little child is your only true democrat. Tom, now, is a hero to Eva. His stories are wonders in her eyes, his songs and Methodist hymns are better than an opera, and the traps and little bits of trash in his pocket a mine of jewels, and he the most wonderful Tom that ever wore a black skin."

In Tom's external situation, at this time, there was, as the world says, nothing to complain of. Little Eva's fancy for him

had led her to petition her father that he might be her special attendant whenever she needed the escort of a servant in her walks or rides. And Tom had general orders to let everything else go and attend to Miss Eva whenever she wanted him— orders which were far from disagreeable to him. He was kept well dressed, for St. Clare was particular on this point. His stable services consisted simply in a daily care and inspection, and directing an under-servant in his duties. For Marie St. Clare declared that she could not have any smell of the horses about him when he came near her. Tom, therefore, in his well-brushed broadcloth suit, smooth silk hat, glossy boots, fault-less wristbands and collar, with his grave, good-natured black face, looked respectable enough to be a Bishop of Carthage, as men of his color were in other ages.

Then, too, he was in a beautiful place, and he did enjoy with a quiet joy the birds, the flowers, the fountains, the perfume, and light and beauty of the court, the silken hangings, and pictures, and chandeliers, and statuettes, and gilding that made the parlors within a kind of Aladdin's palace to him.

On Sundays Tom was at Marie's service, for she made a great point of being pious. And on Sunday morning she stood now, gorgeously dressed, on the verandah, clasping a diamond bracelet on her slender wrist. Marie patronized good things, and she was going now, in full force—diamonds, silk, lace, jewels, and all—to a fashionable church, to be very religious. There she stood, so slender, so elegant, her lace scarf enveloping her like a mist. She looked a graceful creature, and she felt very good and very elegant indeed. Miss Ophelia stood at her side, a perfect contrast. It was not that she had not as handsome a silk dress and shawl and as fine a pocket handkerchief, but stiffness and squareness and bolt-uprightness enveloped her.

"Where's Eva?" said Marie.

"The child stopped on the stairs to say something to Mammy."

And what was Eva saying to Mammy on the stairs? Listen, reader, and you will hear though Marie does not.

"Dear Mammy, I know your head is aching dreadfully."

"Lord bless you, Miss Eva! My head allers aches lately. You don't need to worry."

"Well, I'm glad you're going out. And here, Mammy"— and the little girl threw her arms around her—"you shall take my vinaigrette."

"What! Your beautiful gold smelling-bottle thar, with them diamonds! Lor, Miss, 'twouldn't be proper, no ways."

"Why not? You need it, and I don't. Mama always uses it for headache, and it'll make you feel better. No, you shall take it, to please me, now."

"Do hear the darlin' talk!" said Mammy as Eva thrust it into her bosom, and kissing her, ran downstairs to her mother.

"What were you stopping for?"

"I was just stopping to give Mammy my vinaigrette to take to church with her."

"Eva!" said Marie, stamping impatiently. "Your gold vinaigrette to *Mammy!* When will you learn what's proper? Go and take it right back, this moment!"

Eva looked downcast and turned slowly.

"I say, Marie, let the child alone. She shall do as she pleases," said St. Clare.

"St. Clare, how will she ever get along in the world?" said Marie.

"The Lord knows," said St. Clare. "But she'll get along in heaven better than you or I."

"Oh, Papa, don't," said Eva, softly touching his elbow. "It troubles Mother."

"Well, Cousin, are you ready to go to meeting?" said Miss Ophelia, turning square about on St. Clare.

"I'm not going, thank you."

"I do wish St. Clare ever would go to church," said Marie. "But he hasn't a particle of religion about him. It really isn't respectable."

"I know it," said St. Clare. "You ladies go to church to learn how to get along in the world, I suppose, and your piety sheds respectability on us. If I did go at all, I would go where Mammy goes. There's something to keep a fellow awake there, at least."

"What! Those shouting Methodists? Horrible!" said Marie.

"Anything but the dead sea of your respectable churches, Marie. Positively, it's too much to ask of a man. Eva, do you like to go? Come, stay at home and play with me."

"Thank you, Papa, but I'd rather go to church."

"Isn't it dreadful tiresome?" said St. Clare.

"I think it is tiresome, some," said Eva, "and I am sleepy, too, but I try to keep awake."

"What do you go for, then?"

"Why, you know, Papa," she said in a whisper, "Cousin told me that God wants to have us. And He gives us everything, you know, and it isn't much to do it if He wants us to.

It isn't so very tiresome, after all."

"You sweet little obliging soul!" said St. Clare, kissing her. "Go along, that's a good girl, and pray for me."

"Certainly, I always do," said the child as she sprang after her mother into the carriage.

St. Clare stood on the steps and kissed his hand to her as the carriage drove away. Large tears were in his eyes.

"You see, Evangeline," said her mother, "it's always right and proper to be kind to servants, but it isn't proper to treat them *just* as we would our relations, or people in our own class of life. Now, if Mammy was sick, you wouldn't want to put her in your own bed."

"I should feel just like it, Mamma," said Eva, "because then it would be handier to take care of her, and because, you know, my bed is better than hers."

Marie was in utter despair.

"What can I do to make this child understand me?" she said.

"Nothing," said Miss Ophelia significantly.

"Well, ladies," said St. Clare as they were comfortably seated at the dinner table, "and what was the bill of fare at church today?"

"Oh, Dr. G—— preached a splendid sermon," said Marie. "It was just such a sermon as you ought to hear. It expressed all my views exactly."

"It must have been very improving," said St. Clare.

"Well, I mean all my views about society, and such things," said Marie. "The text was: 'He hath made everything beautiful in its season.' And he showed how all the orders and distinctions in society came from God, and that it was so appropriate, you know, and beautiful, that some should be high and some low, and that some were born to rule and some to serve, and all that, you know. And he applied it so well to all this ridiculous fuss that is made about slavery, and he proved distinctly that the Bible was on our side, and supported all our institutions so convincingly. I only wish you'd heard him."

"Oh, I didn't need it," said St. Clare. "I can learn what does me as much good as that from the *Picayune* any time, and smoke a cigar besides, which I can't do, you know, in a church."

"Why," said Miss Ophelia, "don't you believe in these views?"

"Who—I? If I was to say anything on this slavery matter, I would say out, fair and square, 'We're in for it. We've got 'em, and mean to keep 'em—it's for our convenience and our interest.' For that's the long and short of it—that's just the whole of what all this sanctified stuff amounts to, after all."

"Well," said Miss Ophelia, "do you think slavery right or wrong?"

"I'm not going to have any of your horrid New England directness, Cousin," said St. Clare gayly. "If I answer that question, I know you'll be at me with a half a dozen others, each one harder than the last, and I'm not going to define my position. I am one of the sort that lives by throwing stones at other people's glass houses, but I never mean to put up one for them to stone."

"That's just the way he's always talking," said Marie. "You can't get any satisfaction out of him. I believe it's just because he don't like religion that he's always running out in this way he's been doing."

"Religion!" said St. Clare in a tone that made both ladies look at him. "Religion! Is what you hear at church religion? Is that which can bend and turn, and descend and ascend, to fit every crooked phase of selfish, worldly society, religion?"

"Then you don't believe that the Bible justifies slavery," said Miss Ophelia.

"The Bible was my *mother's* book," said St. Clare. "By it she lived and died, and I would be very sorry to think it did. I'd as soon desire to have it proved that my mother could drink brandy, chew tobacco, and swear, by way of satisfying me that I did right in doing the same. In short, you see," said he, suddenly resuming his gay tone, "all I want is that different things be kept in different boxes. Now, when anyone speaks up like a man and says slavery is necessary to us, we can't get along without it, we should be beggared if we give it up, and, of course, we mean to hold on to it—that is strong, clear, well-defined language. It has the respectability of truth to it. But when he begins to put on a long face, and snuffle, and quote Scripture, I incline to think he isn't much better than he should be."

"Well, at any rate," said Marie, as she reclined herself on a lounge, "I'm thankful I'm born where slavery exists. And I believe it's right—indeed, I feel it must be. And, at any rate, I'm sure I couldn't get along without it."

"I say, what do you think, Pussy?" said her father to Eva, who came in at this moment with a flower in her hand.

"What about, Papa?"

"Why, which do you like the best—to live as they do at your uncle's up in Vermont, or to have a houseful of servants as we do?"

"Oh, of course, our way is the pleasantest," said Eva.

"Why so?" said St. Clare, stroking her head.

"Why, it makes so many more round you to love, you know," said Eva, looking up earnestly.

"Now, that's just like Eva," said Marie. "Just one of her odd speeches."

"Is it an odd speech, Papa?" said Eva, whisperingly, as she got upon his knee.

"Rather, as this world goes, Pussy," said St. Clare. "But where has my little Eva been all dinner-time?"

"Oh, I've been up in Tom's room, hearing him sing, and Aunt Dinah gave me my dinner."

"Hearing Tom sing, hey?"

"Oh, yes! He sings such beautiful things about the New Jerusalem, and bright angels, and the land of Canaan."

"I dare say. It's better than the opera, isn't it?"

"Yes, and he's going to teach them to me."

"Singing lessons, hey? You *are* coming on."

"Yes, he sings for me, and I read to him in my Bible. And he explains what it means, you know."

"On my word," said Marie, laughing, "that is the latest joke of the season."

"Tom isn't a bad hand, now, at explaining Scripture, I'll dare swear," said St. Clare. "Tom has a natural genius for religion. I wanted the horses out early this morning, and I stole up to Tom's room there, over the stables, and there I heard him holding a meeting by himself. And, in fact, I haven't heard anything quite so savory as Tom's prayer this some time. He put in for me with a zeal that was quite apostolic."

"Perhaps he guessed you were listening. I've heard of the trick before."

"If he did, he wasn't very prudent. For he gave the Lord his opinion of me pretty freely. Tom seemed to think there was decidedly room for improvement in me and seemed very earnest that I should be converted."

"I hope you'll lay it to heart," said Miss Ophelia.

"I suppose you are much of the same opinion," said St. Clare. "Well, we shall see—shan't we, Eva?"

The Free Man's Defense

THERE was a gentle bustle at the Quaker house as the afternoon drew to a close. Rachel Halliday moved quietly to and fro, collecting from her household stores such necessities as could be arranged in the smallest space for the wanderers who were to go forth that night. George and his wife were in the little bedroom. He was sitting with his child on his knee and his wife's hand in his. Both looked thoughtful, and traces of tears were on their cheeks.

"Yes, Eliza," said George, "I know all you say is true, and I will try to act worthy of a free man. I'll try to feel like a Christian. I'll forget all the past and put away every hard and bitter feeling, read my Bible and learn to be a good man."

"And when we get to Canada," said Eliza, "I can help you. I can do dressmaking very well, and I understand fine washing and ironing. And between us we can find something to live on."

"Yes, Eliza, so long as we have each other and our boy. Oh, Eliza, if these people only knew what a blessing it is for a man to feel that his wife and child belong to *him!* I've often wondered to see men that could call their wives and children *their own* fretting and worrying about anything else. Why, I feel rich and strong though we have nothing but our bare hands. I feel as if I could scarcely ask God for any more. Yes, though I've worked hard every day till I am twenty-five years old and have not a cent of money, nor a roof to cover me, nor a spot of land to call my own, yet, if they will only let me alone now, I will be satisfied—thankful. I will work and send back the money for you and my boy. As to my old master, he has been paid five times over for all he ever spent for me. I don't owe him anything."

"But yet we are not quite out of danger," said Eliza. "We are not yet in Canada."

"True," said George, "but it seems as if I smelt the free air, and it makes me strong."

At this moment voices were heard in the outer apartment in earnest conversation, and very soon a rap was heard on the door. Eliza started and opened it.

Simeon Halliday was there, and with him a tall, red-haired, shrewd-looking Quaker brother, whom he introduced as Phineas Fletcher.

"Our friend Phineas hath discovered something of importance to the interests of thee and thy party, George," said Simeon. "It were well for thee to hear it."

"That I have," said Phineas, "and it shows the use of a man's always sleeping with one ear open, in certain places, as I've always said. Last night I stopped at a little lone tavern back on the road. Well, I was tired with hard driving, and after my supper, I stretched myself down on a pile of bags in the corner and pulled a buffalo skin over me, to wait till my bed was ready. And what does I do but get fast asleep."

"With one ear open, Phineas?" said Simeon quietly.

"No, I slept, ears and all, for an hour or two, for I was pretty well tired. But when I came to myself a little, I found that there were some men in the room, sitting round a table, drinking and talking. And I thought I'd just see what they were up to, especially as I heard them say something about the Quakers.

" 'So,' says one, 'they are up in the Quaker settlement, no doubt.' Then I listened with both ears, and I found that they were talking about this very party. So I lay and heard them lay off all their plans. This young man, they said, was to be sent back to Kentucky, to his master, who was going to make an example of him, to keep all niggers from running away. And his wife two of them were going to run down to New Orleans and sell on their own account, and they calculated to get sixteen or eighteen hundred dollars for her. And the child, they said, was going to a trader, who had bought him. And then there was the boy, Jim, and his mother—they were to go back to their masters in Kentucky. They said that there were two constables in a town a little piece ahead who would go in with 'em to get 'em taken up, and the young woman was to be taken before a judge. And one of the fellows, who is small and smooth-spoken, was to swear to her for his property, and get her delivered over to him to take South. They've got a right notion of the track we are going tonight, and they'll be down after us, six or eight strong. So, now, what's to be done?"

"What *shall* we do, George?" said Eliza faintly.

"I know what *I* shall do," said George as he stepped into the little room and began examining his pistols.

"Ay, ay," said Phineas, nodding his head to Simeon. "Thou seest, Simeon, how it will work."

"I see," said Simeon, sighing. "I pray it come not to that."

"I don't want to involve anyone with or for me," said George. "If you will lend me your vehicle and direct me, I will drive alone to the next stand. Jim is a giant in strength, and brave as death and despair, and so am I."

"Ah, well, friend," said Phineas, "but thee'll need a driver, for all that. Thee's quite welcome to do all the fighting, thee knows. But I know a thing or two about the road that thee doesn't."

"But I don't want to involve you," said George.

"Involve," said Phineas, with a curious and keen expression of face. "When thee does involve me, please to let me know."

"Phineas is a wise and skillful man," said Simeon. "Thee does well, George, to abide by his judgment. And," he added, laying his hand kindly on George's shoulder and pointing to the pistols, "be not over-hasty with these—young blood is hot."

"I will attack no man," said George. "All I ask of this country is to be let alone, and I will go out peaceably. But"—he paused and his brow darkened and his face worked—"am I going to stand by and see them take my wife and sell her when God has given me a pair of strong arms to defend her? No, God help me! I'll fight to the last breath before they shall take my wife and son. Can you blame me?"

"Mortal man cannot blame thee, George," said Simeon. "But the leaders of our people taught a more excellent way. Let us pray the Lord that we be not tempted."

"And so *I* do," said Phineas, "But if we are tempted too much, why, let them look out, that's all."

"It's quite plain thee wasn't born a Friend," said Simeon, smiling. "The old nature hath its way in thee pretty strong as yet."

To tell the truth, Phineas had been a hearty, two-fisted backwoodsman, a vigorous hunter and a dead shot at a buck. But having wooed a pretty Quakeress, he had been moved by the power of her charms to join the society in his neighborhood.

"Friend Phineas will ever have ways of his own," said Rachel Halliday, smiling, "but we all think that his heart is in the right place, after all."

"Well," said George, "isn't it best that we hasten our flight?"

"I got up at four o'clock and came on with all speed full two or three hours ahead of them, if they start at the time they planned. It isn't safe to start till dark at any rate, for there are some evil persons in the villages ahead that might be disposed to meddle with us if they saw our wagon, and that would delay us more than the waiting. But in two hours I think we may venture. I will go over to Michael Cross and engage him to come behind on his swift nag, and keep a bright look-out on the road, and warn us if any company of men come on. I am going out now to warn Jim and the old woman to be in readiness, and to see about the horses. We have a pretty fair start and stand a good chance to get to the stand before they come up with us. So have good courage, friend George. This isn't the first ugly scrape that I've been in with thy people," said Phineas as he closed the door.

"Phineas is pretty shrewd," said Simeon. "He will do the best that can be done for thee, George."

"All I am sorry for," said George, "is the risk to you."

"Thee'll much oblige us, friend George, to say no more about that. What we do we are conscience bound to do—we can do no other way. And now, mother," said he, turning to Rachel, "hurry thy preparations for these friends, for we must not send them away fasting."

And while Rachel and her children were busy making corn cake, and cooking ham and chicken, and hurrying on the et ceteras of the evening meal, George and his wife sat in their little room with their arms folded about each other, in such talk as husband and wife have when they know that a few hours may part them forever.

"Eliza," said George, "my heart was all withered up till I met you. And your loving me—why, it was almost like raising one from the dead. I've been a new man ever since. And now, Eliza, I'll give my last drop of blood, but they *shall not* take you from me. Whoever gets you must walk over my dead body."

"Oh, Lord, have mercy!" said Eliza. "If He will only let us get out of this country together, that is all we ask."

Rachel now came in, took Eliza's hand kindly, and led the way to the supper table. As they were sitting down, a light tap sounded and Ruth entered.

"I just ran in," she said, "with these little stockings for the boy—three pair, nice, warm woolen ones. It will be so cold, thee knows, in Canada. Does thee keep up good courage, Eliza?" she added, tripping round to Eliza's side of the table, and shaking her warmly by the hand, and slipping a seed-cake into Harry's hand. "I brought a little parcel of these for him," she said, tugging at her pocket to get out the package. "Children, thee knows, will always be eating."

"Oh, thank you. You are too kind," said Eliza.

"Come, Ruth, sit down to supper," said Rachel.

"I couldn't. I left John with the baby, and some biscuits in the oven. So good-by, Eliza. Good-by, George. The Lord grant thee a safe journey." And with a few tripping steps, Ruth was out.

A little while after supper, a large covered wagon drew up before the door, and Phineas jumped briskly down from his seat to arrange his passengers. George walked out of the door with his child on one arm and his wife on the other. His step was firm, his face settled and resolute. Rachael and Simeon came out after them.

"You get out a moment," said Phineas to those inside, "and

let me fix the back of the wagon for the womenfolks and the boy."

"Here are two buffalo skins," said Rachel. "Make the seats as comfortable as may be—it is hard riding all night."

Jim came out first and carefully assisted out his old mother, who clung to his arm and looked anxiously about as if she expected the pursuer every moment.

"Jim, are your pistols all in order?" said George in a low, firm voice.

"Yes, indeed," said Jim.

"And you've no doubt what you shall do if they come?"

"I rather think I haven't," said Jim, throwing open his broad chest and taking a deep breath.

During this brief conversation, Eliza had been taking her leave of her kind friend Rachel, and was handed into the carriage by Simeon. Creeping into the back part with her boy, she sat down among the buffalo skins. The old woman was next handed in and seated. George and Jim sat down on a rough board seat in front of them, while Phineas mounted in front.

"Farewell, my friends," said Simeon from without.

"God bless you!" answered all from within.

And the wagon drove off, rattling and jolting over the frozen road.

There was no opportunity for conversation on account of the roughness of the way and the noise of the wheels. The vehicle rumbled on through long, dark stretches of woodland, over wide, dreary plains, up hills and down valleys—and on, on, on they jogged, hour after hour. The child soon fell asleep and lay heavily in his mother's lap. The poor, frightened old woman at last forgot her fears, and even Eliza, as the night waned, found all her anxieties insufficient to keep her eyes from closing. Phineas seemed, on the whole, the briskest of the company, and beguiled his long drive with whistling certain very un-Quaker-like songs as he went on.

But about three o'clock George's ear caught the hasty and

decided click of a horse's hoofs coming behind them at some distance. He jogged Phineas, who pulled up his horses and listened.

"That must be Michael," he said. "I think I know the sound of his gallop." And he rose up and stretched his head anxiously back over the road.

A man riding in hot haste was now dimly descried at the top of a distant hill.

"There he is, I do believe!" said Phineas.

George and Jim both sprang out of the wagon before they knew what they were doing. All stood intensely silent, with their faces turned toward the expected messenger. Now he went down into a valley, then at last they saw him emerge on the top of a height, within hail.

"Yes, that's Michael," said Phineas. And raising his voice, he called, "Halloa, there, Michael!"

"Phineas! Is that thee?"

"Yes. What news—they coming?"

"Right on behind, eight or ten of them, hot with brandy, swearing and foaming like so many wolves."

And just as he spoke, a breeze brought the faint sound of galloping horsemen toward them.

"In with you—quick, boys, *in!*" said Phineas. "If you must fight, wait till I get you a piece ahead."

Both jumped in, and Phineas lashed the horses to a run, the horseman keeping close beside them. The wagon rattled, jumped, almost flew over the frozen ground, but plainer, and still plainer, came the noise of pursuing horsemen. The women heard it, and looking anxiously out, saw far in the rear, on the brow of a distant hill, a party of men looming up against the red-streaked sky of early dawn. Another hill, and their pursuers had evidently caught sight of their wagon, whose white cloth-covered top made it conspicuous at some distance. A loud yell of brutal triumph came forward on the wind. Eliza sickened and strained her child closer to her bosom. The old woman prayed and groaned, and George and Jim clenched their pistols with the grasp of despair.

The pursuers were gaining on them fast when the wagon made a sudden turn and brought them near a ledge of a steep overhanging rock that rose in an isolated clump. This isolated pile rose up black and heavy against the brightening sky and seemed to promise shelter and concealment. It was a place well known to Phineas, who had been familiar with the spot in his hunting days. It was to gain this point that he had been racing his horses.

"Now for it!" said he, suddenly checking his horses and springing from his seat to the ground. "Out with you, every-one, and up into these rocks with me. Michael, thee tie thy horse to the wagon and drive ahead to Amariah's, and get him and his boys to come back and talk to these fellows."

In a twinkling they were all out of the wagon.

"There," said Phineas, catching up Harry, "you each of you see to the women. And run *now*, if you ever *did* run!"

Quicker than we can say it, the whole party were over the fence, making with all speed for the rocks, while Michael, throwing himself from his horse and fastening the bridle to the wagon, began driving it rapidly away.

"Come ahead," said Phineas as they reached the rocks and saw, in the mingled starlight and dawn, the traces of a rude but plainly marked footpath leading up among them. "This is one of our old hunting-dens. Come up!"

Phineas went before, springing up the rocks like a goat, with the boy in his arms. Jim came second, bearing his trembling old mother over his shoulder, and George and Eliza brought up the rear. The party of horsemen came to the fence and with mingled shouts and oaths were dismounting to prepare to follow them. A few moments' scrambling brought them to the top of the ledge. The path then passed between a narrow defile, where only one could walk at a time, till suddenly they came to a rift or chasm more than a yard in breadth, and beyond which lay a pile of rocks, separate from the rest of the ledge, standing full thirty feet high, with its sides steep as those of a castle. Phineas easily leaped the chasm and set down the boy on a smooth, flat platform of moss that covered the top of the rock.

"Over with you!" he called. "Spring, now, once for your lives!" said he, as one after another sprang across. Several fragments of loose stone formed a kind of breastwork, which sheltered their position from the observation of those below.

"Well, here we all are," said Phineas, peeping over the stone breastwork to watch the assailants, who were coming noisily up under the rocks. "Let 'em get us if they can. Whoever comes here has to walk single file between those two rocks, in fair range of your pistols, boys, d'ye see?"

"I do see," said George. "And now, as this matter is ours, let us take all the risk and do all the fighting."

"Thee's quite welcome to do the fighting, George," said Phineas, chewing checkerberry leaves as he spoke. "But I may have the fun of looking on, I suppose. See, these fellows are kinder debating down there, and looking up like hens when they are going to fly up on the roost. Hadn't thee better give 'em a word o' advice before they come up, just to tell 'em handsomely they'll be shot if they do?"

The party beneath, now more apparent in the light of the dawn, consisted of our old acquaintances Tom Loker and Marks, with two constables, and a posse consisting of such rowdies as could be engaged at the last tavern by a little brandy, to go and help the fun of trapping a set of niggers.

"Well, Tom, yer coons are fa'rly treed," said one.

"Yes, I see 'em go up right here," said Tom. "And here's a path. I'm for going right up. They can't jump down in a hurry, and it won't take long to ferret 'em out."

"But, Tom, they might fire at us from behind the rocks," said Marks. "That would be ugly, you know."

"Ugh!" said Tom with a sneer. "Always for saving your skin, Marks! No danger! Niggers are too plaguey scared."

"I don't know why I *shouldn't* save my skin," said Marks. "It's the best I've got, and niggers *do* fight like the devil sometimes."

At this moment, George appeared on the top of a rock above them, and speaking in a calm, clear voice, said:

"Gentlemen, who are you down there, and what do you want?"

"We want a party of runaway niggers," said Tom Loker. "One George Harris, and Eliza Harris, and their son, and Jim Selden, and an old woman. We've got the officers here and a warrant to take 'em, and we're going to have 'em, too. D'ye hear? An't you George Harris that belongs to Mr. Harris of Shelby county, Kentucky?"

"I am George Harris. A Mr. Harris of Kentucky did call me his property. But now I'm a free man, standing on God's free soil. And my wife and my child I claim as mine. Jim and his mother are here. We have arms to defend ourselves, and we mean to do it. You can come up if you like. But the first one of you that comes within the range of our bullets is a dead man, and the next, and the next, and so on till the last."

"Oh, come, come!" said a short, puffy man, stepping forward and blowing his nose as he did so. "Young man, this an't no kind of talk at all for you. You see, we're officers of justice. We've got the law on our side, and the power, and so forth. So you'd better give up peaceably, you see. For you'll certainly have to give up at last."

"I know very well that you've got the law on your side, and the power," said George bitterly. "You mean to take my wife to sell in New Orleans, and put my boy like a calf in a trader's pen, and send Jim's old mother to the brute that whipped and abused her before because he couldn't abuse her son. You want to send Jim and me back to be whipped and tortured and ground down under the heels of them that you call masters. And your laws *will* bear you out in it—more shame for you and them! But you haven't got us. We don't own your laws, we don't own your country. We stand here as free, under God's sky, as you are. And by the great God that made us, we'll fight for our liberty till we die."

George stood out in fair sight on the top of the rock as he made his declaration of independence. The glow of dawn gave a flush to his swarthy cheek, and bitter indignation and despair gave fire to his dark eye, and, as if appealing from man to the justice of God, he raised his hand to heaven as he spoke. The attitude, eye, voice, manner of the speaker for a moment struck the party below to silence. There is something in boldness and determination that for a time hushes even the rudest nature. Marks was the only one who remained wholly untouched. He was deliberately cocking his pistol, and in the momentary silence that followed George's speech, fired at him.

"Ye see, ye get jist as much for dead as alive in Kentucky," he said coolly as he wiped his pistol on his coat sleeve.

George sprang backward, Eliza uttered a shriek. The ball had passed close to his hair, had nearly grazed the cheek of his wife, and struck in the tree above.

"It's nothing, Eliza," said George quickly.

"Thee'd better keep out of sight with thy speechifying," said Phineas. "They're mean scamps."

"Now, Jim," said George, "look that your pistols are all right, and watch that pass with me. The first man that shows himself I fire at. You take the second, and so on. It won't do, you know, to waste two shots on one."

"But what if you don't hit?"

"I *shall* hit," said George coolly.

The party below, after Marks had fired, stood for a moment rather undecided.

"I think you must have hit some on 'em," said one of the men. "I heard a squeal!"

"I'm going right up for one," said Tom. "I never was afraid of niggers, and I an't going to be now. Who goes after?" he said, springing up the rocks.

George heard the words distinctly. He drew up his pistol,

examined it, and pointed it toward that point in the defile where the first man would appear.

One of the most courageous of the party followed Tom, and the way being thus made, the whole party began pushing up the rock—the hindermost pushing the front ones faster than they would have gone of themselves. On they came, and in a moment the burly form of Tom appeared in sight, almost at the verge of the chasm.

George fired—the shot entered Tom's side. But though wounded, he would not retreat, and with a yell like that of a mad bull, he was leaping right across the chasm into the party.

"Friend," said Phineas, suddenly stepping to the front and meeting him with a push from his long arms, "thee isn't wanted here."

Down he fell into the chasm, crackling down among trees,

bushes, logs, loose stones, till he lay, bruised and groaning, thirty feet below. The fall might have killed him, had it not been broken by his clothes catching in the branches of a tree. But he came down with some force.

"Lord help us, they are perfect devils!" said Marks, heading the retreat down the rocks with much more of a will than he had joined the ascent, while all the party came tumbling after him.

"I say, fellers," said Marks, "you jist go round and pick up Tom, there, while I run and get on to my horse to go back for help." And without minding the hootings and jeers of his company, Marks was as good as his word and was soon seen galloping away.

"Was ever such a sneaking varmint?" said one of the men. "To come on his business, and he clear out and leaves us this yer way!"

"Well, we must pick up that feller," said another. "Cuss me if I much care whether he is dead or alive."

Led by the groans of Tom, the men scrambled and crackled through stumps, logs, and bushes to where that hero lay groaning and swearing.

"Ye keep it a-going pretty loud, Tom," said one. "Ye much hurt?"

"Don't know. Get me up, can't ye? Blast that infernal Quaker! If it hadn't been for him, I'd a pitched some on 'em down here, to see how they liked it."

With much labor and groaning Tom was assisted to rise, and they got him as far as the horses.

"If you could only get me a mile back to that ar tavern. Give me a handkerchief or something to stuff into this place and stop this infernal bleeding."

George looked over the rocks and saw them trying to lift the burly form of Tom into the saddle. After two or three efforts, he reeled and fell heavily to the ground.

"Oh, I hope he isn't killed!" said Eliza, who, with all the party, stood watching the proceeding.

"Why not?" said Phineas. "Serves him right."

"Because after death comes the judgment," said Eliza.

"Yes," said the old woman, who had been groaning and praying in her Methodist fashion during all the encounter, "it's an awful case for the poor crittur's soul."

"On my word, they're leaving him, I do believe," said Phineas.

It was true. For after some appearance of irresolution, the whole party got on their horses and rode away. When they were quite out of sight, Phineas began to bestir himself.

"Well, we must go down and walk a piece," he said. "I told Michael to go forward and bring help and be back here with the wagon. The Lord grant he be along soon. We an't much more than two miles from our stopping-place."

As the party neared the fence, they discovered in the distance their own wagon coming back, accompanied by some men on horseback.

"Well, now, there's Michael, and Stephen, and Amariah," exclaimed Phineas joyfully. "Now we *are* made—as safe as if we'd got there."

"Well, do stop, then," said Eliza, "and do something for that poor man—he's groaning dreadfully."

"It would be no more than Christian," said George. "Let's take him up and carry him on."

"And doctor him up among the Quakers," said Phineas. "Well, I don't care if we do. Here, let's have a look at him." And Phineas, who in the course of his hunting and backwoods life had acquired some rude experience of surgery, kneeled down by the wounded man and began a careful examination of his condition.

"Marks," said Tom feebly, "is that you, Marks?"

"No, I reckon 'tan't, friend," said Phineas. "Much Marks cares for thee if his own skin's safe. He's off long ago."

"I believe I'm done for," said Tom. "The cussed sneaking dog, to leave me to die alone. My poor old mother always told me 'twould be so."

"La sakes! Jist hear the poor crittur. He's got a mammy,

now," said the old Negress. "I can't help kinder pityin' on him."

"Softly, softly. Don't thee snap and snarl, friend," said Phineas as Tom winced and pushed his hand away. "Thee has no chance unless I stop the bleeding." And Phineas busied himself with making some off-hand surgical arrangements with his own pocket handkerchief and such as could be mustered in the company.

"You pushed me down there," said Tom faintly.

"Well, if I hadn't, thee would have pushed us down, thee sees," said Phineas as he stooped to apply his bandage. "There, there—we mean well to thee. We bear no malice. Thee shall be taken to a house where they'll nurse thee first rate—as well as thy own mother could."

Tom groaned and shut his eyes.

The other party now came up. The seats were taken out of the wagon, the buffalo skins, doubled in fours, spread all along one side, and four men with great difficulty lifted the heavy form of Tom into it. Before he was gotten in, he fainted entirely. The old Negro woman sat down on the bottom and took his head in her lap. Eliza, George, and Jim bestowed themselves in the remaining place, and the whole party set forward.

"What do you think of him?" said George, who sat by Phineas in front.

"Well, it's only a pretty deep flesh-wound. But then, tumbling down that place didn't help much. It has bled pretty freely—but he'll get over it, and may be learn a thing or two by it."

"I'm glad to hear you say so," said George. "It would always be a heavy thought to me if I'd caused his death, even in a just cause."

"Yes," said Phineas, "killing is an ugly operation, any way they'll fix it—man or beast."

"What shall you do with this poor fellow?" said George.

"Oh, carry him along to Amariah's. There's old Aunt

Dorcas there—she's most an amazin' nurse. We may reckon on turning him over to her for a fortnight or so."

A ride of about an hour more brought the party to a neat farmhouse, where the weary travelers were received to an abundant breakfast. Tom Loker was soon carefully deposited in a much cleaner and softer bed than he had ever been in the habit of occupying. His wound was carefully dressed and bandaged, and he lay languidly opening and shutting his eyes on the white window-curtains and gently-gliding figures of his sickroom, like a weary child. And here, for the present, we shall take our leave of the party.

Miss Ophelia's Experiences and Opinions

OUR friend Tom, in his simple musings often compared his lot with that of Joseph in Egypt. And, in fact, as time went on, the strength of the parallel increased.

St. Clare was indolent and careless of money. Hitherto the providing and marketing had been principally done by Adolph, who was as careless and extravagant as his master. Tom saw, with an uneasiness he could scarcely repress, the wasteful expenditure of the establishment, and in a quiet, indirect way would sometimes make his own suggestions. St. Clare at first employed him occasionally, but struck with his good business capacity, he confided in him more and more, till gradually all the marketing and providing for the family were entrusted to him.

"No, no, Adolph," he said one day, "let Tom alone. You only understand what you want. Tom understands cost and come to—and there may be some end to money, bye and bye, if we don't let somebody do that."

Trusted to an unlimited extent by a careless master, who handed him a bill without looking at it, and pocketed the change without counting it, Tom had every opportunity and temptation to dishonesty. But to that nature, the very unbounded trust reposed in him was bond and seal for the most scrupulous accuracy.

Tom regarded his gay, airy, handsome young master with an odd mixture of loyalty, reverence, and fatherly concern. That he never read the Bible; never went to church; that he jested and made free with any and everything that came in the way of his wit; that he spent his Sunday evenings at the opera or theater; that he went to wine parties, and clubs, and suppers oftener than was at all expedient—were all things that Tom could see as plainly as anybody, and on which he based a conviction that "Mas'r wasn't a Christian." This conviction he would have been very slow to express to anyone else, but on it he founded many prayers when he was by himself in his little room.

Not that Tom had not his own way of speaking his mind occasionally. For example, the very day after the Sabbath we have described, St. Clare was invited out to a convivial party of choice spirits and was helped home, between one and two o'clock at night, in a condition when the physical had decidedly attained the upper hand of the intellectual. Tom and Adolph assisted to get him composed for the night, the latter in high spirits, evidently regarding the matter as a good joke, and laughing heartily at Tom's horror, who really was simple enough to lie awake most of the rest of the night, praying for his young master.

"Well, Tom, what are you waiting for?" said St. Clare the next day as he sat in his library in dressing gown and slippers. St. Clare had just been entrusting Tom with some money and various commissions.

"Isn't all right there, Tom?" he added as Tom still stood waiting.

"I'm 'fraid not, Mas'r," said Tom with a grave face.

St. Clare laid down his paper, set down his coffee-cup, and looked at Tom.

"Why, Tom, what's the case? You look as solemn as a coffin."

"I feel very bad, Mas'r. I al'ays have thought that Mas'r would be good to everybody."

"Well, Tom, haven't I been? Come, now, what do you want? There's something you haven't got, I suppose, and this is the preface."

"Mas'r al'ays been good to me. I haven't nothing to complain of on that head. But there is one that Mas'r isn't good to."

"Why, Tom, what's got into you? Speak out. What do you mean?"

"Last night, between one and two, I thought so. I studied upon the matter then. Mas'r isn't good to *himself*."

Tom said this with his back to his master and his hand on the doorknob. St. Clare felt his face flush crimson, but he laughed.

"Oh, that's all, is it?" he said gaily.

"All!" said Tom, turning suddenly round and falling on his knees. "Oh, my dear young Mas'r! I'm 'fraid it will be loss of *all—all*—body and soul. The good Book says, 'it biteth like a serpent and stingeth like an adder,' my dear Mas'r!"

Tom's voice choked, and the tears ran down his cheeks.

"You poor, silly fool!" said St. Clare, with tears in his own eyes. "Get up, Tom. I'm not worth crying over."

But Tom wouldn't rise, and looked imploring.

"Well, I won't go to any more of their cursed nonsense, Tom," said St. Clare. "On my honor, I won't. I don't know why I haven't stopped long ago. I've always despised *it*, and myself for it—so now, Tom, wipe up your eyes and go about your errands. Come, come," he added, "no blessings. I'm not so wonderfully good, now," he said as he gently pushed Tom to the door. "There, I'll pledge my honor to you, Tom, you don't see me so again," he said. And Tom went off, wiping his eyes with great satisfaction.

"I'll keep my faith with him, too," said St. Clare as he closed the door. And he did so.

But, all this time, who shall detail the trials manifold of our friend Miss Ophelia, who had begun the labors of a Southern housekeeper?

The first morning of her rule, Miss Ophelia was up at four o'clock. And having attended to all the adjustments of her own chamber, as she had done ever since she came there—to the great amazement of the chambermaid—she prepared for a vigorous onslaught on the cupboards and closets of the establishment of which she had the keys.

The storeroom, the linen presses, the china closet, the kitchen and cellar that day all went under an awful review. Hidden things of darkness were brought to light to an extent that alarmed all the powers of kitchen and chamber, and caused many wonderings and murmurings about "dese yer Northern ladies."

Old Dinah, the head cook, was a self-taught genius, and, like geniuses in general, was positive and opinionated to the last degree. No possible amount of talent, or authority, or explanation could ever make her believe that any other way was better than her own, or that the course she had purused in the smallest matter could be in the least modified. Indeed, it was an axiom with her that the cook could do no wrong. If any part of the dinner was a failure, there were fifty indisputably good reasons for it, and it was the fault of fifty other people, whom Dinah berated with unsparing zeal.

But it was very seldom that there was any failure in Dinah's last results. Though her mode of doing everything was without any sort of calculation as to time and place—though her kitchen generally looked as if it had been arranged by a hurricane blowing through it, and she had about as many places for each cooking utensil as there were days in the year—yet, if one would have patience to wait her own good time, up would come her dinner in perfect order and in a style of preparation with which an epicure could find no fault.

It was now the season of beginning preparation for dinner. Dinah, who required large intervals of reflection and repose, was seated on the kitchen floor, smoking a short, stumpy pipe, to which she was much addicted, and which she always kindled up whenever she felt the need of an inspiration in her arrangements.

Seated around her were various members of that rising race with which a Southern household abounds, engaged in shelling peas, peeling potatoes, picking pinfeathers out of fowls, and other preparatory arrangements—Dinah every once in a while interrupting her meditations to give a poke, or a rap on the head, to some of the young operators, with the pudding-stick that lay by her side. In fact, Dinah ruled over the woolly heads of the younger members with a rod of iron and seemed to consider them born for no earthly purpose but to "save her steps," as she phrased it.

Miss Ophelia, after passing on her tour through all the other parts of the establishment, now entered the kitchen. Dinah had heard, from various sources, what was going on, and was resolved to stand on defensive ground, determined to oppose and ignore every new measure, without any actual contest.

The kitchen was a large, brick-floored apartment, with a great, old-fashioned fireplace stretching along one side of it— an arrangement which St. Clare had vainly tried to persuade Dinah to exchange for the convenience of a modern cook-stove. Not she. When St. Clare had first returned from the North, impressed with the system and order of his uncle's kitchen, he had provided his own with an array of cupboards, drawers, and various apparatus. He might as well have provided them for a squirrel or a magpie. The more drawers and closets there were, the more hiding-holes could Dinah make for the accommodation of old rags, hair combs, old shoes,

ribbons, castoff artificial flowers, and other articles wherein her soul delighted.

When Miss Ophelia entered the kitchen, Dinah did not rise, but smoked on in sublime tranquillity, regarding her movements out of the corner of her eye, but apparently intent only on the operations around her.

Miss Ophelia commenced opening a set of drawers.

"What is this drawer for, Dinah?" she said.

"It's handy for most anythin', Missis," said Dinah. So it appeared to be. From the variety it contained, Miss Ophelia pulled out first a fine damask tablecloth stained with blood, having evidently been used to wrap raw meat.

"What's this, Dinah? You don't wrap up meat in your mistress' best tablecloths?"

"Oh, Lor, Missis, no. The towels was all a-missin' so I jest did it. I laid out to wash that ar—that's why I put it thar."

"Shif'less!" said Miss Ophelia to herself, proceeding to tumble over the drawer, where she found a nutmeg-grater and two or three nutmegs, a Methodist hymnbook, a couple of soiled Madras handkerchiefs, some yarn and knitting-work, a paper of tobacco and a pipe, a few crackers, one or two gilded china saucers with some pomade in them, one or two thin old shoes, a piece of flannel carefully pinned up enclosing some small white onions, several damask table-napkins, some coarse crash towels, some twine and darning needles, and several broken papers, from which sundry sweet herbs were sifting into the drawer.

"Where do you keep your nutmegs, Dinah?" said Miss Ophelia, with the air of one who prayed for patience.

"Most anywhar, Missis. There's some in that cracked teacup up thar, and there's some over in that ar cupboard."

"Here are some in the grater," said Miss Ophelia, holding them up.

"Laws, yes, I put 'em thar this mornin'—I likes to keep my things handy," said Dinah. "You, Jake! What are you stoppin' for? You'll cotch it! Be still, thar!" she added, with a dive of her stick at the criminal.

"What's this?" said Miss Ophelia, holding up the saucer of pomade.

"Laws, it's my ha'r grease. I put it thar to have it handy."

"Do you use your mistress' best saucers for that?"

"Law! It was cause I was driv and in sich a hurry. I was gwine to change it this very day."

"Here are two damask table-napkins."

"Them table-napkins I put thar to get 'em washed out some day."

"Don't you have some place here on purpose for things to be washed?"

"Well, Mas'r St. Clare got dat ar chest, he said, for dat. But I likes to mix up biscuit and hev my things on it some days, and then it an't handy a-liftin' up the lid."

"Why don't you mix your biscuits on the pastry table there?"

"Law, Missis, it gets sot so full of dishes and one thing and another, der an't no room, noways—"

"But you should *wash* your dishes and clear them away."

"Wash my dishes!" said Dinah in a high key, as her wrath began to rise over her habitual respect of manner. "What does ladies know 'bout work, I want to know? When'd Mas'r ever get his dinner if I was to spend all my time a-washin' and a-puttin' up dishes? Miss Marie never telled me so, nohow."

"Well, here are these onions."

"Laws, yes!" said Dinah. "Thar *is* whar I put 'em, now. I couldn't 'member. Them's particular onions I was a-savin' for dis yer very stew. I'd forgot they was in dat ar old flannel."

Miss Ophelia lifted out the sifting papers of sweet herbs.

"I wish Missis wouldn't touch dem ar. I likes to keep my things whar I knows whar to go to 'em," said Dinah rather decidedly.

"But you don't want these holes in the papers."

"Them's handy for siftin' on 't out," said Dinah.

"But you see it spills all over the drawer."

"Laws, yes! If Missis will go a-tumblin' things up so, it will. Missis has spilt lots dat ar way," said Dinah, coming uneasily to the drawers. "If Missis only will go up sta'rs till my clarin' up time comes, I'll have everythin' right. But I can't do nothin' when ladies is round a-henderin'. You, Sam, don't you gib the baby dat ar sugar bowl! I'll crack ye over, if ye don't mind!"

"I'm going through the kitchen and going to put every-thing in order *once*, Dinah. And then I'll expect you to *keep* it so."

"Lor, now, Miss Phelia! Dat ar an't no way for ladies to do. I never did see ladies doin' no sich. My old Missis nor Miss Marie never did, and I don't see no kinder need on 't." And Dinah stalked indignantly about while Miss Ophelia piled and sorted dishes, emptied dozens of scattering bowls of sugar into one receptacle, sorted napkins, tablecloths, and towels for washing—washing, wiping, and arranging with her own hands, and with a speed which perfectly amazed Dinah.

"Lor, now! If dat are de way dem Northern ladies do, dey an't ladies, nohow," she said to some of her satellites when at a safe hearing distance. "I has things as straight as anybody when my clarin' up time comes. But I don't want ladies round, a-henderin' and gettin' my things all whar I can't find 'em."

To do Dinah justice, she had, at irregular periods, fits of reformation and arrangement, which she called "clarin' up times," when she would begin with great zeal, and turn every drawer and closet wrong side outward on to the floor or tables, and make the confusion sevenfold more confounded. Then she would light her pipe, and leisurely go over her arrangements, looking things over and discoursing upon them—making all the young fry scour most vigorously on the tin things, and keeping up for several hours a most energetic state of confusion, which she would explain by the remark that she was "clarin' up." "She couldn't hev things a-gwine on so as they had been, and she was gwine to make these yer young ones keep better order."

For Dinah herself, somehow, indulged the illusion that she, herself, was the soul of order, and it was only the young uns, and everybody else in the house, that were the cause of anything that fell short of perfection in this respect. When all the tins were scoured, and the tables scrubbed snowy white, and everything that could offend tucked out of sight in holes and corners, Dinah would dress herself up in a smart dress, clean apron, and high, brilliant Madras turban, and tell all marauding "young uns" to keep out of the kitchen, for she was gwine to have things kept nice.

Miss Ophelia in a few days thoroughly reformed every department of the house to a systematic pattern. But her labors in all departments that depended on the cooperation of servants were like those of Sisyphus. In despair, she one day appealed to St. Clare.

"There is no such thing as getting anything like system in this family!"

"To be sure there isn't," said St. Clare.

"Such shiftless management, such waste, such confusion I never saw!"

"I daresay you didn't."

"You would not take it so coolly if you were house-keeper."

"My dear Cousin, you may as well understand, once for all, that we masters are divided into two classes, oppressors and oppressed. We who are good-natured and hate severity make up our minds to a good deal of inconvenience. If we *will* keep a shambling, loose, untaught set in the community for our convenience, why we must take the consequence. Some rare cases I have seen of persons who, by a peculiar tact, can produce order and system without severity, but I'm not one of them. So I made up my mind, long ago, to let things go just as they do. I will not have the poor devils thrashed and cut to pieces, and they know it—and, of course, they know the staff is in their own hands."

"But to have no time, no place, no order—all going on in this shiftless way!"

"My dear Vermont, you natives up by the North Pole set an extravagant value on time. What on earth is the use of time to a fellow who has twice as much of it as he knows what to do with? As to order and system, where there is nothing to be done but to lounge on the sofa and read, an hour sooner or later in breakfast or dinner isn't of much account. Now, there's Dinah gets you a capital dinner—soup, ragout, roast fowl, dessert, ice creams and all—and she creates it all out of chaos and old night down there in that kitchen. I think it really sublime the way she manages. But, Heaven bless us! If we are to go down there, and view all the smoking and squatting about and hurry-scurryation of the preparatory process, we should never eat more. My good Cousin, let Dinah go her own way."

"But, Augustine, you don't know how I found things."

"Don't I? Don't I know that the rolling pin is under her bed, and the nutmeg-grater in her pocket with her tobacco, that there are sixty-five different sugar bowls, one in every hole in the house, that she washes dishes with a dinner-napkin one day and with a fragment of an old petticoat the next? But the upshot is, she gets up glorious dinners, makes superb coffee. And you must judge her as warriors and statesmen are judged—by *her success.*"

"But the waste, the expense!"

"Oh, well. Lock everything you can, and keep the key. Give out by driblets, and never inquire for odds and ends—it isn't best."

"That troubles me, Augustine. I can't help feeling as if these servants were not *strictly honest.* Are you sure they can be relied on?"

Augustine laughed immoderately at the grave and anxious face with which Miss Ophelia propounded the question.

"Oh, Cousin, that's too good—*honest.* As if that's a thing to be expected! Honest! Why, of course, they aren't. Why should they be? What upon earth is to make them so?"

"Why don't you instruct?"

"Instruct! Oh, fiddlestick! What instructing do you think I should do? I look like it! As to Marie, she has spirit enough, to be sure, to kill off a whole plantation, if I'd let her manage. But she wouldn't get the cheatery out of them."

"Are there no honest ones?"

"Well, now and then one, whom Nature makes so impracticably simple, truthful, and faithful that the worst possible influence can't destroy it. But, you see, from the mother's breast the colored child feels and sees that there are none but underhand ways open to it. It can get along no other way with its parents, its mistress, its young master and missy playfellows. Cunning and deception become necessary habits. It

isn't fair to expect anything else of him. He ought not to be
punished for it. As to honesty, the slave is kept in that dependent, semi-childish state that there is no making him realize
the rights of property, or feel that his master's goods are not
his own if he can get them. For my part, I don't see how they
can be honest. Such a fellow as Tom, here, is—is a moral
miracle!"

"And what becomes of their souls?" said Miss Ophelia.

"That isn't my affair, as I know of," said St. Clare. "I am
only dealing in facts of the present life. The fact is that the
whole race are pretty generally understood to be turned over
to the devil, for our benefit in this world, however it may
turn out in another."

"This is perfectly horrible!" said Miss Ophelia. "You ought
to be ashamed of yourselves!"

"I don't know as I am. We are in pretty good company, for
all that," said St. Clare. "Look at the high and the low all
the world over, and it's the same story—the lower class used
up, body, soul, and spirit for the good of the upper. It is so in
England. It is so everywhere. And yet all Christendom stands
aghast with virtuous indignation because we do the thing in
a little different shape from what they do it."

"It isn't so in Vermont."

"Ah, well, in New England and in the free states you have
the better of us, I grant. But there is the bell. So, Cousin, let us
come out to dinner."

As Miss Ophelia was in the kitchen in the latter part of the
afternoon, some of the sable children called out, "La, sakes!
Thar's Prue a comin', gruntin' along like she allers does."

A tall, bony, colored woman now entered the kitchen,
bearing on her head a basket of rusks and hot rolls.

"Ho, Prue! You've come," said Dinah.

Prue had a peculiar scowling expression of countenance
and a sullen, grumbling voice. She set down her basket,
squatted herself down, and resting her elbows on her knees
said:

"Oh, Lord! I wish't I's dead!'"

"Why do you wish you were dead?" said Miss Ophelia.

"I'd be out o' my misery," said the woman gruffly, without taking her eyes from the floor.

"What need you getting drunk, then, and cutting up, Prue?" said a spruce quadroon chambermaid, dangling, as she spoke, a pair of coral eardrops.

The woman looked at her with a sour, surly glance.

"Maybe you'll come to it one of these yer days. I'd be glad to see you, I would. Then you'll be glad of a drop, like me, to forget your misery."

"Come, Prue," said Dinah, "let's look at your rusks. Here's Missis will pay for them."

Miss Ophelia took out a couple of dozen.

"Thar's some tickets in that ar old cracked jug on the top shelf," said Dinah. "You, Jake, climb up and get it down."

"Tickets—what are they for?" said Miss Ophelia.

"We buys tickets of her Mas'r, and she gives us bread for 'em."

"And they counts my money and tickets when I gets home, to see if I's got the change, and if I han't, they half kills me."

"And serves you right," said Jane, the pert chambermaid, "if you will take their money to get drunk on. That's what she does, Missis."

"And that's what I *will* do—I can't live no other ways—drink and forget my misery."

"You are very wicked and very foolish," said Miss Ophelia, "to steal your master's money to make yourself a brute with."

"It's mighty likely, Missis. But I will do it—yes, I will. Oh, Lord! I wish I's dead, I do. I wish I's dead and out of my misery!" And slowly and stiffly the old creature rose and got her basket on her head again. But before she went out, she looked at the quadroon girl, who still stood playing with her eardrops.

"Ye think ye're mighty fine with them ar, a-frolickin' and

a-tossin' your head, and a-lookin' down on everybody. Well, never mind—you may live to be a poor, old, cut-up crittur like me. Hope to the Lord ye will, I do. Then see if you won't drink, drink, drink yerself into torment. And sarve ye right, too—ugh!" And the woman left the room.

"Disgusting old beast!" said Adolph, who was getting his master's shaving water. "If I was her master, I'd cut her up worse than she is."

"Ye couldn't do that ar, no ways," said Dinah. "Her back's a fa'r sight now—she can't never get a dress together over it."

"I think such low creatures ought not to be allowed to go round to genteel families," said Miss Jane. "What do you think, Mr. St. Clare?" she said, coquettishly tossing her head at Adolph.

"I'm certainly of your opinion, Miss Benoir," said Adolph. (Benoir was the name of Marie St. Clare's family, and Jane was one of her servants.)

"Pray, Miss Benoir, may I be allowed to ask if those drops are for the ball tomorrow night? They are certainly bewitching!"

"I wonder, now, Mr. St. Clare, what the impudence of you men will come to!" said Jane, tossing her pretty head till the eardrops twinkled again. "I shan't dance with you for a whole evening if you go to asking me any more questions."

"Oh, you couldn't be so cruel, now! I was just dying to know whether you would appear in your pink tarlatane," said Adolph.

"What is it?" said Rosa, a bright, attractive little quadroon, who came skipping downstairs at this moment.

"Why, Mr. St. Clare's so impudent!"

"On my honor," said Adolph, "I'll leave it to Miss Rosa, now."

"I know he's always a saucy creature," said Rosa, poising herself on one of her little feet and looking maliciously at Adolph. "He's always getting me so angry with him."

"Oh, ladies, ladies! You will certainly break my heart between you," and Adolph.

"Do hear the horrid creature talk!" said both ladies, laughing.

"Come—clar out, you! I can't have you cluttering up the kitchen," said Dinah. "In my way, foolin' round here."

"Aunt Dinah's glum because she can't go to the ball," said Rosa.

"Don't want none o' your light-colored balls," said Dinah. "Cuttin' round, makin' b'lieve you's white folks. Arter all, you's niggers, much as I am."

"Aunt Dinah greases her wool stiff every day to make it lie straight," said Jane.

"And it will be wool, after all," said Rosa, maliciously shaking down her long, silky curls.

"Well, in the Lord's sight an't wool as good as ha'r any time?" said Dinah. "I'd like to have Missis say which is worth the most—a couple such as you, or one like me. Get out wid ye, ye trumpery—I won't have ye round!"

Here the conversation was interrupted in a two-fold manner. St. Clare's voice was heard at the head of the stairs, asking Adolph if he meant to stay all night with his shaving water, and Miss Ophelia, coming out of the dining-room, said:

"Jane and Rosa, what are you wasting your time for here? Go in and attend to your muslins."

Our friend Tom, who had been in the kitchen during the conversation with the old rusk-woman, had followed her out into the street. He saw her go on, giving every once in a while a suppressed groan. At last she set her basket down on a door-step and began arranging the old, faded shawl which covered her shoulders.

"I'll carry your basket a piece," said Tom compassionately.

"Why should ye?" said the woman. "I don't want no help."

"You seem to be sick, or in trouble, or somethin'," said Tom.

"I an't sick," said the woman shortly.

"I wish," said Tom, looking at her earnestly, "I wish I could persuade you to leave off drinking. Don't you know it will be ruin of ye, body and soul?"

"I knows I'm gwine to torment," said the woman sullenly. "Ye don't need to tell me that ar. I's ugly, I's wicked, I's gwine straight to torment. Oh, Lord! I wish I's thar!"

Tom shuddered at these frightful words, spoken with a sullen, impassioned earnestness.

"Oh, Lord have mercy on ye, poor crittur! Han't ye never heard of Jesus Christ?"

"Jesus Christ—who's he?"

"Why, He's *the Lord*," said Tom.

"I think I've hearn tell o' the Lord, and the judgment, and torment. I've hearn o' that."

"But didn't anybody ever tell you of the Lord Jesus, that loved us poor sinners, and died for us?"

"Don't know nothin' 'bout that," said the woman. "Nobody han't never loved me since my old man died."

"Where was you raised?" said Tom.

"Up in Kentuck. A man kept me to breed chil'en for market, and sold 'em as fast as they got big enough. Last of all, he sold me to a speculator, and my Mas'r got me o' him."

"What set you into this bad way of drinkin'?"

"To get shet o' my misery. I had one child after I come here, and I thought then I'd have one to raise, cause Mas'r wasn't a speculator. It was de peartest little thing! And Missis she seemed to think a heap on 't at first. It never cried—it was likely and fat. But Missis tuck sick, and I tended her. And I tuck the fever, and my milk all left me, and the child it pined to skin and bone, and Missis wouldn't buy milk for it. She wouldn't hear to me when I told her I hadn't milk. She said she knowed I could feed it on what other folks eat. And the child kinder pined, and cried, and cried, and cried, day and night, and got all gone to skin and bone, and Missis got sot agin it, and she said 'twan't nothin' but crossness. She wished it was dead, she said. And she wouldn't let me have it o' nights cause, she said, it kept me awake and made me good for nothing. She made me sleep in her room, and I had to put it away off in a little kind o' garret, and thar it cried itself to death one night. It did. And I tuck to drinkin' to keep its crying out of my ears! I did—and I will drink! I will, if I do go to torment for it! Mas'r says I shall go to torment, and I tell him I've got thar now!"

"Oh, ye poor crittur!" said Tom. "Han't nobody never telled ye how the Lord Jesus loved ye, and died for ye? Han't they telled ye that He'll help ye, and ye can go to heaven and have rest at last?"

"I looks like gwine to heaven," said the woman. "An't thar where white folks is gwine? S'pose they'd have me thar? I'd rather go to torment and get away from Mas'r and Missis. I had *so*," she said, as with her usual groan she got her basket on her head and walked sullenly away.

Tom turned and walked sorrowfully back to the house. In the court he met little Eva, a crown of tuberoses on her head, and her eyes radiant with delight.

"Oh, Tom! Here you are. I'm glad I've found you. Papa says you may get out the ponies and take me in my little new carriage," she said, catching his hand. "But what's the matter, Tom? You look sober."

"I feel bad, Miss Eva," said Tom sorrowfully. "But I'll get the horses for you."

"But do tell me, Tom, what is the matter. I saw you talking to cross old Prue."

Tom, in simple, earnest phrase, told Eva the woman's history. She did not exclaim, or wonder, or weep. Her cheeks grew pale, and a deep, earnest shadow passed over her eyes. She laid both hands on her bosom and sighed heavily.

Miss Ophelia's Experiences and Opinions (Continued)

"Tom, you needn't get me the horses. I don't want to go," she said.

"Why not, Miss Eva?"

"These things sink into my heart, Tom," said Eva. "They sink into my heart," she repeated earnestly. "I don't want to go." And she turned from Tom and went into the house.

A few days after, another woman came in old Prue's place to bring the rusks. Miss Ophelia was in the kitchen.

"Lor!" said Dinah: "What's got Prue?"

"Prue isn't coming any more," said the woman mysteriously.

"Why not?" said Dinah. "She an't dead, is she?"

"We doesn't exactly know. She's down cellar," said the woman, glancing at Miss Ophelia.

After Miss Ophelia had taken the rusks, Dinah followed the woman to the door.

"What *has* got Prue, anyhow?" she said.

The woman seemed desirous, yet reluctant, to speak, and answered in a low, mysterious tone.

"Well, you mustn't tell nobody. Prue, she got drunk agin—and they had her down cellar. And thar they left her all day. And I hearn 'em saying that the *flies had got to her*—and *she's dead!*"

Dinah held up her hands and, turning, saw close by her side the spirit-like form of Evangeline, her large eyes dilated with horror, and every drop of blood driven from her lips and cheeks.

"Lor bless us! Miss Eva's gwine to faint away! What got us all to let her h'ar such talk? Her pa'll be rael mad."

"I shan't faint, Dinah," said the child firmly. "And why shouldn't I hear it? It an't so much for me to hear it as for poor Prue to suffer it."

"Lor sakes! It isn't for sweet, delicate young ladies like you, these yer stories isn't. It's enough to kill 'em!"

Eva sighed again and walked upstairs with a slow and melancholy step.

Miss Ophelia anxiously inquired the woman's story. Dinah gave a version of it, to which Tom added the particulars which he had drawn from her that morning.

"An abominable business—perfectly horrible!" she exclaimed as she entered the room where St. Clare lay reading his paper.

"Pray, what wickedness has turned up now?" said he.

"What now? Why, those folks have whipped Prue to death!" said Miss Ophelia, going on, with great strength of detail, into the story, and enlarging on its most shocking particulars.

"I thought it would come to that sometime," said St. Clare, going on with his paper.

"Thought so! An't you going to *do* anything about it?" said Miss Ophelia. "Haven't you got any *selectmen*, or anybody, to interfere and look after such matters?"

"It's commonly supposed that the property interest is a sufficient guard in these cases. If people choose to ruin their own possessions, I don't know what's to be done. It seems the poor creature was a thief and a drunkard, and so there won't be much hope to get up sympathy for her."

"It is perfectly outrageous, Augustine! It will certainly bring down vengeance upon you."

"My dear Cousin, I didn't do it, and I can't help it. I would if I could. If low-minded, brutal people will act like themselves, what am I to do? They have absolute control, they are irresponsible despots. There would be no use interfering—

there is no law that amounts to anything practically for such a case. The best we can do is to shut our eyes and ears and let it alone. It's the only resource left us."

"How can you shut your eyes and ears? How can you let such thing alone?"

"My dear child, what do you expect? What can a man of honorable and humane feeling do but shut his eyes all he can and harden his heart? I can't buy every poor wretch I see. I can't turn knight-errant and undertake to redress every individual case of wrong in such a city as this. The most I can do is to try and keep out of the way of it."

St. Clare's fine countenance was for a moment overcast. He looked annoyed, but suddenly calling up a gay smile, he said:

"Come, Cousin, don't stand there looking like one of the Fates. You've only seen a peep through the curtain—a specimen of what is going on, the world over, in some shape or other. If we are to be prying and spying into all the dismals of life, we should have no heart to anything. 'Tis like looking too close into the details of Dinah's kitchen." And St. Clare lay back on the sofa and busied himself with his paper.

Miss Ophelia sat down and pulled out her knitting-work, and sat there grim with indignation. She knit and knit, but while she mused, the fire burned. At last she broke out:

"I tell you, Augustine, I can't get over things so, if you can. It's a perfect abomination for you to defend such a system— that's *my* mind!"

"What now?" said St. Clare, looking up. "At it again, hey?"

"I say it's perfectly abominable for you to defend such a system!" said Miss Ophelia with increasing warmth.

"I defend it, my dear lady? Who ever said I did defend it?" said St. Clare.

"Of course you defend it—you all do—all you Southerners. What do you have slaves for, if you don't?"

"Are you such a sweet innocent as to suppose nobody in

this world ever does what they don't think is right? Don't you, or didn't you ever, do anything that you did not think quite right?"

"If I do, I repent of it, I hope," said Miss Ophelia, rattling her needles with energy.

"So do I," said St. Clare, peeling an orange. "I'm repenting of it all the time."

"What do you keep on doing it for?"

"Didn't you ever keep on doing wrong after you'd repented, my good Cousin?"

"Well, only when I've been very much tempted," said Miss Ophelia.

"Well, I'm very much tempted," said St. Clare. "That's just my difficulty."

"But I always resolve I won't, and I try to break off."

"Well, I have been resolving I won't, off and on, these ten years," said St. Clare. "But I haven't, somehow, got clear. Have you got clear of all your sins, Cousin?"

"Cousin Augustine," said Miss Ophelia seriously, and laying down her knitting-work, "I suppose I deserve that you should reprove my shortcomings. I know all you say is true enough. Nobody feels them more than I do. But it does seem to me, after all, there is some difference between me and you. It seems to me I would cut off my right hand sooner than keep on, from day to day, doing what I thought was wrong. But then, my conduct is so inconsistent with my profession, I don't wonder you reprove me."

"Oh, now, Cousin," said Augustine, sitting down on the floor and laying his head back in her lap, "don't take on so awfully serious! You know what a good-for-nothing saucy boy I always was. I love to poke you up—that's all—just to see you get earnest. I do think you are desperately, distressingly good. It tires me to death to think of it."

"But this is a serious subject, my boy Auguste," said Miss Ophelia, laying her hand on his forehead.

"Dismally so," said he. "And I—well, I never want to talk

seriously in hot weather. What with mosquitoes and all, a fellow can't get himself up to any very sublime moral flights."

"Oh, Auguste, you are a sad rattle-brain!"

"Am I? Well, so I am, I suppose. But for once I will be serious now. But you must hand me that basket of oranges. Now," said Augustine, drawing the basket up, "I'll begin: When, in the course of human events, it becomes necessary for a fellow to hold two or three dozen of his fellow-worms in captivity, a decent regard to the opinions of society requires—"

"I don't see that you are growing more serious," said Miss Ophelia.

"Wait—I'm coming on—you'll hear. The short of the matter is, Cousin," said he, his handsome face suddenly settling into an earnest and serious expression, "on this abstract question of slavery there can, as I think, be but one opinion. It comes from the devil, that's the short of it—and to my mind, it's a pretty respectable specimen of what he can do in his own line."

Miss Ophelia stopped her knitting and looked surprised. And St. Clare, apparently enjoying her astonishment, went on.

"You seem to wonder. But if you get me fairly at it, I'll make a clean breast of it. This cursed business, accursed of God and man, what is it? Strip it of all its ornament, and what is it? Why, because my brother Quashy is ignorant and weak, and I am intelligent and strong—because I know how, and *can* do it—therefore I may steal all he has, keep it, and give him only such and so much as suits my fancy. Whatever is too hard, too dirty, too disagreeable for me, I may set Quashy to doing. Because I don't like work, Quashy shall work. Because the sun burns me, Quashy shall stay in the sun. Quashy shall earn the money, and I will spend it. Quashy shall lie down in every puddle, that I may walk over dryshod. Quashy shall do my will, and not his, all the days of his mortal life, and have such chance of getting to heaven, at last, as I find convenient.

"This I take to be about what slavery *is*. I defy anybody on earth to read our slave code as it stands in our law books and make anything else of it. Talk of the *abuses* of slavery! Humbug! The *thing itself* is the essence of all abuse! And the only reason why the land don't sink under it is because slavery is *used* in a way infinitely better than it is. For pity's sake, for shame's sake, because we are men born of women and not savage beasts, many of us do not, and dare not—we would *scorn* to use the full power which our savage laws put into our hands. And he who goes the furthest, and does the worst, only uses within limits the power that the law gives him."

St. Clare had started up and was walking, with hurried steps, up and down the floor. His fine face seemed actually to burn with the fervor of his feelings. His large blue eyes flashed, and he gestured with an unconscious eagerness. Miss Ophelia had never seen him in this mood before, and she sat perfectly silent.

"I declare to you," said he, suddenly stopping before his cousin, "there have been times when I have thought, if the whole country would sink and hide all this injustice and misery from the light, I would willingly sink with it. When I have been traveling up and down on our boats, or about on my collecting tours, and reflected that every brutal, disgusting, mean, low-lived fellow I met was allowed by our laws to become absolute despot of as many men, women, and children as he could cheat, steal, or gamble money enough to buy—when I have seen such men in actual ownership of helpless children, of young girls and women—I have been ready to curse my country, to curse the human race!"

"Augustine! Augustine!" said Miss Ophelia. "I'm sure you've said enough. I never in my life heard anything like this, even at the North."

"At the North!" said St. Clare with a sudden change of expression, and resuming something of his habitual careless tone. "Pooh! Your Northern folks are cold-blooded. You are cool in everything. You can't begin to curse up hill and down as we can when we get fairly at it."

"Well, but the question is—" said Miss Ophelia.

"Oh, yes, to be sure, the *question is*—and a deuce of a question it is. How come *you* in this state of sin and misery? Well, I shall answer in the good old words you used to teach me Sundays. I came so by ordinary generation. My servants were my father's and, what is more, my mother's. And now they are mine, they and their increase, which bids fair to be a pretty considerable item.

"My father, you know, came first from New England. And he was just such another man as your father—a regular old Roman—upright, energetic, noble-minded, with an iron will. Your father settled down in New England to rule over rocks and stones and to force an existence out of Nature. And mine settled in Louisiana, to rule over men and women and force existence out of them. My mother," said St. Clare, getting up and walking to a picture at the end of the room, "*she was divine!* Don't look at me so! You know what I mean. She probably was of mortal birth, but as far as ever I could observe, there was no trace of any human weakness or error about her. Cousin, that mother has been all that has stood between me and utter unbelief for years. Oh, mother! mother!" said St. Clare, clasping his hands. And then suddenly checking himself, he came back, and seating himself on an ottoman, he went on:

"My brother and I were twins, and they say, you know, that twins ought to resemble each other. But we were in all points a contrast. He was active and observing, I dreamy and inactive. He was generous to his friends and equals, but proud, dominant, overbearing to inferiors and utterly unmerciful to whatever set itself up against him. We loved each other about as boys generally do—off and on, and in general. He was my father's pet, and I my mother's.

"My father was a born aristocrat. Now, an aristocrat, you know, the world over, has no human sympathies beyond a certain line in society. My father's dividing line was that of color. Among his *equals*, never was a man more just and generous. But he considered the Negro, through all possible gradations of color, as an intermediate link between man and animals. I suppose, to be sure, if anybody had asked him, plump and fair, whether they had human immortal souls, he might have hemmed and hawed and said yes. But my father was not a man much troubled with religious sentiment. He had none, beyond a veneration for God as decidedly the head of the upper classes.

"Well, my father worked some five hundred Negroes. He was an inflexible, driving businessman. Everything was to move by system—to be sustained with unfailing accuracy and precision. Now, if you take into account that all this was to be worked out by a set of lazy, twaddling, shiftless laborers, who had grown up all their lives in the absence of every possible motive to learn how to do anything but 'shirk,' as you Vermonters say, and you'll see that there might naturally be, on his plantation, a great many things that looked horrible and distressing to a sensitive child like me.

"Besides all, he had an overseer who had gone through a regular apprenticeship in hardness and brutality and taken his degree to be admitted to practice. My mother never could endure him, nor I. But this man was the absolute despot of the estate.

"I was a little fellow then, but I had the same love that I have now for all kinds of human things. I was found in the cabins and among the field hands a great deal and, of course, was a great favorite, and all sorts of complaints and grievances were breathed in my ear. And I told them to my mother. Between us we hindered and repressed a great deal of cruelty. We congratulated ourselves on doing a vast deal of good till, as often happens, my zeal overacted. Stubbs complained to my father that he couldn't manage the hands and must resign his position. Father was a fond, indulgent husband, but a man that never flinched from anything that he thought necessary.

And so he put down his foot, like a rock, between us and the field hands. He told my mother that over the house servants she should be entire mistress, but that with the field hands he could allow no interference. He revered and respected her above all living beings, but he would have said it all the same to the Virgin Mary herself, if she had come in the way of his system.

"I used sometimes to hear my mother reasoning cases with him—endeavoring to excite his sympathies. He would listen to the most pathetic appeals with the most discouraging politeness. 'It all resolves itself into this,' he would say. 'Must I part with Stubbs, or keep him? Stubbs is the soul of punctuality, honesty, and efficiency, a thorough business hand, and as humane as the general run. We can't have perfection.' After he had said *that*, he commonly drew up his feet on the sofa, like a man that has disposed of a business, and betook himself to a nap, or the newspaper, as the case might be.

"What remained for mother but to train her children in her own views and sentiments? Well, after all you say about training, children will grow up substantially what they *are* by nature, and only that. From the cradle, Alfred was an aristocrat. And as he grew up, all his sympathies and all his reasonings were in that line, and all mother's words went to the winds. As to me, they sunk deep into me. She never contradicted, in form, anything that my father said, or seemed directly to differ from him. But she burnt into my very soul, with all the force of her deep, earnest nature, an idea of the dignity and worth of the meanest human soul. If I had lived to grow up under her care, she might have stimulated me to I know not what of enthusiasm. I might have been a saint, reformer, martyr. But, alas! alas! I went from her when I was only thirteen, and I never saw her again."

St. Clare rested his head on his hands and did not speak for some minutes. After a while he looked up and went on:

"When my father died, he left the whole property to us twin boys, to be divided as we should agree. There does not breathe on God's earth a nobler-souled, more generous fellow than Alfred, in all that concerns his equals. We got on admirably with this property question, without a single unbrotherly word or feeling. We undertook to work the plantation together. And Alfred became an enthusiastic planter, and a wonderfully successful one.

"But two years' trial satisfied me that I could not be a partner in that matter. To have a great gang of seven hundred, whom I could not know personally, or feel any individual interest in, bought and driven, housed, fed, worked like so many horned cattle, the *necessity* of drivers and overseers, the ever-necessary whip—first, last, and only argument—the whole thing was insufferably disgusting and loathsome to me. And when I thought of my mother's estimate of one poor human soul, it became even frightful.

"It's all nonsense to talk to me about slaves *enjoying* all this! To this day, I have no patience with the unutterable trash that some of your patronizing Northerners have made up in their zeal to apologize for our sins. We all know better. Tell me that any man living wants to work all his days, from day-dawn till dark, under the constant eye of a master, on the same dreary, monotonous, unchanging toil, and all for two pairs of pantaloons and a pair of shoes a year, with enough food and shelter to keep him in working order! Any man who thinks that a human being can, as a general thing, be made about as comfortable that way as any other, I wish he might try it. I'd buy the dog, and work him with a clear conscience!"

"I always have supposed," said Miss Ophelia, "that you, all of you, approved of these things, and thought them *right*—according to Scripture."

"Humbug! We are not quite reduced to that yet. Alfred, who is as determined a despot as ever walked, does not pretend to this kind of defense. No, he stands, high and haughty, on that good old respectable ground *the right of the strongest*. And he says, and I think quite sensibly, that the American planter is 'only doing, in another form, what the English aristocracy and capitalists are doing to the lower classes.' That is, I take it, appropriating them, body and bone, soul and spirit, to their use and convenience. He defends both—and I think at least *consistently*. He says that there can be no high civilization without enslavement of the masses. There must, he says, be a lower class, given up to physical toil and confined to an animal nature. A higher one thereby acquires leisure and wealth for a more expanded intelligence and improvement, and becomes the directing soul of the lower. So he reasons because, as I said, he is born an aristocrat. So I don't believe, because I was born a democrat."

"How in the world can the two things be compared?" said Miss Ophelia. "The English laborer is not sold, traded, parted from his family, whipped."

"He is as much at the will of his employer as if he were sold to him. The slave-owner can whip his refractory slave to death—the capitalist can starve him to death. As to family security, it is hard to say which is the worst—to have one's children sold, or see them starve to death at home."

"But it's no kind of apology for slavery, to prove that it isn't worse than some other bad thing."

"I didn't give it for one—nay, I'll say, besides, that ours is the more bold infringement of human rights. Actually buying a man up, like a horse, looking at his teeth, cracking his joints, and trying his paces, and then paying down for him—having speculators, breeders, traders, and brokers in human bodies and souls—sets the thing before the eyes of the civilized world in a more tangible form, though the thing done be, after all, in its nature, the same: that is, appropriating one set of human beings to the use and improvement of another, without any regard to their own."

"I never thought of the matter in this light," said Miss Ophelia.

"Well, I've traveled in England some, and I've looked over a good many documents as to the state of their lower classes.

And I really think there is no denying Alfred when he says that his slaves are better off than a large class of the population of England. You see, you must not infer, from what I have told you, that Alfred is what is called a hard master, for he isn't. In general, he takes a sort of pride in having his slaves comfortably fed and accommodated."

"Well," said Miss Ophelia, "how came you to give up your plantation life?"

"Well, we jogged on together some time, till Alfred saw plainly that I was no planter. He thought it absurd, after he had reformed and altered and improved everywhere to suit my notions, that I still remained unsatisfied. The fact was, it was after all the THING that I hated—the using these men and women just to make money for me.

"Besides, I was always interfering in the details. Being myself one of the laziest of mortals, I had altogether too much fellow feeling for the lazy. And when poor, shiftless dogs put stones at the bottom of their cotton-baskets to make them weigh heavier, or filled their sacks with dirt, with cotton at the top, it seemed so exactly like what I should do if I were they, I couldn't and wouldn't have them flogged for it. Well, of course, there was an end of plantation discipline. And Alf and I came to about the same point that I and my respected father did years before. So he told me that I would never do for business life, and advised me to take the bank-stock and the New Orleans family mansion, and go to writing poetry, and let him manage the plantation. So we parted, and I came here."

"But why didn't you free your slaves?"

"Well, I wasn't up to that. To hold them as tools for money-making, I could not. Have them to help spend money, you know, didn't look quite so ugly to me. Some of them were old house-servants, to whom I was much attached, and the younger ones were children to the old. All were well satisfied to be as they were." He paused and walked reflectively up and down the room.

"There was," said St. Clare, "a time in my life when I had plans and hopes of doing something in this world, more than to float and drift. I had vague, indistinct yearnings to be a sort of emancipator—to free my native land from this spot and stain. All young men have had such fever fits, I suppose, some time—but then. . . ."

"Why didn't you?" said Miss Ophelia. "You ought not to put your hand to the plow and look back."

"Oh, well, things didn't go with me as I expected, and I got the despair of living that Solomon did. I became a piece of driftwood, and have been floating and eddying about ever since."

"My dear Cousin, can you be satisfied with such a way?"

"Satisfied! Was I not just telling you I despised it? But then, to come back to this point—we were on this liberation business. I don't think my feelings about slavery are peculiar. I find many men who, in their hearts, think of it just as I do. The land groans under it. And bad as it is for the slave, it is worse, if anything, for the master. It takes no spectacles to see that a great class of vicious, improvident, degraded people among us are an evil to us as well as to themselves.

"The capitalist and aristocrat of England cannot feel that as we do because they do not mingle with the class they degrade as we do. They are in our houses. They are the associates of our children, and they form their minds faster than we can, for they are a race that children always will cling to and assimilate with. If Eva, now, was not more angel than ordinary, she would be ruined. We might as well allow the small-pox to run among them, and think our children would not take it, as to let them be uninstructed and vicious, and think our children will not be affected by that. Yet our laws positively and utterly forbid any efficient general educational system, and they do it wisely, too. For just begin and thoroughly educate one generation, and the whole thing would be blown sky high. If we did not give them liberty, they would take it."

"And what do you think will be the end of this?" said Miss Ophelia.

"I don't know. One thing is certain—that there is a mustering among the masses, the world over. And there is a day of wrath coming on, sooner or later. The same thing is working in Europe, in England, and in this country. My mother used to tell me of a millennium that was coming, when Christ should reign, and all men should be free and happy. And she taught me, when I was a boy, to pray, 'Thy kingdom come.' "

"Augustine, sometimes I think you are not far from the kingdom," said Miss Ophelia, laying down her knitting and looking anxiously at her cousin.

"Thank you for your good opinion. But it's up and down with me—up to heaven's gate in theory, down in earth's dust in practice. But there's the tea-bell—do let's go—and don't say, now, I haven't had one downright serious talk for once in my life."

At table Marie alluded to the incident of Prue. "I suppose you'll think, Cousin," she said, "that we are all barbarians."

"I think that's a barbarous thing," said Miss Ophelia, "but I don't think you are all barbarians."

"Well, now," said Marie, "I know it's impossible to get along with some of these creatures. They are so bad they ought not to live. I don't feel a particle of sympathy for such cases. If they'd only behave themselves, it would not happen."

"But, Mamma," said Eva, "the poor creature was unhappy. That's what made her drink."

"Oh, fiddlestick! As if that were any excuse! I'm unhappy, very often. I presume," she said pensively, "that I've had greater trials than ever she had. It's just because they are so bad. There's some of them that you cannot break in by any kind of severity. I remember Father had a man that was so lazy he would run away just to get rid of work, and lie around in the swamps, stealing and doing all sorts of horrid things. That man was caught and whipped time and again, and it never did him any good. And the last time he crawled off, though he couldn't but just go, and died in the swamp. There was no sort of reason for it, for Father's hands were always treated kindly."

"I broke a fellow in once," said St. Clare, "that all the overseers and masters had tried their hands on in vain."

"You!" said Marie. "Well, I'd be glad to know when *you* ever did anything of the sort."

"Well, he was a powerful, gigantic fellow—a native-born African—and he appeared to have the rude instinct of freedom in him to an uncommon degree. He was a regular African lion. They called him Scipio. Nobody could do anything with him, and he was sold round from overseer to overseer, till at last Alfred bought him because he thought he could manage him. Well, one day he knocked down the overseer and was fairly off into the swamps. I was on a visit to Alf's plantation, for it was after we had dissolved partnership. Alfred was greatly exasperated. But I told him that it was his own fault, and laid him any wager that I could break the man. And finally it was agreed that if I caught him, I should have him to experiment on. So they mustered out a party of some six or seven, with guns and dogs, for the hunt. People, you know, can get up just as much enthusiasm in hunting a man as a deer, if it is only customary. In fact, I got a little excited myself, though I had only put in as a sort of mediator, in case he was caught.

"Well, the dogs bayed and howled, and we rode and scampered, and finally we started him. He ran and bounded like a buck, and kept us well in the rear for some time. But at last he got caught in an impenetrable thicket of cane. Then he turned to bay, and I tell you he fought the dogs right gallantly. He dashed them to right and left, and actually killed three of them with only his naked fists, when a shot from a gun brought him down, and he fell, wounded and bleeding, almost at my feet. The poor fellow looked up at me with manhood and despair both in his eyes. I kept back the dogs and the

party and claimed him as my prisoner. It was all I could do to keep them from shooting him, in the flush of success. But I persisted in my bargain, and Alfred sold him to me. Well, I took him in hand, and in one fortnight I had him tamed down as submissive and tractable as heart could desire."

"What in the world did you do to him?" said Marie.

"Well, it was quite a simple process. I took him to my own room, had a good bed made for him, dressed his wounds, and tended him myself until he got fairly on his feet again. And in process of time, I had free papers made out for him and told him he might go where he liked."

"And did he go?" said Miss Ophelia.

"No. The foolish fellow tore the paper in two and absolutely refused to leave me. I never had a braver, better fellow —trusty and true as steel. He embraced Christianity afterwards and became as gentle as a child. He used to oversee my place on the lake, and did it capitally, too. I lost him the first cholera season. In fact, he laid down his life for me. For I was sick almost to death, and when, through the panic, everybody else fled, Scipio worked for me like a giant, and actually brought me back into life again. But, poor fellow, he was taken right after, and there was no saving him. I never felt anybody's loss more."

Eva had come gradually nearer and nearer to her father, as he told the story—her lips apart, her eyes wide and earnest with absorbed interest. As he finished, she suddenly threw her arms around his neck, burst into tears, and sobbed convulsively.

"Eva, dear child! What is the matter?" said St. Clare as the child's small frame trembled and shook with the violence of her feelings. "This child," he added, "ought not to hear any of this kind of thing—she's nervous."

"No, Papa, I'm not nervous," said Eva, controlling herself suddenly. "I'm not nervous, but these things *sink into my heart*."

"What do you mean, Eva?"

"I can't tell you, Papa. I think a great many thoughts. Perhaps some day I shall tell you."

"Well, think away, dear—only don't cry and worry your papa," said St. Clare. "Look here—see what a beautiful peach I have got for you!"

Eva took it and smiled, though there was still a nervous twitching about the corners of her mouth.

"Come look at the goldfish," said St. Clare, taking her hand and stepping on to the verandah. A few moments, and merry laughs were heard through the silken curtains as Eva and St. Clare were pelting each other with roses, and chasing each other among the alleys of the court.

There is danger that our humble friend Tom be neglected amid the adventures of the higher born. But if our readers will accompany us up to a little loft over the stable, they may, perhaps learn a little of his affairs. It was a decent room, containing a bed, a chair, and a small, rough stand, where lay Tom's Bible and hymnbook, and where he sits, at present, with his slate before him, intent on something that seems to cost him a great deal of anxious thought.

The fact was, that Tom's home-yearnings had become so strong that he had begged a sheet of writing paper of Eva, and mustering up all his small stock of literary attainment, acquired by Mas'r George's instructions, he conceived the bold idea of writing a letter. And he was busy now, on his slate, getting out his first draft. Tom was in a good deal of trouble, for the forms of some of the letters he had forgotten entirely, and of those he did remember, he didn't know exactly which to use. And when he was working, and breathing very hard, Eva alighted like a bird on the round of his chair behind him and peeped over his shoulder.

"Oh, Uncle Tom! What funny things you *are* making there!"

"I'm trying to write to my poor old woman, Miss Eva, and my little chil'en," said Tom, drawing the back of his hand over his eyes. "But somehow I'm feared I shan't make it out."

"I wish I could help you, Tom! I've learnt to write some. Last year I could make all the letters, but I'm afraid I've forgotten."

So Eva put her little golden head close to his, and the two commenced a grave and anxious discussion. And with a deal of consulting and advising over every word, the composition began, as they both felt, to look quite like writing.

"Yes, Uncle Tom, it really begins to look beautiful," said Eva, gazing delightedly on it. "How pleased your wife'll be, and the poor little children. Oh, it's a shame you ever had to go away from them! I mean to ask Papa to let you go back some time."

"Missis said that she would send down money for me as soon as they could get it together," said Tom. "I'm 'spectin' she will. Young Mas'r George, he said he'd come for me, and he gave me this yer dollar as a sign." And Tom drew from under his clothes the precious dollar.

"Oh, he'll certainly come, then," said Eva. "I'm so glad!"

"And I wanted to send a letter, you know, to let 'em know whar I was, and tell poor Chloe that I was well off—cause she felt so drefful, poor soul!"

"I say, Tom!" said St. Clare, coming up and looking at the slate.

Tom and Eva both started.

"Oh, it's Tom's letter. I'm helping him to write it," said Eva. "Isn't it nice?"

"I wouldn't discourage either of you," said St. Clare, "but I rather think, Tom, you'd better get me to write your letter for you. I'll do it when I come home from my ride."

"It's very important he should write," said Eva, "because his mistress is going to send down money to redeem him, you know, Papa. He told me they told him so."

St. Clare thought, in his heart, that this was probably only one of those things which good-natured owners say to their servants without any intention of fulfilling the expectation thus excited. But he did not make any comment upon it. And that evening Tom's letter was written in due form and safely lodged in the post office.

Topsy

ONE morning while Miss Ophelia was busy in some of her domestic cares, St. Clare's voice was heard calling her at the foot of the stairs.

"Come down here, Cousin. I've something to show you."

"What is it?" said Miss Ophelia, coming down with her sewing in her hand.

"I've made a purchase for your department—see here," said St. Clare. And with the word, he pulled along a little Negro girl, about eight or nine years of age.

She was one of the blackest of her race, and her round, shining eyes, glittering as glass beads, moved with quick and restless glances over everything in the room. Her mouth, half open with astonishment at the wonders of the new Mas'r's parlor, displayed a white and brilliant set of teeth. Her woolly hair was braided in sundry little tails, which stuck out in every direction. The expression of her face was an odd mixture of shrewdness and cunning, over which was oddly drawn, like a kind of veil, an expression of the most doleful gravity. She was dressed in a single filthy, ragged garment, made of bagging, and stood with her hands demurely folded before her. Altogether, there was something odd and goblin-like about her appearance—something, as Miss Ophelia afterward said, "so heathenish" as to inspire that good lady with utter dismay. And turning to St. Clare, she said:

"Augustine, what in the world have you brought that thing here for?"

"For you to educate, to be sure, and train in the way she should go. I thought she was rather a funny specimen. Here, Topsy," he added, giving a whistle, as a man would to call the attention of a dog, "give us a song, now, and show us some of your dancing."

The black, glassy eyes glittered with a kind of wicked drollery, and the thing struck up, in a clear shrill voice, an odd Negro melody, to which she kept time with her hands and feet, spinning round, clapping her hands, knocking her knees together, in a wild, fantastic sort of time, and producing odd guttural sounds in her throat. And finally, turning a somerset or two, and giving a prolonged closing note as odd and unearthly as that of a steam whistle, she came suddenly down on the carpet, and stood with her hands folded and an expression of meekness and solemnity over her face, only broken by the cunning glances which she shot from the corners of her eyes.

Miss Ophelia stood silent, perfectly paralyzed with amazement.

St. Clare appeared to enjoy her astonishment, and addressing the child again, said:

"Topsy, this is your new mistress. I'm going to give you up to her. See now that you behave yourself."

"Yes, Mas'r," said Topsy with holy gravity, her wicked eyes twinkling as she spoke.

"You're going to be good, Topsy, you understand," said St. Clare.

"Oh, yes, Mas'r," said Topsy with another twinkle, her hands still devoutly folded.

"Now, Augustine, what upon earth is this for?" said Miss Ophelia. "Your house is so full of these little plagues now that a body can't set down their foot without treading on 'em. I get up in the morning and find one asleep behind the door, and see one black head poking out from under the table, one lying on the door mat—they are mopping and mowing and grinning between all the railings and tumbling over the kitchen floor! What on earth did you want to bring this one for?"

"For you to educate—didn't I tell you? You're always preaching about educating. I thought I would make you a present of a fresh-caught specimen, and let you try your hand on her, and bring her up in the way she should go."

"*I* don't want her, I am sure—I have more to do with 'em now than I want to."

"That's you Christians, all over! You'll get up a society, and get some poor missionary to spend all his days among just such heathen. But let me see one of you that would take one into your house with you, and take the labor of their conversion on yourselves! No, when it comes to that, they are dirty and disagreeable, and it's too much care, and so on."

"Augustine, you know I didn't think of it in that light," said

Miss Ophelia, evidently softening. "Well, it might be a real missionary work," said she, looking rather more favorably on the child. "But," she added, "I really didn't see the need of buying this one—there are enough now, in your house, to take all my time and skill."

"Well, then, Cousin," said St. Clare, drawing her aside, "the fact is, this concern belonged to a couple of drunken creatures that keep a low restaurant that I have to pass by every day. And I was tired of hearing her screaming, and them beating and swearing at her. She looked bright and funny, too, as if something might be made of her. So I bought her, and I'll give her to you. Try, now, and give her a good New England bringing up and see what it'll make of her. You know I haven't any gift that way. But I'd like you to try."

"Well, I'll do what I can," said Miss Ophelia. And she approached her new subject very much as a person might be supposed to approach a black spider, supposing them to have benevolent designs toward it.

"She's dreadfully dirty, and half naked," she said.

"Well, take her downstairs, and make some of them clean and clothe her up."

Miss Ophelia carried her to the kitchen regions.

"Don't see what Mas'r St. Clare wants of 'nother nigger!" said Dinah, surveying the new arrival with no friendly air. "Won't have her round under *my* feet, *I* know!"

"Pah!" said Rosa and Jane with supreme disgust. "Let her keep out of our way! What in the world Mas'r wanted another of these low niggers for, I can't see!"

"You go long! No more nigger dan you be, Miss Rosa," said Dinah, who felt this last remark a reflection on herself. "You seem to think yourself white folks. You an't nerry one, black *nor* white. I'd like to be one or turrer."

Miss Ophelia saw that there was nobody in the camp that would undertake to oversee the cleansing and dressing of the new arrival, and so she was forced to do it herself, with some very ungracious and reluctant assistance from Jane.

It is not for ears polite to hear the particulars of the first toilet of a neglected, abused child. Miss Ophelia had a good, strong, practical deal of resolution, and she went through all the disgusting details with heroic thoroughness, though, it must be confessed, with no very gracious air. When she saw, on the back and shoulders of the child, great welts and calloused spots—ineffaceable marks of the system under which she had grown up thus far—her heart became pitiful within her.

"See there!" said Jane, pointing to the marks. "Don't that show she's a limb? We'll have fine works with her, I reckon. I hate these nigger young uns. So disgusting! I wonder that Mas'r would buy her!"

The "young un" alluded to heard all these comments with the subdued and doleful air which seemed habitual to her, only scanning, with a keen and furtive glance of her flickering eyes, the ornaments which Jane wore in her ears. When arrayed at last in a suit of decent and whole clothing, her hair cropped short to her head, Miss Ophelia, with some satisfaction, said she looked more Christian-like than she had, and in her own mind began to mature some plans for her instruction.

Sitting down before her, she began to question her.

"How old are you, Topsy?"

"Dunno, Missis," said the image, with a grin that showed all her teeth.

"Don't know how old you are? Didn't anybody ever tell you? Who was your mother?"

"Never had none!" said the child, with another grin.

"Never had any mother? What do you mean? Where were you born?"

"Never was born!" persisted Topsy with another grin, that looked so goblin-like that if Miss Ophelia had been at all nervous, she might have fancied that she had got hold of some sooty gnome. But Miss Ophelia was not nervous, and she said with some sternness:

"You mustn't answer me in that way, child. I'm not playing with you. Tell me where you were born, and who your father and mother were."

"Never was born," repeated the creature, more emphatically. "Never had no father nor mother, nor nothin'. I was raised by a speculator, with lots of others. Old Aunt Sue used to take car' on us."

The child was evidently sincere, and Jane, breaking into a short laugh, said:

"Laws, Missis, there's heaps of 'em. Speculators buys 'em up cheap when they's little, and gets 'em raised for market."

"How long have you lived with your master and mistress?"

"Dunno, Missis."

"Is it a year, or more, or less?"

"Dunno, Missis."

"Laws, Missis, those low Negroes—they can't tell. They don't know anything about time," said Jane. "They don't know what a year is. They don't know their own ages."

"Have you ever heard anything about God, Topsy?"

The child looked bewildered, but grinned as usual.

"Do you know who made you?"

"Nobody as I knows on," said the child, with a short laugh.

The idea appeared to amuse her considerably, for her eyes twinkled, and she added:

"I spect I grow'd. Don't think nobody never made me."

"Do you know how to sew?" said Miss Ophelia, who thought she would turn her inquiries to something more tangible.

"No, Missis."

"What can you do? What did you do for your master and mistress?"

"Fetch water, and wash dishes, and rub knives, and wait on folks."

"Were they good to you?"

"Spect they was," said the child, scanning Miss Ophelia cunningly.

Miss Ophelia rose. St. Clare was leaning over the back of her chair.

"You find virgin soil there, Cousin. Put in your own ideas —you won't find many to pull up."

Miss Ophelia's ideas of children's education, like all her other ideas, were very set and definite, and of the kind that prevailed in New England a century ago, and which are still preserved in some very retired parts where there are no railroads. As nearly as could be expressed, they could be comprised in very few words: to teach them to mind when they were spoken to; to teach them the catechism, sewing, and reading; and to whip them if they told lies. Miss Ophelia knew of nothing else to do and, therefore, applied her mind to her heathen with the best diligence she could command.

The child was announced and considered in the family as Miss Ophelia's girl. And as she was looked upon with no gracious eye in the kitchen, Miss Ophelia resolved to confine her sphere of operation to her own chamber. Behold, then, Topsy, washed and shorn of all the little braided tails wherein her heart had delighted, arrayed in a clean gown, with well-starched apron, standing reverently before Miss Ophelia.

"Now, Topsy, I'm going to show you just how my bed is to be made. I am very particular about my bed. You must learn exactly how to do it."

"Yes, Ma'am," said Topsy with a deep sigh and a face of woeful earnestness.

"Now, Topsy, look here. This is the hem of the sheet—this is the right side of the sheet, and this is the wrong. Will you remember?"

"Yes, ma'am," says Topsy with another sigh.

"Well, now, the under sheet you must bring over the bolster—so—and tuck it clear down under the mattress nice and smooth—so—do you see?"

"Yes, ma'am," said Topsy, with profound attention.

"But the upper sheet," said Miss Ophelia, "must be brought down in this way, and tucked under firm and smooth at the foot—so—the narrow hem at the foot."

"Yes, ma'am," said Topsy, as before. But we will add, what

Miss Ophelia did not see, that during the time when the good lady's back was turned, the young disciple had contrived to snatch a pair of gloves and a ribbon, which she had adroitly slipped into her sleeves, and stood with her hands dutifully folded, as before.

"Now, Topsy, let's see *you* do this," said Miss Ophelia, pulling off the clothes and seating herself.

Topsy, with great gravity and adroitness, went through the exercise completely to Miss Ophelia's satisfaction, smoothing the sheets, patting out every wrinkle, and exhibiting through the whole process a gravity and seriousness with which her instructress was greatly pleased. By an unlucky slip, however, a fluttering fragment of the ribbon hung out of one of her sleeves just as she was finishing, and caught Miss Ophelia's attention. Instantly she pounced upon it.

"What's this? You naughty, wicked child—you've been stealing this!"

The ribbon was pulled out of Topsy's own sleeve, yet she was not in the least disconcerted. She only looked at it with an air of the most surprised and unconscious innocence.

"Laws! Why, that ar's Miss Feely's ribbon, an't it? How could it a got caught in my sleeve?"

"Topsy, you naughty girl, don't you tell me a lie—you stole that ribbon!"

"Missis, I declar for't, I didn't. Never seed it till dis yer blessed minnit."

"Topsy," said Miss Ophelia, "don't you know it's wicked to tell lies?"

"I never tells no lies, Miss Feely," said Topsy, with virtuous gravity. "It's jist the truth I've been a-tellin' now, and an't nothin' else."

"Topsy, I shall have to whip you, if you tell lies so."

"Laws, Missis, if you's to whip all day, couldn't say no other way," said Topsy, beginning to blubber. "I never seed dat ar—it must a got caught in my sleeve. Miss Feely must have left it on the bed, and it got caught in the clothes, and so got in my sleeve."

Miss Ophelia was so indignant at the barefaced lie that she caught the child and shook her.

"Don't you tell me that again!"

The shake brought the gloves on to the floor, from the other sleeve.

"There, you!" said Miss Ophelia. "Will you tell me now that you didn't steal the ribbon?"

Topsy now confessed to the gloves, but still persisted in denying the ribbon.

"Now, Topsy," said Miss Ophelia, "if you'll confess all about it, I won't whip you this time." Thus entreated, Topsy confessed to the ribbon and gloves, with woeful protestations of penitence.

"Well, now, tell me. I know you must have taken other things since you have been in the house, for I let you run about all day yesterday. Now, tell me if you took anything, and I shan't whip you."

"Laws, Missis! I took Miss Eva's red thing she wars on her neck."

"You did, you naughty child!—Well, what else?"

"I took Rosa's yerrings—them red ones."

"Go bring them to me this minute, both of 'em."

"Laws, Missis! I can't—they's burnt up!"

"Burnt up! What a story! Go get 'em, or I'll whip you."

Topsy, with loud protestations and tears and groans declared that she *could* not. "They's burnt up—they was."

"What did you burn 'em up for?" said Miss Ophelia.

"Cause I's wicked—I is. I's mighty wicked, anyhow. I can't help it."

Just at this moment Eva came innocently into the room, with the identical coral necklace on her neck.

"Why, Eva, where did you get your necklace?" said Miss Ophelia.

"Get it? Why, I've had it on all day," said Eva.

"Did you have it on yesterday?"

"Yes, and what is funny, Aunty, I had it on all night. I forgot to take it off when I went to bed."

Miss Ophelia looked perfectly bewildered, the more so as Rosa at that instant came into the room with a basket of newly ironed linen poised on her head and the coral eardrops shaking in her ears.

"I'm sure I can't tell anything what to do with such a child!" she said in despair. "What in the world did you tell me you took those things for, Topsy?"

"Why, Missis said I must 'fess, and I couldn't think of nothin' else to 'fess," said Topsy, rubbing her eyes.

"But, of course, I didn't want you to confess things you didn't do," said Miss Ophelia. "That's telling a lie, just as much as the other."

"Laws, now, is it?" said Topsy, with an air of innocent wonder.

"La, there an't any such thing as truth in that limb," said Rosa, looking indignantly at Topsy. "If I was Mas'r St. Clare, I'd whip her till the blood run. I would—I'd let her catch it!"

"No, no, Rosa," said Eva, with an air of command which the child could assume at times. "You mustn't talk so, Rosa. I can't bear to hear it."

"La sakes! Miss Eva, you's so good, you don't know nothing how to get along with niggers. There's no way but to cut 'em well up, I tell ye."

"Rosa!" said Eva. "Hush! Don't you say another word of that sort!" and the eye of the child flashed, and her cheek deepened its color.

Rosa was cowed in a moment.

"Miss Eva has got the St. Clare blood in her, that's plain. She can speak, for all the world, just like her papa," she said as she passed out of the room.

Eva stood looking at Topsy.

"Poor Topsy, why need you steal? You're going to be taken good care of now. I'm sure I'd rather give you anything of mine than have you steal it," said Eva.

It was the first word of kindness the child had ever heard in her life, and the sweet tone and manner struck strangely on the wild, rude heart, and a sparkle of something like a tear shone in the keen, round, glittering eyes. But it was followed by the short laugh and habitual grin. Topsy only thought Eva's speech something funny and inexplicable—she did not believe it.

But what was to be done with Topsy? Miss Ophelia found the case a puzzler. Her rules for bringing up didn't seem to apply. She thought she would take time to think of it, and by way of gaining time, shut Topsy up in a dark closet till she had arranged her ideas further on the subject.

"I don't see," said Miss Ophelia to St. Clare, "how I'm going to manage that child without whipping her."

"Oh, well, certainly," said St. Clare. "Do as you think best. Only I'll make one suggestion: I've seen this child whipped with a poker, knocked down with the shovel or tongs, whichever came handiest, et cetera. And seeing that she is used to that style of operation, I think your whippings will have to be pretty energetic to make much impression."

"What is to be done with her, then?" said Miss Ophelia.

"You have started a serious question," said St Clare. "I wish you'd answer it. What is to be done with a human being that can be governed only by the lash—it's a very common state of things down here!"

"I'm sure I don't know. I never saw such a child as this."

"Such children are very common among us, and such men and women, too. How are they to be governed?" said St. Clare.

"I'm sure it's more than I can say," said Miss Ophelia.

"Or I either," said St. Clare. "The horrid cruelties and outrages that once in a while find their way into the papers—such cases as Prue's, for example—what do they come from? In many cases it is a gradual hardening process on both sides—the owner growing more and more cruel as the servant more and more callous. I saw this very early when I became an owner, and I resolved never to begin, because I did not know when I should stop. I resolved, at least, to protect my own moral nature. The consequence is that my servants act like spoiled children. But I think that better than for us both to be brutalized together. You have talked a great deal about our responsibilities in educating, Cousin. I really wanted you to *try* with one child, who is a specimen of thousands among us."

"It is your system makes such children," said Miss Ophelia.

"I know it. But they are *made*—they exist—and what *is* to be done with them?"

"Well, I can't say I thank you for the experiment. But then, as it appears to be a duty, I shall persevere and try, and do the best I can," said Miss Ophelia. And after this she did labor on her new subject. She instituted regular hours and employments for her, and undertook to teach her to read and to sew.

In the former art the child was quick enough. She learned her letters as if by magic, and was very soon able to read plain reading. But the sewing was a more difficult matter. The creature was active as a monkey, and the confinement of sewing was her abomination. So she broke her needles, threw them slyly out of windows, or down in chinks of the walls. She tangled, broke, and dirtied her thread, or with a sly movement would throw a spool away altogether. Her motions were almost as quick as those of a practiced conjurer, and her command of her face quite as great. And though Miss Ophelia could not help feeling that so many accidents could not possibly happen in succession, yet she could not detect her.

Topsy was soon a noted character in the establishment. Her talent for every species of drollery, grimace, and mimicry—for dancing, tumbling, climbing, singing, whistling, imitating every sound that hit her fancy—seemed inexhaustible. In her play hours, she invariably had every child in the establishment at her heels, open-mouthed with admiration and wonder—not excepting Miss Eva, who appeared to be fascinated by her as a dove is sometimes charmed by a glittering serpent. Miss Ophelia was uneasy that Eva should fancy Topsy's society so much, and implored St. Clare to forbid it.

"Poh! Let the child alone," said St. Clare. "Topsy will do her good. Evil rolls off Eva's mind like dew off a cabbage leaf. If she could have been spoiled, it would have been done years ago."

Topsy was at first despised by the upper servants. They soon found reason to alter their opinion. It was very soon discovered that whoever cast an indignity on Topsy was sure to meet with some inconvenient accident shortly after. Either a pair of earrings or some cherished trinket would be missing, or an article of dress would be suddenly found utterly ruined, or the person would stumble accidentally into a pail of hot water, or dirty slop would unaccountably deluge them from above when in full gala dress. Nobody in the world ever doubted who did the things, but not a scrap of any direct evidence could be found to establish the suppositions, and Miss Ophelia was too just to feel at liberty to proceed to any lengths about it. In short, Topsy soon made the household understand the propriety of letting her alone, and she was let alone, accordingly.

In all manual operations, Topsy was smart and energetic. With a few lessons, she had learned to do the work of Miss Ophelia's chamber in a way with which even that particular lady could find no fault. Mortal hands could not lay spread smoother, adjust pillows more accurately, sweep and dust and arrange more perfectly than Topsy when she chose—but she didn't very often choose. If Miss Ophelia, after three or four days of careful and patient supervision, was so hopeful as to suppose that Topsy could do without overlooking, and so go off and busy herself about something else, Topsy would hold a perfect carnival of confusion for some one or two hours. Instead of making the bed, she would amuse herself with pulling off the pillowcases and butting her woolly head among the pillows. She would climb the posts and hang head downward from the tops, flourish the sheets and spreads over the apartment, dress the bolster up in Miss Ophelia's night clothes —singing and whistling and making grimaces at herself in the looking-glass the while.

"Topsy!" Miss Ophelia would say when at the end of all patience. "What does make you act so?"

"Dunno, Missis. I spects cause I's so wicked!"

"I don't know anything what I shall do with you, Topsy."

"Law, Missis, you must whip me. My old Missis allers whipped me. I ain't used to workin' unless I gets whipped."

"Why, Topsy, I don't want to whip you. You can do well if you've a mind to. What is the reason you won't?"

"Laws, Missis, I's used to whippin'. I spects it's good for me."

Miss Ophelia tried the recipe, and Topsy invariably made a terrible commotion, screaming, groaning, and imploring, though half an hour afterward, when roosted on some projection of the balcony and surrounded by a flock of admiring "young uns," she would express the utmost contempt of the whole affair.

"Law, Miss Feely whip! Wouldn't kill a skeeter her whippin's. Oughter see how old Mas'r made the flesh fly. Old Mas'r know'd how!"

Topsy always made great capital of her own sins, evidently considering them as something peculiarly distinguishing.

"Law, you niggers," she would say to some of her auditors, "does you know you's all sinners? Well, you is—everybody is. White folks is sinners too—Miss Feely says so. But I spects niggers is the biggest ones. But lor! Ye an't any on ye up to me. I's so awful wicked there can't nobody do nothin' with me. I used to keep old Missis a swarin' at me half de time. I spects I's the wickedest crittur in the world." And Topsy would cut a somerset, and come up brisk and shining on to a higher perch, and evidently plume herself on the distinction.

St. Clare took the same kind of amusement in the child that a man might in the tricks of a parrot or a pointer. Topsy, whenever her sins brought her into disgrace in other quarters, always took refuge behind his chair. And St. Clare, in one way or another, would make peace for her. From him she got many a stray picayune, which she laid out in nuts and candies, and distributed with careless generosity to all the children in the family. For Topsy, to do her justice, was good-natured and liberal, and only spiteful in self-defense.

Kentuck

OUR readers may not be unwilling to glance back, for a brief interval, at Uncle Tom's cabin on the Kentucky farm and see what has been transpiring among those whom he had left behind.

It was late in the summer afternoon, and the doors and windows of the large parlor all stood open to invite any stray breeze that might feel in a good humor to enter. Mr. Shelby sat in a large hall opening into the room and running through the whole length of the house to a balcony on either end. Leisurely tipped back in one chair, with his heels in another, he was enjoying his after-dinner cigar. Mrs. Shelby sat in the door, busy about some fine sewing. She seemed like one who had something on her mind, which she was seeking an opportunity to introduce.

"Do you know," she said, "that Chloe has had a letter from Tom?"

"Ah, has she? Tom's got some friend there, it seems. How is the old boy?"

"He has been bought by a very fine family, I should think," said Mrs. Shelby, "is kindly treated, and has not much to do."

"Ah, well, I am glad of it, very glad," said Mr. Shelby heartily. "Tom, I suppose, will get reconciled to a Southern residence—hardly want to come up here again."

"On the contrary, he inquires very anxiously," said Mrs. Shelby, "when the money for his redemption is to be raised."

"I'm sure *I* don't know," said Mr. Shelby. "Once get business running wrong, there does seem to be no end to it. It's like jumping from one bog to another all through a swamp.

Borrow of one to pay another, and then borrow of another to
pay one. And these confounded notes falling due before a
man has time to smoke a cigar and turn round."

"It does seem to me, my dear, that something might be
done to straighten matters. Suppose we sell off all the horses,
and sell one of your farms, and pay up square?"

"Oh, ridiculous, Emily! You are the finest woman in Kentucky, but still you haven't sense to know that you don't
understand business. Women never do, and never can."

"But," said Mrs. Shelby, "could not you give me some little
insight into yours—a list of all your debts, at least, and of all
that is owed to you, and let me try and see if I can't help you
to economize?"

"Oh, bother! Don't plague me, Emily! I can't tell
exactly. I know somewhere about what things are likely to be.
But there's no trimming and squaring my affairs as Chloe
trims crust off her pies. You don't know anything about business, I tell you." And Mr. Shelby, not knowing any other
way of enforcing his ideas, raised his voice.

Mrs. Shelby ceased talking, with something of a sigh. Her
heart was set on performing her promise to Tom and Aunt
Chloe, and she sighed as discouragements thickened around
her.

"Don't you think we might in some way contrive to raise
that money? Poor Aunt Chloe! Her heart is so set on it!"

"I'm sorry if it is. I think I was premature in promising. I'm
not sure, now, but it's the best way to tell Chloe, and let her
make up her mind to it. Tom'll have another wife in a year or
two, and she had better take up with somebody else."

"Mr. Shelby, I have taught my people that their marriages
are as sacred as ours. I never could think of giving Chloe such
advice."

"Well, well, Emily, I don't pretend to interfere with your
religious notions. Only they seem extremely unfitted for
people in that condition."

"They are, indeed," said Mrs. Shelby, "and that is why,

from my soul, I hate the whole thing. I tell you, my dear, *I* cannot absolve myself from the promises I make to these help-less creatures. If I can get the money no other way, I will take music scholars—I could get enough, I know, and earn the money myself."

"You wouldn't degrade yourself that way, Emily? I never could consent to it."

"Degrade! Would it degrade me as much as to break my faith with the helpless? No, indeed."

Here the conversation was interrupted by the appearance of Aunt Chloe at the end of the verandah.

"If you please, Missis," said she.

"Well, Chloe, what is it?" said her mistress, rising and going to the end of the balcony.

"If Missis would come and look at dis yer lot o' poetry."

Mrs. Shelby smiled as she saw a prostrate lot of chickens and ducks, over which Chloe stood with a very grave face of consideration.

"I'm a-thinkin' whether Missis would be a-havin' a chicken pie o' dese yer."

"Really, Aunt Chloe, I don't much care. Serve them any way you like.

Chloe stood handling them over distractedly. It was quite evident that the chickens were not what she was thinking of. At last, with a short laugh, she said:

"Laws me, Missis! What should Mas'r and Missis be a troublin' theirselves 'bout de money, and not a-usin' what's right in der hands?" And Chloe laughed again.

"I don't understand you, Chloe," said Mrs. Shelby, nothing doubting that Chloe had heard every word of the conversa-tion that had passed between her and her husband.

"Why, laws me, Missis!" said Chloe. "Other folks hires out der niggers and makes money on 'em."

"Well, Chloe, who do you propose that we should hire out?"

"Law! I an't proposin' nothin'. Only Sam he said der was

one of dese yer *perfectioners* dey calls 'em, in Louisville, said he wanted a good hand at cake and pastry, and said he'd give four dollars a week to one, he did."

"Well, Chloe."

"Well, laws, I's a thinkin', Missis, it's time Sally was put along to be doin' something. Sally's been under my care, now, dis some time, and she does most as well as me, considerin'. And if Missis would only let me go, I would help fetch up de money. I an't afraid to put my cake, nor pies nother, 'longside no *perfectioner's*."

"But, Chloe, do you want to leave your children?"

"Laws, Missis. De boys is big enough to do day's works. Dey does well enough. And Sally, she'll take de baby—she's such a peart young un, she won't take no lookin' arter."

"Louisville is a good way off."

"Law sakes! Who's afeard? It's down river, somer near my old man, perhaps?" said Chloe, speaking the last in the tone of a question.

"No, Chloe. It's many a hundred miles off," said Mrs. Shelby.

Chloe's countenance fell.

"Never mind. Your going there shall bring you nearer, Chloe. Yes, you may go, and your wages shall every cent of them be laid aside for your husband's redemption."

As when a bright sunbeam turns a dark cloud to silver, so Chloe's dark face brightened immediately—it really shone.

"Laws! If Missis isn't too good! I was thinkin' of dat ar very thing, 'cause I shouldn't need no clothes, nor shoes, nor nothin'—I could save every cent. How many weeks is der in a year, Missis"?

"Fifty-two," said Mrs. Shelby.

"Laws, now! Dere is? And four dollars for each on 'em. Why how much'd dat ar be?"

"Two hundred and eight dollars," said Mrs. Shelby.

"Why-e!" said Chloe, with an accent of surprise and delight. "And how long would it take me to work it out, Missis?"

"Some four or five years, Chloe. But, then, you needn't do it all—I shall add something to it."

"I wouldn't hear to Missis givin' lessons nor nothin'. Mas'r's quite right in dat ar—'twouldn't do, no ways. I hope none our family ever be brought to dat ar while I's got hands."

"Don't fear, Chloe. I'll take care of the honor of the family," said Mrs. Shelby, smiling. "But when do you expect to go?"

"Well, I warn't spectin' nothin', only Sam, he's a gwine to de river with some colts, and he said I could go long with him. So I jes put my things together. If Missis was willin', I'd go with Sam tomorrow morning, if Missis would write my pass and write me a commendation."

"Well, Chloe, I'll attend to it, if Mr. Shelby has no objections. I must speak to him."

Mrs. Shelby went upstairs, and Aunt Chloe, delighted, went out to her cabin to make her preparation.

"Law sakes, Mas'r George! Ye didn't know I's agwine to Louisville tomorrow!" she said to George, as entering her cabin, he found her busy in sorting over her baby's clothes. "I thought I'd jes look over sis's things and get 'em straightened up. But I'm gwine, Mas'r George—gwine to have four dollars a week. And Missis is gwine to lay it all up to buy back my old man agin!"

"Whew!" said George. "Here's a stroke of business, to be sure! How are you going?"

"Tomorrow, wid Sam. And now, Mas'r George, I knows you'll jes sit down and write to my old man, and tell him all about it, won't ye?"

"To be sure," said George. "Uncle Tom'll be right glad to hear from us. I'll go right in the house for paper and ink. And then, you know, Aunt Chloe, I can tell about the new colts and all."

"Sartin, sartin, Mas'r George. You go 'long, and I'll get ye up a bit o' chicken or some sich. Ye won't have many more suppers wid yer poor old aunty."

"The Grass Withereth—the Flower Fadeth"

LIFE passes with us all a day at a time. So it passed with our friend Tom, till two years were gone.

His letter homeward was in due time answered by Master George, in a good, round, schoolboy hand that Tom said might be read "most acrost the room." It stated how Aunt Chloe had been hired out to a confectioner in Louisville, where her skill in the pastry line was gaining wonderful sums of money, all of which, Tom was informed, was to be laid up to go to make up the sum of his redemption money. Mose and Pete were thriving, and the baby was trotting all about the house, under the care of Sally and the family generally.

The rest of the letter gave a list of George's school studies, each one headed by a flourishing capital. It also told the names of four new colts that appeared on the premises since Tom left, and stated, in the same connection, that Father and Mother were well. Tom thought it the most wonderful specimen of composition that had appeared in modern times and held a council with Eva about getting it framed, to hang up in his room. Nothing but the difficulty of arranging it so that both sides of the page would show at once stood in the way of this undertaking.

The friendship between Tom and Eva had grown with the child's growth. It would be hard to say what place she held in the soft, impressible heart of her faithful attendant. He loved her as something frail and earthly, yet almost worshiped her as something divine. To humor her graceful fancies was Tom's chief delight. In the market, at morning, his eyes were always on the flower-stalls for rare bouquets for her, and the choicest peach or orange was slipped into his pocket to give to her when he came back. And the sight that pleased him most was her sunny head looking out the gate for his distant approach, and her childish question: "Well, Uncle Tom, what have you got for me today?"

—————

At this time in our story, the whole St. Clare establishment is, for the time being, removed to their villa on Lake Pontchartrain. The heat of summer had driven all who were able to leave the sultry and unhealthy city to seek the shores of the lake and its cool breezes.

It is now one of those intensely golden sunsets which kindles the whole horizon into one blaze of glory and makes the water another sky. Tom and Eva were seated on a little mossy seat in an arbor at the foot of the garden. It was Sunday evening, and Eva's Bible lay open on her knee. She read: "And I saw a sea of glass, mingled with fire."

"Tom," said Eva, suddenly stopping and pointing to the lake, "there 'tis."

"What, Miss Eva?"

"Don't you see—there?" said the child, pointing to the glassy water, which reflected the golden glow of the sky. "There's a 'sea of glass, mingled with fire.' "

"True enough, Miss Eva," said Tom. And Tom sang:

> O, had I the wings of the morning,
>   I'd fly away to Canaan's shore;
> Bright angels should convey me home,
>   To the new Jerusalem.

"Where do you suppose new Jerusalem is, Uncle Tom?" said Eva.

"Oh, up in the clouds, Miss Eva."

"Then I think I see it," said Eva. "Look in those clouds—they look like great gates of pearl. And you can see beyond them—far, far off—it's all gold. Tom, sing about 'spirits bright.' "

Tom sung the words of a well known Methodist hymn:

> I see a hand of spirits bright,
>   That taste the glories there;
> They all are robed in spotless white,
>   And conquering palms they bear.

"Uncle Tom, I've seen *them*," said Eva.

Tom had no doubt of it at all; it did not surprise him in the least. If Eva had told him she had been to heaven, he would have thought it entirely probable.

"They come to me sometimes in my sleep, those spirits." And Eva's eyes grew dreamy, and she hummed in a low voice:

> They all are robed in spotless white,
>   And conquering palms they bear.

"Uncle Tom," said Eva, "I'm going there."

"Where, Miss Eva?"

The child rose and pointed her little hand to the sky. The glow of evening lit her golden hair and flushed cheek with a kind of unearthly radiance, and her eyes were raised earnestly to the skies.

"I'm going *there*," she said, "to the spirits bright, Tom. *I'm going, before long.*"

The faithful old heart felt a sudden thrust. And Tom thought how often he had noticed, within six months, that Eva's little hands had grown thinner, and her skin more transparent, and her breath shorter; and how, when she ran or played in the garden, as she once could for hours, she became soon so tired and languid. He had heard Miss Ophelia speak often of a cough that all her medicaments could not cure, and even now that cheek and little hand were burning with hectic fever. And yet the thought that Eva's words suggested had never come to him till now.

The talk between Tom and Eva was interrupted by a hasty call from Miss Ophelia.

"Eva—Eva! Why, child, the dew is falling. You mustn't be out there!"

Eva and Tom hastened in.

Miss Ophelia was skilled in nursing. She had noted the slight, dry cough, the daily brightening cheek. She tried to communicate her fears to St. Clare, but he threw back her suggestions with a restless petulance, unlike his usual careless good humor.

"Don't be croaking, Cousin—I hate it!" he would say. "Don't you see that the child is only growing? Children always lose strength when they grow fast."

"But she has that cough!"

"Oh, nonsense of that cough. It is not anything. She has taken a little cold, perhaps."

"Well, that was just the way Eliza Jane was taken, and Ellen and Maria Sanders."

"Oh, stop these hobgoblin nurse legends! You old hands have got so wise that a child cannot cough or sneeze but you see ruin at hand. Only take care of the child, keep her from the night air, and don't let her play too hard, and she'll do well enough."

So St. Clare said, but he grew nervous and restless. He watched Eva feverishly day by day, as might be told by the frequency with which he repeated over that "the child was quite well, that there wasn't anything in that cough." But he kept by her more than before, took her oftener to ride with him, brought home every few days some receipt or strengthening mixture—"Not," he said, "that the child *needed* it, but then it would not do her any harm."

The thing that struck a deeper pang to his heart than anything else was the daily increasing maturity of the child's mind and feelings. While still retaining all a child's fanciful graces, yet she often dropped words of such a reach of thought that they seemed to be an inspiration. At such times St. Clare would feel a sudden thrill, and clasp her in his arms as if that fond clasp could save her. And his heart rose up with wild determination to keep her, never to let her go.

The child's whole heart and soul seemed absorbed in works of love and kindness. Impulsively generous she had always been, but there was a touching womanly thoughtfulness about her now, that everyone noticed. She still loved to play with Topsy and the various colored children. But she now seemed rather a spectator than an actor of their plays, and she would sit for half an hour at a time laughing at the odd tricks of Topsy—and then a shadow would seem to pass across her face, her eyes grew misty, and her thoughts were afar.

"Mamma," she said suddenly to her mother one day, "why don't we teach our servants to read?"

"What a question, child! People never do."

"Why don't they?" said Eva.

"Because it is no use for them to read. It don't help them to work any better, and they are not made for anything else."

"But they ought to read the Bible, Mamma, to learn God's will."

"Oh, they can get that read to them all *they* need."

"It seems to me, Mamma, the Bible is for everyone to read themselves. They need it a great many times when there is nobody to read it."

"Eva, you are an odd child," said her mother.

"Miss Ophelia has taught Topsy to read," continued Eva.

"Yes, and you see how much good it does. Topsy is the worst creature I ever saw!"

"Here's poor Mammy!" said Eva. "She does love the Bible so much, and wishes so she could read! And what will she do when I can't read to her?"

Marie was busy turning over the contents of a drawer as she answered:

"Well, of course, by and by, Eva, you will have other things to think of besides reading the Bible round to servants. Not but that is very proper—I've done it myself when I had health. But when you come to be dressing and going into company, you won't have time. See here!" she added. "These jewels I'm going to give you when you come out. I wore them to my first ball. I can tell you, Eva, I made a sensation."

Eva took the jewel-case and lifted from it a diamond necklace. Her large, thoughtful eyes rested on them, but it was plain her thoughts were elsewhere.

"How sober you look, child!" said Marie.

"Are these worth a great deal of money, Mamma?"

"To be sure, they are. Father sent to France for them. They are worth a small fortune."

"I wish I had them," said Eva, "to do what I pleased with!"

"What would you do with them?"

"I'd sell them, and buy a place in the free states, and take all our people there, and hire teachers to teach them to read and write."

Eva was cut short by her mother's laughing.

"Set up a boarding school! Wouldn't you teach them to play on the piano, and paint on velvet?"

"I'd teach them to read their own Bible, and write their own letters, and read letters that are written to them," said Eva steadily. "I know, Mamma, it does come very hard on them that they can't do these things. Tom feels it—Mammy does—a great many of them do. I think it's wrong."

"Come, come, Eva, you are only a child. You don't know anything about these things," said Marie. "Besides, your talking makes my head ache."

Eva stole away. But after that she gave Mammy reading lessons.

Henrique

ABOUT this time, St. Clare's brother Alfred with his eldest son, a boy of twelve, spent a day or two with the family at the lake. Nature had made the brothers opposites on every point, yet a mysterious tie seemed to unite them in a closer friendship than ordinary. They were always abusing each other's opinions and practices, and yet never a whit the less absorbed in each other's society.

Henrique, the eldest son of Alfred, was a noble, dark-eyed, princely boy, full of vivacity and spirit, who from the first

moment of introduction seemed to be perfectly fascinated by the graces of his cousin Evangeline.

Eva had a little pet pony, of a snowy whiteness. It was easy as a cradle and as gentle as its little mistress. And this pony was now brought up to the back verandah by Tom, while a little mulatto boy of about thirteen led along a small black Arabian, which had just been imported, at a great expense, for Henrique.

Henrique had a boy's pride in his new possession, and as he advanced and took the reins out of the hands of his little groom, he looked carefully over him, and his brow darkened.

"What's this, Dodo, you little lazy dog! You haven't rubbed my horse down this morning."

"Yes, Mas'r," said Dodo submissively. "He got that dust on his own self."

"You rascal, shut your mouth!" said Henrique, violently raising his riding whip. "How dare you speak?"

The boy was a handsome, bright-eyed mulatto, of just Henrique's size, and his curling hair hung round a high, bold forehead. He had white blood in his veins, as could be seen by the quick flush in his cheeks as he eagerly tried to speak.

"Mas'r Henrique!" he began.

Henrique struck him across the face with his riding whip and seizing one of his arms, forced him on to his knees and beat him till he was out of breath.

"There, you impudent dog! Now will you learn not to answer back when I speak to you? Take the horse back and clean him properly. I'll teach you your place!"

"Young Mas'r," said Tom, "I spects what he was gwine to say was that the horse would roll when he was bringing him up from the stable. He's so full of spirits—that's the way he got that dirt on him. I looked to his cleaning."

"You hold your tongue till you're asked to speak!" said Henrique, turning on his heel and walking up the steps to speak to Eva, who stood in her riding dress.

"Dear Cousin, I'm sorry this stupid fellow has kept you waiting," he said. "Let's sit down here on this seat till they come. What's the matter, Cousin? You look sober."

"How could you be so cruel and wicked to poor Dodo?" said Eva.

"Cruel? Wicked?" said the boy, with unaffected surprise. "What do you mean, dear Eva?"

"I don't want you to call me dear Eva when you do so," said Eva.

"Dear Cousin, you don't know Dodo—it's the only way to manage him, he's so full of lies and excuses. The only way is to put him down at once—not let him open his mouth. That's the way Papa manages."

"But Uncle Tom said it was an accident, and he never tells what isn't true."

"He's an uncommon old nigger, then!" said Henrique. "Dodo will lie as fast as he can speak."

"You frighten him into deceiving if you treat him so."

"Why, Eva, you've really taken such a fancy to Dodo that I shall be jealous."

"But you beat him, and he didn't deserve it."

"Oh, well, it may go for some time when he does, and don't get it. A few cuts never come amiss with Dodo—he's a regular spirit, I can tell you. But I won't beat him again before you if it troubles you."

Eva was not satisfied but found it in vain to try to make her handsome cousin understand her feelings.

Dodo soon appeared with the horses.

"Well, Dodo, you've done pretty well this time," said his young master, with a more gracious air. "Come, now, and hold Miss Eva's horse while I put her on the saddle."

Dodo came and stood by Eva's pony. His face was troubled. His eyes looked as if he had been crying.

Henrique, who valued himself on his gentlemanly adroitness in all matters of gallantry, soon had his fair cousin in the saddle, and gathering the reins, placed them in her hands. But Eva bent to the other side of the horse, where Dodo was standing, and said as he relinquished the reins, "That's a good boy, Dodo. Thank you!"

Dodo looked up in amazement into the sweet young face. The blood rushed to his cheeks, and the tears to his eyes.

"Here, Dodo," said his master imperiously.

Dodo held the horse while his master mounted.

"There's a picayune for you to buy candy with, Dodo," said Henrique. "Go get some." And Henrique cantered down the walk after Eva.

Dodo stood looking after the two children. One had given him money, and one had given him what he wanted far more —a kind word, kindly spoken. Dodo had been only a few months away from his mother. His master had bought him at a slave warehouse for his handsome face, to be a match to the handsome pony. And he was now getting his breaking in at the hands of his young master.

The scene of the beating had been witnessed by the two brothers St. Clare from another part of the garden.

Augustine's cheek flushed, but he only observed, with his usual sarcastic carelessness:

"I suppose that's what we may call republican education, Alfred?"

"Henrique is a devil of a fellow when his blood's up," said Alfred.

"I suppose you consider this an instructive practice for him," said Augustine dryly.

"I couldn't help it if I didn't. Henrique is a regular little tempest. His mother and I have given him up long ago. But then, that Dodo is a perfect sprite—no amount of whipping can hurt him."

"And this by way of teaching Henrique that all men are born free and equal!"

"Poh!" said Alfred. "One of Tom Jefferson's pieces of

French sentiment and humbug. It's perfectly ridiculous to have that going the rounds among us to this day. There's no use in talking, Augustine. I believe we've been round and round this old track five hundred times, more or less. What do you say to a game of backgammon?"

The two brothers ran up the verandah steps and were soon seated at a light bamboo stand, with the backgammon board between them.

"You take the first throw," said Alfred. And the brothers were soon lost in the game and heard no more till the scraping of horses' feet was heard under the verandah.

"There come the children," said Augustine, rising. "Look here, Alf! Did you ever see anything so beautiful?"

And, in truth, it *was* a beautiful sight. Henrique, with his bold brow and dark, glossy curls and glowing cheek, was laughing gaily as he bent toward his fair cousin. She was dressed in a blue riding dress, with a cap of the same color. Exercise had given a brilliant hue to her cheeks and heightened the effect of her singularly transparent skin and golden hair.

"Good heavens! What perfectly dazzling beauty!" said Alfred. "I tell you, Auguste, won't she make some hearts ache, one of these days?"

"She will, too truly—God knows I'm afraid so!" said St. Clare in a tone of sudden bitterness, as he hurried down to take her off her horse.

"Eva, darling!" You're not much tired?" he said as he clasped her in his arms.

"No, Papa," said the child. But her short, hard breathing alarmed her father.

"How could you ride so fast, dear? You know it's bad for you."

"I felt so well, Papa, and liked it so much I forgot."

St. Clare carried her in his arms into the parlor and laid her on the sofa.

"Henrique, you must be careful of Eva," said he. "You mustn't ride fast with her."

"I'll take her under my care," said Henrique, seating himself by the sofa and taking Eva's hand.

Eva soon found herself much better. Her father and uncle resumed their game, and the children were left together.

"Do you know, Eva, I'm so sorry Papa is only going to stay two days here, and then I shan't see you again for ever so long. If I stayed with you, I'd try to be good, and not be cross to Dodo, and so on. I don't mean to treat Dodo ill. But, you know, I've got such a quick temper. I'm not really bad to him, though. I give him a picayune now and then. And you see he dresses well. I think, on the whole, Dodo's pretty well off."

"Would you think you were well off if there were not one creature in this world near you to love you?"

"I? Well, of course not."

"And you have taken Dodo away from all the friends he ever had, and now he has not a creature to love him. Nobody can be good that way."

"Well, I can't help it, as I know of. I can't get his mother, and I can't love him myself, nor anybody else as I know of."

"Why can't you?" said Eva.

"*Love* Dodo! Why, Eva, you wouldn't have me! I may *like* him well enough, but you don't *love* your servants."

"I do, indeed."

"How odd!"

"Don't the Bible say we must love everybody?"

"Oh, the Bible! To be sure, it says a great many such things. But then, nobody ever thinks of doing them—you know, Eva, nobody does."

Eva did not speak. Her eyes were fixed and thoughtful for a few moments.

"At any rate," she said, "dear Cousin, do love poor Dodo, and be kind to him, for my sake!"

"I could love anything for your sake, dear Cousin, for I really think you are the loveliest creature that I ever saw!" And Henrique spoke with an earnestness that flushed his handsome face. Eva received it with perfect simplicity, without even a change of feature, merely saying, "I'm glad you feel so, dear Henrique! I hope you will remember."

The dinner bell put an end to the interview.

Foreshadowings

Two days after this, Alfred St. Clare and Augustine parted, and Eva, who had been stimulated by the society of her young cousin to exertions beyond her strength, began to fail rapidly. St. Clare was at last willing to call in medical advice— a thing from which he had always shrunk because it was an admission of an unwelcome truth.

Marie St. Clare had taken no notice of the child's gradually decaying health and strength, because she was completely absorbed in studying out two or three new forms of disease of which she believed herself a victim. Miss Ophelia had several times tried to awaken her maternal fears about Eva, but to no avail.

"I don't see as anything ails the child," she would say. "She runs about and plays."

"But she has a cough."

"Cough! You don't need to tell *me* about a cough. I've always been subject to a cough, all my days. When I was Eva's age, they thought I was in a consumption. Night after night, Mammy used to sit up with me. Oh, Eva's cough is not anything."

"But she gets weak and is short-breathed."

"Law! I've had that, years and years. It's only a nervous affection."

"But she sweats so, nights."

"Well, I have, these ten years. Very often, night after night, my clothes will be wringing wet. There won't be a dry thread in my night clothes, and the sheets will be so that Mammy has to hang them up to dry. Eva doesn't sweat anything like that!"

Miss Ophelia shut her mouth for the time. But now that Eva was fairly and visibly prostrated, and a doctor called, Marie all of a sudden took a new turn.

She knew it, she said. She always felt it that she was destined to be the most miserable of mothers. Here she was, with her wretched health, and her only darling child going down to the grave before her eyes. And Marie routed up Mammy nights, and rumpussed and scolded with more energy than ever all day, on the strength of this new misery.

"My dear Marie, don't talk so!" said St. Clare. "You ought not to give up the case so, at once."

"You have not a mother's feelings, St. Clare! You never could understand me! You don't now."

"But don't talk so, as if it were a gone case!"

"I can't take it as indifferently as you can, St. Clare. If *you* don't feel when your only child is in this alarming state, *I* do. It's a blow too much for me, with all I was bearing before."

"It's true," said St. Clare, "that Eva is very delicate, *that* I always knew. And that she has grown so rapidly as to exhaust her strength. And that her situation is critical. But now she is only prostrated by the heat of the weather, and by the excitement of her cousin's visit, and the exertions she made. The physician says there is room for hope."

"Well, of course, if you can look on the bright side, pray do. It's a mercy if people haven't sensitive feelings in this world. I am sure I wish I didn't feel as I do—it only makes me completely wretched. I wish I *could* be as easy as the rest of you!"

And the "rest of them" had good reason to breathe the same prayer, for Marie paraded her new misery as the reason and apology for all sorts of inflictions on everyone about her.

In a week or two there was a great improvement of symptoms—one of those deceitful lulls by which her unyielding disease so often beguiles the anxious heart even on the verge of the grave. Eva's step was again in the garden, in the balconies. She played and laughed again, and her father joyfully declared that they should soon have her as hearty as anybody. Miss Ophelia and the physician alone felt no encouragement.

There was one other heart, too, that felt the same certainty, and that was the little heart of Eva. What is it that sometimes speaks in the soul so calmly, so clearly, that its earthly time is short? Be it what it may, it rested in the heart of Eva, a calm, sweet certainty that Heaven was near. She was only troubled by sorrow for those who loved her so dearly. Her father most—for Eva, though she never distinctly thought so, had an instinctive perception that she was more in his heart than any other. She loved her mother because she was so loving a creature, and all the selfishness that she had seen in her only saddened and perplexed her. For she had a child's implicit trust that her mother could not do wrong. There was something about her that Eva never could make out, and she always smoothed it over with thinking that, after all, it was Mamma, and she loved her very dearly indeed.

She felt, too, for those fine, faithful servants to whom she was as daylight and sunshine. Eva was an uncommonly mature child, and the things that she had witnessed of the evils of the system under which they were living had fallen, one by one, into the depths of her thoughtful heart. She had vague longings to do something for them, to bless and save not only them, but all in their condition—longings that contrasted sadly with the feebleness of her little frame.

"Uncle Tom," she said one day when she was reading to

her friend, "I can understand why Jesus *wanted* to die for us."

"Why, Miss Eva?"

"Because I've felt so, too."

"What is it, Miss Eva? I don't understand."

"I can't tell you. But when I saw those poor creatures on the boat, you know, when you came down and I—some had lost their mothers, and some their husbands, and some mothers cried for their little children—and when I heard about poor Prue—oh, wasn't that dreadful!—and a great many other times, I've felt that I would be glad to die if my dying could stop all this misery. I *would die* for them, Tom, if I could," said the child earnestly, laying her little thin hand on his.

Tom looked at the child with awe. And when she, hearing her father's voice, glided away, he wiped his eyes many times as he looked after her.

"It's jest no use tryin' to keep Miss Eva here," he said to Mammy, whom he met a moment after. "She's got the Lord's mark in her forehead."

"Ah, yes, yes," said Mammy, raising her hands. "I've allers said so. She wasn't never like a child that's to live—there was allers something deep in her eyes. I've told Missis so, many the time. It's a-comin' true—we all sees it—dear little, blessed lamb!"

Eva came tripping up the verandah steps to her father. It was late in the afternoon, and the rays of the sun formed a kind of glory behind her as she came forward in her white dress, with her golden hair and glowing cheeks, her eyes unnaturally bright with the slow fever that burned in her veins.

St. Clare had called her to show a statuette that he had been buying for her. But her appearance, as she came on, impressed him suddenly and painfully. There is a kind of beauty so intense, yet so fragile, that we cannot bear to look at it. Her father folded her suddenly in his arms and almost forgot what he was going to tell her.

"Eva, dear, you are better nowadays, are you not?"

"Papa," said Eva, with sudden firmness, "I've had things I wanted to say to you a great while. I want to say them now, before I get weaker."

St. Clare trembled as Eva seated herself in his lap. She laid her head on his bosom and said:

"It's all no use, Papa, to keep it to myself any longer. The time is coming that I am going to leave you. I am going, and never to come back!" And Eva sobbed.

"Oh, now, my dear little Eva!" said St. Clare, trembling as he spoke, but speaking cheerfully, "you've got nervous and low-spirited. You mustn't indulge such gloomy thoughts. See here, I've bought a statuette for you!"

"No, Papa," said Eva, putting it gently away, "don't deceive yourself! I am *not* any better, I know it perfectly well. And I am going, before long. I am not nervous. I am not low-

spirited. If it were not for you, Papa, and my friends, I should be perfectly happy. I want to go—I long to go!"

"Why, dear child, what has made your poor little heart so sad? You have had everything to make you happy that could be given you."

"I had rather be in heaven, though only for my friends' sake I would be willing to live. There are a great many things here that make me sad, that seem dreadful to me. I had rather be there. But I don't want to leave you—it almost breaks my heart!"

"What makes you sad and seems dreadful, Eva?"

"Oh, things that are done, and done all the time. I feel sad for our poor people. They love me dearly, and they are all good and kind to me. I wish, Papa, they were all *free*."

"Why, Eva, child, don't you think they are well enough off now?"

"Oh, but Papa, if anything should happen to you, what would become of them? There are very few men like you, Papa. Uncle Alfred isn't like you, and Mamma isn't. And then, think of old Prue's owners! What horrid things people do, and can do!" Eva shuddered.

"My dear child, you are too sensitive. I'm sorry I ever let you hear such stories."

"Oh, that's what troubles me, Papa. You want me to live so happy, and never to have any pain—never suffer anything—not even hear a sad story, when other poor creatures have nothing but pain and sorrow all their lives. It seems selfish. I ought to know such things, I ought to feel about them! Such things always sank into my heart, they went down deep. I've thought and thought about them. Papa isn't there any way to have all slaves made free?"

"That's a difficult question, dearest. There's no doubt that this way is a very bad one. A great many people think so. I do myself. I heartily wish that there were not a slave in the land. But then, I don't know what is to be done about it!"

"Papa, you are such a good man, and so noble, and kind,

and you always have a way of saying things that is so pleasant, couldn't you go all round and try to persuade people to do right about this? When I am dead, Papa, then you will think of me, and do it for my sake. I would do it if I could."

"When you are dead, Eva," said St. Clare passionately. "Oh, child, don't talk to me so! You are all I have on earth."

"Poor old Prue's child was all that she had—and yet she had to hear it crying, and she couldn't help it. Papa, these poor creatures love their children as much as you do me. Oh, do something for them! There's poor Mammy loves her children. I've seen her cry when she talked about them. And Tom loves his children. And it's dreadful, Papa, that such things are happening all the time!"

"There, there, darling," said St. Clare soothingly. "Only don't distress yourself, and don't talk of dying, and I will do anything you wish."

"And promise me, dear Father, that Tom shall have his freedom as soon as"—she stopped, and said in a hesitating tone—"I am gone!"

"Yes, dear, I will do anything in the world—anything you could ask me to."

"Dear, Papa," said the child, laying her burning cheek against his, "how I wish we could go together!"

"Where, dearest?" said St. Clare.

"To our Saviour's home. It's so sweet and peaceful there—it is all so loving there!" The child spoke unconsciously as of a place where she had often been. "Don't you want to go, Papa?" she said.

St. Clare drew her closer to him, but was silent.

"You will come to me," said the child, speaking in a voice of calm certainty which she often used unconsciously.

"I shall come after you. I shall not forget you."

The shadows of the solemn evening closed round them deeper and deeper as St. Clare sat silently holding the little frail form to his bosom. We can think *much*, very much, in a moment. St. Clare saw and felt many things, but spoke nothing. As it grew darker, he took his child to her bedroom. And when she was prepared for rest, he sent away the attendants, and rocked her in his arms, and sung to her till she was asleep.

The Little Evangelist

IT was Sunday afternoon. St. Clare was stretched on a bamboo lounge in the verandah, solacing himself with a cigar. Marie lay reclined on a sofa opposite the window opening on the verandah, closely secluded, under an awning of transparent gauze, from the outrages of the mosquitoes, and languidly holding in her hand an elegantly bound prayer book. She was holding it because it was Sunday, and she imagined she had been reading it, though, in fact she had been only taking a succession of short naps, with it open in her hand.

Miss Ophelia, who, after some rummaging, had hunted up a small Methodist meeting within riding distance, had gone out, with Tom as driver, to attend it, and Eva had accompanied them.

"I say, Augustine," said Marie after dozing a while, "I must send to the city after my old Doctor Posey. I'm sure I've got the complaint of the heart."

"Well, why need you send for him? This doctor that attends Eva seems skillful."

"I would not trust him in a critical case," said Marie. "And I think I may say mine is becoming so. Believe it or not, my distress about Eva, and the exertions I have made with that dear child, have developed what I have long suspected."

What the *exertions* were which Marie referred to, it would have been difficult to state. St. Clare quietly made this commentary to himself, and went on smoking till a carriage drove up before the verandah, and Eva and Miss Ophelia alighted.

Miss Ophelia marched straight to her own chamber to put away her bonnet and shawl, as was always her manner, before she spoke a word on any subject, while Eva came at St. Clare's call, and was sitting on his knee giving him an account of the services they had heard.

They soon heard loud exclamations from Miss Ophelia's room, and violent reproof addressed to somebody.

"What new witchcraft has Tops been brewing?" asked St. Clare. "That commotion is of her raising, I'll be bound!"

A moment after, Miss Ophelia, in high indignation, came dragging the culprit along.

"Come out here, now!" she said. "I *will* tell your master!"

"What's the case now?" asked Augustine.

"The case is that I cannot be plagued with this child any longer! It's past all bearing. Flesh and blood cannot endure it. Here I locked her up and gave her a hymn to study. And what does she do but spy out where I put my key, and has gone to my bureau, and got a bonnet trimming, and cut it all to pieces to make dolls' jackets! I never saw anything like it in my life!"

"I told you, Cousin," said Marie, "that you'd find out that these creatures can't be brought up without severity. If I had *my* way, now," she said, looking reproachfully at St. Clare, "I'd send that child out and have her thoroughly whipped. I'd have her whipped till she couldn't stand!"

"I don't doubt it," said St. Clare.

"There is no use in this shilly-shally way of yours, St. Clare!" said Marie. "Cousin is a woman of sense, and she sees it now, as plain as I do."

Miss Ophelia's indignation had been pretty actively roused by the trickery and wastefulness of the child, but Marie's words went beyond her.

"I wouldn't have the child treated so for the world," she said. "But I am sure, Augustine, I don't know what to do. I've taught and taught, I've talked till I'm tired. I've whipped her,

I've punished her in every way I can think of, and still she's just what she was at first."

"Come here, Tops, you monkey!" said St. Clare.

Topsy came up, her round, hard eyes glittering and blinking with a mixture of apprehensiveness and their usual odd drollery.

"What makes you behave so?" said St. Clare, who could not help being amused with the child's expression.

"Spects it's my wicked heart," said Topsy demurely. "Miss Feely says so."

"Don't you see how much Miss Ophelia has done for you? She says she has done everything she can think of."

"Lor yes, Mas'r! Old Missis used to say so, too. She whipped me a heap harder, and used to pull my har, and knock my head agin the door. But it didn't do me no good! I spects if they's to pull every spear o' har out o' my head, it wouldn't do no good, neither—I's so wicked! Laws! I's nothin' but a nigger, no ways!"

"Well, I shall have to give her up," said Miss Ophelia. "I can't have that trouble any longer."

"Well, I'd just like to ask one question," said St. Clare.

"What is it?"

"Why, if your Gospel is not strong enough to save one heathen child that you can have at home here all to yourself, what's the use of sending one or two poor missionaries off with it among thousands of just such? I suppose this child is about a fair sample of what thousands of your heathen are."

Miss Ophelia did not make an immediate answer, and Eva, who had stood a silent spectator of the scene thus far, made a silent sign to Topsy to follow her. There was a little glass-room at the corner of the verandah, which St. Clare used as a sort of reading room. And Eva and Topsy disappeared into this place.

"What's Eva going about, now?" said St. Clare. "I mean to see." And advancing on tiptoe, he lifted up a curtain that covered the glass door and looked in. In a moment, laying his

finger on his lips, he made a silent gesture to Miss Ophelia to come and look. There sat the two children on the floor, with their side faces toward them: Topsy with her usual air of careless drollery and unconcern; opposite to her, Eva, her whole face fervent with feeling, and tears in her eyes.

"What does make you so bad, Topsy? Why won't you try and be good? Don't you love *anybody*, Topsy?"

"Dunno nothin' 'bout love. I loves candy and sich, that's all," said Topsy.

"But you love your father and mother."

"Never had none, ye know. I telled ye that, Miss Eva."

"Oh, I know," said Eva sadly. "But hadn't you any brother, or sister, or aunt, or—"

"No, none on 'em—never had nothing nor nobody."

"But, Topsy, if you'd only try to be good, you might—"

"Couldn't never be nothin' but a nigger, if I was ever so

good," said Topsy. "If I could be skinned, and come white, I'd try then."

"But people can love you if you are black, Topsy. Miss Ophelia would love you, if you were good."

Topsy gave the short, blunt laugh that was her common mode of expressing disbelief.

"Don't you think so?" said Eva.

"No. She can't bar me 'cause I'm a nigger! She'd 's soon have a toad touch her! There can't nobody love niggers, and niggers can't do nothin'! *I* don't care," said Topsy, beginning to whistle.

"Oh, Topsy, poor child, *I* love you!" said Eva, with a sudden burst of feeling, and laying her little thin, white hand on Topsy's shoulder. "I love you, because you haven't had any father, or mother, or friends, because you've been a poor, abused child. I love you, and I want you to be good. I am very unwell, Topsy, and I think I shan't live a great while. And it really grieves me to have you be so naughty. I wish you would try to be good, for my sake—it's only a little while I shall be with you."

The round, keen eyes of the black child were overcast with tears. Large, bright drops rolled heavily down, one by one, and fell on the little white hand. Yes, in that moment a ray of real belief, a ray of heavenly love, had penetrated the darkness of her heathen soul. She laid her head down between her knees and wept and sobbed, while the beautiful child, bending over her, looked like the picture of some bright angel stooping to reclaim a sinner.

"Poor Topsy!" said Eva. "Don't you know that Jesus loves all alike? He is just as willing to love you as me. He loves you just as I do—only more, because He is better. He will help you to be good, and you can go to Heaven at last, and be an angel forever, just as much as if you were white. Only think of it, Topsy! *You* can be one of those spirits bright Uncle Tom sings about."

"Oh, dear Miss Eva, dear Miss Eva!" said the child. "I will try, I will try. I never did care nothin' 'bout it before."

St. Clare at this instant dropped the curtain. "It puts me in mind of Mother," he said to Miss Ophelia. "It is true what she told me. If we want to give sight to the blind, we must be willing to do as Christ did—call them to us, and *put our hands on them.*"

"I've always had a prejudice against Negroes," said Miss Ophelia, "and it's a fact, I never could bear to have that child touch me. But I didn't think she knew it."

"Trust any child to find that out," said St. Clare. "There's no keeping it from them. But I believe that all the trying in the world to benefit a child, and all the substantial favors you can do them, will never excite one emotion of gratitude while that feeling of repugnance remains in the heart. It's a queer kind of a fact, but so it is."

"I don't know how I can help it," said Miss Ophelia. "They *are* disagreeable to me—this child in particular. How can I help feeling so?"

"Eva does, it seems."

"Well, she's so loving! After all, though, she's no more than Christ-like," said Miss Ophelia. "I wish I were like her. She might teach me a lesson."

"It wouldn't be the first time a little child had been used to instruct an old disciple if it *were* so," said St. Clare.

Death

THE deceitful strength which had buoyed Eva up for a little while was fast passing away. Seldom and more seldom her light footstep was heard in the verandah, and oftener and oftener she was found reclined on a little lounge by the open window.

It was toward the middle of the afternoon, as she was so reclining—her Bible half open, her little transparent finger lying listlessly between the leaves—suddenly she heard her mother's voice, in sharp tones, on the verandah.

"What now, you baggage! What new piece of mischief! You've been picking the flowers, hey?" And Eva heard the sound of a smart slap.

"Law, Missis! They's for Miss Eva," she heard a voice say, which she knew belonged to Topsy.

"Miss Eva! A pretty excuse! You suppose she wants *your* flowers, you good-for-nothing nigger! Get along, off with you!"

In a moment Eva was off her lounge and on the verandah.

"Oh, don't, Mamma! I should like the flowers. Do give them to me. I want them!"

"Why, Eva, your room is full now."

"I can't have too many," said Eva. "Topsy, do bring them here."

Topsy, who had stood sullenly holding down her head, now came up and offered her flowers. She did it with a look of hesitation and bashfulness, quite unlike the boldness which was usual with her.

"It's a beautiful bouquet!" said Eva, looking at it.

It was rather a singular one—a brilliant scarlet geranium and one single white japonica, with its glossy leaves. It was tied up with an evident eye to the contrast of color, and the arrangement of every leaf had carefully been studied.

Topsy looked pleased as Eva said, "Topsy, you arrange flowers very prettily. Here is this vase I haven't any flowers for. I wish you'd arrange something every day for it."

"Well, that's odd!" said Marie. "What in the world do you want that for?"

"Never mind, Mamma. You'd as lief as not Topsy should do it—had you not?"

"Of course, anything you please, dear. Topsy, you hear your young mistress. See that you mind."

Topsy made a short courtesy and looked down. And as she turned away, Eva saw a tear roll down her dark cheek.

"You see, Mamma, I knew poor Topsy wanted to do something for me," said Eva to her mother.

"Oh, nonsense! It's only because she likes to do mischief. She knows she mustn't pick flowers—so she does it. That's all there is to it. But if you fancy to have her pluck them, so be it."

"Mamma, I think Topsy is different from what she used to be. She's trying to be a good girl."

"She'll have to try a good while before *she* gets to be good," said Marie with a careless laugh.

"Well, you know, Mamma, poor Topsy! Everything has always been against her. It's such a pity—oh, such a pity!" said Eva, looking out on the distant lake and speaking half to herself.

"What's a pity?" said Marie.

"Why, that anyone who could be a bright angel, and live with angels, should go all down, down, down and nobody help them! Oh, dear!"

"Well, we can't help it. It's no use worrying, Eva. I don't know what's to be done. We ought to be thankful for our own advantages."

"I hardly can be," said Eva, "I'm so sorry to think of poor folks that haven't any."

"That's odd enough," said Marie. "I'm sure my religion makes me thankful for my advantages."

"Mamma," said Eva, "I want to have some of my hair cut off—a good deal of it."

"What for?" said Marie.

"Mamma, I want to give some away to my friends, while I **am** able to give it to them myself. Won't you ask Aunty to **come** and cut it for me?"

Marie raised her voice and called Miss Ophelia from the other room.

The child half rose from her pillow as she came in, and shaking down her long golden-brown curls, said playfully, "Come, Aunty, shear the sheep!"

"What's that?" said St. Clare, who just then entered with some fruit he had been out to get for her.

"Papa, I just want Aunty to cut off some of my hair. There's too much of it, and it makes my head hot. Besides, I want to give some of it away."

Miss Ophelia came with her scissors.

"Take care—don't spoil the looks of it!" said her father. "Cut underneath, where it won't show. Eva's curls are my pride."

"Oh, Papa!" said Eva sadly.

"Yes, and I want them kept handsome against the time I take you up to your uncle's plantation to see Cousin Henrique," said St. Clare in a gay tone.

"I shall never go there, Papa. I am going to a better country. Oh, do believe me! Don't you see, Papa, that I get weaker every day?"

"Why do you insist that I shall believe such a cruel thing, Eva?" said her father.

"Only because it is *true*, Papa. And if you will believe it now, perhaps you will get to feel about it as I do."

St. Clare closed his lips and stood gloomily eyeing the long, beautiful curls, which, as they were separated from the child's head, were laid one by one in her lap. She raised them up, looked earnestly at them, twined them around her thin fingers, and looked from time to time anxiously at her father.

"It's just what I've been foreboding!" said Marie. "It's just what has been preying on my health from day to day, bringing me downward to the grave, though nobody regards it. I have seen this long. St. Clare, you will see, after a while, that I was right."

"Which will afford you great consolation, no doubt!" said St. Clare in a dry, bitter tone.

Marie lay back on a lounge and covered her face with her handkerchief.

Eva looked earnestly from one to the other. It was evident she saw, felt, and appreciated the difference between the two.

She beckoned with her hand to her father. He came and sat down by her.

"Papa, my strength fades away every day, and I know I must go. There are some things I want to say and do—that I ought to do. And you are so unwilling to have me speak a word on this subject. But there's no putting it off. Do be willing I should speak now!"

"My child, I *am* willing," said St. Clare, covering his eyes with one hand and holding up Eva's hand with the other.

"Then, I want to see all our people together. I have some things I *must* say to them," said Eva.

"Well," said St. Clare, in a tone of dry endurance.

Miss Ophelia despatched a messenger, and soon the whole of the servants were convened in the room.

Eva lay back on her pillows, her hair hanging loosely about her face, her crimson cheeks contrasting painfully with the intense whiteness of her complexion, and her soul-like eyes fixed earnestly on everyone.

The servants were struck with a sudden emotion. The spiritual face, the long locks of hair cut off and lying by her, her father's averted face, and Marie's sobs struck at once upon the feelings of a sensitive and impressible race. And as they came in, they looked one on another, sighed, and shook their heads. There was a deep silence, like that of a funeral.

Eva raised herself and looked long and earnestly round at everyone.

"I sent for you all, my dear friends," she said, "because I love you. I love you all. And I have something to say to you, which I want you always to remember. . . . I am going to leave you. In a few more weeks you will see me no more—"

Here the child was interrupted by bursts of groans, sobs,

and lamentations, which broke from all present, and in which
her slender voice was lost entirely. She waited a moment, and
then, speaking in a tone that checked the sobs of all, she
said:

"If you love me, you must not interrupt me so. Listen to
what I say. I want to speak to you about your souls. . . . Many
of you, I am afraid, are very careless. You are thinking only
about this world. I want you to remember that there is a
beautiful world, where Jesus is. I am going there, and you can
go there. It is for you, as much as me. But if you want to go
there, you must not live idle, careless, thoughtless lives. You
must be Christians. You must remember that each one of you
can become angels, and be angels forever. . . . If you want to
be Christians, Jesus will help you. You must pray to him. You
must read—"

The child checked herself, looked piteously at them, and
said sorrowfully:

"Oh, dear! You *can't* read, poor souls!" And she hid her
face in the pillow and sobbed, while many a smothered sob
from those she was addressing, who were kneeling on the
floor, aroused her.

"Never mind," she said, raising her face and smiling
brightly through her tears. "I have prayed for you, and I
know Jesus will help you, even if you can't read. Try all to
do the best you can. Pray every day. Ask Him to help you,
and get the Bible read to you whenever you can. And I think
I shall see you all in heaven."

"Amen," was the murmured response from the lips of
Tom and Mammy and some of the elder ones, who belonged
to the Methodist church. The younger and more thoughtless
ones, for the time completely overcome, were sobbing, with
their heads bowed upon their knees.

"I know," said Eva, "you all love me."

"Yes! Oh, yes! Indeed we do! Lord bless her!" was the
answer of all.

"Yes, I know you do! There isn't one of you that hasn't

always been very kind to me. And I want to give you something that, when you look at, you shall always remember me. I'm going to give all of you a curl of my hair, and when you look at it, think that I loved you and am gone to Heaven, and that I want to see you all there."

It is impossible to describe the scene, as with tears and sobs they gathered around the little creature and took from her hands what seemed to them a last mark of her love. They fell on their knees. They sobbed, and prayed, and kissed the hem of her garment. And the older ones poured forth words of endearment, mingled in prayers and blessings.

As each one took their gift, Miss Ophelia, who was apprehensive for the effect of all this excitement on her little patient, signed to each one to pass out of the apartment.

At last all were gone but Mammy and Uncle Tom.

"Here, Uncle Tom," said Eva, "is a beautiful one for you. Oh, I am so happy, Uncle Tom, to think I shall see you in heaven—for I'm sure I shall. And Mammy—dear, kind Mammy!" she said, fondly throwing her arms around her old nurse. "I know you'll be there, too."

"Oh, Miss Eva, don't see how I can live without ye, nohow!" said the faithful creature. " 'Pears like it's just taking everything off the place to oncet!" And Mammy gave way to a passion of grief.

Miss Ophelia pushed her and Tom gently from the apartment, and thought they were all gone. But as she turned, Topsy was standing there.

"Where did you start up from?" she said suddenly.

"I was here," said Topsy, wiping the tears from her eyes. "Oh, Miss Eva, I've been a bad girl, but won't you give *me* one, too?"

"Yes, poor Topsy! To be sure I will. There—every time you look at that, think that I love you, and wanted you to be a good girl."

"Oh, Miss Eva, I *is* tryin'!" said Topsy earnestly. "But,

Lor, it's so hard to be good! 'Pears like I an't used to it, no ways!'"

"Jesus knows it, Topsy. He is sorry for you. He will help you."

Topsy, with her eyes hid in her apron, was silently passed from the apartment by Miss Ophelia. But as she went, she hid the precious curl in her bosom.

All being gone, Miss Ophelia shut the door. That worthy lady had wiped away many tears of her own during the scene, but concern for the consequence of such an excitement to her young charge was uppermost in her mind.

St. Clare had been sitting, during the whole time, with his hand shading his eyes, in the same attitude. When they were all gone, he sat so still.

"Papa!" said Eva gently, laying her hand on his.

He gave a sudden start and shiver, but made no answer.

"Dear Papa!" said Eva.

"I *cannot*," said St. Clare rising, "I *cannot* have it so! The Almighty hath dealt *very bitterly* with me!" And St. Clare pronounced these words with a bitter emphasis indeed.

"Augustine! Has not God a right to do what He will with His own?" said Miss Ophelia.

"Perhaps so. But that doesn't make it any easier to bear," said he with a dry, hard, tearless manner, as he turned away.

"Papa, you break my heart!" said Eva, rising and throwing herself into his arms. "You must not feel so!" And the child sobbed and wept with a violence which alarmed them all, and turned her father's thoughts at once to another channel.

"There, Eva—there, dearest! Hush! hush! I was wrong; I was wicked. I will feel any way, do any way—only don't distress yourself. Don't sob so. I will be resigned. I was wicked to speak as I did."

Eva soon lay like a wearied dove in her father's arms, and he, bending over her, soothed her by every tender word he could think of.

Marie rose and threw herself out of the apartment into her own, where she fell into violent hysterics.

"You didn't give me a curl, Eva," said her father, smiling sadly.

"They are all yours, Papa," said she, smiling—"yours and Mamma's. And you must give dear Aunty as many as she wants. I only gave them to our people myself because you know, Papa, they might be forgotten when I am gone, and because I hoped it might help them remember. . . . You are a Christian, are you not, Papa?" said Eva doubtfully.

"Why do you ask me?"

"I don't know. You are so good, I don't see how you can help it."

"What is being a Christian, Eva?"

"Loving Christ most of all," said Eva.

"Do you, Eva?"

"Certainly I do."

"You never saw Him," said St. Clare.

"That makes no difference," said Eva. "I believe Him and in a few days I shall *see* Him." And the young face grew fervent, radiant with joy.

St. Clare said no more.

Eva, after this, declined rapidly. There was no more any doubt of the event—the fondest hope could not be blinded. Her beautiful room was avowedly a sickroom, and Miss Ophelia day and night performed the duties of a nurse. And never did her friends appreciate her value more than in that capacity. With so well-trained a hand and eye, such perfect adroitness and practice in every art which could promote neatness and comfort, and keep out of sight every disagreeable incident of sickness—with such a perfect sense of time, such a clear, untroubled head, such exact accuracy in remembering every prescription and direction of the doctor's—she was everything to them. They who had shrugged their shoulders at her little peculiarities and setnesses, so unlike the careless freedom of Southern manners, acknowledged that now she was the exact person that was wanted.

Uncle Tom was much in Eva's room. The child suffered from nervous restlessness, and it was a relief to her to be carried. And it was Tom's greatest delight to carry her little frail form in his arms, resting on a pillow, now up and down her room, now out into the verandah. And when the fresh breezes blew from the lake, he would sometimes walk with her under the orange-trees in the garden, or, sitting down in some of their old seats, sing to her their favorite old hymns.

Her father often did the same thing, but his frame was slighter, and when he was weary, Eva would say to him:

"Oh, Papa, let Tom take me. Poor fellow! It pleases him, and, you know, it's all he can do now, and he wants to do something."

"So do I, Eva," said her father.

"Well, Papa, you can do everything, and are everything to me. You read to me, you sit up nights, and Tom has only this one thing, and his singing. And I know, too, he does it easier than you can. He carries me so strong!"

The desire to do something was not confined to Tom. Every servant in the establishment showed the same feeling, and in their way did what they could.

Poor Mammy's heart yearned toward her darling. But she found no opportunity, night or day, as Marie declared that the state of her mind was such it was impossible for her to rest. And, of course, it was against her principles to let anyone else rest.

"I feel it my duty to be particularly careful of myself now," she would say, "feeble as I am, and with the whole care and nursing of that dear child upon me."

"Indeed, my dear," said St. Clare, "I thought our cousin relieved you of that."

"You talk like a man, St. Clare—just as if a mother *could* be relieved of the care of a child in that state. But then, it's all alike—no one ever knows what I feel! I can't throw things off as you do."

St. Clare smiled. You must excuse him, he couldn't help it—for St. Clare could smile yet. For so bright and placid was the farewell voyage of the little spirit that it was impossible to realize that death was approaching. The child felt no pain, only a tranquil, soft weakness, daily increasing. And she was so beautiful, so loving, so trustful, so happy, that one could not resist the soothing influence which seemed to breathe around her. St. Clare found a strange calm coming over him. It was not hope—that was impossible. It was not resignation. It was only a calm resting in the present, which seemed so beautiful that he wished to think of no future.

The friend who knew most of Eva's own imaginings was her faithful bearer, Tom. To him she said what she would not disturb her father by saying. Tom at last would not sleep in his room, but lay all night in the outer verandah, ready to rouse at every call.

"Uncle Tom, what alive have you taken to sleeping anywhere and everywhere, like a dog, for?" said Miss Ophelia. "I thought you was one of the orderly sort, that liked to lie in bed in a Christian way."

"I do, Miss Feely," said Tom mysteriously. "I do, but now—"

"Well, what now?"

"We mustn't speak loud. Mas'r St. Clare won't hear on 't. But, Miss Feely, you know the Lord, he sends his messenger in the soul. I must be thar, Miss Feely. For when that ar blessed child goes into the kingdom, they'll open the door so wide, we'll all get a look in at the glory, Miss Feely."

"Uncle Tom, did Miss Eva say she felt more unwell than usual tonight?"

"No, but she told me, this morning, she was coming nearer—thar's them that tells it to the child, Miss Feely. It's the angels—it's 'the trumpet sound afore the break o' day,' " said Tom, quoting from a favorite hymn.

This dialogue passed between Miss Ophelia and Tom between ten and eleven one evening after her arrangements had all been made for the night, when on going to bolt her outer door, she found Tom stretched along by it in the outer verandah.

She was not nervous, but the solemn, heartfelt manner struck her. Eva had been unusually bright and cheerful that afternoon, and had sat raised in her bed, and looked over all her little trinkets and precious things, and designated the friends to whom she would have them given. And her manner was more animated, and her voice more natural, than they had known it for weeks. Her father had been in, in the evening, and had said that Eva appeared more like her former self than ever she had done since her sickness. And when he kissed her for the night, she said to Miss Ophelia, "Cousin, we may keep her with us, after all. She is certainly better." And he had retired with a lighter heart in his bosom than he had had there for weeks.

But at midnight—strange, mystic hour!—when the veil between the frail present and the eternal future grows thin— then came the messenger!

There was a sound in that chamber, first of one who stepped quickly. It was Miss Ophelia, who had resolved to sit up all night with her little charge, and who, at the turn of the night, had discerned what experienced nurses significantly call "a change." The outer door was quickly opened, and Tom, who was watching outside, was on the alert in a moment.

"Go for the doctor, Tom! Lose not a moment," said Miss Ophelia. And stepping across the room, she rapped at St. Clare's door.

"Cousin," she said, "I wish you would come."

Those words fell on his heart like clods upon a coffin. Why did they? He was up and in the room in an instant and bending over Eva, who still slept.

They stood there so still gazing upon her that even the ticking of the watch seemed too loud. In a few moments Tom returned with the doctor. He entered, gave one look, and stood silent as the rest.

"When did this change take place?" said he, in a low whisper, to Miss Ophelia.

"About the turn of the night," was the reply.

Marie, roused by the entrance of the doctor, appeared hurriedly from the next room.

"Augustine! Cousin!—Oh!—What—" she hurriedly began.

"Hush!" said St. Clare hoarsely. "*She is dying!*"

Mammy heard the words and flew to awaken the servants. The house was roused—lights were seen, footsteps heard, anxious faces thronged the verandah and looked tearfully through the glass doors. But St. Clare heard and saw nothing —he saw only *that look* on the face of the little sleeper.

"Oh, if she would only wake and speak once more!" he said. And stooping over her, he spoke in her ear, "Eva, darling!"

The large blue eyes unclosed—a smile passed over her face. She tried to raise her head and to speak.

"Do you know me, Eva?"

"Dear Papa," said the child, with a last effort, throwing her arms about his neck. In a moment they dropped again. And as

St. Clare raised his head, he saw a spasm of mortal agony pass over the face—she struggled for breath, and threw up her little hands.

"Oh, God, this is dreadful!" he said, turning away in agony and wringing Tom's hand, scarce conscious what he was doing. "Oh, Tom, my boy, it is killing me!"

Tom had his master's hands between his own, and with tears streaming down his dark cheeks, looked up for help where he had always been used to look.

"Pray that this may be cut short!" said St. Clare. "This wrings my heart."

"Oh, bless the Lord! It's over—it's over, dear Mas'r!" said Tom. "Look at her."

The child lay panting on her pillows, as one exhausted—the large clear eyes rolled up and fixed. Ah, what said those eyes, that spoke so much of heaven? Earth was past, and earthly pain. But so solemn, so mysterious was the triumphant brightness of that face that it checked even the sobs of sorrow. They pressed around her in breathless stillness.

"Eva," said St. Clare gently.

She did not hear.

"Oh, Eva, tell us what you see! What is it?" said her father.

A bright, a glorious, smile passed over her face, and she said brokenly, "Oh, love—joy—peace!" gave one sigh, and passed from death unto life.

"This Is the Last of Earth"

THE statuettes and pictures in Eva's room were shrouded in white napkins. Only hushed breathings and muffled footfalls were heard in that chamber, and the light stole in solemnly through windows partially darkened by closed blinds. The bed was draped in white. And there, beneath the drooping angel-figure, lay a sleeping form—sleeping never to awaken.

There she lay, robed in one of the simple white dresses she had been wont to wear when living. The rose-colored light through the curtains cast over the icy coldness of death a warm glow. The heavy eyelashes drooped softly on the pure cheek. The head was turned a little to one side, as if in natural sleep.

St. Clare, with folded arms, stood there gazing. Ah, who shall say what he was thinking? From the hour that voices had said in the dying chamber, "She is gone," it has been all a dreary mist, a heavy "dimness of anguish." He had heard voices around him. He had had questions asked, and answered them. They had asked him when he would have the funeral, and where they should lay her. And he had answered impatiently that he cared not.

Adolph and Rosa had arranged the chamber. Fickle and childish as they generally were, they were soft-hearted and full of feeling, and while Miss Ophelia presided over the general details of order and neatness, it was their hands that added those soft, poetic touches to the arrangements that took from the death room the grim and ghastly air which too often marks a New England funeral.

There were still flowers on the shelves—all white, delicate and fragrant. Eva's little table, covered with white, bore on it her favorite vase, with a single white moss rosebud in it. The folds of the drapery, the fall of the curtains, had been arranged and rearranged by Adolph and Rosa. Even now, while St. Clare stood there thinking, little Rosa tripped softly into the chamber with a basket of white flowers. She stepped back when she saw St. Clare and stopped respectfully. But seeing that he did not observe her, she came forward to place them around the dead. St. Clare saw her as in a dream while she placed in the small hands a fair cape jessamine, and with admirable taste disposed other flowers around the couch.

The door opened again, and Topsy, her eyes swelled with crying, appeared, holding something under her apron. Rosa made a quick, forbidding gesture, but she took a step into the room.

"You must go out," said Rosa in a sharp, positive whisper. "*You* haven't any business here!"

"Oh, do let me! I brought a flower—such a pretty one!" said Topsy, holding up a half-blown tea rosebud. "Do let me put just one there."

"Get along!" said Rosa, more decidedly.

"Let her stay!" said St. Clare, suddenly stamping his foot. "She shall come."

Rosa suddenly retreated, and Topsy came forward and laid her offering at the feet of the corpse. Then suddenly, with a wild and bitter cry, she threw herself on the floor alongside the bed, and wept, and moaned aloud.

Miss Ophelia hastened into the room and tried to raise and silence her, but in vain.

"Oh, Miss Eva, Oh, Miss Eva! I wish I's dead, too—I do!"

There was a piercing wildness in the cry. The blood flushed into St. Clare's white, marble-like face, and the first tears he had shed since Eva died stood in his eyes.

"Get up, child," said Miss Ophelia in a softened voice. "Don't cry so. Miss Eva is gone to heaven. She is an angel."

"But I can't see her!" said Topsy. "I never shall see her!" and she sobbed again.

They all stood a moment in silence.

"*She* said she *loved* me," said Topsy, "she did! Oh, dear! oh dear! There an't *nobody* left now—there ain't!"

"That's true enough," said St. Clare. "But do," he said to Miss Ophelia, "see if you can't comfort the poor creature."

"I jest wish I hadn't never been born," said Topsy. "I didn't want to be born, no ways. And I don't see no use on 't."

Miss Ophelia raised her gently, but firmly, and took her

from the room. But as she did so, some tears fell from her eyes.

"Topsy, you poor child," she said as she led her into her room, "don't give up! *I* can love you, though I am not like that dear little child. I hope I've learnt something of the love of Christ from her. I can love you. I do, and I'll try to help you to grow up a good Christian girl."

Miss Ophelia's voice was more than her words, and more than that were the honest tears that fell down her face. From that hour she acquired an influence over the mind of the destitute child that she never lost.

"Oh, my Eva, whose little hour on earth did so much of good," thought St. Clare, "what account have I to give for my long years?"

There were, for a while, soft whisperings and footfalls in the chamber, as one after another stole in to look at the dead. And then came the little coffin. And then there was a funeral, and carriages drove to the door, and strangers came and were seated. And there were white scarfs and ribbons, and crape bands, and mourners dressed in black crape. And there were words read from the Bible, and prayers offered.

And St. Clare lived, and walked, and moved, as one who has shed every tear. To the last he saw only one thing—that golden head in the coffin. But then he saw the cloth spread over it, the lid of the coffin closed. And he walked, when he was put beside the others, down to a little place at the bottom of the garden, and there, by the mossy seat where she and Tom had talked, and sung, and read so often, was the little grave. St. Clare stood beside it—looked vacantly down. He saw them lower the little coffin. He heard, dimly, the solemn words: "I am the resurrection and the Life; he that believeth in me, though he were dead, yet shall he live." And as the earth was cast in and filled up the grave, he could not realize that it was Eva that they were hiding from his sight.

And then all were gone, and the mourners went back to the place which should know her no more. And Marie's room was darkened, and she lay on the bed, sobbing and moaning in uncontrollable grief, and calling every moment for the attentions of all her servants. Of course, they had no time to cry—why should they? The grief was *her* grief, and she was fully convinced that nobody on earth did, could, or would feel it as she did.

"St. Clare did not shed a tear," she said. "He didn't sympathize with her. It was perfectly wonderful to think how hardhearted and unfeeling he was, when he must know how she suffered."

So much are people the slave of their eye and ear, that many of the servants really thought that Missis was the principal sufferer in the case, especially as Marie began to have hysterical spasms, and sent for the doctor, and at last declared herself dying. And in the running and scampering, and bringing up hot bottles, and heating of flannels, and chafing, and fussing that ensued, there was quite a diversion.

Tom, however, had a feeling at his own heart that drew him to his master. He followed him wherever he walked, wistfully and sadly. And when he saw him sitting, so pale and quiet, in Eva's room, holding before his eyes her little open Bible, though seeing no letter or word of what was in it, there was more sorrow to Tom in that still, fixed, tearless eye than in all Marie's moans and lamentations.

In a few days Augustine, with the restlessness of grief, longed for another scene to change the current of his thoughts. So they left the house, and the garden with its little grave, and came back to New Orleans. And St. Clare walked the streets busily, and strove to fill up the chasm in his heart with hurry and bustle and change of place. And people who saw him in the street, or met him at the café, knew of his loss only by the weed on his hat. For there he was, smiling and talking, and reading the newspaper, and speculating on politics, and attending to business matters. And who could see that all this smiling outside was but a hollow shell over a heart that was a dark and silent sepulcher?

"Mr. St. Clare is a singular man," said Marie to Miss Ophelia in a complaining tone. "I used to think if there was anything in the world he did love, it was our dear little Eva. But he seems to be forgetting her very easily. I cannot ever get him to talk about her. I really did think he would show more feeling!"

"Still waters run deepest, they used to tell me," said Miss Ophelia.

"Oh, I don't believe in such things. It's all talk. If people have feeling, they will show it—they can't help it. But then, it's a great misfortune to have feeling. I'd rather have been made like St. Clare. My feelings prey upon me so!"

"Sure, Missis, Mas'r St. Clare is gettin' thin as a shader. They say he don't never eat nothin'," said Mammy. "I know he don't forget Miss Eva. I know there couldn't nobody— dear little blessed cretur!" she added, wiping her eyes.

"Well, at all events, he has no consideration for me," said Marie. "He hasn't spoken one word of sympathy, and he must know how much more a mother feels than any man can."

"The heart knoweth its own bitterness," said Miss Ophelia gravely.

"That's just what I think. I know just what I feel—nobody else seems to. Eva used to, but she is gone!" And Marie lay back on her lounge and began to sob disconsolately.

While this conversation was taking place in the parlor, another was going on in St. Clare's library.

Tom had seen him go to his library some hours before, and after vainly waiting for him to come out, determined at last to make an errand in. He entered softly. St. Clare lay on his lounge, at the further end of the room. He was lying on his face, with Eva's Bible open before him, at a little distance. Tom walked up and stood by the sofa. He hesitated, and while he was hesitating, St. Clare suddenly raised himself up. The honest face, so full of grief, and with such an imploring expression of affection and sympathy, struck his master. He laid his hand on Tom's and bowed down his forehead on it.

"Oh, Tom, my boy, the whole world is as empty as an eggshell."

"I know it, Mas'r, I know it," said Tom. "But oh, if Mas'r could only look up—up where our dear Miss Eva is—up to the dear Lord Jesus!"

"Ah, Tom! I do look up, but the trouble is, I don't see anything when I do. I wish I could."

Tom sighed heavily.

"It seems to be given to children and poor, honest fellows, like you, to see what we can't," said St. Clare. "How comes it?"

"Thou hast 'hid from the wise and prudent, and revealed unto babes,' " murmured Tom. " 'Even so, Father, for so it seemed good in thy sight.' "

"Tom, I don't believe—I can't believe—I've got the habit of doubting," said St. Clare. "I want to believe this Bible—and I can't."

"Dear Mas'r, pray to the good Lord—'Lord, I believe; help thou my unbelief.' "

"Who knows anything about anything?" said St. Clare, his eyes wandering dreamily, and speaking to himself. "Was all that beautiful love and faith only one of the ever-shifting phases of human feeling, passing away with the breath? And is there no more Eva—no heaven—no Christ—nothing?"

"Oh, dear Mas'r, there is! I know it, I'm sure of it," said Tom, falling on his knees. "Do, do, dear Mas'r, believe it!"

"How do you know there's any Christ, Tom? You never saw the Lord."

"Felt Him in my soul, Mas'r—feel Him now! Oh, Mas'r, when I was sold away from my old woman and the chil'en, I was jest a'most broke up. I felt as if there warn't nothin' left. And then the good Lord, He stood by me, and He said, 'Fear not, Tom.' And He brings light and joy into a poor feller's soul—makes all peace. And I's so happy, and loves every-body, and feels willin' jest to be the Lord's, and have the Lord's will done, and be put jest where the Lord wants to put me. I know it couldn't come from me, cause I's a poor, com-plainin' cretur. It comes from the Lord. And I know He's willin' to do for Mas'r."

Tom spoke with fast-running tears and choking voice. St. Clare leaned his head on his shoulder, and wrung the hard, faithful, black hand.

"Tom, you love me," he said.

"I's willin' to lay down my life, this blessed day, to see Mas'r a Christian."

"Poor, foolish boy!" said St. Clare, half-raising himself. "I'm not worth the love of one good, honest heart like yours."

"Oh, Mas'r, dere's more than me love you—the blessed Lord Jesus loves you."

"How do you know that, Tom?" said St. Clare.

"Feels it in my soul. Oh, Mas'r, 'The love of Christ, that passeth knowledge.' "

"Singular," said St. Clare, turning away, "that the story of a man that lived and died eighteen hundred years ago can affect people so yet! But he was no man," he added suddenly. "No man ever had such long and living power! Oh that I could believe what my mother taught me, and pray as I did when I was a boy!"

"If Mas'r pleases," said Tom, "Miss Eva used to read this so beautifully. I wish Mas'r be so good as read it. Don't get no readin', hardly, now Miss Eva's gone."

The chapter was the eleventh of John, the touching ac-count of the raising of Lazarus. St. Clare read it aloud, often pausing to wrestle down feelings which were roused by the pathos of the story. Tom knelt before him, with clasped hands, and with an absorbed expression of love, trust, adora-tion, on his quiet face.

"Tom," said his master, "this is all *real* to you!"

"I can jest fairly *see* it, Mas'r," said Tom.

"I wish I had your eyes, Tom."

"I wish to the dear Lord, Mas'r had!"

"But, Tom, you know that I have a great deal more knowledge than you. What if I should tell you that I don't believe this Bible?"

"Oh, Mas'r!" said Tom, holding up his hands with a disapproving gesture.

"Wouldn't it shake your faith some, Tom?"

"Not a grain," said Tom.

"Why, Tom, you must know I know the most."

"Oh, Mas'r, haven't you jest read how He hides from the wise, and prudent, and reveals unto babes? But Mas'r wasn't in earnest, for sartin, now?" said Tom anxiously.

"No, Tom, I was not. I don't disbelieve, and I think there is reason to believe. And still I don't. It's a troublesome bad habit I've got, Tom."

"If Mas'r would only pray!"

"How do you know I don't, Tom?"

"Does Mas'r?"

"I would, Tom, if there was anybody there when I pray. But it's all speaking unto nothing, when I do. But come, Tom, you pray, now, and show me how."

Tom's heart was full. He poured it out in prayer, like waters that have been long suppressed. One thing was plain enough: Tom *thought* there was somebody to hear, whether there was or not. In fact, St. Clare felt himself borne, on the tide of his faith and feeling, almost to the gates of that heaven he seemed so vividly to conceive. It seemed to bring him nearer to Eva.

"Thank you, my boy," said St. Clare when Tom rose. "I like to hear you, Tom. But go, now, and leave me alone. Some other time I'll talk more."

Tom silently left the room.

Reunion

Week after week glided away, and the waves of life settled back to their usual flow. For still must we eat, and drink, and sleep, and wake again, after all vital interest in living has fled.

All the interests and hopes of St. Clare's life had unconsciously wound themselves around his child. It was for Eva that he had managed his property. It was for Eva that he had planned the disposal of his time. And to do this and that for Eva—to buy, improve, alter, and arrange, or dispose something for her—had been so long his habit, that now she was gone, there seemed nothing to be thought of, and nothing to be done. He read his little Eva's Bible seriously and honestly. He thought more soberly and practically of his relations to his servants—enough to make him extremely dissatisfied with both his past and present course. And one thing he did, soon after his return to New Orleans, was to commence the legal steps necessary to Tom's emancipation, which was to be perfected as soon as he could get through the necessary formalities.

Meanwhile, he attached himself to Tom more and more every day. In all the wide world, there was nothing that seemed to remind him so much of Eva. And he would insist on keeping him constantly about him. Unapproachable as he was with regard to his deeper feelings, he almost thought aloud to Tom. Nor would anyone have wondered at it who had seen the expression of affection and devotion with which Tom continually followed his young master.

"Well, Tom," said St. Clare, the day after he had commenced the legal formalities for his enfranchisement, "I'm going to make a free man of you. So have your trunk packed, and get ready to set out for Kentuck."

The sudden light of joy that shone in Tom's face as he raised his hands to heaven, his emphatic "Bless the Lord!" rather discomposed St. Clare. He did not like it that Tom should be so ready to leave him.

"You haven't had such very bad times here that you need be in such a rapture, Tom," he said dryly.

"No, no, Mas's! 'Tan't that—it's bein' a *free man!* That's what I'm joyin' for."

"Why, Tom, don't you think, for your own part, you've been better off than to be free?"

"*No, indeed,* Mas'r St. Clare," said Tom, with a flash of energy. "No, indeed!"

"Why, Tom, you couldn't possibly have earned, by your work, such clothes and such living as I have given you."

"Knows all that, Mas'r St. Clare. Mas'r's been too good. But, Mas'r, I'd rather have poor clothes, poor house, poor everything and have 'em *mine,* than have the best and have 'em any man's else—I had *so,* Mas'r. I think it's natur, Mas'r."

"I suppose so, Tom, and you'll be going off and leaving me in a month or so," he added, rather discontentedly. "Though why you shouldn't, no mortal knows," he said in a gayer tone. And getting up, he began to walk the floor.

"Not while Mas'r is in trouble," said Tom. "I'll stay with Mas'r as long as he wants me—so as I can be any use."

"Not while I'm in trouble, Tom?" said St. Clare, looking sadly out of the window. . . . "And when *will* my trouble be over?"

"When Mas'r St. Clare's a Christian," said Tom.

"And you really mean to stay by till that day comes?" said St. Clare, half smiling, as he turned from the window and laid his hand on Tom's shoulder. "Ah, Tom, you soft, silly boy! I won't keep you till that day. Go home to your wife and children, and give my love to all."

"I's faith to believe that day will come," said Tom earnestly and with tears in his eyes. "The Lord has a work for Mas'r."

"A work, hey?" said St. Clare. "Well, now, Tom, give me your views on what sort of a work it is—let's hear."

"Why, even a poor fellow like me has a work from the Lord. And Mas'r St. Clare, that has larnin', and riches, and friends—how much he might do for the Lord!"

"Tom, you seem to think the Lord needs a great deal done for him," said St. Clare, smiling.

"We does for the Lord when we does for his critturs," said Tom.

"Good theology, Tom. Better than Dr. B. preaches, I dare swear," said St. Clare.

The conversation was here interrupted by the announcement of some visitors.

Marie St. Clare felt the loss of Eva as deeply as she could feel anything. And as she was a woman that had a great faculty of making everybody unhappy when she was, her immediate attendants had still stronger reason to regret the loss of their young mistress. Poor old Mammy, in particular, whose heart, severed from all natural domestic ties, had consoled itself with this one beautiful being, was almost heartbroken. She cried day and night and was, from excess of sorrow, less skillful and alert, which drew down a constant storm on her defenseless head.

Miss Ophelia felt the loss, but in her good and honest heart it bore fruit unto everlasting life. She was more softened, more gentle. She was more diligent in teaching Topsy and did not any longer shrink from her touch, or manifest an ill-repressed disgust, because she felt none. She saw in Topsy now only an immortal creature whom God had sent to be led by her to glory and virtue. Topsy did not become at once a saint. But the life and death of Eva did work a marked change in her. The callous indifference was gone. There was now hope, desire, and striving for good—a strife irregular, interrupted oft, but yet renewed again.

One day, when Topsy had been sent for by Miss Ophelia, she came hastily thrusting something into her bosom.

"What are you doing there, you limb? You've been stealing something, I'll be bound," said the imperious little Rosa, who had been sent to call her, seizing her at the same time roughly by the arm.

"You go 'long, Miss Rosa!" said Topsy, pulling from her. " 'Tan't none o' your business!"

"None o' your sa'ce!" said Rosa. "I saw you hiding something—I know yer tricks." And Rosa seized her arm and tried to force her hand into her bosom, while Topsy, enraged, kicked and fought valiantly for what she considered her rights. The clamor of the battle drew Miss Ophelia and St. Clare both to the spot.

"She's been stealing!" said Rosa.

"I han't neither!" sobbed Topsy.

"Give me that, whatever it is!" said Miss Ophelia firmly.

Topsy hesitated. But, on a second order, pulled out of her bosom a little parcel done up in the foot of one of her own old stockings.

Miss Ophelia turned it out. There was a small book, which had been given to Topsy by Eva, containing a single verse of Scripture arranged for every day in the year, and in a paper the curl of hair that she had given her on that memorable day when she had taken her last farewell.

St. Clare was a good deal affected at the sight of it. The little book had been rolled in a long strip of black crape, torn from the funeral weeds.

"What did you wrap *this* round the book for?" said St. Clare, holding up the crape.

"Cause—cause—cause 'twas Miss Eva's. Oh, don't take 'em away, please!" she said. And sitting flat down on the floor and putting her apron over her head, she began to sob with passion.

"Come, come, don't cry—you shall have them!" said St. Clare, and drew Miss Ophelia with him into the parlor.

"I really think you can make something of that concern," he said, pointing with his thumb backward over his shoulder. "Any mind that is capable of a *real sorrow* is capable of good. You must try and do something with her."

"The child has improved greatly," said Miss Ophelia. "I have great hopes of her. But, Augustine," she said, laying her hand on his arm, "one thing I want to ask. Whose is this child to be—yours or mine?"

"Why, I gave her to *you*," said Augustine.

"But not legally. I want her to be mine legally," said Miss Ophelia.

"Whew! Cousin!" said Augustine. "What will the Abolition Society think? They'll have a day of fasting appointed for this backsliding, if you become a slaveholder!"

"Oh, nonsense! I want her mine that I may have a right to take her to the free states and give her her liberty, that all I am trying to do be not undone."

"Oh, Cousin, what an awful 'doing evil that good may come!' I can't encourage it."

"I don't want you to joke, but to reason," said Miss Ophelia. "There is no use in my trying to make this child a Christian child unless I save her from all the chances and reverses of slavery. And if you really are willing I should have her, I want you to give me a deed of gift, or some legal paper."

"Well, well," said St. Clare, "I will." And he sat down and unfolded a newspaper to read.

"But I want it done now," said Miss Ophelia.

"What's your hurry?"

"Because now is the only time there ever is to do a thing in," said Miss Ophelia. "Come, now, here's paper, pen, and ink. Just write a paper."

St. Clare was considerably annoyed by Miss Ophelia's downrightness.

"Why, what's the matter?" said he. "Can't you take my word?"

"I want to make sure of it," said Miss Ophelia. "You may die, or fail, and then Topsy be hustled off to auction, spite of all I can do."

"Really, you are quite provident. Well, seeing I'm in the hands of a Yankee, there is nothing for it but to concede." And St. Clair rapidly wrote off a deed of gift and signed his name to it in sprawling capitals, concluding by a tremendous flourish.

"There, isn't that black and white now, Miss Vermont?" he said as he handed it to her.

"Good boy," said Miss Ophelia, smiling. "But must it not be witnessed?"

"Oh, bother, yes! Here," he said, opening the door into Marie's apartment, "Marie, Cousin wants your autograph. Just put your name down here."

"What's this?" said Marie, as she ran over the paper. "Ridiculous! I thought Cousin was too pious for such horrid things," she added, as she carelessly wrote her name. "But if she has a fancy for that article, I am sure she's welcome."

"There, now, she's yours, body and soul," said St. Clare, handing the paper.

"No more mine now than she was before," said Miss Ophelia. "Nobody but God has a right to give her to me. But I can protect her now."

St. Clare turned back into the parlor, and Miss Ophelia, who seldom sat much in Marie's company, followed him, having first carefully laid away the paper.

"Augustine," she said suddenly as she sat knitting while he read his paper, "have you ever made any provision for your servants in case of your death?"

"No," said St. Clare, as he read on.

"Then all your indulgence to them may prove a great cruelty by and by."

St. Clare had often thought the same thing himself, but he answered carelessly:

"Well, I mean to make a provision by and by."

"When?" said Miss Ophelia.

"Oh, one of these days."

"What if you should die first?"

"Cousin, what's the matter?" said St. Clare, laying down his paper and looking at her. "Do you think I show symptoms of yellow fever or cholera that you are making post mortem arrangements with such zeal?"

" 'In the midst of life we are in death,' " said Miss Ophelia.

St. Clare rose up and walked to the door that stood open on the verandah, to put an end to a conversation that was not agreeable to him. Mechanically he repeated the last word again—"*Death!* Strange that there should be such a word," he said, "and such a thing, and we ever forget it—that one should be living, warm and beautiful, full of hopes, desires, and wants one day, and the next be gone, utterly gone, and forever!"

St. Clare was absent and thoughtful all tea-time. After tea, he and Marie and Miss Ophelia took possession of the parlor almost in silence.

Marie disposed herself on a lounge, under a silken mosquito curtain, and was soon sound asleep. Miss Ophelia silently busied herself with her knitting. St. Clare sat down to the piano and began playing a sort of melancholy movement. He seemed in a deep reverie. After a little, he opened one of the drawers, took out an old music book whose leaves were yellow with age, and began turning it over.

"There," he said to Miss Ophelia. "This was one of my mother's books—and here is her handwriting—come and look at it. She copied and arranged this from Mozart's Requiem. It was something she used to sing often—I think I can hear her now."

He struck a few majestic chords and began singing.

Tom, who was listening in the outer verandah, was drawn by the sound to the very door, where he stood earnestly. He did not understand the Latin words, of course, but the music and manner of singing appeared to affect him strongly.

When St. Clare had done singing, he sat leaning his head upon his hand a few moments, and then began walking up and down the floor.

"I don't know what makes me think of my mother so much tonight," he said. "I have a strange kind of feeling, as if she were near me. I keep thinking of things she used to say. Strange, what brings these past things so vividly back to us sometimes!"

St. Clare walked up and down the room for some minutes more, and then said:

"I believe I'll go down street a few moments and hear the news tonight."

He took his hat and passed out.

Tom followed him to the passage, out of the court, and asked if he should attend him.

"No, my boy," said St. Clare. "I shall be back in an hour."

Tom sat down in the verandah. It was a beautiful moonlight evening, and he sat watching the rising and falling spray of the fountain, and listening to its murmur. Tom thought of his home, and that he should soon be a free man and able to return to it at will. He thought how he should work to buy his wife and boys. He felt the muscles of his brawny arms with a sort of joy, as he thought they would soon belong to himself, and how much they could do to work out the freedom of his family. Then he thought of his noble young master, and ever, second to that, came the prayer that he had always offered for him. And then his thoughts passed on to the beautiful Eva, whom he now thought of among the angels, and he thought till he almost fancied that that bright face and golden hair were looking upon him out of the spray of the fountain. And so musing, he fell asleep.

Tom was awakened by a loud knocking and a sound of many voices at the gate. He hastened to undo it. And with smothered voices and heavy tread, came several men, bringing a body, wrapped in a cloak and lying on a shutter. The light of the lamp fell full on the face, and Tom gave a wild cry of amazement and despair that rang through all the galleries, as the men advanced with their burden to the open parlor door, where Miss Ophelia sat knitting.

St. Clare had turned into a café to look over an evening paper. As he was reading, an affray arose between two gentlemen in the room, who were both partially intoxicated. St. Clare and one or two others made an effort to separate them, and St. Clare received a fatal stab in the side with a bowie knife, which he was attempting to wrest from one of them.

The house was full of cries and lamentations, shrieks and screams, servants frantically tearing their hair, throwing themselves on the ground, or running distractedly about, lamenting. Tom and Miss Ophelia alone seemed to have any presence of mind, for Marie was in strong hysteric convulsions. At Miss Ophelia's direction, one of the lounges in the parlor was hastily prepared, and the bleeding form laid upon it. St. Clare had fainted, through pain and loss of blood. But as Miss Ophelia applied restoratives, he revived, opened his eyes, and looked earnestly around the room. His eyes, traveling wistfully over every object, finally rested on his mother's picture.

The physician now arrived and made his examination. It was evident from the expression of his face that there was no hope. But he applied himself to dressing the wound, and he and Miss Ophelia and Tom proceeded composedly with this work amid the lamentations and sobs and cries of the affrighted servants, who had clustered about the doors and windows of the verandah.

"Now," said the physician, "we must turn all these creatures out. All depends on his being kept quiet."

St. Clare opened his eyes and looked fixedly on the distressed beings whom Miss Ophelia and the doctor were trying to urge from the apartment. "Poor creatures!" he said, and an expression of bitter self-reproach passed over his face. Adolph absolutely refused to go. Terror had deprived him of all presence of mind. He threw himself on the floor, and nothing could persuade him to rise. The rest yielded to Miss Ophelia's urgent representations that their master's safety depended on their stillness and obedience.

St. Clare could say but little. He lay with his eyes shut, but it was evident that he wrestled with bitter thoughts. After a while he laid his hand on Tom's, who was kneeling beside him, and said, "Tom, poor fellow!"

"What, Mas'r?" said Tom earnestly.

"I am dying!" said St. Clare, pressing his hand. "Pray."

"If you would like a clergyman—"said the physician.

St. Clare hastily shook his head and said again to Tom, more earnestly, "Pray!"

And Tom did pray, with all his mind and strength, for the soul that was passing—the soul that seemed looking so steadily and mournfully from those large, melancholy blue eyes.

When Tom ceased to speak, St. Clare reached out and took his hand, looking earnestly at him, but saying nothing. He closed his eyes, but still retained his hold. For in the gates of eternity the black hand and the white hold each other with equal clasp.

He murmured softly to himself at broken intervals. It was evident that the words he had been singing that evening were passing through his mind—words of entreaty addressed to Infinite Pity. His lips moved as parts of the hymn fell brokenly from them.

"His mind is wandering," said the doctor.

"No! It is coming HOME at last!" said St. Clare. "At last! At last!"

The effect of speaking exhausted him. The sinking paleness of death fell on him. But with it there fell, as if shed from the wings of some pitying spirit, a beautiful expression of peace, like that of a wearied child who sleeps.

So he lay for a few moments. They saw that the mighty hand was on him. Just before the spirit parted, he opened his eyes with a sudden light as of joy and recognition, said "Mother!" and then was gone.

The Unprotected

WE hear often of the distress of the Negro servants on the loss of a kind master. And with good reason. For no creature on God's earth is left more utterly unprotected and desolate than the slave in these circumstances.

The child who has lost a father has still the protection of friends, and of the law. He is something, and can do something—has acknowledged rights and position. The slave has none. The law regards him in every respect as devoid of rights as a bale of merchandise. He feels that there are ten chances of his finding an abusive and tyrannical master, to one of his finding a considerate and kind one. Therefore is it that the wail over a kind master is loud and long, as well it may be.

When St. Clare breathed his last, terror took hold of all his household. He had been stricken down so in a moment, in the flower and strength of his youth! Every room and gallery of the house resounded with sobs and shrieks of despair.

Marie, whose nervous system had been weakened by constant self-indulgence, had nothing to support the terror of the shock, and at the time her husband breathed his last, was passing from one fainting fit to another. Thus he to whom she had been joined in the mysterious tie of marriage passed from her forever without the possibility of even a parting word.

Miss Ophelia had remained with her kinsman to the last—all eye, all ear, all attention—doing everything of the little that could be done, and joining with her whole soul in the tender and impassioned prayers which the poor slave had poured forth for the soul of his dying master.

Tom's whole soul was filled with thoughts of eternity. And

while he ministered around the lifeless clay, he did not once think that the sudden stroke had left him in hopeless slavery. He felt at peace about his master. For in that hour when he had poured forth his prayer into the bosom of his Father, he had found an answer of quietness and assurance springing up within himself. Tom hoped and trusted, and was at peace.

But the funeral passed, with all its pageant of black crape, and prayers, and solemn faces. And back rolled the cool, muddy waves of everyday life, and up came the everlasting hard inquiry of "What's to be done next?"

It rose to the mind of Marie, as, surrounded by anxious servants, she sat up in a great easy chair and inspected samples of crape and bombazine. It rose to Miss Ophelia, who began to turn her thoughts towards her Northern home. It rose, in silent terrors, to the minds of the servants, who well knew the unfeeling, tyrannical character of the mistress in whose hands they were left.

It was about a fortnight after the funeral that Miss Ophelia, busied in her apartment, heard a gentle tap at the door. She opened it, and there stood Rosa, the pretty young quadroon, her hair in disorder, and her eyes swelled with crying.

"Oh, Miss Feely," she said, falling to her knees and catching the skirt of her dress, "*do, do go* to Miss Marie for me! Do plead for me! She's goin' to send me out to be whipped—look there!" and she handed to Miss Ophelia a paper.

It was an order, written in Marie's delicate Italian hand, to the master of a whipping establishment, to give the bearer fifteen lashes.

"What have you been doing?" said Miss Ophelia.

"You know, Miss Feely, I've got such a bad temper. It's very bad of me. I was trying on Miss Marie's dress, and she slapped my face, and I spoke out before I thought and was saucy. And she said that she'd bring me down, and have me know, once and for all, that I wasn't going to be so topping as I had been. And she wrote this, and says I shall carry it. I'd rather she'd kill me, right out."

Miss Ophelia stood considering, with the paper in her hand.

"You see, Miss Feely," said Rosa, "I don't mind the whipping so much, if Miss Marie or you was to do it. But to be sent to a *man!* And such a horrid man—the shame of it, Miss Feely!"

Miss Ophelia well knew that it was the universal custom to send women and young girls to whipping-houses, to the hands of the lowest of men—men vile enough to make this their profession—there to be subjected to shameful exposure and brutal correction. She had *known* it before. But hitherto she had never realized it, till she saw the slender form of Rosa almost convulsed with distress. All the honest blood of womanhood, the strong New England blood of liberty, flushed to her cheeks and throbbed bitterly in her indignant heart. But with habitual prudence and self-control, she mastered herself, and crushing the paper firmly in her hand, she merely said to Rosa:

"Sit down, child, while I go to your mistress."

"Shameful, monstrous, outrageous!" she said to herself as she was crossing the parlor.

She found Marie sitting up in her easy chair, with Mammy standing by her, combing her hair. Jane sat on the ground before her, busy in chafing her feet.

"How do you find yourself today?" said Miss Ophelia.

A deep sigh and a closing of the eyes was the only reply for a moment. Then Marie answered, "Oh, I don't know, Cousin. I suppose I'm as well as I ever shall be!" And Marie wiped her eyes with a cambric handkerchief, bordered with an inch deep of black.

"I came," said Miss Ophelia, with a short, dry cough, such as commonly introduces a difficult subject, "I came to speak with you about poor Rosa."

Marie's eyes were open wide enough now, and a flush rose to her sallow cheeks as she answered sharply:

"Well, what about her?"

"She is very sorry for her fault."

"She is, is she? She'll be sorrier before I've done with her! I've endured that child's impudence long enough. And now I'll bring her down—I'll make her lie in the dust!"

"But could not you punish her some other way—some way that would be less shameful?"

"I mean to shame her—that's just what I want. She has all her life presumed on her delicacy, and her good looks, and her lady-like airs, till she forgets who she is—and I'll give her one lesson that will bring her down, I fancy!"

"But, Cousin, consider that if you destroy delicacy and a sense of shame in a young girl, you deprave her very fast."

"Delicacy!" said Marie with a scornful laugh. "A fine word for such as she! I'll teach her, with all her airs, that she's no better than the raggedest black wench that walks the streets! She'll take no more airs with me!"

"You will answer to God for such cruelty!" said Miss Ophelia with energy.

"Cruelty? I'd like to know what the cruelty is! I wrote orders for only fifteen lashes, and told him to put them on lightly. I'm sure there's no cruelty there!"

"No cruelty!" said Miss Ophelia. "I'm sure any girl might rather be killed outright!"

"It might seem so to anybody with your feeling. But all these creatures get used to it. It's the only way they can be kept in order. Once let them feel that they are to take any airs about delicacy, and all that, and they'll run all over you, just as my servants always have. I've begun now to bring them under. And I'll have them all to know that I'll send one out to be whipped as soon as another, if they don't mind themselves!" said Marie, looking around her decidedly.

Jane hung her head and cowered at this, for she felt as if it was particularly directed to her. Miss Ophelia sat for a moment as if she had swallowed some explosive mixture and were ready to burst. Then recollecting the utter uselessness of contention with such a nature, she shut her lips resolutely, gathered herself up, and walked out of the room.

It was hard to go back and tell Rosa that she could do nothing for her. And shortly after, one of the man-servants came to say that her mistress had ordered him to take Rosa with him to the whipping-house, whither she was hurried, in spite of her tears and entreaties.

A few days after, Tom was standing musing by the balconies, when he was joined by Adolph, who, since the death of his master, had been entirely crestfallen and disconsolate. Adolph knew that he had always been an object of dislike to Marie, but while his master lived, he had paid but little attention to it. Now that he was gone, he had moved about in daily dread and trembling, not knowing what might befall him next. Marie had held several consultations with her lawyer. After communicating with St. Clare's brother, it was determined to sell the place and all the servants, except her own personal property, and these she intended to take with her and go back to her father's plantation.

"Do ye know, Tom, that we've all got to be sold?" said Adolph.

"How did you hear that?" said Tom.

"I hid myself behind the curtains when Missis was talking with her lawyer. In a few days we shall all be sent off to auction, Tom."

"The Lord's will be done!" said Tom, folding his arms and sighing heavily.

"We'll never get another such a master," said Adolph apprehensively. "But I'd rather be sold than take my chance under Missis."

Tom turned away—his heart was full. The hope of liberty, the thought of distant wife and children, rose up before his patient soul, as to the mariner shipwrecked almost in port rises the vision of the church-spire and loving roofs of his native village, seen over the top of some black wave only for one last farewell. He drew his arms tightly over his bosom, and choked back the bitter tears, and tried to pray. The poor old soul had such a singular, unaccountable prejudice in favor of liberty that it was a hard wrench for him. And the more he said "Thy will be done," the worse he felt.

He sought Miss Ophelia, who ever since Eva's death had treated him with marked and respectful kindness.

"Miss Feely," he said, "Mas'r St. Clare promised me my freedom. He told me that he had begun to take it out for me. And now, perhaps, if Miss Feely would be good enough to speak about it to Missis, she would feel like goin' on with it, as it was Mas'r St. Clare's wish."

"I'll speak for you, Tom, and do my best," said Miss Ophelia. "But if it depends on Mrs. St. Clare, I can't hope much for you. Nevertheless, I will try."

This incident occurred a few days after that of Rosa, while Miss Ophelia was busied in preparations to return North.

Seriously reflecting within herself, she considered that perhaps she had shown too hasty a warmth of language in her former interview with Marie, and she now resolved to be as agreeable as possible, and negotiate Tom's case with all the diplomatic skill of which she was mistress.

She found Marie reclining upon a lounge, supporting herself on one elbow by pillows, while Jane, who had been out shopping, was displaying before her certain samples of thin black stuffs.

"That will do," said Marie, selecting one. "Only I'm not sure about its being properly mourning."

"Laws, Missis," said Jane. "Mrs. General Derbennon wore just this very thing, after the General died last summer. It makes up lovely!"

"What do you think?" said Marie to Miss Ophelia.

"It's a matter of custom, I suppose," said Miss Ophelia. "You can judge about it better than I."

"The fact is," said Marie, "that I haven't a dress in the world that I can wear. And as I am going to break up the establishment and go off next week, I must decide upon something."

"Are you going so soon?"

"Yes. St. Clare's brother has written, and he and the lawyer think that the servants and furniture had better be put up at auction, and the place left with our lawyer."

"There's one thing I wanted to speak with you about," said Miss Ophelia. "Augustine promised Tom his liberty, and began the legal forms necessary to it. I hope you will use your influence to have it perfected."

"Indeed, I shall do no such thing!" said Marie sharply. "Tom is one of the most valuable servants on the place—it couldn't be afforded. Besides, what does he want of liberty? He's a great deal better off as he is."

"But he does desire it, very earnestly, and his master promised it," said Miss Ophelia.

"I dare say he does want it," said Marie. "They all want it, just because they are a discontented lot—always wanting what they haven't got. Now, I'm principled against emancipating in any case. Keep a Negro under the care of a master, and he does well enough and is respectable. But set them free, and they get lazy, and won't work, and take to drinking, and go all down to be mean, worthless fellows. I've seen it tried, hundreds of times. It's no favor to set them free."

"But Tom is so steady, industrious, and pious."

"Oh, you needn't tell me! I've seen a hundred like him. He'll do very well as long as he's taken care of—that's all."

"But then consider," said Miss Ophelia, "when you set him up for sale, the chances of his getting a bad master."

"Oh, that's all humbug!" said Marie. "It isn't one time in a hundred that a good fellow gets a bad master. Most masters are good, for all the talk that is made. I've lived and grown up here, in the South, and I never yet was acquainted with a master that didn't treat his servants well—quite as well as is worth while. I don't feel any fears on that head."

"Well," said Miss Ophelia energetically, "I know it was one of the last wishes of your husband that Tom should have his liberty. It was one of the promises that he made to dear little Eva on her deathbed, and I should not think you would feel at liberty to disregard it."

Marie had her face covered with her handkerchief at this appeal, and began sobbing and using her smelling-bottle with great energy.

"Everybody goes against me!" she said. "Everybody is so inconsiderate! I shouldn't have expected that *you* would bring up all these remembrances of my troubles to me—it's so inconsiderate! But nobody ever does consider—my trials are so peculiar. It's so hard, that when I had only one daughter, she should have been taken! And when I had a husband that just exactly suited me—and I'm so hard to be suited!—he should be taken! And you seem to have so little feeling for me, and keep bringing it up to me so carelessly, when you know how it overcomes me!" and Marie sobbed, and gasped for breath, and called Mammy to open the window, and to bring her the camphor bottle, and to bathe her head, and unhook her dress. And, in the general confusion that ensued Miss Ophelia made her escape to her apartment.

She saw at once that it would do no good to say anything

more. Miss Ophelia, therefore, did the next best thing she could for Tom—she wrote a letter to Mrs. Shelby for him, stating his troubles, and urging them to send to his relief.

The next day Tom and Adolph and some half a dozen other servants were marched down to a slave warehouse, to await the convenience of the trader, who was going to make up a lot for auction.

The Slave Warehouse

A SLAVE warehouse! Perhaps some of my readers conjure up horrible visions of such a place. But no, innocent friends. Human property is high in the market, and is, therefore, well fed, well cleaned, tended, and looked after, that it may come to sale sleek and strong and shining. A slave warehouse in New Orleans is a house externally not much unlike many others, kept with neatness—and where every day you may see arranged, under a sort of shed along the outside, rows of men and women, who stand there as a sign of the property sold within.

Then you shall be courteously entreated to call and examine and shall find an abundance of husbands, wives, brothers, sisters, fathers, mothers, and young children, to be "sold separately, or in lots to suit the convenience of the purchaser."

It was a day or two after the conversation between Marie and Miss Ophelia that Tom, Adolph, and about half a dozen others of the St. Clare estate were turned over to the loving kindness of Mr. Skeggs, the keeper of a depot on ——Street, to await the auction next day.

Tom had with him quite a sizable trunk full of clothing, as had most others of them. They were ushered, for the night, into a long room, where many other men of all ages, sizes, and shades of complexion were assembled, and from which roars of laughter and unthinking merriment were proceeding.

"Aha! That's right. Go it, boys, go it!" said Mr. Skeggs. "My people are always so merry! Sambo, I see!" he said, speaking approvingly to a burly Negro who was performing tricks of low buffoonery, which occasioned the shouts which Tom had heard.

As might be imagined, Tom was in no humor to join these proceedings. Setting his trunk as far as possible from the noisy group, he sat down on it and leaned his face against the wall.

"What dat ar nigger doin' here?" said Sambo, coming up to Tom after Mr. Skeggs had left the room. Sambo was a full black, of great size, very lively, glib, and full of trick and grimace.

"What you doin' here?" said Sambo, coming up to Tom, and poking him facetiously in the side. "Meditatin', eh?"

"I am to be sold at auction tomorrow," said Tom quietly.

"Sold at auction—haw! haw! Boys, an't this yer fun? I wish't I was gwine that ar way! Tell ye, wouldn't I make 'em laugh? But how is it—dis yer whole lot gwine tomorrow?" said Sambo, laying his hand freely on Adolph's shoulder.

"Please to let me alone!" said Adolph fiercely, straightening himself up with extreme disgust.

"Law, now, boys! Dis yer's one o' yer white niggers—kind o' cream color, ye know, scented!" said he, snuffing. "Oh, Lor! He'd do for a tobaccer-shop. They could keep him to scent snuff! Lor, he'd keep a whole shop a-gwine, he would!"

"I say, keep off, can't you?" said Adolph, enraged.

"Lor, now, how touchy we is—we white niggers! Look at us, now!" And Sambo gave a humorous imitation of Adolph's manner. "Here's de airs and graces. We's been in a good family, I spects."

"Yes," said Adolph. "I had a master that could have bought you all for old truck!"

"Lor, you did! Be hanged if they aren't lucky to get shet of

ye. Spects they's gwine to trade ye off with a lot o' cracked teapots and sich like!" said Sambo with a provoking grin.

Adolph, enraged at this taunt, flew furiously at his adversary, swearing and striking on every side of him. The rest laughed and shouted, and the uproar brought the keeper to the door.

"What now, boys? Order, order!" he said, coming in and flourishing a large whip.

All fled in different directions except Sambo, who, presuming on the favor which the keeper had to him, stood his ground, ducking his head with a grin whenever the master made a dive at him.

"Lor, Mas'r, 'tan't us—we's reglar stiddy. It's these yer new hands. They's real aggravatin'—kinder pickin' at us all time!"

The keeper at this turned upon Tom and Adolph, and distributing a few kicks and cuffs without much inquiry, and leaving general orders for all to be good boys and go to sleep, left the apartment.

While this scene was going on in the men's sleeping room, the reader may be curious to take a peep at the corresponding apartment allotted to the women. Stretched out in various attitudes over the floor, he may see numberless sleeping forms of every shade and complexion, from the purest ebony to white, and of all years, from childhood to old age, lying now asleep. Here is a fine bright girl of ten years, whose mother was sold out yesterday, and who tonight cried herself to sleep when nobody was looking at her. Here a worn old Negro woman, whose thin arms and calloused fingers tell of hard toil, waiting to be sold tomorrow, as a castoff article, for what can be got for her. And some forty or fifty others, with heads variously enveloped in blankets or articles of clothing, lie stretched around them.

But in a corner, sitting apart from the rest, are two females of a more interesting appearance than common. One of these is a respectably dressed mulatto woman, between forty and fifty, with soft eyes and a gentle, pleasant face. She has on her head a high-raised turban, made of a gay red Madras handkerchief of the first quality, and her dress is neatly fitted and of good material, showing that she has been provided for with a careful hand. By her side, and nestling closely to her, is a young girl of fifteen—her daughter. She is a quadroon, as may be seen from her fairer complexion, though her likeness to her mother is quite discernible. She has the same soft, dark eyes, with longer lashes, and her curling hair is of a luxuriant brown. She also is dressed with great neatness, and her white, delicate hands betray very little acquaintance with servile toil.

These two, whom we shall call Susan and Emmeline, had been the personal attendants of an amiable and pious lady of New Orleans, by whom they had been carefully and piously instructed and trained. They had been taught to read and write, diligently instructed in the truths of religion, and their lot had been as happy a one as in their condition it was possible to be. But the only son of their protectress had the management of her property, and by carelessness and extravagance involved it to a large amount, and at last failed. Both are weeping, but each quietly, that the other may not hear.

"Mother, just lay your head on my lap and see if you can't sleep a little," says the girl, trying to appear calm.

"I haven't any heart to sleep, Em. I can't. It's the last night we may be together!"

"Oh, Mother, don't say so! Perhaps we shall get sold together—who knows?"

"If 'twas anybody's else case, I should say so, too, Em," said the woman. "But I'm so feard of losin' you that I don't see anything but the danger."

"Why, Mother, the man said we were both likely, and would sell well."

Susan remembered the man's looks and words. With a deadly sickness at her heart, she remembered how he had looked at Emmeline's hands, and lifted up her curly hair, and pronounced her a first-rate article.

"Mother, I think we might do first rate if you could get a place as cook, and I as chambermaid or seamstress, in some family. I dare say we shall. Let's both look as bright and lively as we can, and tell all we can do, and perhaps we shall," said Emmeline.

"I want you to brush your hair all back straight tomorrow," said Susan.

"What for, Mother? I don't look near so well that way."

"Yes, but you'll sell better so."

"I don't see why!" said the child.

"Respectable families would be more apt to buy you if they saw you looked plain and decent, as if you wasn't trying to look handsome. I know their ways better'n you do," said Susan.

"Well, mother, then I will."

"And, Emmeline, if we shouldn't ever see each other again after tomorrow, if I'm sold way up on a plantation somewhere, and you somewhere else, always remember how you've been brought up, and all Missis has told you. Take your Bible with you, and your hymnbook. And if you're faithful to the Lord, he'll be faithful to you."

So speaks the poor soul in sore discouragement. For she knows that tomorrow any man, however vile and brutal, however godless and merciless, if he only has money to pay for her, may become owner of her daugher, body and soul. And then, how is the child to be faithful? She thinks of all this as she holds her daughter in her arms, and wishes that she were not handsome.

The soft, earnest, quiet moonbeam looks in fixedly, marking the bars of the grated windows on the prostrate, sleeping forms. The mother and daughter are singing together a wild and melancholy dirge, common as a funeral hymn among the slaves:

> Oh, where is weeping Mary?
> Oh, where is weeping Mary?
> 'Rived in the goodly land.

> She is dead and gone to Heaven;
> She is dead and gone to Heaven;
> 'Rived in the goodly land.

Sing on, poor souls! The night is short, and the morning will part you forever!

But now it is morning, and everybody is astir, and the worthy Mr. Skeggs is busy and bright, for a lot of goods is to be fitted out for auction. Orders are passed around to everyone to put on their best face and be spry. And now all are arranged in a circle for a last review before they are marched up to the Bourse.

Mr. Skeggs, with his palmetto on and his cigar in his mouth, walks around to put farewell touches on his wares.

"How's this?" he said, stepping in front of Susan and Emmeline. "Where's your curls, gal?"

The girl looked timidly at her mother, who, with the smooth adroitness common among her class, answered:

"I was telling her, last night, to put up her hair smooth and neat, and not havin' it flying about in curls—looks more respectable so."

"Bother!" said the man, turning to the girl. "You go right along and curl yourself real smart! Be back in quick time, too!" he added, giving a crack to a rattan he held in his hand. "You go and help her," he said to the mother. "Them curls may make a hundred dollars' difference in the sale of her."

Beneath a splendid dome were men of all nations, moving to and fro over the marble pave. On every side of the circular area were little tribunes, or stations, for the use of speakers and auctioneers. Two of these, on opposite sides of the area, were now occupied by brilliant and talented gentlemen, enthusiastically forcing up the bids of connoisseurs in their various wares. A third one, on the other side, still unoccupied, was surrounded by a group waiting the moment of sale to begin. And here we may recognize the St. Clare servants—Tom, Adolph, and others. And there, too, Susan and Emmeline, awaiting their turn with anxious and dejected faces. Various spectators, intending to purchase, or not intending, as the case might be, gathered around the group, handling, examining, and commenting on their various points and faces with the same freedom that a set of jockeys discuss the merits of a horse.

"Hulloa, Alf! What brings you here?" said a young exquisite, slapping the shoulder of a sprucely-dressed young man who was examining Adolph through an eyeglass.

"Well, I was wanting a valet, and I heard that St. Clare's lot was going. I thought I'd just look at his—"

"Catch me ever buying any of St. Clare's people! Spoilt niggers, every one. Impudent as the devil!" said the other.

"Never fear that!" said the first. "If I get 'em, I'll soon have their airs out of them. They'll soon find that they've another kind of master to deal with than Monsieur St. Clare. 'Pon my word, I'll buy that fellow. I like the shape of him."

"You'll find it'll take all you've got to keep him. He's deucedly extravagant!"

"Yes, but my lord will find that he *can't* be extravagant with *me*. Just let him be sent to the calaboose a few times and thoroughly dressed down! I'll tell you if it don't bring him to a sense of his ways. Oh, I'll reform him, up hill and down— you'll see. I buy him, that's flat!"

Tom had been standing wistfully examining the multitude of faces thronging around him for one whom he would wish to call master. And if you should ever be under the necessity, sir, of selecting, out of two hundred men, one who was to become your absolute owner and disposer, you would, perhaps, realize just as Tom did how few there were that you would feel at all comfortable in being made over to. Tom saw abundance of men—great, burly, gruff men; little chirping, dried men; long-favored, lank, hard men; and every variety of stubbed-looking, commonplace men, who pick up their fellowmen as one picks up chips, putting them into the fire or a basket with equal unconcern, according to their convenience. But he saw no St. Clare.

A little before the sale commenced, a short, broad, muscular man, in a checked shirt considerably open at the bosom, and pantaloons much the worse for dirt and wear, elbowed his way through the crowd, like one who is going actively into a business. And coming up to the group, he began to examine them systematically.

From the moment that Tom saw him approaching, he felt an immediate and revolting horror at him, that increased as he came near. He was evidently, though short, of gigantic strength. His round bullet head, large, light-gray eyes with their shaggy, sandy eyebrows, and stiff, wiry, sunburned hair, were rather unprepossessing items, it is to be confessed. His large, coarse mouth was distended with tobacco, the juice of which, from time to time, he ejected from him with great decision and explosive force. His hands were immensely large, hairy, sunburned, freckled, and dirty, and garnished with long nails in a very foul condition. This man proceeded to a very free personal examination of the lot. He seized Tom by the jaw and pulled open his mouth to inspect his teeth; made him strip up his sleeve to show his muscle; turned him round; made him jump and spring to show his paces.

"Where was you raised?" he added briefly.

"In Kentuck, Mas'r," said Tom, looking about as if for deliverance.

"What have you done?"

"Had care of Mas'r's farm," said Tom.

"Likely story!" said the other shortly as he passed on. He paused a moment before Adolph. Then spitting a discharge of tobacco juice on his well-blacked boots, and giving a contemptuous "umph," he walked on. Again he stopped before Susan and Emmeline. He put out his heavy, dirty hand and drew the girl toward him, passed it over her neck and bust, felt her arms, looked at her teeth, and then pushed her back against her mother, whose patient face showed the suffering she had been going through at every motion of the hideous stranger.

The girl was frightened and began to cry.

"Stop that, you minx!" said the salesman. "No whimpering here—the sale is going to begin." And accordingly the sale began.

Adolph was knocked off, at a good sum, to the young gentleman who had previously stated his intention of buying him. And the other servants of the St. Clare lot went to various bidders.

"Now, up with you, boy—d'ye hear?" said the auctioneer to Tom.

Tom stepped upon the block, gave a few anxious looks round. All seemed mingled in a common, indistinct noise—the clatter of the salesman crying off his qualifications in French and English, the quick fire of French and English bids. And almost in a moment came the final thump of the hammer, and the clear ring on the last syllable of the word "dollars," as the auctioneer announced his price, and Tom was made over. He had a master!

He was pushed from the block. The short, bullet-headed man, seizing him roughly by the shoulder, pushed him to one side, saying in a harsh voice, "Stand there, *you!*"

Tom hardly realized anything. But still the bidding went on, rattling, clattering, now French, now English. Down goes the hammer again—Susan is sold. She goes down from the block, stops, looks wistfully back—her daughter stretches her hands toward her. She looks with agony in the face of the man who has bought her—a respectable middle-aged man of benevolent countenance.

"Oh, Mas'r, please do buy my daughter!"

"I'd like to, but I'm afraid I can't afford it!" said the gentleman, looking with painful interest as the young girl mounted the block and looked around her with a frightened and timid glance.

The blood flushes painfully in her otherwise colorless cheek, her eye has a feverish fire, and her mother groans to see that she looks more beautiful than she ever saw her before. Bids rise in rapid succession.

"I'll do anything in reason," said the benevolent-looking gentleman, pressing in and joining with the bids. In a few moments they have run beyond his purse. He is silent. The auctioneer grows warmer. But bids gradually drop off. It lies now between an aristocratic old citizen and our bullet-headed acquaintance. The citizen bids for a few turns, contemptuously measuring his opponent. But the bullet-head has the advantage over him, both in obstinacy and concealed length of purse, and the controversy lasts but a moment. The ham-

mer falls—he has got the girl, body and soul, unless God help
her!

Her master is Mr. Legree, who owns a cotton plantation
on the Red River. She is pushed along into the same lot with
Tom and two other men, and goes off, weeping as she goes.

The benevolent gentleman is sorry. But then, the thing
happens every day. One sees girls and mothers crying at these
sales *always*. It can't be helped, et cetera. And he walks off
with his purchase in another direction.

The Middle Passage

On the lower part of a small, mean boat on the Red River,
Tom sat, chains on his wrists, chains on his feet, and a weight
heavier than chains on his heart. All had faded from his sky.
All had passed by him, as the trees and banks were now passing, to return no more. Kentucky home, with wife and children and indulgent owners; St. Clare home, with all its
refinements and splendors; the golden head of Eva, with its
saint-like eyes; the proud, gay, handsome, seemingly careless
yet ever kind St. Clare; hours of ease and indulgent leisure—all
gone. And in place thereof, *what* remains?

Mr. Simon Legree, Tom's master had purchased slaves at
one place and another in New Orleans to the number of
eight, and driven them, handcuffed, in couples of two and
two, down to the good steamer *Pirate*, which lay at the levee,
ready for a trip up the Red River. Having got them fairly on
board, and the boat being off, he came round to take a review
of them. Stopping opposite Tom, who had been attired for
sale in his best broadcloth suit, with well-starched linen and
shining boots, he briefly expressed himself as follows:

"Stand up!"

Tom stood up.

"Take off that stock!" And as Tom, encumbered by his fetters, proceeded to do it, he assisted him by pulling it, with no gentle hand, from his neck, and putting it in his pocket.

Legree now turned to Tom's trunk, and taking from it a pair of old pantaloons and a dilapidated coat, which Tom had been wont to put on about his stable-work, he said, liberating Tom's hands from the handcuffs and pointing to a recess in among the boxes:

"You go there and put these on."

Tom obeyed, and in a few moments returned.

"Take off your boots," said Mr. Legree.

Tom did so.

"There," said the former, throwing him a pair of coarse, stout shoes, such as were common among the slaves. "Put these on."

In Tom's hurried exchange, he had not forgotten to transfer his cherished Bible to his pocket. It was well he did so, for Mr. Legree, having refitted Tom's handcuffs, proceeded to investigate the contents of his pockets. He drew out a silk handkerchief and put it into his own pocket. Several little trifles, which Tom had treasured chiefly because they had amused Eva, he looked upon with a contemptuous grunt and tossed them over his shoulder into the river.

Tom's Methodist hymnbook, which in his hurry he had forgotten, Legree now held up and turned over.

"Humph! Pious, to be sure. So, what's yer name, you belong to the church, eh?"

"Yes, Mas'r," said Tom firmly.

"Well, I'll soon have *that* out of you. I have none o' yer bawling, praying, singing niggers on my place. So remember. Now, mind yourself," he said with a stamp and a fierce glance of his gray eye directed at Tom, "*I'm* your church now! You understand—you've got to be as *I* say."

Something within the silent black man answered *No!* And

as if repeated by an invisible voice, came the words: "Fear not! for I have redeemed thee. I have called thee by my name. Thou art MINE!"

But Simon Legree heard no voice. He only glared for a moment on the downcast face of Tom and walked off. He took Tom's trunk, which contained a very neat and abundant wardrobe, to the forecastle, where it was soon surrounded by various hands of the boat. With much laughing at the expense of niggers who tried to be gentlemen, the articles very readily were sold to one and another, and the empty trunk finally put up at auction. It was a good joke, they all thought, especially to see how Tom looked after his things as they were going this way and that. And then the auction of the trunk—that was funnier than all.

This little affair being over, Simon sauntered up again to his property.

"Now, Tom, I've relieved you of any extra baggage, you see. Take mighty good care of them clothes. It'll be long enough 'fore you get more. I go in for making niggers careful. One suit has to do for one year on my place."

Simon next walked up to the place where Emmeline was sitting, chained to another woman.

"Well, my dear," he said, chucking her under the chin, "keep up your spirits."

The involuntary look of horror and fright with which the girl regarded him did not escape his eye. He frowned fiercely.

"None o' your shines, gal! You's got to keep a pleasant face when I speak to ye—d'ye hear? And you, you old yellow poco moonshine!" he said, giving a shove to the mulatto woman to whom Emmeline was chained. "Don't you carry that sort of face! You's got to look chipper, I tell ye!

"I say, all on ye," he said, retreating a pace or two, "look at me—look at me—look me right in the eye—*straight*, now!" said he, stamping his foot at every pause.

As by a fascination, every eye was now directed to the glaring greenish-gray eyes of Simon.

"Now," said he, doubling his great, heavy fist into something resembling a blacksmith's hammer, "d'ye see this fist? Heft it!" he said, bringing it down on Tom's hand. "Look at these yer bones! Well, I tell ye this yer fist has got as hard as iron *knocking down niggers.* I never see the nigger yet I couldn't bring down with one crack," said he, bringing his fist down so near to the face of Tom that he winked and drew back. "I don't keep none o' yer cussed overseers. I does my own overseeing. And I tell you things *is* seen to. You's every one on ye got to toe the mark, I tell ye—quick, straight, the moment I speak. That's the way to keep in with me. Ye won't find no soft spot in me nowhere. So now, mind yerselves, for I don't show no mercy!"

The women involuntarily drew in their breath, and the whole gang sat with downcast, dejected faces. Meanwhile

Simon turned on his heel and marched up to the bar of the boat for a dram.

"That's the way I begin with my niggers," he said to a gentlemanly man who had stood by him during his speech. "It's my system to begin strong—just let 'em know what to expect."

"Indeed!" said the stranger, looking upon him with the curiosity of a naturalist studying some out-of-the-way specimen.

"Yes, indeed. I'm none o' yer gentlemen planters with lily fingers, to slop round and be cheated by some old cuss of an overseer. Just feel of my knuckles, now. Look at my fist. Tell ye, sir, the flesh on't has come jest like a stone, practicing on niggers—feel on it."

The stranger applied his fingers to the implement in question and simply said:

" 'Tis hard enough. And I suppose," he added, "practice has made your heart just like it."

"Why, yes, I may say so," said Simon with a hearty laugh. "I reckon there's as little soft in me as in anyone going. Tell you, nobody comes it over me! Niggers never gets round me, neither with squalling nor soft soap—that's a fact."

"You have a fine lot there."

"Real," said Simon. "There's that Tom, they telled me he was suthin' uncommon. I paid a little high for him, tendin' him for a driver and a managing chap. Only get the notions out that he's larnt by bein' treated as niggers never ought to be, he'll do prime! The yellow woman I got took in on. I rayther think she's sickly, but I shall put her through for what she's worth. She may last a year or two. I don't go for savin' niggers. Use up and buy more, it's my way. Makes you less trouble, and I'm quite sure it comes cheaper in the end." And Simon sipped his glass.

"And how long do they generally last?" said the stranger.

"Well, dunno. 'Cordin as their constitution is. Stout fellers last six or seven years, trashy ones get worked up in two or three. I used to, when I fust begun, have considerable trouble fussin' on 'em and trying to make 'em hold out—doctorin' on 'em up when they's sick, and givin' on 'em clothes and blankets, and what not, tryin' to keep 'em all sort o' decent and comfortable. Law, 'twas heaps o' trouble. Now, you see, I just put 'em straight through, sick or well. When one nigger's dead, I buy another. And I find it comes cheaper and easier every way."

The stranger turned away and seated himself beside a gentleman who had been listening to the conversation with repressed uneasiness.

"You must not take that fellow to be any specimen of Southern planters," said he.

"I should hope not," said the young gentleman with emphasis.

"He is a mean, low, brutal fellow!" said the other.

"And yet your laws allow him to hold any number of human beings subject to his absolute will, without even a shadow of protection. And low as he is, you cannot say that there are not many such."

"Well," said the other, "there are also many considerate and humane men among planters."

"Granted," said the young man. "But in my opinion, it is you considerate, humane men that are responsible for all the brutality and outrage wrought by these wretches. Because if it were not for your sanction and influence, the whole system could not keep foothold for an hour."

"You certainly have a high opinion of my good nature," said the planter, smiling. "But I advise you not to talk quite so loud, as there are people on board the boat who might not be quite so tolerant as I am."

The young gentleman colored and smiled, and the two were soon busy in a game of backgammon. Meanwhile another conversation was going on in the lower part of the boat, between Emmeline and the mulatto woman with whom she was confined. As was natural, they were exchanging with each other some particulars of their history.

"Who did you belong to?" said Emmeline.

"Well, my Mas'r was Mr. Ellis—lived on Levee Street. P'raps you've seen the house."

"Was he good to you?" said Emmeline.

"Mostly, till he tuk sick. He's lain sick, off and on, more than six months, and been orful oneasy. 'Pears like he warn't willin' to have nobody rest day nor night, and got so curis, there couldn't nobody suit him. 'Pears like he just grew crosser every day. Kep' me up nights till I got fa'rly beat out, and couldn't keep awake no longer. And cause I got to sleep one night, Lors, he talk so orful to me, and he tell me he'd sell me to just the hardest master he could find. And he'd promised me my freedom, too, when he died."

"Had you any friends?" said Emmeline.

"Yes, my husband—he's a blacksmith. Mas'r gen'ly hired him out. They took me off so quick, I didn't even have time to see him. And I's got four children. Oh, dear me!" said the woman, covering her face with her hands.

Emmeline wanted to say something, but she could not think of anything to say. What was there to be said? As by a common consent, they both avoided, with fear and dread, all mention of the horrible man who was now their master.

The boat moved on—freighted with its weight of sorrow —up the red, muddy, turbid current, through the abrupt, tortuous windings of the Red River. And sad eyes gazed wearily on the steep red-clay banks, as they glided by in dreary sameness. At last the boat stopped at a small town, and Legree, with his party, disembarked.

Dark Places

TRAILING wearily behind a rude wagon, and over a ruder road, Tom and his associates paced onward.

In the wagon was seated Simon Legree. The two women, still fettered together, were stowed away with some baggage in the back part of it. And the whole company were seeking Legree's plantation, which lay a good distance off.

It was a wild, forsaken road, now winding through dreary pine barrens, where the wind whispered mournfully, and now over log causeways and through cypress swamps. The doleful trees rose out of the slimy, spongy ground, hung with long wreaths of funereal black moss, while ever and anon the loathsome form of the moccasin snake might be seen sliding among broken stumps and shattered branches that lay rotting in the water.

It is disconsolate enough, this riding, to the stranger who, with well-filled pocket and well-appointed horse, threads the lonely way on some errand of business. But it is wilder, drearier, to the man enthralled, whom every weary step bears further from all that man loves and prays for.

So one should have thought that witnessed the sunken and dejected expression on those dark faces, the wistful, patient weariness with which those sad eyes rested on object after object that passed them in their sad journey.

Simon rode on, however, apparently well pleased, occasionally pulling away at a flask of spirit, which he kept in his pocket.

"I say, *you!*" he said, as he turned back and caught a glance at the dispirited faces behind him. "Strike up a song, boys—come!"

The men looked at each other, and the "come" was repeated, with a smart crack of the whip which the driver carried in his hands. Tom began a Methodist hymn:

> Jerusalem, my happy home,
> Name ever dear to me!
> When shall my sorrows have an end,
> Thy joy when shall—

"Shut up, you black cuss!" roared Legree. "Did ye think I wanted any o' yer infernal old Methodism? I say, tune up, now, something real rowdy—quick!"

One of the other men struck up one of the those unmeaning songs common among the slaves.

> Mas'r seed me cotch a coon,
> High boys, high!
> He laughed to split—d'ye see the moon?
> Hi! ho! ho! boys, ho!
> Ho! yo! hi—e! oh!

The singer appeared to make up the song to his own pleasure, generally hitting on rhyme, without much attempt at reason. And all the party took up the chorus, at intervals:

> Ho! ho ho! boys, ho!
> High—e—oh! High—e—oh!

It was sung with a forced attempt at merriment, but no wail of despair could have had such a depth of woe in it as the wild notes of the chorus. There was a prayer in it, which Simon could not hear. He only heard the boys singing noisily, and was well pleased—he was making them "keep up their spirits."

"Well, my little dear," said he, turning to Emmeline and laying his hand on her shoulder, "we're almost home!"

When Legree scolded and stormed, Emmeline was terrified. But when he laid his hand on her and spoke as he now did, she felt as if she had rather he would strike her. The expression of his eyes made her soul sick, and her flesh creep. Involuntarily she clung closer to the mulatto woman by her side, as if she were her mother.

"You didn't ever wear earrings," he said, taking hold of her small ear with his coarse fingers.

"No, Mas'r!" said Emmeline, trembling and looking down.

"Well, I'll give you a pair, when we get home, if you're a good girl. You needn't be so frightened. I don't mean to make you work very hard. You'll have fine times with me, and live like a lady—only be a good girl."

It was about this time that the enclosures of the plantation rose to view.

The estate had formerly belonged to a gentleman of wealth and taste, who had bestowed some considerable attention to the adornment of his grounds. It had been purchased at a bargain by Legree, who used it, as he did everything else, merely as an implement for money-making. The place had been left to go to utter decay.

What was once a smooth-shaven lawn before the house, dotted here and there with ornamental shrubs, was now covered with frowsy, tangled grass, with horse-posts set up here and there in it, where the turf was stamped away, and the ground littered with broken pails, cobs of corn and other slovenly remains. Here and there a mildewed jessamine or honeysuckle hung raggedly from some ornamental support, which had been pushed to one side by being used as a horse-post. What once was a large garden was now all grown over with weeds. What had been a conservatory had now no window sashes, and on the moldering shelves stood some dry, forsaken flowerpots, with sticks in them, whose dried leaves showed they had once been plants.

The house had been large and handsome. It was built in a manner common in the South—a wide verandah of two stories running round every part of the house, into which every outer door opened, the lower tier being supported by brick pillars. But the place looked desolate and uncomfortable. Some windows were stopped up with boards, some with shattered panes, and shutters hung by a single hinge. All told of coarse neglect and discomfort.

Three or four ferocious-looking dogs, roused by the sound of the wagon wheels, came tearing out, and were with difficulty restrained from laying hold of Tom and his companions by the effort of the ragged servants who came after them.

"Ye see what ye'd get!" said Legree, caressing the dogs with grim satisfaction and turning to Tom and his companions. "Ye see what ye'd get, if ye try to run off. These yer dogs has been raised to track niggers, and they'd just as soon chaw one on ye up as eat their supper. So mind yourself! How now, Sambo!" he said to a ragged fellow without any brim to his hat, who was officious in his attentions. "How have things been going?"

"Fust rate, Mas'r."

"Quimbo," said Legree to another, who was making zealous demonstrations to attract his attention, "ye minded what I telled ye?"

"Guess I did, didn't I?"

These two colored men were the two principal hands on the plantation. Legree had trained them in savageness and brutality as systematically as he had his bulldogs. And by long practice in hardness and cruelty, he had brought their whole nature to about the same range of capacities. Sambo and Quimbo cordially hated each other. The plantation hands, one and all, cordially hated them. And by playing off one against another, Legree was pretty sure, through one or the other of the three parties, to get informed of whatever was on foot in the place.

Nobody can live entirely without social intercourse, and Legree encouraged his two black satellites to a kind of coarse familiarity with him—familiarity, however, at any moment liable to get one or the other of them into trouble. For on the slightest provocation, one of them always stood ready, at a nod, to be a minister of his vengeance on the other.

As they stood there now by Legree, they seemed an apt illustration of the fact that brutal men are lower even than animals. Their coarse, dark, heavy features, their great eyes, rolling enviously on each other, their barbarous, guttural, half-brute intonation—all were in admirable keeping with the vile character of everything about the place.

"Here, you, Sambo," said Legree, "take these yer boys down to the quarters. And here's a gal I've got for *you*," said he, as he separated the mulatto woman from Emmeline and pushed her toward him. "I promised to bring you one, you know."

The woman gave a sudden start, and drawing back, said suddenly:

"Oh, Mas'r! I left my old man in New Orleans."

"What of that, you ——. Won't you want one here? None o' your words—go long!" said Legree, raising his whip.

"Come, mistress," he said to Emmeline, "you go in here with me."

A dark, wild face was seen for a moment at the window of the house, and as Legree opened the door, a female voice said something in a quick, imperative tone. Tom, who was looking with anxious interest after Emmeline, as she went in, noticed this and heard Legree answer angrily, "You may hold your tongue! I'll do as I please, for all you!"

Tom heard no more, for he was soon following Sambo.

The quarters was a little sort of street of rude shanties in a row, in a part of the plantation far off from the house. They had a forlorn, brutal, forsaken air. Tom's heart sank when he saw them. He had been comforting himself with the thought of a cottage, rude indeed, but one which he might make neat and quiet, and where he might have a shelf for his Bible and a place to be alone out of his laboring hours. He looked into several. They were mere rude shells, destitute of any furniture except a heap of straw, foul with dirt, spread confusedly over the floor, which was merely the bare ground, trodden hard by the tramping of innumerable feet.

"Which of these will be mine?" said he to Sambo submissively.

"Dunno. Ken turn in here, I spose," said Sambo. "Spects thar's room for another thar. Thar's a pretty smart heap o' niggers to each on 'em now. Sure, I dunno what I's to do with more."

It was late in the evening when the weary occupants of the shanties came flocking home—men and women in soiled and tattered garments, surly and uncomfortable, and in no mood to look pleasantly on newcomers. The small village was alive with no inviting sounds. Hoarse, guttural voices contended at the hand-mills where their morsel of hard corn was yet to be ground into meal, to fit it for the cake that was to constitute their only supper. From the earliest dawn of the day they had been in the fields, pressed to work under the driving lash. For it was now in the very heat and hurry of the season, and no means was left untried to press everyone up to the top of their capabilities.

Tom looked in vain among the gang, as they poured along, for companionable faces. He saw only sullen, scowling, brutish men and feeble, discouraged women. To a late hour in the night the sound of the grinding was protracted, for the mills were few in number, compared with the grinders, and the weary and feeble ones were driven back by the strong and came on last in their turn.

"Ho yo!" said Sambo, coming to the mulatto woman and throwing down a bag of corn before her. "What a cuss yo name?"

"Lucy," said the woman.

"Wal, Lucy, you my woman now. Yo grinds dis yer corn, and get *my* supper baked, ye har?"

"I an't your woman, and I won't be!" said the woman, with the sharp, sudden courage of despair. "You go long!"

"I'll kick you, then!" said Sambo, raising his foot threateningly.

"Ye may kill me if ye choose—the sooner the better. Wish't I was dead!" said she.

"I say, Sambo, you go to spilin' the hands, I'll tell Mas'r o' you," said Quimbo, who was busy at the mill, from which he had viciously driven two or three tired women, who were waiting to grind their corn.

"And I'll tell him ye won't let the women come to the mills, yo old nigger!" said Sambo. "Yo jest keep to yo own row."

Tom was hungry with his day's journey and almost faint for want of food.

"Thar, yo!" said Quimbo, throwing down a coarse bag which contained a peck of corn. "Thar, nigger, grab, take car' on 't—you won't get no more *dis* yer week."

Tom waited till a late hour to get a place at the mills. And then, moved by the utter weariness of two women whom he saw trying to grind their corn there, he ground for them, put together the decaying brands of the fire, where many had baked cakes before them, and then went about getting his own supper. It was a new kind of work there—a deed of charity, small as it was. But it woke an answering touch in their hearts. An expression of womanly kindness came over their hard faces. They mixed his cake for him, and tended its baking. And Tom sat down by the light of the fire and drew out his Bible—for he had need of comfort.

"What's that?" said one of the women.

"A Bible," said Tom.

"Good Lord! Han't seen un since I was in Kentuck."

"Was you raised in Kentuck?" said Tom with interest.

"Yes, and well raised, too. Never spected to come to dis yer!" said the woman, sighing.

"What's dat ar book, anyway?" said the other woman.

"Why, the Bible."

"Laws a me! What's dat?" said the woman.

"Do tell! You never hearn on 't?" said the other woman. "I used to hear Missis a readin' on 't, sometimes, in Kentuck. But laws o' me! We don't har nothin' here but crackin' and swarin'."

"Read a piece, anyways," said the first woman, curiously, seeing Tom attentively poring over it.

Tom read: " 'Come unto Me, all ye that labor and are heavy laden, and I will give you rest.' "

"Them's good words enough," said the woman. "Who says 'em?"

"The Lord," said Tom.

"I jest wish I know'd whar to find Him," said the woman. "I would go. 'Pears like I never should get rested agin. My flesh is fairly sore, and I tremble all over, every day, and Sambo's allers a-jawin' at me cause I doesn't pick faster. And nights it's most midnight 'fore I can get my supper. And den 'pears like I don't turn over and shut my eyes 'fore I hear de horn blow to get up, and at it agin in de mornin'. If I knew whar de Lor was, I'd tell him."

"He's here, He's everywhere," said Tom.

"Lor, you an't gwine to make me believe dat ar! I know de Lor an't here," said the woman. " 'Tan't no use talking, though. I's jest gwine to camp down and sleep while I ken."

The women went off to their cabins, and Tom sat alone by the smoldering fire that flickered up redly in his face.

The silver, fair-browed moon rose in the purple sky and looked down, calm and silent, as God looks on the scene of misery and oppression—looked calmly on the lone black man as he sat with his arms folded and his Bible on his knee.

"Is god here?"

In Tom's simple heart waged a fierce conflict. The crushing sense of wrong, the foreshadowing of a whole life of future misery, the wreck of all past hopes, mournfully tossed in his soul. He rose, disconsolate, and stumbled into the cabin that had been allotted to him.

The floor was already strewn with weary sleepers, and the foul air of the place almost repelled him. But the heavy night dews were chill, and his limbs weary, and wrapping about him a tattered blanket, which formed his only bedclothing, he stretched in the straw and fell asleep.

Cassy

It took but a short time to familiarize Tom with all that was to be hoped or feared in his new way of life. He was an expert and efficient workman in whatever he undertook, and from habit and principle prompt and faithful. Quiet and peaceable in his disposition, he hoped, by unremitting diligence, to avert from himself at least a portion of the evils of his condition. He saw enough of abuse and misery to make him sick and weary, but he determined to toil on, with religious patience, not without hope that some way of escape might yet be opened to him.

Legree took silent note of Tom's ability. He rated him as a first-class hand. And yet he felt a secret dislike to him—the native opposition of bad to good. He saw plainly that when his violence and brutality fell on the helpless, Tom took notice of it. And the opinion even of a slave may annoy a master. Tom in various ways showed a tenderness of feeling for his fellow-sufferers, strange and new to them, which was watched with a jealous eye by Legree. He had purchased Tom with a view of eventually making him a sort of overseer, with whom he might, at times, entrust his affairs in short absences. And in his view, the first, second, and third requisite for that place was *hardness*. Legree made up his mind to harden Tom forthwith, and some few weeks after he had been on the place, determined to commence the process.

One morning, when the hands were mustered for the field, Tom noticed, with surprise, a newcomer among them whose appearance excited his attention. It was a woman, tall and slenderly formed, with remarkably delicate hands and feet, and dressed in neat and respectable garments. By the appear-

ance of her face, she might have been between thirty-five
and forty. And it was a face that, once seen, could never be
forgotten—one of those that, at a glance, seemed to convey to
us an idea of a wild, painful, and romantic history.

Her forehead was high, and her eyebrows marked with
beautiful clearness. Her straight, well-formed nose, her finely-
cut mouth, and the graceful contour of her head and neck
showed that she must once have been beautiful. But her face
was deeply wrinkled with lines of pain, and of proud and
bitter endurance. Her complexion was sallow and unhealthy,
her cheeks thin, her features sharp, and her whole form
emaciated. But her eyes were the most remarkable feature—
large, heavily black, overshadowed by long lashes of equal
darkness, and wildly, mournfully despairing.

Where she came from, or who she was, Tom did not know.
The first he did know, she was walking by his side, erect and
proud, in the dim gray of the dawn. To the gang, however,
she was known. For there was much looking and turning of
heads and smothered exultation among the miserable, ragged,
half-starved creatures by whom she was surrounded.

"Got to come to it at last—glad of it!" said one.

"He! he! he!" said another. "You'll know how good it is,
Misse!"

"We'll see her work!"

The woman took no notice of these taunts but walked on
with the same expression of angry scorn, as if she heard nothing. Tom had always lived among refined and cultivated
people, and he felt intuitively, from her air and bearing, that
she belonged to that class. But how or why she could be fallen
to those degrading circumstances, he could not tell. The
woman neither looked at him nor spoke to him, though all the
way to the field she kept close at his side.

Tom was soon busy at his work, but as the woman was at
no great distance from him, he often glanced at her. He saw at
a glance that a native adroitness made the task to her an easier
one than it proved to many. She picked very fast and very

clean, and with an air of scorn, as if she despised both the work and the disgrace and humiliation of the circumstances in which she was placed.

In the course of the day, Tom was working near the mulatto woman who had been bought in the same lot with himself. She was evidently in a condition of great suffering, and Tom often heard her praying, as she wavered and trembled and seemed about to fall down. Tom silently, as he came near to her, transferred several handfuls of cotton from his own sack to hers.

"Oh, don't, don't," said the woman, looking surprised. "It'll get you into trouble."

Just then Sambo came up. He seemed to have a special spite against this woman, and flourishing his whip, said in brutal tones, "What dis yer, Luce—foolin' a?" And kicking the woman with his heavy cowhide shoe, he struck Tom across the face with his whip.

Tom silently resumed his task. But the woman, before at the last point of exhaustion, fainted.

"I'll bring her to!" said the driver, with a brutal grin. "I'll give her something better than camphire!" And taking a pin from his coat-sleeve, he buried it to the head in her flesh. The woman groaned and half rose. "Get up, you beast, and work, will yer, or I'll show yer a trick more!"

The woman seemed stimulated, for a few moments, to an unnatural strength, and worked with desperate eagerness.

"See that you keep to dat ar," said the man, "or yer'll wish yer's dead tonight, I reckin!"

"That I do now!" Tom heard her say.

At the risk of all that he might suffer, Tom came forward again and put all the cotton in his sack into the woman's.

"Oh, you mustn't. You dunno what they'll do to ye!" said the woman.

"I can b'ar it," said Tom, "better'n you." And he was at his place again. It passed in a moment.

Suddenly the stranger woman whom we have described,

and who had, in the course of her work come near enough
to hear Tom's last words, raised her heavy black eyes and
fixed them, for a second, on him. Then, taking a quantity of
cotton from her basket, she placed it in his.

"You know nothing about this place," she said, "or you
wouldn't have done that. When you've been here a month,
you'll be done helping anybody. You'll find it hard enough to
take care of your own skin!"

"The Lord forbid, Missis!" said Tom, using instinctively
the respectful form proper to the high bred with whom he
had lived.

"The Lord never visits these parts," said the woman bitterly, as she went nimbly forward with her work. And again
the scornful smile curled her lips.

But the action of the woman had been seen by the driver
across the field, and flourishing his whip, he came up to her.

"What! what!" he said to the woman, with an air of triumph. "YOU a foolin'? Go long! Yer under me now—mind
yerself, or yer'll cotch it!"

A glance like sheet-lightning suddenly flashed from those
black eyes, and facing about with quivering lip and dilated
nostrils, she drew herself up and fixed a glance, blazing
with rage and scorn, on the driver.

"Dog!" she said. "Touch *me*, if you dare! I've power
enough yet to have you torn by the dogs, burnt alive, cut to
inches! I've only to say the word!"

"What de devil you here for, den?" said the man, evidently
cowed, and sullenly retreating a step or two. "Didn't mean no
harm, Misse Cassy!"

"Keep your distance, then!" said the woman. And, in truth,
the man seemed greatly inclined to attend to something at
the other end of the field.

The woman turned to her work and labored with dispatch
that was perfectly astonishing to Tom. She seemed to work
by magic. Before the day was through, her basket was filled,
crowded down, and piled, and she had several times put

largely into Tom's. Long after dusk, the whole weary train, with their baskets on their heads, filed up to the building appropriated to storing and weighing the cotton. Legree was there, busily conversing with the two drivers.

"Dat ar Tom's gwine to make a powerful deal o' trouble. Kept puttin' into Lucy's basket. One o' these yer dat will get all der niggers to feelin' 'bused, if Mas'r don't watch him!" said Sambo.

"Hey-dey! The black cuss!" said Legree. "He'll have to get a breakin' in, won't he, boys?"

Both Negroes grinned a horrid grin at this.

"Ay, ay! Let Mas'r Legree alone for breakin' in! De debil heself couldn't beat Mas'r at dat!" said Quimbo.

"Wal, boys, the best way is to give him the flogging to do, till he gets over his notions. Break him in!"

"Lord, Mas'r'll have hard work to get dat out o' him!"

"It'll have to come out of him, though!" said Legree, as he rolled his tobacco in his mouth.

"Now, dar's Lucy—de aggravatinest, ugliest wench on de place!" pursued Sambo.

"Take care, Sam. I shall begin to think what's the reason for your spite agin Lucy."

"Well, Mas'r knows she sot herself up agin Mas'r, and wouldn't have me, when he telled her to."

"I'd a flogged her into 't," said Legree, spitting, "only there's such a press o' work. It don't seem wuth while to upset her jest now. She's slender. But these yer slender gals will bear half killin' to get their own way!"

"Wal, Lucy was real aggravatin' and lazy, sulkin' round— wouldn't do nothin'. And Tom he tuck up for her."

"He did, eh! Wal, then, Tom shall have the pleasure of flogging her. It'll be a good practice for him, and he won't put it onto the gal like you devils, neither."

"Ho! Ho! Haw! Haw! Haw!" laughed both the sooty wretches.

"Wal, but Mas'r, Tom and Misse Cassy, dey among 'em filled Lucy's basket. I guess der weight's in it, Mas'r!"

"*I do the weighing!*" said Legree emphatically.

Both the drivers again laughed their diabolical laugh.

"So!" he added. "Misse Cassy did her day's work."

"She picks like de debil and all his angels!"

"She's got 'em all in her, I believe!" said Legree. And growling a brutal oath, he proceeded to the weighing-room.

––––––––

Slowly the weary, dispirited creatures wound their way into the room, and with crouching reluctance presented their baskets to be weighed.

Legree noted on a slate, on the side of which was pasted a list of names, the amount.

Tom's basket was weighed and approved, and he looked, with an anxious glance, for the success of the woman he had befriended.

Tottering with weakness, she came forward and delivered her basket. It was of full weight, as Legree well perceived. But affecting anger, he said:

"What, you lazy beast! Short again! Stand aside! You'll catch it pretty soon!"

The woman gave a groan of utter despair and sat down on a board.

The person who had been called Misse Cassy now came forward and with a haughty, careless air delivered her basket. As she delivered it, Legree looked in her eyes with a sneering yet inquiring glance.

She fixed her black eyes steadily on him, her lips moved slightly, and she said something in French. What it was, no one knew, but Legree's face became perfectly demoniacal in its expression as she spoke. He half raised his hand, as if to strike—a gesture which she regarded with fierce disdain as she turned and walked away.

"And now," said Legree, "come here, you Tom. You see, I

telled ye I didn't buy ye jest for the common work. I mean to promote ye, and make a driver of ye. And tonight ye may jest as well begin to get yer hand in. Now ye jest take this yer gal and flog her—ye've seen enough on't to know how."

"I beg Mas'r's pardon," said Tom. "Hopes Mas'r won't set me at that. It's what I an't used to—never did—and can't do, no way possible."

"Ye'll larn a pretty smart chance of things ye never did know, before I've done with ye!" said Legree, taking up a cowhide and striking Tom a heavy blow across the cheek, and following up the infliction by a shower of blows.

"There!" he said as he stopped to rest. "Now will ye tell me ye can't do it?"

"Yes, Mas'r," said Tom, putting up his hand to wipe the blood that trickled down his face. "I'm willin' to work night and day, and work while there's life and breath in me. But this yer thing I can't feel it right to do. And, Mas'r, I *never* shall do it—*never!*"

Tom had a remarkably smooth, soft voice, and a habitually respectful manner that had given Legree an idea that he would be cowardly and easily subdued. When he spoke these last words, a thrill of amazement went through everyone. The poor woman clasped her hands and said, "Oh Lord!" and everyone involuntarily looked at each other and drew in their breath, as if to prepare for the storm that was about to burst.

Legree looked stupefied and confounded, but at last burst forth:

"What! Ye blasted black beast! Tell *me* ye don't think it *right* to do what I tell ye! What have any of you cussed cattle to do with thinking what's right? I'll put a stop to it! Why, what do ye think ye are? Maybe ye think yer a gentleman, master Tom, to be a-telling your master what's right, and what an't! So you pretend it's wrong to flog the gal!"

"I think so, Mas'r," said Tom. "The poor crittur's sick and feeble. 'Twould be downright cruel, and it's what I never will do, nor begin to. Mas'r, if you mean to kill me, kill me. But as to my raising my hand agin anyone here, I never shall—I'll die first!"

Tom spoke in a mild voice, but with a decision that could not be mistaken. Legree shook with anger. His greenish eyes glared fiercely, and his very whiskers seemed to curl with passion. But like some ferocious beast that plays with its victim before he devours it, he kept back his strong impulse to proceed to immediate violence, and broke out into bitter raillery.

"Well, here's a pious dog, at last, let down among us sinners! A saint, a gentleman, and no less, to talk to us sinners about our sins! Powerful holy crittur, he must be! Here, you rascal, you make believe to be so pious—didn't you never hear, out of yer Bible, 'Servants, obey yer masters?' An't I yer master? Didn't I pay down twelve hundred dollars, cash, for all there is inside yer old cussed black shell? An't yer mine now, body and soul?" he said, giving Tom a violent kick with his heavy boot. "Tell me!"

In the very depth of physical suffering, bowed by brutal oppression, this question shot a gleam of joy and triumph through Tom's soul. He suddenly stretched himself up, and looking earnestly to heaven, while the tears and blood that flowed down his face mingled, he exclaimed:

"No! no! no! My soul an't yours, Mas'r. You haven't bought it—ye can't buy it. It's been bought and paid for by One that is able to keep it. No matter, no matter, you can't harm me!"

"I can't!" said Legree with a sneer. "We'll see—we'll see! Here, Sambo, Quimbo, give this dog such a breakin' in as he won't get over this month!"

The two gigantic Negroes that now laid hold of Tom, with fiendish exultation in their faces, might have formed no unapt personification of powers of darkness. The poor woman screamed with apprehension, and all rose, as by a general impulse, while they dragged him unresisting from the place.

The Quadroon's Story

It was late at night, and Tom lay groaning and bleeding alone, in an old forsaken room of the gin-house, among pieces of broken machinery, piles of damaged cotton, and other rubbish which had there accumulated.

The night was damp and close. The thick air swarmed with myriads of mosquitoes, which increased the restless torture of his wounds, whilst a burning thirst filled up the uttermost measure of physical anguish.

"Oh, good Lord! *Do* look down. Give me the victory! Give me the victory over all!" prayed poor Tom in his anguish.

A footstep entered the room, and the light of a lantern flashed on his eyes.

"Who's there? Oh, for the Lord's massy, please give me some water!"

The woman Cassy—for it was she—set down her lantern, and pouring water from a bottle, raised his head and gave him drink. Another and another cup was drained, with feverish eagerness.

"Drink all ye want," she said. "I knew how it would be. It isn't the first time I've been out in the night, carrying water to such as you."

"Thank you, Missis," said Tom when he had done drinking.

"Don't call me Missis! I'm a miserable slave like yourself—a lower one than you can ever be!" said she bitterly. "But now," said she, going to the door and dragging in a small straw mattress, over which she had spread linen cloths wet with cold water, "try, my poor fellow, to roll yourself on to this."

Stiff with wounds and bruises, Tom was a long time in accomplishing this movement. But when done, he felt a considerable relief from the cooling application to his wounds.

The woman, whom long practice with the victims of brutality had made familiar with many healing arts, went on to make repeated applications to Tom's wounds, by means of which he was soon somewhat relieved.

"Now," said the woman, when she had raised his head on a roll of damaged cotton, "there's the best I can do for you."

Tom thanked her, and Cassy, sitting down on the floor, drew up her knees, and embracing them with her arms, looked fixedly before her with a bitter and painful expression of countenance.

"It's no use, my poor fellow!" she broke out at last. "It's of no use, this you've been trying to do. You were a brave fellow—you had the right on your side. But it's all in vain for you to struggle. You are in the devil's hands. He is the strongest, and you must give up!"

Give up! And had not human weakness and physical agony whispered that before? Tom started. For the bitter woman, with her wild eyes and melancholy voice, seemed to him an embodiment of the temptation with which he had been wrestling.

"Oh Lord! Oh Lord!" he groaned. "How can I give up?"

"There's no use calling on the Lord—he never hears," said the woman steadily. "There isn't any God, I believe. Or, if there is, he's taken sides against us. All goes against us, heaven and earth. Everything is pushing us into hell. Why shouldn't we go?"

Tom closed his eyes and shuddered at the dark words.

"You see," said the woman, "*you* don't know anything about it. I do. I've been on this place five years, body and soul under this man's foot. And I hate him as I do the devil! Here you are, on a lone plantation, ten miles from any other, in the swamps. Not a white person here who could testify, if you were burned alive, if you were scalded, cut into inch pieces, set up for the dogs to tear, or hung up and whipped to death. There's no law here, of God or man, that can do you, or any one of us, the least good.

"And this man! There's no earthly thing that he's too good to do. I could make anyone's hair rise and their teeth chatter if I should only tell what I've seen and been knowing to here— and it's no use resisting. Did I *want* to live with him? Wasn't I a woman delicately bred? And he—God in heaven!—what was he, and is he? And yet I've lived with him these five years, and cursed every moment of my life, night and day! And now, he's got a new one—a young thing only fifteen, and she brought up, she says, piously. Her good mistress taught her to read the Bible. And she's brought her Bible here—to hell—with her!" And the woman laughed a wild and doleful laugh, that rang with a strange, supernatural sound through the old ruined shed.

Tom folded his hands. All was darkness and horror.

"Oh Jesus! Lord Jesus! Have you quite forgot us poor critturs?" burst forth at last. "Help, Lord, I perish!"

The woman sternly continued:

"And what are these miserable low dogs you work with, that you should suffer on their account? Every one of them would turn against you the first time they got a chance. They are all of 'em as low and cruel to each other as they can be. There's no use in your suffering to keep from hurting them."

"Poor critturs!" said Tom. "What made 'em cruel? And if I give out, I shall get used to 't, and grow, little by little, just like 'em. No, no, Missis! I've lost everything—wife, and chil'en, and home, and a kind Mas'r—and he would have set me free if he'd only lived a week longer. I've lost everything in *this* world, and it's clean gone, forever—and now I *can't* lose Heaven, too! No, I can't get to be wicked, besides all!"

"But it can't be that the Lord will lay sin to our account," said the woman. "He won't charge it to us when we're forced to it. He'll charge it to them that drove us to it."

"Yes," said Tom, "but that won't keep us from growing wicked. If I get to be as hard-hearted as that ar Sambo, and as wicked, it won't make much odds to me how I come so. It's *bein'* so—that ar's I'm a-dreadin'."

The woman fixed a wild and startled look on Tom, as if a new thought had struck her, and then, heavily groaning, said:

"Oh God a mercy! You speak the truth! Oh—oh—oh!" And with groans, she fell on the floor.

There was a silence a while, in which the breathing of both parties could be heard, when Tom faintly said, "Oh, please, Missis!"

The woman suddenly rose up, with her face composed to its usual stern, melancholy expression.

"Please, Missis, I saw 'em throw my coat in that ar corner, and in my coat pocket is my Bible. If Missis would please get it for me."

Cassy went and got it. Tom opened, at once, to a heavily marked passage, much worn, of the last scenes in the life of Him by whose stripes we are healed.

"If Missis would only be so good as read that ar—it's better than water."

Cassy took the book with a dry, proud air, and looked over the passage. She then read aloud in a soft voice that touching account of anguish and of glory. Often, as she read, her voice faltered, and sometimes failed her altogether. She would stop then, with an air of frigid composure, till she had mastered herself. When she came to the touching words, "Father, forgive them, for they know not what they do," she threw down the book, and burying her face in the heavy masses of her hair, sobbed aloud.

Tom was weeping also, and occasionally uttering a smothered exclamation.

"If we only could keep up to that ar!" said Tom. "It seemed to come so natural to Him, and we have to fight so hard for 't! Oh Lord, help us! Oh Blessed Lord Jesus, do help us!"

"Missis," said Tom after a while, "I can see that, somehow, you're quite 'bove me in everything. But there's one thing Missis might learn even from poor Tom. Ye said the Lord took sides against us, because He lets us be 'bused and knocked round. But ye see what come on His own Son—the blessed Lord of Glory—wan't He al'ays poor? And have we, any on us, yet come so low as He come? The Lord han't forgot us—I'm sartin o' that ar! If we suffer with Him, we shall also reign, Scripture says, but if we deny Him, He also will deny us. Didn't they all suffer—the Lord and all his? It tells how they were stoned and sawn asunder, and wandered about in sheepskins and goatskins, and was destitute, afflicted, tormented. Sufferin' an't no reason to make us think the Lord's turned agin us, but jest the contrary, if only we hold on to Him, and doesn't give up to sin."

"But why does He put us where we can't help but sin?" said the woman.

"I think we *can* help it," said Tom.

"You'll see," said Cassy. "What'll you do? Tomorrow they'll be at you again. I know 'em. I've seen all their doings. I can't bear to think of all they'll bring you to—and they'll make you give out, at last!"

"Lord Jesus!" said Tom. "You *will* take care of my soul? Oh Lord, do! Don't let me give out!"

"Oh dear!" said Cassy. "I've heard all this crying and praying before, and yet they've been broken down and brought under. There's Emmeline, she's trying to hold on, and you're trying—but what use? You must give up, or be killed by inches."

"Well, then, I *will* die!" said Tom. "Spin it out as long as they can, they can't help my dying sometime! And after that, they can't do no more. I'm clar, I'm set! I *know* the Lord'll help me and bring me through."

The woman did not answer. She sat with her black eyes intently fixed on the floor.

"May be it's the way," she murmured to herself. "But those that *have* given up, there's no hope for them—none. We live in filth, and grow loathsome, till we loathe ourselves. And we long to die, and we don't dare to kill ourselves. No hope! no hope! no hope! This girl, now—just as old as I was!

"You see me now," she said to Tom. "See what I am! Well, I was brought up in luxury." And speaking very rapidly, Cassy poured out to Tom the terrible story of her life.

She was born, she said, the daughter of a wealthy white man of New Orleans and a slave woman. Educated in a convent, she had left it at fourteen to attend the funeral of her father, who had died very suddenly. She never went back. For when the property came to be settled, it was found there was scarcely enough to cover the debts, and though her father had always meant to set her free, he had not done so. Cassy was sold.

A young man of wealth and breeding bought her for a great price, and she went to him willingly, for she loved him, as he did her. This man surrounded her with everything that money could buy. But he refused to marry her and convinced her that marriage was impossible. Yet she was happy—she loved—and seven joyous years followed, in which two children were born to her.

The eldest was a boy beautiful as his father, the younger a girl who looked like her. She thought herself as happy as anyone could be. But then came evil times. The children's father, led on by a scheming cousin of his—a man named Butler—began to gamble, involved himself in debts, and fell in love with a woman of his own class. His debts stood in the way of marrying as he wished; so to satisfy his creditors, he secretly sold both Cassy and her children—to his scheming cousin.

When her new owner came to take possession and showed her the papers, she told him she'd die sooner than live with him.

"Just as you please," said he, "but if you don't behave reasonably, I'll sell both the children where you shall never see them again."

Cassy gave in then, for her hands were tied. Whenever she resisted his will, he would talk of selling little Henry and Elise. In the end he did so anyway. And by telling her from day to day that perhaps he would buy them back, he made her submit.

One day as she was out walking and passed by the calaboose, she saw a crowd about the gate and heard a child's voice. And suddenly her little Henry broke away from two or three men who were holding him, and ran, screaming, and caught her dress. They came up to him swearing, while one man told him that he would not get away so, that he was going with him into the calaboose, and he'd get a lesson there he'd never forget.

"I tried to beg and plead," Cassy went on, "but they only laughed. The poor boy screamed and looked into my face, and held on to me, until in tearing him off, they tore the skirt of my dress half away. And they carried him in screaming, 'Mother! Mother! Mother!' There was one man stood there seemed to pity me. I offered him all the money I had if he'd only interefere. He shook his head and said that the man said the boy had been impudent and disobedient ever since he bought him, and that he was going to break him in, once for all. I turned and ran. And every step of the way I thought that I heard him scream. I got into the house, ran to the parlor, where I found Butler. I told him and begged him to go and interfere. He only laughed and told me the boy had got his deserts. He'd got to be broken in—the sooner the better.

"It seemed to me something in my head snapped at that moment. I felt dizzy and furious. I remember seeing a great sharp bowie knife on the table. I remember something about catching it and flying upon him. And then all grew dark, and I didn't know any more—not for days and days."

When she came to herself, Cassy was in a room not her own. An old black woman tended her, and a doctor came to see her, and a great deal of care was taken of her. After a while she learned that she had been left here to be sold, and that was why such pains were taken with her.

Many men came to look at her, and at last one Captain Stuart bought her. He seemed to have some feeling for her and promised to do all he could to find and buy back her children.

"He went to the hotel where my Henry was," Cassy told Tom. "They told him he had been sold to a planter up on Pearl River. That was the last I ever heard. Then he found where my daughter was, but they would not sell her. Captain

Stuart was very kind to me. He had a splendid plantation and took me to it. In the course of a year, I had a son born. But I had made up my mind—yes, I had. I would never again let a child live to grow up! I took the little fellow in my arms when he was two weeks old, and kissed him, and cried over him. And then I gave him laudanum, and held him close while he slept to death. How I mourned and cried over it! And who ever dreamed that it was anything but a mistake that had made me give it the laudanum? But it's one of the few things that I'm glad of now. I am not sorry, to this day—he, at least, is out of pain. What better than death could I give him, poor child! After a while the cholera came, and Captain Stuart died. Everybody died that wanted to live—and I—I, though I went down to death's door, *I lived!* Then I was sold and passed from hand to hand, till I grew faded and wrinkled, and I had a fever. And then this wretch bought me and brought me here—and here I am!"

Cassy stopped. She had hurried on through her story with a wild, passionate utterance, sometimes seeming to address it to Tom, and sometimes speaking as if to herself. So overpowering was the force with which she spoke that for a while Tom was beguiled even from the pain of his wounds, and raising himself on one elbow, watched her as she paced restlessly up and down, her long black hair swaying heavily about her as she moved.

"You tell me," she said after a pause, "that there is a God— a God that looks down and sees all these things. Maybe it's so. The sisters in the convent used to tell me of a day of judgment, when everything is coming to light. Won't there be vengeance then!

"They think it's nothing, what we suffer—nothing what our children suffer! It's all a small matter. Yet I've walked the streets when it seemed as if I had misery enough in my own heart to sink the city. I've wished the houses would fall on me, or the stones sink under me. Yes! And in the judgment day, I will stand up before God, a witness against those that have ruined me and my children, body and soul!

"When I was a girl, I used to love God and prayer. Now I'm a lost soul, pursued by devils that torment me day and night. They keep pushing me on and on—and I'll do it, too, some of these days!" she said, clenching her hand. "I'll send him where he belongs—a short way, too—one of these nights, if they burn me alive for it!" A wild, long laugh rang through the shed and ended in a hysterical sob. She threw herself on the floor, sobbing.

In a few moments the fit seemed to pass off. Cassy rose slowly and seemed to collect herself.

"Can I do anything more for you, my poor fellow?" she said, approaching where Tom lay. "Shall I give you some more water?"

There was a graceful and compassionate sweetness in her voice and manner as she said this, that formed a strange contrast to her former wildness.

Tom drank the water and looked earnestly and pitifully into her face.

"Oh, Missis, I wish you'd go to Him that can give you living waters!"

"Go to him! Where is he? Who is he?" said Cassy.

"Him that you read of to me—the Lord'"

"I used to see the picture of Him, over the altar, when I was a girl," said Cassy mournfully. "But *He isn't here.* There's nothing here but sin and long, long, long despair!" She laid her hand on her breast and drew in her breath, as if to lift a heavy weight.

Tom looked as if he would speak again, but she cut him short with a decided gesture.

"Don't talk, my poor fellow. Try to sleep, if you can." And placing water in his reach, and making whatever little arrangements for his comfort she could, Cassy left the shed.

The Tokens

THE sitting room of Legree's establishment was a large, long room with a wide, ample fireplace. It had once been hung with a showy and expensive paper, which now hung moldering, torn, and discolored from the damp walls. The place had that peculiar sickening smell which one often notices in close old houses. In the fireplace stood a brazier full of burning charcoal. For though the weather was not cold, the evenings always seemed damp and chilly in that great room. Legree, moreover, wanted a place to light his cigars and heat his water for punch. The ruddy glare of the charcoal displayed the confused aspect of the room—saddles, bridles, several sorts of harness, riding whips, overcoats, and various articles of clothing scattered up and down the room. And the dogs had encamped themselves among them.

Legree was just mixing himself a tumbler of punch, pouring his hot water from a cracked and broken-nosed pitcher, grumbling as he did so:

"Plague on that Sambo, to kick up this yer row between me and the new hands! The fellow won't be fit to work for a week now—right in the press of the season."

"Yes, just like you," said a voice behind his chair. It was the woman Cassy, who had stolen upon his soliloquy.

"Hah! You she-devil! You've come back, have you?"

"Yes, I have," she said coolly. "Come to have my own way, too."

"You lie, you jade. I'll be up to my word. Either behave yourself, or stay down to the quarters, and fare and work with the rest."

"I'd rather, ten thousand times," said the woman, "live in the dirtiest hole at the quarters than be under your roof!"

"But you are under my roof, for all that," said he, turning upon her with a savage grin. "That's one comfort. So sit down here on my knee, my dear, and hear to reason," said he, laying hold of her wrist.

"Simon Legree, take care!" said the woman, with a sharp flash of her eye, a glance so wild as to be almost appalling. "You're afraid of me, Simon," she said deliberately. "And you've reason to be! Be careful, for I've got the devil in me!"

The last words she whispered in a hissing tone, close to his ear.

"Get out! I believe, to my soul, you have!" said Legree, pushing her from him and looking uncomfortably at her. "After all, Cassy," he said, "why can't you be friends with me, as you used to?"

"Used to!" said she, a world of bitter feelings choking her.

Cassy had always kept over Legree the kind of influence that a strong, impassioned woman can ever keep over the most brutal man. But of late she had grown more and more irritable and restless, and her irritability, at times, broke out into raving insanity. This liability made her a sort of object of dread to Legree, who had that superstitious horror of insane persons which is common to coarse, uninstructed minds. When Legree brought Emmeline to the house, all the smoldering embers of womanly feeling flashed up in the worn heart of Cassy. She took part with the girl, and a fierce quarrel ensued between her and Legree. Legree swore she should be put to field service if she would not be peaceable. Cassy, with proud scorn, declared she *would* go to the field. And she worked there one day, as we have described, to show how perfectly she scorned the threat.

Legree was secretly uneasy all day. When Cassy presented her basket at the scales, he had hoped for some concession, and addressed her in a sort of conciliatory, half scornful tone. And she had answered with the bitterest contempt. The outrageous treatment of poor Tom had roused her still more, and she had followed Legree to the house to upbraid him for his brutality.

"I wish, Cassy," said Legree, "you'd behave yourself decently."

"*You* talk about behaving decently! And what have you been doing? You, who haven't even sense enough to keep from spoiling one of your best hands, right in the most pressing season, just for your devilish temper!"

"I was a fool, it's a fact, to let any such brangle come up," said Legree. "But when the boy set up his will, he had to be broke in."

"I reckon you won't break *him* in!"

"Won't I?" said Legree, rising passionately. "I'd like to know if I won't? He'll be the first nigger that ever came it round me! I'll break every bone in his body, but he *shall* give up!"

Just then the door opened, and Sambo entered. He came forward, bowing, and holding out something in a paper.

"What's that, you dog?" said Legree.

"It's a witch thing, Mas'r!"

"A what?"

"Something that niggers gets from witches. Keeps 'em from feelin' when they's flogged. He had it tied round his neck with a black string."

Legree, like most godless and cruel men, was superstitious. He opened the paper uneasily.

There dropped out of it a silver dollar and a long, shining curl of fair hair—hair which, like a living thing, twined itself round his fingers.

"Damnation!" he screamed in sudden passion, stamping on the floor, and pulling furiously at the hair, as if it burned him. "Where did this come from? Take it off! Burn it up! Burn it up! What did you bring it to me for?" and he threw it into the charcoal.

Sambo stood with his heavy mouth wide open and aghast with wonder, while Cassy, who was preparing to leave the apartment, stopped and looked at him in perfect amazement.

"Don't you bring me any more of your devilish things!" he shouted, shaking his fist at Sambo, who retreated hastily toward the door. Picking up the silver dollar, Legree sent it smashing through the windowpane, out into the darkness.

Sambo was glad to make his escape. When he was gone, Legree seemed a little ashamed of his fit of alarm. He sat doggedly down in his chair and began sullenly sipping his tumbler of punch.

Cassy prepared herself for going out, unobserved by him, and slipped away to minister to poor Tom, as we have already related.

And what was the matter with Legree? And what was there in a curl of fair hair to appall that brutal man, familiar with every form of cruelty? To answer this, we must carry the reader backward in his history.

Hard and godless man as he seemed now, there had been a time when a fair-haired woman had led him, at the sound of Sabbath bell, to worship and to pray. Far in New England that mother had trained her only son with long, unwearied love and patient prayers. But Legree had followed in the steps of his hard-tempered sire. Boisterous and tyrannical, he despised all her counsel, would none of her reproof, and at an early age broke from her to seek his fortunes at sea. He never came home but once after. And then his mother clung to him and sought to win him from a life of sin.

That day Legree was almost persuaded—mercy held him by the hand. But sin got the victory. And one night, when his mother in the last agony of her despair knelt at his feet, he spurned her from him, and with brutal curses fled to his ship.

The next Legree heard of her was when, one night, as he was carousing among drunken companions, a letter was put into his hand. He opened it, and a lock of long, curling hair fell from it and twined about his fingers. The letter told him his mother was dead and that, dying, she blessed and forgave him.

Legree had burned the hair and burned the letter. And when he saw them hissing and crackling in the flame, he had shuddered as he thought of everlasting fires. He tried to drink and revel and swear away the memory. But often in the deep night he had seen that pale mother rising by his bedside, and felt the soft twining of that hair around his finger.

"Blast it!" said Legree to himself, as he sipped his liquor. "Where did he get that? If it didn't look just like—whoo! I thought I'd forgot that. Curse me if I think there's any such thing as forgetting anything, anyhow. Hang it! I'm lonesome! I'll call Em. She hates me—the monkey! I don't care—I'll make her come!"

Legree stepped out into a large entry, which went upstairs by what had formerly been a superb, winding staircase. But the passageway was dirty and dreary and lumbered with boxes and unsightly litter. In the gloom the uncarpeted stairs seemed winding up to nobody knew where.

Legree stopped at the foot and heard a voice singing. It seemed strange and ghostlike in that dreary old house, perhaps because of the already tremulous state of his nerves.

O there'll be mourning, mourning, mourning,
O there'll be mourning, at the judgment-seat of Christ!

"Blast the girl!" said Legree. "I'll choke her—Em! Em!" he called harshly. But only a mocking echo from the walls answered him. The sweet voice still sang on:

Parents and children there shall part!
Parents and children there shall part!
Shall part to meet no more!

And clear and loud swelled through the empty halls the refrain:

O there'll be mourning, mourning, mourning,
O there'll be mourning, at the judgment-seat of Christ!

Legree stopped. He would have been ashamed to tell of it, but large drops of sweat stood on his forehead, his heart beat heavy and thick with fear. He even thought he saw something white rising and glimmering in that gloom before him, and shuddered to think what if the form of his dead mother should suddenly appear to him.

"I know one thing," he said to himself, as he stumbled back into the sitting room and sat down, "I'll let that fellow alone after this! I b'lieve I am bewitched, sure enough! I've been shivering and sweating ever since. Where did he get that hair? It couldn't have been *that!* I burnt *that* up, I know I did! It would be a joke if hair could rise from the dead!

"I say," said Legree, stamping and whistling to the dogs, "wake up, some of you, and keep me company!" But the dogs only opened one eye at him sleepily and closed it again.

"I'll have Sambo and Quimbo up here to sing and dance one of their hell dances, and keep off these horrid notions," said Legree. And putting on his hat, he went on to the verandah and blew a horn, with which he commonly summoned his two drivers.

It was between one and two o'clock at night, as Cassy was returning from her ministrations to poor Tom, that she heard the sound of wild shrieking, whooping, halloing, and singing from the sitting room, mingled with the barking of dogs and other symptoms of general uproar.

She came up on the verandah steps and looked in. Legree and both the drivers, in a state of furious intoxication, were singing, whooping, upsetting chairs, and making all manner of grimaces at each other.

She rested her hand on the window-blind and looked fixedly at them—there was a world of anguish, scorn, and fierce bitterness in her black eyes as she did so. "Would it be a sin to rid the world of such a wretch?" she said to herself.

She turned hurriedly away, and passing round to a back door, glided upstairs and tapped at Emmeline's door.

Emmeline and Cassy

CASSY entered the room and found Emmeline sitting, pale with fear, in the furthest corner of it. The girl started up nervously, but on seeing who it was, rushed forward, and catching her arm, said, "Oh, Cassy, is it you? I'm so glad you've come! I was afraid it was—Oh, you don't know what a horrid noise there has been down stairs all this evening!"

"I ought to know," said Cassy dryly. "I've heard it often enough."

"Oh, Cassy, do tell me! Couldn't we get away from this place? I don't care where—into the swamp among the snakes —anywhere! *Couldn't* we get *somewhere* away from here?"

"Nowhere but into our graves," said Cassy.

"Did you ever try?"

"I've seen enough of trying, and what comes of it."

"I'd be willing to live in the swamps, and gnaw the bark from trees. I an't afraid of snakes! I'd rather have one near me than him," said Emmeline eagerly.

"There have been a good many here of your opinion," said Cassy. "But you couldn't stay in the swamps—you'd be tracked by the dogs and brought back, and then—"

"What would he do?" said the girl, looking with breathless interest into her face.

"What *wouldn't* he do, you'd better ask," said Cassy. "He's learned his trade well among the pirates in the West Indies.

You wouldn't sleep much if I should tell you things I've seen —things that he tells of sometimes for good jokes. I've heard screams here that I haven't been able to get out of my head for weeks and weeks. There's a place way out down by the quarters, where you can see a black, blasted tree, and the ground all covered with black ashes. Ask anyone what was done there, and see if they will dare to tell you."

"Oh, what do you mean?"

"I won't tell you. I hate to think of it. And I tell you, the Lord only knows what we may see tomorrow, if that poor fellow holds out as he's begun."

"Horrid!" said Emmeline, every drop of blood receding from her cheeks. "Oh, Cassy, do tell me what I shall do!"

"What I've done. Do the best you can—do what you must —and make it up in hating and cursing."

"He wanted to make me drink some of his hateful brandy," said Emmeline, "and I hate it so—"

"You'd better drink," said Cassy. "I hated it, too, and now I can't live without it. One must have something—things don't look so dreadful when you take that."

"Mother used to tell me never to touch any such thing," said Emmeline.

"*Mother* told you!" Cassy said with bitter emphasis. "What use is it for mothers to say anything? You are all to be bought and paid for, and your souls belong to whoever gets you. That's the way it goes. I say, *drink* brandy. Drink all you can get, and it'll make things come easier."

"Oh, Cassy! Do pity me!"

"Pity you! Don't I? Haven't I a daughter—Lord knows where she is, and whose she is now—going the way her mother went before her, I suppose, and that her children must go, after her! There's no end to the curse—forever!"

"I wish I'd never been born!" said Emmeline, wringing her hands.

"That's an old wish with me," said Cassy. "I've got used to wishing that. I'd die if I dared to," she said, looking out into the darkness with that still, fixed despair which was the habitual expression of her face when at rest.

"It would be wicked to kill one's self," said Emmeline.

"I don't know why—no wickeder than things we live and do, day after day. But the sisters told me things when I was in the convent that make me afraid to die. If it would only be the end of us, why, then. . . ."

Emmeline turned away and hid her face in her hands.

While this conversation was passing in the chamber, Simon Legree, overcome with his carouse, had sunk to sleep in the room below. Legree was not a habitual drunkard. His coarse, strong nature craved, and could endure, a continual stimulation, but a deep spirit of cautiousness prevented his often yielding to appetite in such measure as to lose control of himself.

This night, however, in his feverish efforts to banish the thoughts which rose within him, he had indulged more than common, so that when he had discharged his attendants, he fell heavily on a settle in the room and was soon sound asleep.

He woke at dawn with an oath and a curse. Stumbling forward, he poured out a tumbler of brandy and drank half of it.

"I've had a h——l of a night!" he said to Cassy, who just then entered from an opposite door.

"You'll get plenty of the same sort, by and by," she said dryly.

"What do you mean, you minx?"

"You'll find out, one of these days," returned Cassy in the same tone. "Now, Simon, I've one piece of advice to give you."

"The devil, you have!"

"My advice is," said Cassy steadily, as she began adjusting some things about the room, "that you let Tom alone."

"What business is 't of yours?"

"What? To be sure, I don't know what it should be. If you want to pay twelve hundred for a fellow and use him right up in the press of the season, just to serve your own spite, it's no business of mine. I've done what I could for him."

"You have? What business have you meddling in my matters?"

"None, to be sure. I've saved you some thousands of dollars, at different times, by taking care of your hands—that's all the thanks I get. If your crop comes shorter into market than any of theirs, you won't lose your bet, I suppose? Tompkins won't lord it over you, I suppose—you'll pay down your money like a lady, won't you?"

Legree, like many other planters, had but one form of ambition—to have in the heaviest crop of the season—and he had several bets on this very present season pending in the next town. Cassy, therefore, touched the only string that could be made to vibrate.

"Well, I'll let him off at what he's got," said Legree. "But he shall beg my pardon, and promise better fashions."

"That he won't do," said Cassy.

"Won't, eh?"

"No, he won't."

"I'd like to know *why*, Mistress," said Legree, in the extreme of scorn.

"Because he's done right, and he knows it, and won't say he's done wrong."

"Who a cuss cares what he knows? The nigger shall say what I please, or—"

"Or you'll lose your bet on the cotton crop by keeping him out of the field just at the very press."

"But he *will* give up—course he will. Don't I know what niggers is? He'll beg like a dog this morning."

"He won't, Simon. You don't know this kind. You may kill him by inches—you won't get the first word of confession out of him."

"We'll see. Where is he?" said Legree, starting out.

"In the waste room of the gin-house," said Cassy.

Legree, though he talked so stoutly to Cassy, still sallied

forth from the house with a degree of misgiving which was not common with him. His dreams of the past night, mingled with Cassy's words, considerably affected his mind. He resolved that nobody should be witness to his encounter with Tom, and determined, if he could not subdue him by bullying, to defer his vengeance, to be wreaked in a more convenient season.

The solemn light of dawn had looked in through the rude window of the shed where Tom was lying. He did not know but that the day of his death was dawning in the sky. Far from discouraging his soul, the mysterious warnings of Cassy had in the end roused it as with a heavenly call, and his heart throbbed with solemn joy as he thought that the wondrous *all* of which he had often pondered—the great white throne, with its ever-radiant rainbow; the white-robed multitude, with voices as many waters; the crowns, the palms, the harps —might all break upon his vision before that sun should set again. Therefore, without shuddering or trembling, he heard the voice of his persecutor as he drew near.

"Well, my boy," said Legree, with a contemptuous kick, "how do you find yourself? Didn't I tell yer I could larn yer a thing or two? How do yer like it—eh? How did yer whaling agree with yer, Tom? An't quite so crank as ye was last night. Ye couldn't treat a poor sinner, now, to a bit of sermon, could ye—eh?"

Tom answered nothing.

"Get up, you beast!" said Legree, kicking him again.

This was a difficult matter for one so bruised and faint, and as Tom made efforts to do so, Legree laughed brutally.

"What makes ye so spry this morning, Tom? Cotched cold, may be, last night."

Tom by this time had gained his feet and was confronting his master with a steady, unmoved front.

"The devil, you can!" said Legree, looking him over. "I believe you haven't got enough yet. Now, Tom, get right

down on yer knees and beg my pardon for yer shines last
night."

Tom did not move.

"Down, you dog!" said Legree, striking him with his riding
whip.

"Mas'r Legree," said Tom, "I can't do it. I did only what I
thought was right. I shall do jest so again, if ever the time
comes. I never will do a cruel thing, come what may."

"Yes, but ye don't know what may come, Master Tom. Ye
think what you've got is something. I tell you 'tan't anything—
nothing 'tall. How would ye like to be tied to a tree and have
a slow fire lit up around ye—wouldn't that be pleasant, eh
Tom?"

"Mas'r," said Tom, "I know ye can do dreadful things.
But"—he stretched himself upward and clasped his hands—
"but after ye've killed the body, there an't no more ye can do.

And oh, there's all ETERNITY to come, after that!"

ETERNITY—the word thrilled through the black man's soul with light and power as he spoke. It thrilled through the sinner's soul, too, like the bite of a scorpion. Legree gnashed his teeth, but rage kept him silent, and Tom, like a man disenthralled, spoke in a clear and cheerful voice:

"Mas'r Legree, as ye bought me, I'll be a true and faithful servant to ye. I'll give ye all the work of my hands, all my time, all my strength. But my soul I won't give up to mortal man. I will hold on to the Lord, and put his commands before all—die or live. You may be sure on 't. Mas'r Legree, I an't a grain afeared to die. I'd as soon die as not. Ye may whip me, starve me, burn me—it'll only send me sooner where I want to go."

"I'll make ye give out, though, 'fore I've done!" Legree said in a rage.

"I shall have *help*," said Tom. "You'll never do it."

"Who the devil's going to help you?"

"The Lord Almighty," said Tom.

"D——n you!" and with one blow of his fist Legree felled Tom to the earth.

A cold, soft hand fell on Legree's at this moment. He turned—it was Cassy.

"Will you be a fool?" she said in French. "Let him go! Let me alone to get him fit to be in the field again. Isn't it just as I told you?"

"Well, have it your own way," Legree said doggedly to Cassy. Then, "Hark ye!" he said to Tom. "I won't deal with ye now, because the business is pressing, and I want all my hands. But I *never* forget. I'll score it against ye, and sometime I'll have my pay out o' yer old black hide—mind ye!"

He turned and went out.

"There you go," said Cassy, looking darkly after him. "Your reckoning's to come yet!—My poor fellow, how are you?"

"The Lord God hath sent his angel and shut the lion's mouth, for this time," said Tom.

"For this time, to be sure," said Cassy. "But now you've got his ill will upon you, to follow you day in, day out, hanging like a dog on your throat—sucking your blood, bleeding away your life, drop by drop. I know the man."

Liberty

A WHILE we must leave Tom in the hands of his persecutors, while we turn to pursue the fortunes of George and his wife, whom we left in friendly hands in a farmhouse on the roadside.

Tom Loker we left, too, groaning in a most immaculately clean Quaker bed, under the motherly supervision of Aunt Dorcas, who found him to the full as tractable a patient as a sick bison.

Imagine a tall, dignified, spiritual woman, whose white muslin cap shades silvery hair, parted on a broad, clear forehead, which overarches thoughtful gray eyes. A snowy handkerchief of lisse crape is folded neatly across her bosom. Her glossy brown silk dress rustles peacefully as she glides up and down the chamber.

"The devil!" says Tom Loker, giving a great throw to the bedclothes.

"I must request thee, Thomas, not to use such language," said Aunt Dorcas, as she quietly rearranged the bed.

"Well, I won't, granny, if I can help it," says Tom. "But it is enough to make a fellow swear—so cursedly hot!"

Dorcas removed a comforter from the bed, straightened the

clothes again, and tucked them in till Tom looked something like a chrysalis.

"I wish, friend, thee would leave off cursing and swearing, and think upon thy ways," she remarked.

"What the devil," said Tom, "should I think of *them* for? Last thing ever *I* want to think of—hang it all!" And Tom flounced over, untucking and disarranging everything.

"That fellow and gal are here, I s'pose," said he sullenly, after a pause.

"They are so," said Dorcas.

"They'd better be off up to the lake," said Tom, "the quicker the better."

"Probably they will do so," said Aunt Dorcas, knitting peacefully.

"And hark ye," said Tom. "We've got correspondents in Sandusky, that watch the boats for us. I don't care if I tell, now. I hope they *will* get away, just to spite Marks—the cursed puppy! D——n him!"

"Thomas!" said Dorcas.

"I tell you, granny, if you bottle a fellow up too tight, I shall split," said Tom. "But about the gal—tell 'em to dress her up some way so's to alter her. Her description's out in Sandusky."

"We will attend to that matter," said Dorcas with composure.

As we at this place take leave of Tom Loker, we may as well say that, having lain three weeks at the Quaker dwelling, sick with rheumatic fever, which set in along with his other afflictions, Tom arose from his bed a somewhat sadder and wiser man. And in place of slave-catching, he betook himself to life in one of the new settlements, where his talents developed themselves more happily in trapping bears, wolves, and other inhabitants of the forest, in which he made himself quite a name in the land.

As Tom had informed them that their party would be

looked for in Sandusky, it was thought prudent to divide them. Jim, with his old mother, was forwarded separately. And a night or two after, George and Eliza, with their child, were driven privately into Sandusky and lodged beneath a hospitable roof, preparatory to taking their last passage on the lake.

Their night was now far spent, and the morning star of liberty rose fair before them. Liberty! What is it? Is there anything more in it than a name? Why, men and women of America, does your heart's blood thrill at that word, for which your fathers bled, and your braver mothers were willing that their noblest and best should die?

What is freedom to that young man, who sits there with his arms folded over his broad chest, the tint of African blood in his cheek, its dark fires in his eyes—what is freedom to George Harris? To your fathers, freedom was the right of a nation to be a nation. To him, it is the right of a man to be a man, and not a brute; the right to call the wife of his bosom his wife, and to protect her from lawless violence; the right to protect and educate his child; the right to have a home of his own, a religion of his own, a character of his own, unsubject to the will of another. All these thoughts were rolling and seething in George's breast as he watched his wife adapting to her slender form the articles of man's attire in which it was deemed safest she should make her escape.

"Now for it," said Eliza, as she stood before the glass and shook down her mass of silky, curly hair. "I say, George, it's almost a pity, isn't it—pity it's all got to come off?"

George smiled sadly and made no answer.

Eliza turned resolutely to the glass, and the scissors glittered as one long lock after another was detached from her head.

"Now for a few fancy touches," she said, taking up a hairbrush. "There now, an't I a pretty young fellow?" And Eliza turned to her husband, laughing and blushing at the same time.

"You always will be pretty, do what you will," said George.

"What does make you so sober?" said Eliza, kneeling on one knee and laying her hand on his. "We are only within twenty-four hours of Canada, they say. Only a day and a night on the lake, and then—oh, then—!"

"Oh, Eliza!" said George, drawing her toward him. "That is it. Now my fate is all narrowing down to a point. To come so near, to be almost in sight, and then lose all. I should never live under it, Eliza."

"Don't fear," said his wife. "The good Lord would not have brought us so far if he didn't mean to carry us through. I seem to feel him with us, George. I feel that God is going to bring us out of bondage this very day."

"I will believe you, Eliza," said George, rising. "I will believe. Come, let's be off. Put on your cap. So—a little to one side. That crop of little curls is quite becoming—I never saw you look so pretty. But it's almost time for the carriage. I wonder if Mrs. Smyth has got Harry rigged?"

The door opened, and a middle-aged woman entered, leading little Harry, dressed in girl's clothes.

"What a pretty girl he makes!" cried Eliza admiringly.

The child stood gravely regarding his mother in her strange attire, observing a profound silence, and peeping at her from under his dark curls.

"Does Harry know Mamma?" said Eliza, stretching her hands toward him.

The child clung shyly to the woman.

"Come, Eliza, why do you try to coax him when you know that he has got to be kept away from you?"

"I know it's foolish," said Eliza, "yet I can't bear to have him turn away from me. But come—where's my cloak? And these gloves! Mercy upon us!" said Eliza. "Why, my hands are lost in them."

"I advise you to keep them on pretty strictly," said George. "Your little slender paw might bring us all out. Now, Mrs.

Smyth, you are to go under our charge and be our aunty—
you mind."

"I've heard," said Mrs. Smyth, "that there have been men
down, warning all the packet captains against a man and
woman with a little boy."

"They have!" said George. "Well, if we see any such
people, we can tell them."

A hack now drove to the door, and the friendly family
who had received the fugitives crowded around them with
farewell greetings.

The disguises the party had assumed were in accordance
with the hints of Tom Loker. Mrs. Smyth, a woman from the
settlement in Canada to which they were fleeing, being fortu-
nately about to cross the lake to return thither, had consented
to appear as the aunt of little Harry. In order to attach him to
her, he had been allowed to remain, the last two days, under

her sole charge. And an extra amount of petting, joined to an indefinite amount of seed-cakes and candy, had cemented a very close attachment on the part of the young gentleman.

The hack drove to the wharf. The two young men, as they appeared, walked up the plank into the boat, Eliza gallantly giving her arm to Mrs. Smyth, and George attending to their baggage.

George was standing at the captain's office, settling for his party, when he overheard two men talking by his side.

"I've watched everyone that came on board," said one, "and I know they're not on this boat."

The voice was that of the clerk of the boat. The speaker whom he addressed was our sometime friend Marks, who had come on to Sandusky, seeking whom he might devour.

"You would scarcely know the woman from a white one," said Marks. "The man is a very light mullato. He has a brand in one of his hands."

The hand with which George was taking the tickets and change trembled a little. But he turned coolly around, fixed an unconcerned glance on the face of the speaker, and walked leisurely toward another part of the boat, where Eliza stood waiting for him. Mrs. Smyth, with little Harry, had meantime sought the seclusion of the ladies' cabin.

The bell rang out its farewell peal. Marks walked down the plank to the shore. And George drew a long sigh of relief as the boat put a returnless distance between them.

Oh, what an untold world there is in one human heart! Who thought, as George walked calmly up and down the deck of the steamer with his shy companion at his side, of all that was burning in his bosom? The mighty good that seemed approaching seemed too good, too fair, to be a reality. He felt a jealous dread, every moment of the day, that something would rise to snatch it from him. But the boat swept on. Hours fleeted, and at last, clear and full rose the blessed English shores.

George and his wife stood arm in arm as the boat neared

the small town of Amherstberg. His breath grew thick and
short, and a mist gathered before his eyes. Silently he pressed
the little hand that lay trembling on his arm. The bell rang,
the boat stopped. Scarcely seeing what he did, he looked out
his baggage and gathered his party. The little company were
landed on the shore. They stood still till the boat had cleared,
and then, with tears and embracings, the husband and wife,
with their wondering child in their arms, knelt down and
lifted up their hearts to God.

A moment after, George and Eliza were guided by Mrs.
Smyth to the hospitable abode of a good missionary, whom
Christian charity has placed here as a shepherd to the outcast
and wandering who are constantly finding an asylum on this
shore.

Who can speak the blessedness of that first day of freedom? Is not the *sense* of liberty a higher and a finer one than
any of the five? To move, speak, and breathe—go out and
come in unwatched and free from danger! Who can speak the
blessings of that rest which comes down on the free man's
pillow, under laws which ensure to him the rights that God
has given to man? How fair and precious to that mother was
that sleeping child's face, endeared by the memory of a thousand dangers! How impossible was it to sleep, in the possession of such blessedness! And yet, these two had not one acre
of ground—not a roof that they could call their own—they
had spent their all, to the last dollar. They had nothing more
than the birds of the air, or the flowers of the field—yet they
could not sleep for joy.

"Oh, ye who take freedom from man, with what words
shall ye answer it to God?"

The Victory

WHEN Tom stood face to face with his persecutor, and heard his threats, and thought that his hour was come, his heart swelled bravely in him, and he thought he could bear torture and fire, bear anything, with the vision of Jesus and heaven but just a step beyond. But when he was gone, and the excitement passed off, came back the pain of his bruised and weary limbs—came back the sense of his utterly hopeless, forlorn estate. And the day passed wearily enough.

Long before his wounds were healed, Legree insisted that he should be put to the regular field work. And then came day after day of pain and weariness, aggravated by every kind of injustice and indignity that the ill will of a mean and malicious mind could devise.

Tom no longer wondered at the habitual surliness of his associates. Nay, he found the placid, sunny temper, which had been the habit of his life, sorely strained by the inroads of the same thing. He had flattered himself on leisure to read his Bible, but there was no such thing as leisure there. In the height of the season, Legree did not hesitate to press all his hands through, Sundays and weekdays alike. Why shouldn't he? He made more cotton by it and gained his wager. And if it wore out a few more hands, he could buy better ones. At first Tom used to read a verse or two of his Bible by the flicker of the fire, after he had returned from his daily toil. But after the cruel treatment he received, he used to come home so exhausted that his head swam and his eyes failed when he tried to read. He was obliged to stretch himself down with the others, in utter exhaustion.

Is it strange that the religious peace and trust which had

upborne him hitherto should give way to tossings of soul and despondent darkness? It was weeks and months that Tom wrestled in his soul. He thought of Miss Ophelia's letter to his Kentucky friends and would pray earnestly that God would send him deliverance. Then he would watch, day after day, in the vague hope of seeing somebody sent to redeem him. When nobody came, he would crush back bitter thoughts— that it was vain to serve God, that God had forgotten him.

One evening he was sitting in utter dejection by a few decaying brands where his coarse supper was baking. He put a few bits of brushwood on the fire, and strove to raise the light, and then drew his worn Bible from his pocket. There were all the marked passages which had thrilled his soul so often. Had the word lost its power, or could the failing eye and weary sense no longer answer to the touch of that mighty inspiration? Heavily sighing, he put it in his pocket.

A coarse laugh roused him. He looked up—Legree was standing opposite to him.

"Well, old boy," he said, "you find your religion don't work, it seems! I thought I should get that through your wool at last!"

The cruel taunt was more than hunger and cold and nakedness. Tom was silent.

"You were a fool," said Legree, "for I meant to do well by you when I bought you. You might have been better off than Sambo, or Quimbo either, and had easy times. And instead of getting cut up and thrashed every day or two, ye might have had liberty to lord it round and cut up the other niggers. And ye might have had, now and then, a good warming of whiskey punch. Come, Tom, don't you think you'd better be reasonable? Heave that ar old pack of trash in the fire, and join my church!"

"The Lord forbid!" said Tom fervently.

"You see the Lord an't going to help you. If he had been, he wouldn't have let *me* get you! This yer religion is all a mess of lying trumpery, Tom. I know all about it. Ye'd better hold to me. I'm somebody, and can do something!"

"No, Mas'r," said Tom. "I'll hold on. The Lord may help me, or not help. But I'll hold to Him, and believe Him to the last!"

"The more fool you!" said Legree, spitting scornfully at him and spurning him with his foot. "Never mind. I'll chase you down yet and bring you under—you'll see!" And Legree turned away.

Tom sat like one stunned at the fire. Suddenly everything around him seemed to fade, and a vision rose before him of one crowned with thorns, buffeted and bleeding. Tom gazed in awe and wonder at the majestic patience of the face. The deep, pathetic eyes thrilled him. His soul awoke as with floods of emotion he stretched out his hands and fell upon his knees—when gradually the vision changed. The sharp thorns became rays of glory. And in splendor inconceivable, he saw that same face bending compassionately toward him, and a voice said: "He that overcometh shall sit down with me on my throne, even as I also overcame, and am set down with my Father on His throne."

How long Tom lay there, he knew not. When he came to himself, the fire was gone out, his clothes were wet with the chill and drenching dews. But the dread soul-crisis was past, and in the joy that filled him, he no longer felt hunger, cold, degradation, disappointment, wretchedness. Tom looked up to the silent, ever-living stars—and the solitude of the night rang with the triumphant words of a hymn which he had sung often in happier days, but never with such feeling as now:

> The earth shall be dissolved like snow,
>   The sun shall cease to shine;
> But God, who called me here below,
>   Shall be forever mine.

And when this mortal life shall fail,
And flesh and sense shall cease,
I shall possess within the veil
A life of joy and peace.

When the dim gray of dawn woke the slumberers to go forth to the field, there was among those tattered and shivering wretches one who walked with an exultant tread. For firmer than the ground he trod on, was his strong faith in Almighty, eternal love.

From this time, peace encircled the lowly heart of the oppressed one. Past now the earthly regrets, past its fluctuations of hope and fear and desire—the human will was now entirely merged in the Divine. So short now seemed the remaining voyage of life that uttermost woes fell from him unharming.

All noticed the change in his appearance. Cheerfulness and alertness seemed to return to him, and a quietness which no insult or injury could ruffle seemed to possess him.

"What the devil's got into Tom?" Legree said to Sambo. "A while ago he was all down in the mouth, and now he's peart as a cricket."

"Dunno, Mas'r. Gwine to run off, mebbe."

"Like to see him try that," said Legree, with a savage grin, "wouldn't we, Sambo?"

"Guess we would! Haw! haw! ho!" said Sambo, laughing. "Lord, de fun! To see him stickin' in de mud—chasin' and tarin' through de bushes, dogs a-holdin' on to him! Lord, I laughed fit to split, dat ar time we cotched Molly. I thought they'd a had her all stripped up afore I could get 'em off. She car's de marks o' dat ar spree yet."

"I reckon she will to her grave," said Legree. "But now, Sambo, you look sharp. If the nigger's got anything of this sort going, trip him up."

"Mas'r, let me lone for dat," said Sambo. "I'll tree de coon. Ho, ho, ho!"

This was spoken as Legree was getting on to his horse, to go to the neighboring town. That night, as he was returning, he thought he would turn his horse and ride round the quarters and see if all was safe.

It was a superb moonlit night. The shadows of the graceful china trees lay minutely pencilled on the turf below, and there was that stillness in the air which it seems almost unholy to disturb. Legree was at a little distance from the quarters when he heard the voice of someone singing. It was not a usual sound there, and he paused to listen. A musical tenor voice sang:

> When I can read my title clear
> To mansions in the skies,
> I'll bid farewell to every fear,
> And wipe my weeping eyes.
>
> Should earth against my soul engage,
> And hellish darts be hurled,
> Then I can smile at Satan's rage,
> And face a frowning world.
>
> Let cares like a wild deluge come,
> And storms of sorrow fall,
> May I but safely reach my home,
> My God, my Heaven, my All.

"So ho!" said Legree to himself. "He thinks so, does he? How I hate these cursed Methodist hymns! Here, you nigger," said he, coming suddenly out upon Tom and raising his riding whip, "how dare you be gettin' up this yer row, when you ought to be in bed? Shut yer old black gash, and get along in with you!"

"Yes, Mas'r," said Tom with ready cheerfulness, as he rose to go in.

Legree was provoked beyond measure by Tom's evident happiness, and riding up to him, belabored him over his head and shoulders.

"There, you dog!" he said. "See if you'll feel so comfortable after that!"

But the blows fell now only on the outer man, and not, as before, on the heart. Tom stood perfectly submissive. And yet Legree could not hide from himself that his power over his thrall was somehow gone. And as Tom disappeared in his cabin, and he wheeled his horse suddenly round, he understood full well that it was God who was standing between him and his victim, and he cursed Him.

Tom's whole soul overflowed with compassion and sympathy for the poor wretches by whom he was surrounded. To him it seemed as if his life-sorrows were now over. And out of that strange treasury of peace and joy with which he had been endowed from above, he longed to pour out something for the relief of their woes. It is true, opportunities were scanty. But on the way to the fields and back again, and during the hours of labor, chances fell in his way of extending a helping hand to the weary and disheartened.

The poor, worn-down, brutalized creatures at first could scarce comprehend this. But when it was continued week after week and month after month, it began to awaken long-silent chords in their benumbed hearts. Gradually the strange, silent, patient man, who was ready to bear everyone's burden and sought help from none, who stood aside for all, and came last, and took least, yet was foremost to share his little all with any who needed, the man who, on cold nights, would give up his tattered blanket to add to the comfort of some woman who shivered with sickness, and who filled the baskets of the weaker ones in the field at the terrible risk of coming short in his own measure—this man at last began to have a strange power over them. When the more pressing season was past, and they were allowed again their Sundays for their own use, many would gather together to hear from him of Jesus. And who can speak the simple joy with which some of those poor outcasts, to whom life was a joyless journey to a dark unknown, heard of a compassionate Redeemer and a heavenly home?

One night, after all in Tom's cabin were sunk in sleep, he was suddenly aroused by seeing Cassy's face at the hole between the logs that served for a window. She made a silent gesture for him to come out.

Tom came out the door. It was between one and two o'clock at night—broad, calm, still moonlight. Tom remarked, as the light of the moon fell upon Cassy's large, black eyes, that there was a wild and peculiar glare in them, unlike their wonted fixed despair.

"Come, Father Tom," she said, laying her small hand on his wrist and drawing him forward with a force as if the hand were of steel. "Come—I've news for you."

"What, Misse Cassy?" said Tom anxiously.

"Tom, wouldn't you like your liberty?"

"I shall have it, Missy, in God's time," said Tom.

"Ay, but you may have it tonight," said Cassy with a flash of sudden energy. "Come on."

Tom hesitated.

"Come!" said she in a whisper, fixing her eyes on him. "Come along! He's asleep—sound. I put enough into his brandy to keep him so. I wish I'd had more—I shouldn't have wanted you. But come, the back door is unlocked. There's an axe there—I put it there. His room door is open. I'll show you the way. I'd done it myself, only my arms are so weak. Come along!"

"Not for ten thousand worlds, Misse!" said Tom firmly, stopping and holding her back as she was pressing forward.

"But think of all these poor creatures," said Cassy. "We might set them all free, and go somewhere in the swamps, and find an island, and live by ourselves. I've heard of its being done. Any life is better than this."

"No!" said Tom. "No! Good never comes of wickedness. I'd sooner chop my right hand off!"

"Then *I* shall do it," said Cassy, turning.

"No, no, no!" said Tom, holding her small clenched hands. "No, ye poor, lost soul, that ye mustn't do. The dear, blessed Lord never shed no blood but His own, and that He poured out for us when we was enemies. Lord, help us to follow His steps and love our enemies."

"Love!" said Cassy with a fierce glare. "Love *such* enemies! It isn't in flesh and blood."

"No, Misse, it isn't," said Tom, looking up. "But *He* gives it to us, and that's the *victory*. When we can love and pray over all and through all, the battle's past, and the victory's come—glory be to God!" And with streaming eyes and choking voice, the black man looked up to heaven.

The deep fervor of Tom's feeling, the softness of his voice, his tears, fell like dew on the wild, unsettled spirit of the poor woman. A softness gathered over the fires of her eye. She looked down, and Tom could feel the relaxing muscles of her hands as she said:

"Didn't I tell you that evil spirits followed me? Oh, Father Tom, I can't pray. I wish I could. I never have prayed since my children were sold. What you say must be right—I know it must. But when I try to pray, I can only hate and curse. I can't pray."

"Poor soul!" said Tom compassionately. "Satan desires to have ye, and sift ye as wheat. I pray the Lord for ye. Oh, Misse Cassy, turn to the dear Lord Jesus. He came to bind up the broken-hearted and comfort all that mourn."

Cassy stood silent, while large, heavy tears dropped from her downcast eyes.

"Misse Cassy," said Tom in a hesitating tone after surveying her a moment in silence, "if ye only could get away from here—if the thing was possible—I'd 'vise ye and Emmeline to do it. That is, if ye could go without blood-guiltiness—not otherwise."

"Would you try it with us, Father Tom?"

"No," said Tom. "Time was when I would. But the Lord's given me a work among these yer poor souls, and I'll stay with 'em and bear my cross with 'em till the end. It's different with you. It's a snare to you—it's more'n you can stand—and you'd better go, if you can."

"I know no way but through the grave," said Cassy.

"There's no beast or bird but can find a home somewhere—
even snakes and alligators have their places to lie down and be
quiet. But there's no place for us. Down in the darkest
swamps their dogs will hunt us out and find us. Everybody
and everything is against us. Even the beasts side against us—
and where shall we go?"

Tom stood silent. At length he said:

"Him that saved Daniel in the den of lions, that saved the
children in the fiery furnace—Him that walked on the sea and
bade the winds be still—He's alive yet. And I've faith to believe He can deliver you. Try it, and I'll pray with all my
might for you."

By what strange law of mind is it that an idea long overlooked, and trodden underfoot as a useless stone, suddenly
sparkles out in new light, as a discovered diamond?

Cassy had often revolved, for hours, all possible or probable schemes of escape, and dismissed them all as hopeless and
impracticable. But at this moment there flashed through her
mind a plan so simple and feasible in all its details as to awaken
an instant hope.

"Father Tom, I'll try it!" she said suddenly.

"Amen! said Tom. "The Lord help ye!"

The Stratagem

THE garret of the house that Legree occupied, like most other
garrets, was a desolate space, dusty, hung with cobwebs, and
littered with castoff lumber. The rich family that had inhab-
ited the house in the days of its splendor had imported a great
deal of splendid furniture, some of which they had taken
away with them, while some remained standing in moldering,
unoccupied rooms, or stored away in this place. One or two

immense packing-boxes, in which this furniture was brought, stood against the sides of the garret. There was a small window there, which let in, through its dingy, dusty panes, a scanty, uncertain light on the tall, high-backed chairs and dusty tables that had once seen better days. Altogether it was a weird and ghostly place.

But ghostly as it was, it wanted not in legends among the superstitious Negroes to increase its terrors. Some few years before, a Negro woman who had incurred Legree's displeasure was confined there for several weeks. What passed there, we do not say—the Negroes used to whisper darkly to each other. But it was known that the body of the unfortunate creature was one day taken down from there and buried. And after that, it was said that oaths and cursings and the sound of violent blows used to ring through that old garret and mingle with wailings and groans of despair. Once when Legree chanced to overhear something of this kind, he flew into a violent passion and swore that the next one that told stories about the garret should have an opportunity of knowing what was there, for he would chain them up there for a week. This hint was enough to repress talking, though, of course, it did not disturb the credit of the story in the least.

The sleeping room of Cassy was directly under the garret. One day, without consulting Legree, she suddenly took it upon herself to change all the furniture of the room to one at some considerable distance. The under-servants, who were called on to effect this movement, were running and bustling about with great zeal and confusion when Legree returned from a ride.

"Hallo, you Cass!" said Legree. "What's in the wind now?"

"Nothing. Only I choose to have another room," said Cassy.

"And what for, pray?" said Legree.

"I choose to," said Cassy.

"The devil you do! And what for?"

"I'd like to get some sleep now and then."

"Sleep! Well, what hinders your sleeping?"

"I could tell, I suppose, if you want to hear," said Cassy dryly.

"Speak out, you minx!" said Legree.

"Oh, nothing. I suppose it wouldn't disturb *you*. Only groans, and people scuffling and rolling round on the garret floor, half the night, from twelve to morning!"

"People up garret!" said Legree uneasily, but forcing a laugh. "Who are they, Cassy?"

Cassy raised her sharp, black eyes and looked in the face of Legree with an expression that went through his bones as she said, "To be sure, Simon, who are they? I'd like to have *you* tell me. You don't know, I suppose!"

With an oath, Legree struck at her with his riding whip. But she glided to one side and passed through the door, and looking back, said, "If you'll sleep in that room, you'll know all about it. Perhaps you'd better try it." And then immediately she shut and locked the door.

Legree blustered and swore, and threatened to break down the door, but apparently thought better of it and walked uneasily into the sitting room. Cassy perceived that her shaft had struck home. And from that hour she never ceased to continue the train of influences she had begun.

In a knothole in the garret she had inserted the neck of an old bottle in such a manner that when there was the least wind, most doleful wailing sounds proceeded from it, which, in a high wind, increased to a perfect shriek, such as to superstitious ears might easily seem to be that of horror and despair.

These sounds were, from time to time, heard by the servants, and revived in full force the memory of the old ghost legend. A superstitious, creeping horror seemed to fill the house, and though no one dared to breathe it to Legree, he found himself surrounded by it, as by an atmosphere.

A night or two after this, Legree was sitting in the old sitting room, by the side of a flickering wood fire. It was a stormy, windy night, such as raises whole squadrons of nondescript noises in rickety old houses. Windows were rattling, shutters flapping, the wind carousing and tumbling down the chimney and every once in a while puffing out smoke and ashes, as if a legion of spirits were coming after them. Legree had been casting up accounts and reading newspapers for some hours, while Cassy sat in the corner, sullenly looking into the fire. Legree laid down his paper, and seeing an old book lying on the table, which he had noticed Cassy reading the first part of the evening, took it up and began to turn it over. It was one of those collections of stories of bloody murders, ghostly legends, and supernatural visitations which have a strange fascination for one who once begins to read them.

Legree poohed and pished, but read, turning page after page, till finally he threw down the book with an oath.

"You don't believe in ghosts, do you, Cass?" said he, taking the tongs and settling the fire. "I thought you'd more sense than to let noises scare *you*."

"No matter what I believe," said Cassy sullenly.

"Fellows used to try to frighten me with their yarns at sea," said Legree. "Never come it round me that way. I'm too tough for any such trash, tell ye."

Cassy sat looking intensely at him in the shadow of the corner. There was that strange light in her eyes that always impressed Legree with uneasiness.

"Them noises was nothing but rats and wind," said Legree. "Rats will make a devil of a noise. I used to hear 'em sometimes down in the hold of the ship. And wind—Lord's sake! Ye can make anything out o' wind."

Cassy knew Legree was uneasy under her eyes, and therefore she made no answer, but sat fixing them on him, with that strange, unearthly expression as before.

"Come, speak out, woman—don't you think so?" said Legree.

"Can rats walk down stairs, and come walking through the entry, and open a door when you've locked it and set a chair against it?" said Cassy. "And come walk, walk, walking right up to your bed, and put out their hand—so?"

Cassy kept her glittering eyes fixed on Legree as she spoke, and he stared at her like a man in the nightmare, till when she finished by laying her hand, icy cold, on his, he sprang back with an oath.

"Woman! What do you mean? Nobody did?"

"Oh, no—of course not—did I say they did?" said Cassy with a smile of chilling mockery.

"But—did—have you really seen? Come, Cass, what is it, now—speak out!"

"You may sleep there yourself," said Cassy, "if you want to know."

"Did it come from the garret, Cassy?"

"*It*—what?" said Cassy.

"Why, what you told of—"

"I didn't tell you anything," said Cassy, with dogged sullenness. Legree walked up and down the room uneasily.

"I'll have this yer thing examined. I'll look into it this very night. I'll take my pistols—"

"Do," said Cassy. "Sleep in that room. I'd like to see you doing it. Fire your pistols—do!"

Legree stamped his foot and swore violently.

"Don't swear," said Cassy. "Nobody knows who may be hearing you. Hark! What was that?"

"What?" said Legree, starting.

A heavy old Dutch clock that stood in the corner of the room began and slowly struck twelve.

For some reason or other, Legree neither spoke nor moved. A vague horror fell on him—while Cassy, with a keen, sneering glitter in her eyes, stood looking at him, counting the strokes.

"Twelve o'clock. Well, *now* we'll see," said she, turning and opening the door into the passageway, and standing as if listening.

"Hark! What's that?" said she, raising her finger.

"It's only the wind," said Legree. "Don't you hear how cursedly it blows?"

"Simon, come here" said Cassy in a whisper, laying her hand on his and leading him to the foot of the stairs. "Do you know what *that* is? Hark!"

A wild shriek came pealing down the stairway. It came from the garret. Legree's knees knocked together. His face grew white with fear.

"Hadn't you better get your pistols?" said Cassy, with a sneer that froze Legree's blood. "It's time this thing was looked into, you know. I'd like to have you go up now. *They're at it.*"

"I won't go," said Legree with an oath.

"Why not? There an't any such thing as ghosts, you know! Come!" And Cassy flitted up the winding stairway, laughing, and looking back after him. "Come on."

"I believe you *are* the devil!" said Legree. "Come back, you hag—come back, Cass! You shan't go!"

But Cassy laughed wildly and fled on. He heard her open the entry doors that led to the garret. A wild gust of wind swept down, extinguishing the candle he held in his hand, and with it came the fearful, unearthly screams. They seemed to be shrieked in his very ear.

Legree fled frantically into the parlor, whither in a few moments he was followed by Cassy, pale, calm, cold as an avenging spirit, and with that same fearful light in her eye.

"I hope you are satisfied," said she.

"Blast you, Cass!" said Legree.

"What for?" said Cassy. "I only went up and shut the doors. *What's the matter with that garret*, Simon, do you suppose?" said she.

"None of your business!" said Legree.

"Oh, it an't? Well," said Cassy, "at any rate, I'm glad *I* don't sleep under it."

Anticipating the rising of the wind, that very evening Cassy had been up and opened the garret window. Of course, the moment the doors were opened, the wind had drafted down and extinguished the light.

This may serve as a specimen of the game that Cassy played with Legree, until he would sooner have put his head into a lion's mouth than to have explored that garret. Meanwhile, in the night, when everybody else was asleep, Cassy slowly and carefully accumulated there a stock of provisions sufficient to afford subsistence for some time. She transferred, article by article, a greater part of her own and Emmeline's wardrobe. All things being arranged, they only waited a fitting opportunity to put their plan in execution.

By cajoling Legree and taking advantage of a good-natured interval, Cassy had got him to take her with him to the neighboring town, which was situated directly on the Red River. She remarked every turn in the road, and formed an estimate of the time to be occupied in traversing it.

At the time when all was matured for action, our readers may, perhaps, like to look behind the scenes and see the final measure.

It was now near evening. Legree had been absent on a ride to a neighboring farm. For many days Cassy had been unusually gracious and accommodating, and Legree and she had been, apparently, on the best of terms. At present we may behold her and Emmeline in the room of the latter, busy in sorting and arranging two small bundles.

"There, these will be large enough," said Cassy. "Now put on your bonnet, and let's start—it's just about the right time."

"Why, they can see us yet," said Emmeline.

"I mean they shall," said Cassy coolly. "Don't you know that they must have their chase after us, at any rate? The way of the thing is to be just this: We will steal out of the back door and run down by the quarters. Sambo or Quimbo will be sure to see us. They will give chase, and we will get into the swamp. Then they can't follow us any further till they go up and give the alarm, and turn out the dogs, and so on. And while they are blundering round, and tumbling over each other, as they always do, you and I will just slip along to the creek that runs back of the house, and wade along in it till we get opposite the back door. That will put the dogs all at fault, for scent won't lie in the water. Everyone will run out of the house to look after us, and then we'll whip in at the back door, and up into the garret, where I've got a nice bed made up in one of the great boxes. We must stay in that garret a good while, for I tell you he will raise heaven and earth after us. He'll muster some of those old overseers on the other plantations, and have a great hunt. And they'll go over every inch of ground in that swamp. He makes it his boast that nobody ever got away from him. So let him hunt at his leisure."

"Cassy, how well you have planned it!" said Emmeline. "Who ever would have thought of it, but you?"

There was neither pleasure nor exultation in Cassy's eyes—only a despairing firmness.

"Come," she said, reaching her hand to Emmeline.

The two fugitives glided noiselessly from the house and flitted, through the gathering shadows of the evening, along by the quarters. As Cassy expected, when quite near the verge of the swamps that encircled the plantation, they heard a voice calling to them to stop. It was not Sambo, however, but Legree, who was pursuing them with violent curses. At the sound, the feebler spirit of Emmeline gave way, and laying hold of Cassy's arm, she said, "Oh, Cassy, I'm going to faint!"

"If you do, I'll kill you!" said Cassy, drawing a small, glittering stiletto and flashing it before the eyes of the girl.

The words and action accomplished the purpose. Emmeline did not faint, and succeeded in plunging with Cassy into a part of the labyrinth of swamp so deep and dark that it was perfectly hopeless for Legree to think of following them without assistance.

"Well," said he, chuckling brutally, "at any rate, they've got themselves into a trap now—the baggages! They're safe enough. They shall sweat for it!"

"Hulloa, there! Sambo! Quimbo! All hands!" called Legree, coming to the quarters when the men and women were just returning from work. "There's two runaways in the swamps. I'll give five dollars to any nigger as catches 'em. Turn out the dogs! Turn out Tiger and Fury and the rest!"

The sensation produced by this news was immediate. Many of the men sprang forward to offer their services. Some ran one way, and some another. Some were for getting flambeaux of pineknots. Some were uncoupling the dogs, whose hoarse, savage bay added not a little to the animation of the scene.

"Mas'r, shall we shoot 'em, if we can't cotch 'em?" said Sambo, to whom his master brought out a rifle.

"You may fire on Cass, if you like—it's time she was gone to the devil, where she belongs—but the gal, not," said Legree. "And now, boys, be spry and smart. Five dollars for him that gets 'em, and a glass of spirits to every one of you, anyhow."

The whole band, with the glare of blazing torches and whoop and shout and savage yell of man and beast, proceeded down to the swamp, followed at some distance by every servant in the house. The establishment was, of a consequence, wholly deserted when Cassy and Emmeline glided into it the back way. The whooping and shouts of their pursuers were still filling the air. And looking from the sitting room windows, Cassy and Emmeline could see the troop, with their flambeaux, just dispersing themselves along the edge of the swamp.

"See there!" said Emmeline, pointing. "The hunt has begun! Look how those lights dance about! Hark! The dogs! If we were *there*—! Oh, for pity's sake, do let's hide ourselves! Quick!"

"There's no occasion for hurry," said Cassy coolly. "They are all out after the hunt—that's the amusement of the evening! We'll go upstairs by and by. Meanwhile," said she, deliberately taking a key from the pocket of a coat that Legree had thrown down in his hurry, "meanwhile I shall take something to pay our passage."

She unlocked the desk and took from it a roll of bills, which she counted over rapidly.

"Oh, don't let's do that!" said Emmeline.

"Don't!" said Cassy. "Why not? Would you have us starve in the swamps, or have that which will pay our way to the free states? Money will do anything, girl." And as she spoke, she put the money in her bosom.

"It would be stealing," said Emmeline in a distressed whisper.

"Stealing!" said Cassy with a scornful laugh. "They who steal body and soul needn't talk to us. Every one of these bills is stolen—stolen from poor, starving, sweating creatures, who must go to the devil at last for his profit. Let *him* talk about stealing! But come, we may as well go up garret. I've got a stock of candles there and some books to pass away the time. You may be pretty sure they won't come *there* to inquire after us. If they do, I'll play ghost for them."

When Emmeline reached the garret, she found an immense box turned on its side so that the opening faced the wall, or rather the eaves. Cassy lit a small lamp, and creeping round under the eaves, they established themselves in it. It was spread with a couple of small mattresses and some pillows. A box near by was plentifully stored with candles, provisions, and all the clothing necessary to their journey, which Cassy had arranged into bundles of an astonishingly small compass.

"There," said Cassy as she fixed the lamp into a small hook which she had driven into the side of the box for that purpose. "This is to be our home for the present. How do you like it?"

"Are you sure they won't come and search the garret?"

"I'd like to see Simon Legree doing that," said Cassy. "No, indeed. He will be too glad to keep away. As to the servants, they would any of them stand and be shot, sooner than show their faces here."

Somewhat reassured, Emmeline settled herself back on her pillow.

"What did you mean, Cassy, by saying you would kill me?" she said simply.

"I meant to stop your fainting," said Cassy. "And I did do it. And now I tell you, Emmeline, you must make up your mind *not* to faint, let what will come. There's no sort of need of it. If I had not stopped you, that wretch might have had his hands on you now."

Emmeline shuddered.

The two remained some time in silence. Cassy busied herself with a French book. Emmeline, overcome with exhaustion, fell into a doze and slept some time. She was awakened by loud shouts and outcries, the tramp of horse's feet, and the baying of dogs. She started up with a faint shriek.

"Only the hunt coming back," said Cassy coolly. "Never

fear. Look out of this knothole. See 'em all down there? Simon has to give it up for this night. Look how muddy his horse is, flouncing about in the swamp. The dogs, too, look rather crestfallen. Ah, my good sir, you'll have to try the race again and again—the game isn't there."

"Oh, don't speak a word!" said Emmeline. "What if they should hear you?"

"If they do hear anything, it will make them very particular to keep away," said Cassy. "No danger. We may make any noise we please, and it will only add to the effect."

At length the stillness of midnight settled down over the house. Legree, cursing his ill luck, and vowing dire vengeance on the morrow, went to bed.

The Martyr

THE escape of Cassy and Emmeline irritated the before surly temper of Legree to the last degree. And his fury, as was to be expected, fell upon the defenseless head of Tom. When he hurriedly announced the tidings among his hands, there was a sudden light in Tom's eye, a sudden upraising of his hands, that did not escape him. He saw that Tom did not join the pursuers. Legree thought of forcing him to do it. But having had, of old, experience of his inflexibility when commanded to take part in any deed of inhumanity, he would not, in his hurry, stop to enter into any conflict with him.

Tom, therefore, remained behind, with a few who had learned of him to pray, and offered up prayers for the escape of the fugitives.

When Legree returned, baffled and disappointed, all the long-working hatred of his soul toward his slave began to gather in a deadly form. Had not this man braved him—steadily, powerfully, resistlessly—ever since he bought him?

"I *hate* him!" said Legree that night as he sat up in his bed. "I *hate* him! And isn't he MINE? Can't I do what I like with him? Who's to hinder?" And Legree clenched his fist and shook it, as if he had something in his hands that he could rend in pieces.

But then, Tom was a faithful, valuable servant, and although Legree hated him the more for that, yet the consideration was still somewhat of a restraint to him.

The next morning he determined to say nothing, as yet. He would assemble a party from some neighboring plantations, with dogs and guns, surround the swamp, and go about the hunt systematically. If it succeeded, well and good. If not, he would summon Tom before him, and—his teeth clenched and his blood boiled—*then* he would break that fellow down, or. . . . There was a dire inward whisper, to which his soul assented.

"Well," said Cassy the next day as she took a survey through the knothole, "the hunt's going to begin again today."

Three or four mounted horsemen were curvetting about on the space in front of the house. And one or two leashes of strange dogs were struggling with the Negroes who held them, baying and barking at each other.

Two of the men were overseers of plantations in the vicinity. Others were some of Legree's associates at the tavern bar of a neighboring city, who had come for the interest of the sport. A more hard-faced set, perhaps, could not be imagined. Legree was serving brandy, profusely, round among them, as also among the Negroes who had been detailed from the various plantations for this service. For it was an object to make every service of this kind among the Negroes as much of a holiday as possible.

Cassy placed her ear to the knothole and could overhear a good deal of the conversation. A grave sneer overcast the

dark, severe gravity of her face as she listened and heard them divide out the ground, discuss the rival merits of the dogs, give orders about firing, and the treatment of each, in case of capture.

"If it wasn't for *you*, child," she said, looking at Emmeline, "I'd *go* out to them. And I'd thank any one of them that *would* shoot me down. For what use will freedom be to me? Can it give me back my children, or make me what I used to be?"

Emmeline, in her childlike simplicity, was half afraid of the dark moods of Cassy. She looked perplexed, but made no answer. She only took her hand, with a gentle, caressing movement.

"Don't!" said Cassy, trying to draw it away. "You'll get me to loving you. And I never mean to love anything again."

"Poor Cassy!" said Emmeline. "Don't feel so! If the Lord

gives us liberty, perhaps he'll give you back your daughter. At any rate, I'll be like a daughter to you. I know I'll never see my poor mother again! I shall love you, Cassy, whether you love me or not."

The gentle, childlike spirit conquered. Cassy sat down by her, put her arm round her neck, and stroked the soft, brown hair.

"Oh, Em," she said, "I've hungered for my children, and thirsted for them, and my eyes fail with longing for them! Here! here!" she said, striking her breast. "It's all desolate, all empty! If God would give me back my children, then I could pray."

"You must trust Him, Cassy," said Emmeline. "He is our Father."

"His wrath is upon us," said Cassy. "He has turned away in anger."

"No, Cassy! He will be good to us! Let us hope in Him," said Emmeline. "I always have had hope."

The hunt was long, animated, and thorough, but unsuccessful. Weary and dispirited, Legree alighted from his horse.

"Now, Quimbo," he said as he stretched himself down in the sitting room, "you jest go and walk that Tom up here, right away! The old cuss is at the bottom of this yer whole matter. And I'll have it out of his old black hide, or I'll know the reason why!"

Sambo and Quimbo, though hating each other, were joined by a no less cordial hatred of Tom. Quimbo, therefore, departed with a will to execute his orders.

Tom heard the message with a forewarning heart, for he knew all the plan of the fugitives' escape, and the place of their present concealment. He knew the deadly character of the man he had to deal with, and his despotic power. But he felt strong in God to meet death rather than betray the help-less.

He set his basket down by the row and, looking up, said, "Into thy hands I commend my spirit! Thou hast redeemed me, oh Lord God of truth!" Then he quietly yielded himself to the brutal grasp with which Quimbo seized him.

"Ay, ay!" said the giant, as he dragged him along. "Ye'll cotch it now! I'll be boun' Mas'r's back's up *high!* No sneakin' out now! Tell ye, ye'll get it, and no mistake! See how ye'll look now, helpin' Mas'r's niggers to run away! See what ye'll get!"

The savage words—none of them reached that ear. A higher voice there was saying, "Fear not them that kill the body, and, after that, have no more that they can do." Nerve and bone of that poor man's body vibrated to those words, as if touched by the finger of God, and he felt the strength of a thousand souls in one. As he passed along, the trees and bushes, the huts of his servitude, the whole scene of his degra-dation, seemed to whirl by him as the landscape by the rush-ing car. His soul throbbed—his home was in sight, and the hour of release at hand.

"Well, Tom!" said Legree, walking up and seizing him grimly by the collar of his coat, and speaking through his teeth in a paroxysm of determined rage. "Do you know, I've made up my mind to KILL you?"

"It's very likely, Mas'r," said Tom calmly.

"I *have*," said Legree with grim, terrible calmness, "*done— just—that—thing*, Tom, unless you'll tell me what you know about these yer gals!"

Tom stood silent.

"D'ye hear?" said Legree, stamping, with a roar like that of an incensed lion. "Speak!"

"*I han't got nothing to tell, Mas'r*," said Tom, with a slow, firm, deliberate utterance.

"Do you dare to tell me, ye old black Christian, ye don't *know?*" said Legree.

Tom was silent.

"Speak!" thundered Legree, striking him furiously. "Do you know anything?"

"I know, Mas'r, but I can't tell anything. *I can die!*"

Legree drew in a long breath, and suppressing his rage, took Tom by the arm, and approaching his face almost to his, said in a terrible voice:

"Hark ye, Tom! Ye think cause I've let you off before, I don't mean what I say. But this time I've *made up my mind*, and counted the cost. You've always stood it out agin me. Now I'll *conquer ye or kill ye*—one or t'other! I'll count every drop of blood there is in you, and take 'em, one by one, till ye give up!"

Tom looked up to his master and answered, "Mas'r, if you was sick, or in trouble, or dying, and I could save ye, I'd *give* ye my heart's blood. And if taking every drop of blood in this poor old body would save your precious soul, I'd give 'em freely, as the Lord gave his for me. Oh, Mas'r! Don't bring this great sin on your soul! It will hurt you more than 'twill me! Do the worst you can, my troubles'll be over soon. But if ye don't repent, yours won't *never* end!"

Like a strange snatch of heavenly music, heard in the lull of a tempest, this burst of feeling made a moment's blank pause. Legree stood aghast and looked at Tom. And there was such a silence that the tick of the old clock could be heard.

It was but a moment. There was one hesitating pause—one irresolute, relenting thrill—and the spirit of evil came back with sevenfold force. Legree, foaming with rage, smote his victim to the ground.

Scenes of blood and cruelty are shocking to our ear and heart. What man has nerve to do, man has not nerve to hear. What brother-man and brother-Christian must suffer cannot be told us, even in our secret chamber, it so harrows up the soul. And yet, oh my country, these things are done under the shadow of thy laws! Oh, Christ! Thy church sees them almost in silence!

Was he alone, that long night, whose brave, loving spirit was bearing up in that old shed against brutal stripes?

Nay! There stood by him ONE—seen by him alone—"like unto the Son of God."

The tempter stood by him, too, every moment pressing him to shun that agony by the betrayal of the innocent. But the brave, true heart was firm on the Eternal Rock. Like his Master, he knew that if he saved others, himself he could not save. Nor could utmost extremity wring from him words, save of prayer and holy trust.

"He's most gone, Mas'r," said Sambo, touched in spite of himself by the patience of his victim.

"Pay away till he give up! Give it to him, give it to him!" shouted Legree. "I'll take every drop of blood he has, unless he confesses!"

Tom opened his eyes and looked upon his master. "Ye poor, miserable crittur!" he said. "There an't no more ye can do! I forgive ye, with all my soul!" and he fainted entirely away.

"I b'lieve, my soul, he's done for finally," said Legree, stepping forward to look at him. "Yes, he is! Well, his mouth's shut up at last—that's one comfort!"

Yes, Legree, but who shall shut up that voice in thy soul?

Yet Tom was not quite gone. His wondrous words and pious prayers had struck upon the hearts of the imbruted blacks who had been the instruments of cruelty upon him. And the instant Legree withdrew, they took him down, and in their ignorance sought to call him back to life—as if *that* were any favor to him.

"Sartin, we's been doin' a dreadful wicked thing!" said Sambo. "Hopes Mas'r'll have to 'count for it, and not we."

They washed his wounds. They provided a rude bed of

some refuse cotton for him to lie down on. And one of them, stealing up to the house, begged a drink of brandy of Legree, pretending that he was tired and wanted it for himself. He brought it back and poured it down Tom's throat.

"Oh, Tom!" said Quimbo. "We's been awful wicked to ye!"

"I forgive ye, with all my heart!" said Tom faintly.

"Oh, Tom! Do tell us who is *Jesus,* anyhow," said Sambo, "Jesus, that's been a standin' by you so all this night? Who is He?"

The word roused the failing, fainting spirit. He poured forth a few sentences of that wondrous One—His life, His death, His everlasting presence, and power to save.

They wept—both the two savage men.

"Why didn't I never hear this before?" said Sambo. "But I do believe! I can't help it! Lord Jesus, have mercy on us!"

"Poor critturs!" said Tom. "I'd be willing to b'ar all I have, if it'll only bring ye to Christ! Oh, Lord, give me these two more souls, I pray!"

That prayer was answered.

The Young Master

Two days after, a young man drove a light wagon up through the avenue of china trees, and throwing the reins hastily on the horses' necks, sprang out and inquired for the owner of the place.

It was George Shelby. To show how he came to be there, we must go back in our story.

The letter of Miss Ophelia to Mrs. Shelby had, by some unfortunate accident, been detained for a month or two at some remote post office, before it reached its destination. And, of course, before it was received, Tom was already lost to view among the distant swamps of the Red River.

Mrs. Shelby read the news with the deepest concern. But any immediate action upon it was an impossibility. She was then in attendance on the sickbed of her husband, who lay delirious in the crisis of a fever. Master George Shelby, who in the interval had changed from a boy to a tall young man, was her constant assistant and only reliance in superintending his father's affairs. Miss Ophelia had taken the precaution to send them the name of the lawyer who did business for the St. Clares, and the most that, in the emergency, could be done, was to address a letter of inquiry to him. The sudden death of Mr. Shelby a few days after brought, of course, an absorbing pressure of other interests for a time.

Mrs. Shelby, as sole executrix of the estate, applied herself to the work of straightening the entangled web of affairs. For some time she and George were occupied with selling property and settling debts. In the meantime, they received a letter from the lawyer in New Orleans, saying that he knew nothing of the matter—the man was sold at a public auction, and, beyond receiving the money, he knew nothing of the affair.

Neither George nor Mrs. Shelby could be easy at this result. And some six months later, George, having business for his mother down the river, resolved to visit New Orleans in person and push his inquiries.

After some months of unsuccessful search, by the merest accident George fell in with a man who happened to possess the desired information. And with his money in his pocket, our hero took steamboat for Red River, resolving to find and repurchase his old friend.

Legree received the stranger with a kind of surly hospitality.

"I understand," said the young man, "that you bought, in New Orleans, a boy named Tom. He used to be on my father's place, and I came to see if I couldn't buy him back."

Legree's brow grew dark, and he broke out passionately: "Yes, I did buy such a fellow—and a h——l of a bargain I had of it, too! The most rebellious, saucy, impudent dog! Set up my niggers to run away. Got off two gals worth eight hundred or a thousand dollars apiece. He owned to that, and when I bid him tell me where they was, he up and said he knew, but he wouldn't tell, and stood to it, though I gave him the cussedest flogging I ever gave a nigger yet. I b'lieve he's trying to die. But I don't know as he'll make it out."

"Where is he?" said George. "Let me see him." The cheeks of the young man were crimson, and his eyes flashed fire, but he prudently said nothing, as yet.

"He's in dat ar shed," said a little fellow who stood holding George's horse.

Legree kicked the boy and swore at him. But George, without saying another word, turned and strode to the spot.

Tom had been lying two days since the fatal night—not suffering, for every nerve of suffering was blunted and destroyed. He lay, for the most part, in a quiet stupor, for the laws of a powerful and well-knit frame would not at once release the imprisoned spirit. By stealth, there had been there, in the darkness of the night, poor desolated creatures, who stole from their scanty hours' rest that they might repay to him some of those ministrations of love in which he had always been so abundant. Truly those poor disciples had little to give—only the cup of cold water—but it was given with full hearts.

Cassy, who had glided out of her place of concealment and, by overhearing, learned the sacrifice that had been made for her and Emmeline, had been there the night before, defying the danger of detection. And moved by the few last words which the affectionate soul had yet strength to breathe, the dark, despairing woman had wept and prayed.

When George entered the shed, he felt his head giddy and his heart sick.

"Is it possible, is it possible?" said he, kneeling down by him. "Uncle Tom, my poor, poor old friend!"

Something in the voice penetrated to the ear of the dying. He moved his head gently, smiled, and said:

> "Jesus can make a dying-bed
> Feel soft as downy pillows are."

Tears which did honor to his manly heart fell from the young man's eyes as he bent over his poor friend.

"Oh, dear Uncle Tom! Do wake—do speak once more! Look up! Here's Mas'r George—your own little Mas'r George. Don't you know me?"

"Mas'r George!" said Tom, opening his eyes and speaking in a feeble voice. "Mas'r George!" He looked bewildered.

Slowly the idea seemed to fill his soul. The vacant eye became fixed and brightened, the whole face lighted up. The hard hands clasped, and tears ran down the cheeks.

"Bless the Lord! It is—it is—it's all I wanted! They haven't forgot me. It warms my soul. It does my old heart good! Now I shall die content! Bless the Lord, oh my soul!"

"You shan't die! You *mustn't* die, nor think of it! I've come to buy you and take you home," said George passionately.

"Oh, Mas'r George, ye're too late. The Lord's bought me, and is going to take me home—and I long to go. Heaven is better than Kentuck."

"Oh, don't die! It'll kill me! It'll break my heart to think what you've suffered—and lying in this old shed, here! Poor, poor fellow!"

"Don't call me poor fellow!" said Tom solemnly. "I *have* been poor fellow. But that's all past and gone now. I'm right in the door, going into glory! Oh, Mas'r George! *Heaven has come!* I've got the victory! The Lord Jesus has given it to me! Glory be to His name!"

George was awe-struck at the force with which these broken sentences were uttered. He sat gazing in silence.

Tom grasped his hand and continued: "Ye mustn't, now,

tell Chloe, poor soul, how ye found me—'twould be so drefful to her. Only tell her ye found me going into glory, and that I couldn't stay for no one. And tell her the Lord's. stood by me everywhere and al'ays, and made everything light and easy. And oh, the poor chil'en, and the baby! My old heart's been most broke for 'em, time and agin! Tell 'em all to follow me—follow me. Give my love to Mas'r, and dear good Missis, and everybody in the place. Ye don't know. 'Pears like I loves 'em all. I loves every crittur everywhar. It's nothing *but* love—Oh, Mas'r George! What a thing 'tis to be a Christian!"

At this moment Legree sauntered up to the door of the shed, looked in with an air of affected carelessness, and turned away.

"The old Satan!" said George. "It's a comfort to think the devil will pay *him* for this, some of these days!"

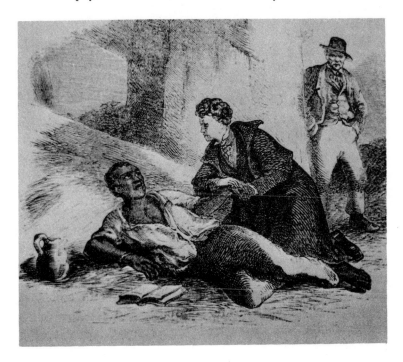

"Oh, don't! Oh, ye mustn't!" said Tom, grasping his hand. "He's a poor mis'able crittur. It's awful to think on't! Oh, if he only could repent, the Lord would forgive him, now. But I'm 'feard he never will."

"I hope he won't!" said George. "I never want to see *him* in Heaven!"

"Hush, Mas'r George! It worries me. Don't feel so! He an't done me no real harm—only opened the gate of the kingdom for me, that's all."

At this moment the sudden flush of strength which the joy of meeting his young master had infused into the dying man gave way. A sudden sinking fell upon him. He closed his eyes, and that mysterious and sublime change passed over his face that told the approach of other worlds.

He began to draw his breath with long, deep inspirations, and his broad chest rose and fell heavily. The expression of his face was that of a conqueror.

"Who—who—who shall separate us from the love of Christ?" he said in a voice that contended with mortal weakness. And with a smile he fell asleep.

George sat fixed with solemn awe. It seemed to him that the place was holy. And as he closed the lifeless eyes, and rose up from the dead, only one thought possessed him—that expressed by Tom: "What a thing it is to be a Christian!"

He turned. Legree was standing behind him.

The presence of the man was simply loathsome to George, and he felt an impulse to get away from him, with as few words as possible. Fixing his eyes on Legree, he pointed to the dead. "You have got all you ever can of him," George said. "What shall I pay you for the body? I will take it away and bury it decently."

"I don't sell dead niggers," said Legree sullenly. "You are welcome to bury him where and when you like."

"Boys," said George in an authoritative tone to two or three Negroes who were looking at the body, "help me lift him up and carry him to my wagon. And get me a spade."

One of them ran for a spade. The other two assisted George to carry the body to the wagon.

George neither spoke to nor looked at Legree, who did not countermand his orders, but stood whistling with an air of unconcern. He sulkily followed them to where the wagon stood at the door.

George spread his cloak in the wagon and had the body carefully disposed of in it, moving the seat so as to give it room. Then he turned, fixed his eyes on Legree, and said with forced composure:

"I have not, as yet, said to you what I think of this most atrocious affair. This is not the time and place. But, sir, this innocent blood shall have justice. I will proclaim this murder. I will go to the very first magistrate and expose you."

"Do!" said Legree, snapping his fingers scornfully. "I'd like to see you doing it. Where you going to get witnesses? How you going to prove it? Come, now!"

George saw, at once, the force of this defiance. There was not a white person on the place, and in all Southern courts the testimony of colored blood is nothing. He felt at that moment as if he could have rent the heavens with his heart's indignant cry for justice. But in vain.

"After all, what a fuss for a dead nigger!" said Legree.

The word was as a spark to a powder magazine. George turned and, with one indignant blow, knocked Legree flat upon his face.

Some men are decidedly bettered by being knocked down. If a man lays them fairly flat in the dust, they seem immediately to conceive a respect for him. Legree was one of this sort. As he rose, therefore, and brushed the dust from his clothes, he eyed the slowly retreating wagon with some evident consideration. Nor did he open his mouth till it was out of sight.

Beyond the boundaries of the plantation, George had noticed a dry, sandy knoll, shaded by a few trees. There they made the grave.

"Shall we take off the cloak, Mas'r?" said the Negroes when the grave was ready.

"No, no—bury it with him. It's all I can give you now, poor Tom, and you shall have it."

They laid him in, and the men shoveled away silently. They banked the grave up and laid green turf over it.

"You may go, boys," said George, slipping a quarter into the hand of each. They lingered about, however.

"If young Mas'r would please buy us—" said one.

"We'd serve him so faithful!" said the other.

"Hard times here, Mas'r!" said the first. "Do, Mas'r buy us, please."

"I can't!—I can't!" said George with difficulty, motioning them off. "It's impossible!"

The poor fellows looked dejected and walked off in silence.

"Witness, eternal God!" said George, kneeling on the grave of his poor friend. "Oh, witness that from this hour I will do *what one man can* to drive out this curse of slavery from my land!"

An Authentic Ghost Story

FOR some remarkable reason, ghostly legends were uncommonly rife, about this time, among the servants on Legree's place.

It was whisperingly asserted that footsteps, in the dead of night, had been heard descending the garret stairs and patrolling the house. In vain the doors of the upper entry had been locked. The ghost either carried a duplicate key in its pocket, or availed itself of a ghost's immemorial privilege of coming through the keyhole.

Authorities were somewhat divided as to the outward form of the spirit. They agreed with each other in no particular except the common family peculiarity of the ghost tribe—the wearing of a *white sheet*. Be it as it may, a tall figure in a white sheet did walk, at the most approved ghostly hours, around the Legree premises—pass the doors, glide about the house, disappear at intervals, and reappearing, pass up the silent stairway into that fatal garret. And in the morning the entry doors were all found shut and locked as firm as ever.

Legree could not help overhearing this whispering. And it was all the more exciting to him from the pains that were taken to conceal it from him. He drank more brandy than usual, held up his head briskly, and swore louder than ever in the daytime. But he had bad dreams. The night after Tom's body had been carried away, he rode to the next town for a carouse, and had a high one. He got home late and tired, locked his door, took out the key, and went to bed.

After all, let a man take what pains he may to hush it down, a human soul is an awful ghostly, unquiet possession for a bad man to have. What a fool is he who locks his door to keep out spirits, who has in his own bosom a spirit he dares not meet alone—whose voice, smothered far down, is yet like the forewarning trumpet of doom!

But Legree locked his door. He set a night-lamp at the head of his bed, and he put his pistols there. He examined the catches and fastenings of the windows, and then swore he "didn't care for the devil and all his angels," and went to sleep.

Well, he slept, for he was tired—slept soundly. But finally there came over his sleep a shadow, a horror, an apprehension of something dreadful hanging over him. It was his mother's shroud, he thought, but Cassy had it, holding it up and showing it to him. He heard a confused noise of screams and groanings. And with it all, he knew he was asleep, and he struggled to wake himself. He was half awake. He was sure something was coming into his room. He knew the door was opening, but he could not stir hand or foot. At last he turned with a start. The door *was* open, and he saw a hand putting out his light.

It was a cloudy, misty moonlight, and there he saw it—something white! He heard the still rustle of its ghostly garments. It stood still by his bed—a cold hand touched his. A voice said three times, in a low, fearful whisper, "Come! come! come!" And while he lay sweating with terror, he knew not when or how, the thing was gone. He sprang out of bed and pulled at the door. It was shut and locked, and the man fell down in a swoon.

After this, Legree became a harder drinker than ever before. He no longer drank cautiously, prudently.

There were reports around the country, soon after, that he was sick and dying. Excess had brought on that frightful disease that seems to throw the lurid shadows of a coming retribution back into the present life. None could bear the horrors of that sickroom, when he raved and screamed, and spoke of sights which almost stopped the blood of those who heard him. And at his dying bed stood a stern, white relentless figure, saying, "Come! come! come!"

By a singular coincidence, on the very night that this vision appeared to Legree, the house door was found open in the morning, and some of the Negroes had seen two white figures gliding down the avenue toward the highroad.

It was near sunrise when Cassy and Emmeline paused, for a moment, in a little knot of trees near the town.

Cassy was dressed after the manner of the Creole Spanish ladies—wholly in black. A small black bonnet, covered by a veil thick with embroidery, concealed her face. It had been agreed that in their escape she was to personate the character of a Creole lady, and Emmeline that of her servant.

Brought up, from early life, in connection with the highest society, the language, movements, and air of Cassy were all in agreement with this idea. And she had still enough remaining with her, of a once splendid wardrobe and sets of jewels, to enable her to personate the thing to advantage.

She stopped in the outskirts of the town, where she had noticed trunks for sale, and purchased a handsome one. This she requested the man to send along with her. And, accordingly, thus escorted by a boy wheeling her trunk, and Emmeline behind her, carrying her carpetbag and sundry bundles, she made her appearance at the small tavern like a lady of consideration.

The first person that struck her, after her arrival, was George Shelby, who was staying there, awaiting the next boat.

Cassy had remarked the young man from her knothole in the garret, and seen him bear away the body of Tom, and observed his encounter with Legree. Subsequently she had gathered, from the conversations she had overheard among the Negroes as she glided about in her ghostly disguise after nightfall, who he was, and in what relation he stood to Tom. She, therefore, felt an immediate increase of confidence when she found that he was, like herself, awaiting the next boat.

Cassy's air and manner, speech, and evident command of money prevented any suspicion in the hotel. People never inquire too closely into those who are fair on the main point of paying well—a thing which Cassy had foreseen when she provided herself with money.

In the edge of the evening, a boat was heard coming along. George Shelby, with the politeness which comes naturally to every Kentuckian, handed Cassy aboard and exerted himself to provide her with a good stateroom. On pretext of illness, Cassy kept her room and bed during the whole time they were on Red River, and was waited on with devotion by her attendant.

When they arrived at the Mississippi River, George, having learned that the course of the strange lady was upward, like his own, proposed to take a stateroom for her on the same boat with himself. Behold, therefore, the whole party safely transferred to the good steamer *Cincinnati* and sweeping up the river under a powerful head of steam.

Cassy's health was much better. She sat upon the deck,

came to the table, and was remarked upon in the boat as a lady that must have been very handsome.

From the moment that George got the first glimpse of her face, he was troubled with one of those fleeting and indefinite likenesses which almost everybody can remember, and has been at times perplexed with. He could not keep himself from looking at her, and watching her perpetually. At table, or sitting at her stateroom door, still she would encounter the young man's eyes fixed on her, and politely withdrawn, when she showed that she was sensible of the observation.

Cassy became uneasy. She began to think that he suspected something. Finally she resolved to throw herself entirely on his generosity and entrust him with her whole history.

George was heartily disposed to sympathize with anyone who had escaped from Legree's plantation. And with a courageous disregard of consequences, he assured her that he would do all in his power to protect and bring them through.

The next stateroom to Cassy's was occupied by a French lady named de Thoux. This lady, having gathered from George's conversation that he was from Kentucky, seemed evidently disposed to cultivate his acquaintance. George's chair was often placed at her stateroom door. And Cassy, as she sat upon the deck, could hear their conversation.

Madame de Thoux was very minute in her inquires as to Kentucky, where she said she had resided in a former period of her life. George discovered, to his surprise, that her former residence must have been in his own vicinity. And her inquires showed a knowledge of people and things in his region that was perfectly surprising to him.

"Do you know," said Madame de Thoux to him, one day, "of any man in your neighborhood of the name of Harris?"

"There is an old fellow of that name lives not far from my father's place," said George. "We never had much intercourse with him, though."

"He is a large slave-owner, I believe," said Madame de

Thoux, with a manner which seemed to betray more interest than she was exactly willing to show.

"He is," said George, looking rather surprised at her manner.

"Did you ever know of his having—perhaps you may have heard of his having a mulatto boy named George?"

"Oh, certainly—George Harris—I know him well. He married a servant of my mother's but has escaped now to Canada."

"He has?" said Madame de Thoux quickly. "Thank God!"

George looked a surprised inquiry, but said nothing.

Madame de Thoux leaned her head on her hand and burst into tears.

"He is my brother," she said.

"Madame!" said George, with a strong accent of surprise.

"Yes," said Madame de Thoux, lifting her head proudly and wiping her tears. "Mr. Shelby, George Harris is my brother."

"I am perfectly astonished," said George, pushing back his chair a pace or two, and looking at Madame de Thoux.

"I was sold to the South when he was a boy," said she. "I was bought by a good and generous man. He took me with him to the West Indies, set me free, and married me. It is but lately that he died. And I was coming up to Kentucky to see if I could find and redeem my brother."

"I have heard him speak of a sister Emily that was sold South," said George.

"Yes, indeed! I am the one," said Madame de Thoux. "Tell me what sort of a—"

"A very fine young man," said George, "notwithstanding the curse of slavery that lay on him. He sustained a first-rate character, both for intelligence and principle. I know, you see," he said, "because he married in our family."

"What sort of a girl?" said Madame de Thoux eagerly.

"A treasure," said George, "a beautiful, intelligent, amiable girl. Very pious. My mother had brought her up and trained her as carefully, almost, as a daughter. Eliza could read and write, embroider and sew beautifully—and was a beautiful singer."

"Was she born in your house?" said Madame de Thoux.

"No. Father bought her once, in one of his trips to New Orleans, and brought her up as a present to Mother. She was about eight or nine years old then. Father would never tell Mother what he gave for her. But the other day, in looking over his old papers, we came across the bill of sale. He paid an extravagant sum for her, to be sure. I suppose on account of her extraordinary beauty."

George sat with his back to Cassy and did not see the absorbed expression of her countenance as he was giving these details.

At this point in the story, she touched his arm, and with a face perfectly white with interest, said, "Do you know the name of the people he bought her of?"

"A man of the name of Simmons, I think, was the principal in the transaction. At least, I think that was the name on the bill of sale."

"Oh, my God!" said Cassy, and fell insensible on the floor of the cabin.

Though neither George nor Madame de Thoux could conjecture what was the cause of Cassy's fainting, still they made all the tumult which is proper in such a case, George upsetting a wash-pitcher and breaking two tumblers in the warmth of his humanity.

Poor Cassy! When she recovered, turned her face to the wall, and wept and sobbed like a child—perhaps, mother, you can tell what she was thinking of! Perhaps you cannot. But she felt as sure, in that hour, that God had had mercy on her, and that she should see her daughter, as she did months afterward when—but we anticipate.

Results

THE rest of our story is soon told. On reaching home, George Shelby took pains to send Cassy the bill of sale of Eliza. Its date and name all corresponded with her own knowledge of facts, and left no doubt upon her mind as to the identity of her child. It remained now only for her to trace out the path of the fugitives.

Madame de Thoux and she, thus drawn together by the singular coincidence of their fortunes, proceeded immediately to Canada and began a tour of inquiry among the stations where the numerous fugitives from slavery are located. At Amherstberg they found the missionary with whom George and Eliza had taken shelter on their first arrival in Canada. And through him they were enabled to trace the family to Montreal.

George and Eliza had now been five years free. George had found constant occupation in the shop of a worthy machinist, where he had been earning a competent support for his family, which, in the meantime, had been increased by the addition of a daughter. Little Harry had been put to a good school and was making rapid progress in knowledge.

The worthy missionary was so much interested in the search that he accompanied the two women to Montreal, Madame de Thoux bearing all the expense of the expedition.

The scene now changes to a small, neat tenement in the outskirts of Montreal, the time, evening. A cheerful fire blazes on the hearth. A tea-table, covered with a snowy cloth, stands prepared for the evening meal. In one corner of the room is a table covered with a green cloth, where stands an open writing desk, and over it a shelf of well-selected books.

This was George's study. The same zeal for self-improvement, which led him to steal the much coveted arts of reading and writing amid all the toils and discouragements of his early life, still led him to devote all his leisure time to self-cultivation.

At this present time, he is seated at the table, making notes from a volume of the family library he has been reading.

"Come, George," says Eliza, "you've been gone all day. Do put down that book, and let's talk while I'm getting tea—do."

And little Eliza seconds the effort by toddling up to her father, and trying to pull the book out of his hand, and install herself on his knee as a substitute.

"Oh, you little witch!" says George, yielding, as in such circumstances man always must.

"That's right," says Eliza, and begins to cut a loaf of bread. A little older she looks, her form a little fuller, her air more matronly than of yore, but evidently contented and happy as woman need be.

"Harry, my boy, how did you come on in that sum today?" says George as he laid his hand on his son's head.

Harry has lost his long curls. But he can never lose those eyes and eyelashes, and that fine, bold brow that flushes with triumph as he answers, "I did it, every bit of it, *myself*, Father. And *nobody* helped me!"

"That's right," says his father. "Depend on yourself, my son. You have a better chance than ever your poor father had."

At this moment there is a rap at the door, and Eliza goes and opens it. The delighted "Why! This you!" calls up her husband. The good pastor of Amherstberg is welcomed. There are two women with him, and Eliza asks them to sit down.

Now, if the truth must be told, the honest pastor had arranged a little program, according to which this affair was to

develop itself. And on the way up, all had very prudently cautioned each other not to let things out except according to previous arrangement.

What was the good man's consternation, therefore, just as he had motioned to the ladies to be seated, and was taking out his pocket handkerchief to wipe his mouth so as to proceed to his introductory speech in good order, when Madame de Thoux upset the whole plan by throwing her arms around George's neck and letting all out at once by saying, "Oh, George! Don't you know me? I'm your sister Emily."

Cassy had seated herself more composedly, and would have carried on her part very well, had not little Eliza suddenly appeared before her in the exact shape and form, every outline and curl, just as her daughter was when she saw her last. The little thing peered up in her face. Cassy caught her up in her arms, pressed her to her bosom, and said, what at that moment she really believed, "Darling, I'm your mother!"

In fact, it was a troublesome matter to do up exactly in proper order. But the good pastor, at last, succeeded in getting everybody quiet and delivering the speech with which he had intended to open the exercises. And in this he succeeded so well that his whole audience were sobbing about him.

They knelt together, and the good man prayed. For there are some feelings so tumultuous that they can find rest only by being poured into the bosom of Almighty love. Then, rising up, the new-found family embraced each other, with a holy trust in Him who from such peril and dangers, and by such unknown ways, had brought them together.

And now, having recovered from too great and sudden joy, our friends are seated around the social board, and are getting decidedly companionable. Only Cassy, who keeps little Eliza on her lap, occasionally squeezes the little thing in a manner that rather astonishes her, and obstinately refuses to have her mouth stuffed with cake to the extent the little one desires. She says—what the child rather wonders at—that she has got something better than cake, and doesn't want it.

And, indeed, in two or three days such a change passed over Cassy that our readers would scarcely know her. The despairing, haggard expression of her face had given way to one of gentle trust. She seemed to sink at once into the bosom of the family and to take the little ones into her heart as something for which it long had waited. Indeed, her love seemed to flow more naturally to the little Eliza than to her own daughter, for she was the exact image of the child whom she had lost. The little one was a flowery bond between mother and daughter, through whom grew up acquaintance and affection. Eliza's steady, consistent piety made her a proper guide for the shattered and wearied mind of her mother. Cassy yielded at once, and with her whole soul, to every good influence, and became a devout and tender Christian.

After a day or two, Madame de Thoux told her brother more particularly of her affairs. The death of her husband had left her an ample fortune, which she generously offered to share with the family. When she asked George what way she could best apply it for him, he answered, "Give me an education, Emily. That has always been my heart's desire.

Then I can do all the rest."

It was decided that the whole family should go, for some years, to France, whither they sailed, carrying Emmeline with them. It was a satisfaction to them all that on shipboard the girl's good looks won the affection of the first mate of the vessel. And shortly after entering the port, she became his wife.

George remained four years at a French university. Applying himself with zeal, he obtained a very thorough education there. Political troubles in France, however, led the family again to seek an asylum in this country.

George's feelings and views, as an educated man, may be best expressed in a letter to one of his friends:

I feel somewhat at a loss as to my future course. True, as you have said to me, I might mingle in the circles of the whites in this country, my shade of color is so slight, and that of my wife and family scarce perceptible. But, to tell you the truth, I have no wish to.

My sympathies are not for my father's race, but for my mother's. To him I was no more than a fine dog or horse. To my poor heartbroken mother I was a *child*. And though I never saw her after the cruel sale that separated us, yet I *know* she always loved me dearly. I know it by my own heart. When I think of all she suffered, of my own early sufferings, of the distresses and struggles of my heroic wife, of my sister, sold in the New Orleans slave market— though I hope to have no unchristian sentiments, I may be excused for saying I have no wish to pass for an American, or to identify myself with them.

It is with the oppressed, enslaved African race that I cast in my lot. And if I wished anything, I would wish myself two shades darker rather than one lighter.

The desire and yearning of my soul is for an African *nationality*. I want a people that shall have a tangible, separate existence of its own.

"Where shall I look? On the shores of Africa I see a

republic—a republic formed of picked men, who by energy and self-educating force have in many cases raised themselves above a condition of slavery. Having gone through a preparatory stage of feebleness, Liberia has, at last, become an acknowledged nation on the face of the earth—acknowledged by both France and England. There it is my wish to go and find myself a people.

Do you say that I am deserting my enslaved brethren? I think not. If I forget them one hour, one moment of my life, so may God forget me! But what can I do for them here? Can I break their chains? No, not as an individual. But let me go and form part of a nation, which shall have a voice in the councils of nations, and then we can speak. A nation has a right to argue, remonstrate, implore, and present the cause of its race—which an individual has not.

But, you will tell me, our race have equal rights to mingle in the American republic as the Irishman, the German, the Swede. Granted, they have. We *ought* to be free to meet and mingle—to rise by our individual worth, without any consideration of caste or color. And they who deny us this right are false to their own professed principles of human equality. We ought in particular to be allowed *here*. We have *more* than the rights of common men—we have the claim of an injured race for reparation. But then, *I do not want it.* I want a country, a nation, of my own. I think that the African race has peculiarities yet to be unfolded in the light of civilization and Christianity, which, if not the same with those of the Anglo-Saxon, may prove to be, morally, of even a higher type.

To the Anglo-Saxon race have been intrusted the destinies of the world during its pioneer period of struggle and conflict. But as a Christian, I look for another era to arise. On its borders I trust we stand. And the throes that now convulse the nations are, to my hope, but the birthpangs of an hour of universal peace and brotherhood.

You will call me an enthusiast. You will tell me that I

have not well considered what I am undertaking. But I have considered, and counted the cost. I go to Liberia not as to a place of romance, but as to a *field of work*. I expect to work with both hands, to work *hard*, to work against all sorts of difficulties and discouragements, and to work till I die. This is what I go for. And in this I am quite sure I shall not be disappointed.

Whatever you may think of my determination, believe that, in whatever I do, I act with a heart wholly given to my people.

GEORGE HARRIS

George, with his wife, children, sister, and Eliza's mother, embarked for Africa some few weeks after. If we are not mistaken, the world will yet hear from him there.

Of our other characters we have nothing very particular to write, except a word relating to Miss Ophelia and Topsy, and a farewell chapter which we shall dedicate to George Shelby.

Miss Ophelia took Topsy home to Vermont with her, much to the surprise of her family. At first they thought her an odd and unnecessary addition to their establishment. But Miss Ophelia did her duty by Topsy so conscientiously that the child rapidly grew in grace and in favor with the family and neighborhood. At the age of womanhood, she was, by her own request, baptized, and became a member of the Christian church in the place. She showed so much intelligence, zeal, and desire to do good in the world that she was at last sent as a missionary to one of the stations in Africa, where she is teaching the children of her own country.

P.S.—It will be a satisfaction to some mother, also, to state that some inquiries, set on foot by Madame de Thoux, have resulted recently in the discovery of Cassy's son. Being a young man of energy, he had escaped, some years before his mother, and been received and educated by friends of the oppressed in the North. He will soon follow his family to Africa.

The Liberator

GEORGE Shelby had written to his mother merely a line, stating the day that she might expect him home. Of the death scene of his old friend he had not the heart to write.

Mrs. Shelby, on that day, was seated in her comfortable parlor, where a cheerful hickory fire was dispelling the chill of the late autumn evening. A supper table, glittering with plate and cut glass, was set out, over whose arrangements our old friend Chloe was presiding. Arrayed in a new calico dress, with clean, white apron and high, well-starched turban, her black polished face glowing with satisfaction, she lingered around the arrangements of the table, merely as an excuse for talking a little to her mistress.

"Laws, now. Won't it look natural to him?" she said. "Thar—I set his plate just whar he likes it, round by the fire. Mas'r George allers wants de warm seat. Oh, go away! Why didn't Sally get out de *best* teapot, de little new one Mas'r George got for Missis, Christmas? I'll have it out—Missis has heard from Mas'r George?" she said inquiringly.

"Yes, Chloe. But only a line, just to say he would be home tonight if he could—that's all."

"Didn't say nothin' 'bout my old man, s'pose?" said Chloe, still fidgeting with the teacups.

"No, he didn't. He did not speak of anything, Chloe. He said he would tell all when he got home."

"Just like Mas'r George—he's allers so ferce for tellin' everything hisself. I allers minded dat ar in Mas'r George. Don't see, for my part, how white people gen'lly can b'ar to hev to write things much as they do, writin's such slow, oneasy kind o' work."

Mrs. Shelby smiled.

"I'm a-thinkin' my old man won't know de boys and de baby. Lor! She's de biggest gal, now—good she is, too, and peart, Polly is. She's out to the house, now, watchin' the hoecake. I's got jist de very pattern my old man liked so much, a-bakin'. Jist sich as I gi'n him de mornin' he was took off. Lord bless us! How I felt dat ar mornin'!"

Mrs. Shelby sighed and felt a heavy weight on her heart at this allusion. She had felt uneasy ever since she received her son's letter, lest something should prove to be hidden behind the veil of silence he had drawn.

"Missis has got dem bills?" said Chloe anxiously.

"Yes, Chloe."

"Cause I wants to show my old man dem very bills de *perfectioner* gave me. 'And,' says he, 'Chloe, I wish you'd stay longer.' 'Thank you, Mas'r,' says I, 'I would, only my old man's coming home, and Missis—she can't do without me no longer.' There's jist what I telled him. Bery nice man, dat Mas'r Jones was."

Chloe had insisted that the very bills in which her wages had been paid should be preserved to show to her husband, in memorial of her capability. And Mrs. Shelby had readily consented to humor her in the request.

"He won't know Polly—my old man won't. Laws, it's five year since they tuck him. She was a baby den—couldn't but jist stand. Remember how tickled he used to be cause she would keep a-fallin' over when she sot out to walk. Laws a me!"

The rattling of wheels was now heard.

"Mas'r George!" said Aunt Chloe, starting to the window.

Mrs. Shelby ran to the entry door, and was folded in the arms of her son. Aunt Chloe stood anxiously straining her eyes out into the darkness.

"Oh, *poor* Aunt Chloe!" said George, stopping compassionately and taking her hard, black hand between both his.

"I'd have given all my fortune to have brought him with me, but he's gone to a better country."

There was a passionate exclamation from Mrs. Shelby, but Aunt Chloe said nothing.

The party entered the supper room. The money, of which Chloe was so proud, was still lying on the table.

"Thar," said she, gathering it up and holding it out with a trembling hand to her mistrress. "Don't neber want to see nor hear on 't agin. Jist as I knew 'twould be—sold, and murdered on dem ar old plantations!"

Chloe turned and was walking proudly out of the room. Mrs. Shelby followed her softly and took one of her hands, drew her down into a chair, and sat down by her.

"My poor, good Chloe!" said she.

Chloe leaned her head on her mistress' shoulder and sobbed out, "Oh, Missis! 'Scuse me, my heart's broke—dat's all!"

"I know it is," said Mrs. Shelby, as her tears fell fast. "And *I* cannot heal it, but Jesus can. He healeth the broken-hearted, and bindeth up their wounds."

There was a silence for some time, while all wept together. At last George, sitting down beside the mourner, took her hand, and with simple pathos, repeated the triumphant scene of her husband's death, and his last messages of love.

About a month after this, one morning, all the servants of the Shelby estate were convened together in the great hall that ran through the house, to hear a few words from their young master.

To the surprise of all, he appeared among them with a bundle of papers in his hand, containing a certificate of freedom to everyone on the place. He read each one successively, and presented it amid the sobs and tears and shouts of all present.

Many, however, pressed around him, earnestly begging him not to send them away, and tendering back their free papers.

"We don't want to be no freer than we are. We's allers had

all we wanted. We don't want to leave de old place, and Mas'r and Missis, and de rest!"

"My good friends," said George, as soon as he could get a silence, "there'll be no need for you to leave me. The place wants as many hands to work it as it did before. We need the same about the house that we did before. But you are now free men and free women. I shall pay you wages for your work, such as we shall agree on. The advantage is that in case of my getting in debt, or dying—things that might happen— you cannot now be taken up and sold. I expect to carry on the estate, and to teach you what, perhaps, it will take you some time to learn—how to use the rights I give you as free men and women. I expect you to be good, and willing to learn. And I trust in God that I shall be faithful, and willing to teach. And now, my friends, look up and thank God for the blessing of freedom."

An aged Negro, who had grown gray and blind on the

estate, now rose, and lifting his trembling hand, said, "Let us give thanks unto the Lord!" As all kneeled by one consent, a more touching and hearty Te Deum never ascended to heaven, though borne on the peal of organ, bell, and cannon, than came from that honest old heart.

On rising, another struck up a Methodist hymn, of which the burden was:

> The year of Jubilee is come—
> Return, ye ransomed sinners, home.

"One thing more," said George, as he stopped the congratulations of the throng. "You all remember our good old Uncle Tom?"

George here gave a short narration of the scene of his death, and of his loving farewell to all on the place, and added:

"It was on his grave, my friends, that I resolved, before God, that I would never own another slave while it was possible to free him—that nobody, through me, should ever run the risk of being parted from home and friends and dying on a lonely plantation, as he died. So when you rejoice in your freedom, think that you owe it to that good old soul, and pay it back in kindness to his wife and children. Think of your freedom every time you see UNCLE TOM'S CABIN. And let it be a memorial to put you all in mind to follow in his steps, and be as honest and faithful and Christian as he was."